MW00913025

SUDDENLY A MORTAL SPLENDOR

Alexander Blackburn

Other books by Alexander Blackburn

The Cold War of Kitty Pentacost (Novel)

A Sunrise Brighter Still: The Visionary Novels of Frank Waters (Criticism)

The Myth of the Picaro: Continuity and Transformation of the Picaresque Novel (Criticism)

SUDDENLY A MORTAL SPLENDOR

A NOVEL BY

ALEXANDER BLACKBURN

This book is a work of fiction. Names, characters, places and incidents are either the product of the author's imagination or are used fictitiously. Any resemblance to actual events or locales or persons, living or dead, is entirely coincidental.

BASKERVILLE Publishers, Inc.
7616 LBJ Freeway, Suite 220, Dallas, TX 75251-1008

Part One originally appeared in somewhat different form in *Crosscurrents*

Library of Congress Cataloging-in-Publication Data

Blackburn, Alexander.
Suddenly a mortal splendor : a novel / by Alexander Blackburn.
p. cm.
ISBN 1-880909-23-5 $20.00 ($26.00) Can.)
1. Hungarians--Foreign countries--Fiction. 2. Orphans--Hungary--Fiction. I. Title.
PS3552.L3414S83 1995
813'.54--dc20 94-24638
CIP

Manufactured in the United States of America
First Printing, 1995

For Inés with love

You making haste haste on decay: not blameworthy; life is
good, be it stubbornly long or suddenly
A mortal splendor: meteors are not needed less than mountains:
shine, perishing republic.

—*Robinson Jeffers*

PART ONE

WHEN I returned from Vietnam a month before Christmas, 1973, I was twenty-eight years old, stressed out, and spiritually etiolated, no splendor in the soul.

Bluejean called. South America this time.

After a year of combat duty, I had caught the rotation, reported to Fort Carson, signed up for sixty days of accumulated leave, bought groceries, taken a cab to our ranch-type house in Colorado Springs, and I had scarcely entered the door when the phone was ringing from thousands of miles away. This time the Queen of the Counterculture had taken not just my self-esteem but Teapot, my life.

I had hoped to talk to Bluejean about our duty to care for Teapot. Flying home, I dreamed we would all drive into the High Rockies for a camp-out until the silences up there opened our voices to talking, and talking became healing. We had once had talk and laughter going for us—a marriage. Anyway there was, I remembered, a hot spring on a ranch in the Sangre de Cristo Mountains of the San Luis Valley about thirty dirt-road miles northeast of Alamosa. It was up in the boulders and aspens at the 9,000-foot elevation, this baptismal water bubbling from the Genesis womb of the earth. Especially in the late fall, when Winnebago campers and other conspicuous consumers had departed, you could have the place to yourselves. You could run around in the nude. Not I, though, not with a ten-year-old girl watching her idol. Still, whatever your preference in body exposure, you could float in steaming water and look up to the incredible Colorado sky, bluer than blue by day, blacker than black by night until stippled with stars as an ocean irradiated by the exploding phosphorescence of a billion organisms. And that time of year, the mountains glistening from first snow, the faraway habitations of man sparkling like crystals, the thin cold air clears your head like neat whiskey.

When she was traveling Bluejean usually didn't call to tell me where she was, and she was not, in her jargon, into letters. There was one exception to that rule about letters, one I'll be telling about later. Bluejean, though, never wrote me in Vietnam. As if I'd wanted to fight, or as if there were something dishonorable about serving the country that gave me freedom and opportunity. Bluejean did care for people, though, at depths of grieving; only, my love had failed to show her how to love herself properly, or perhaps it was burdensome to be tied to a man who accommodated himself to life as a cuckold. Teapot wrote. I don't know why I call her Teapot when her name is Christina, but I've been influenced by Bluejean, one of the great nicknamers, Christina to "Tea" to "Teapot" being a fairly mild example of the art. Teapot wrote me postcards in her fourth-grader's hieroglyphic.

We went to the zoo. The giraf liked me. Mommy says i

am a bad girl. i am happy, i don't know why. Luv to Daddy from CHRISTINA.

I wrote Teapot and Bluejean separate letters once a week, funny stories in sentences without subordination for Teapot, matters of life and death for Bluejean. That's how she knew I was coming home and when, down to the precise estimated time of arrival. It was good to exist in her thoughts. Nor had she left me completely alone: she left me Karl Marx. The odor that assaulted my olfactory nerves as I opened the door should have warned me that Karl Marx and I had home to ourselves. Not recognizing me, Karl Marx retreated to the kitchen and pretended to be Charlie in black pajamas. That was all right with me. Except that a split-level ranch-type house in a treeless tract development in the sand and buffalo grass east of Pike's Peak can be depressing even at the best of times.

The line from South America was remarkably clear: American technology fully operational during a revolution. Later it would occur to me that dictatorships like to show off progressive tendencies, the way Mussolini made trains run on time. Bluejean's "Hi, Paul" might have come from the local 7-Eleven store instead of from the country of... Hang on. That name is classified, or that's the way I treat it, and have for years. There are spies everywhere. People in that country have long arms. So... Call it Pacífica—Pacífica, an old democracy of people who work like Germans, play like Italians, and pride themselves on a culture unrivaled by most other countries of its size and population, which is about ten million, take away some thousands who have disappeared. Whatever, Bluejean was calling from the capital... Ciudad de Pacífica, calling from the office of the archbishop in fact, even though Bluejean execrated priests as women's natural enemies. Down there it was spring, I was told, in November, purple jacaranda blooming along avenues, lime and lemon trees ripening in every garden. Crowds of people having visions of the Virgin Mary and taking snapshots of the sun. In Colorado Springs the last golden flames of aspen had flickered out, and Pike's Peak, looming sacrally through mists at 14,000 feet, was snowcapped and sun-scintillant but hugely indifferent. As we talked I kept on my fighter-pilot style sunglasses, but the mountain was still dazzling, framed by the picture window of what once had been the family room. The line was too clear, too full of pain.

Bluejean was in Pacífica, and Pacífica was in the throes of revolution. It was her first encounter with the real thing, but I figured she could take care of herself. Having lost a leg below the knee at an age when most American girls have no greater affliction than dental braces, she had not only coped with life but fairly flung herself at it. While some of us were learning about mortgages and the manual of courts-martial, the Queen of the Counterculture was learning how to make Molotov cocktails, how to overthrow the class enemy and to liberate the oppressed masses—learning from her books—how, in short, to make time fly for the dispossessed. She made it fly for me, too.

Call it coincidence. Knowing that Bluejean's refrigerator would be empty—as I had always done the grocery shopping, she and Teapot and Karl Marx had probably eaten little for a year except Kentucky Fried Chicken and Pizza Hut pizza—I had loaded up on goodies at the PX before taking the cab home, had sighed about Karl Marx's rice-paddy tactics, had replenished the refrigerator (it had been left on and empty, as undefrosted as a Paleolithic cave), had opened a Coors and had turned on the TV *just* as they were broadcasting about revolution in Pacífica. The usual sort of pictures. A jet bombing the presidential palace. Longhaired Latin boys, their faces as inscrutable as those of statues on Easter Island, their American battle fatigues ill-fitting, wildly fired automatic weapons into smoking barricades. Corpses of women and children allegedly terrorists. Then a few macho pronouncements from the dictator of the new military junta. He had slicked-back snow-white hair, a mustache like a septic toothbrush, and a chlorine-yellow uniform with the usual fruit salad of ribbons. Destiny had chosen him, he said. Then the American TV reporter outside the Sheraton Hotel trashed the English language in the usual way. *It is reported that the report of CIA involvement cannot be reported as confirmed as previously reported in our report. As far as democracy, the democratically elected socialist gov—* I switched channels to a football game, my first in a year. Give me a good football game anytime, everything functioning smoothly as the human brain, everybody where they should be in between outbursts of creativity and controlled violence. Bluejean called on third down and goal to go after the two-minute warning. I gazed through my sunglasses at Pike's Peak. I heard the tumult that meant a touchdown. I saw Karl Marx playing Viet Cong on top of the refrigerator, glaring at me, raising hackles and the stub of his chopped-off tail. Bluejean said Jack. I had to think before remembering Jack meant John Woolpack. Bluejean mentioned Grace, and I retrieved her, too, from memory. I didn't know about the Woolpacks' divorce yet at the time of this call. Say Jack and Grace Woolpack to me *then* and I had a memory-bank printout of a middle-aged couple, Jack the American, Grace an Englishwoman, rich people who sometimes lived in London, sometimes at Paradise Ranch near Flagstaff, Arizona, and sometimes on a large estate in Ciudad de Pacífica. There they were, evidently, in Pacífica, and there was Teapot, my heart's delight, staying with Woolpack, Teapot's natural father. If natural was the word. I mean, he'd abandoned Bluejean and his own child.

Bluejean always said I was jealous. I tore off three hair

shirts saying Who Me Jealous. She said jealousy was ruining the Relationship. I wasn't into Fun, she said. It was true. At parties, for instance, I wouldn't strip with her friends. Wild horses couldn't have dragged off my tight-fitting Levis and shitkickers. The sight of naked people coming to you live, as they say, is not fun. Fat people, too, as fat as Bluejean was threatening to become when last I had seen her, full of fast food and mindblowers, stoned on the shag carpet, faces blanked out yet expressing a sort of earnest and funereal lasciviousness, the high-decibel rock beat of my stereo filling the family room with rubbery motions. I could just go up to Teapot's room and watch football on her 19-inch color portable. She freaked out on football. Daddy's girl. But Bluejean mocked me, saying a real man should be a motorcyclist: Harley-Davidson, black leather jacket, the whole nine yards. We were supposed to go helling through the Rockies at a hundred miles per hour and a six-pack of Coors per hundred miles, stopping to relate to leftover Mormon polygamists. Of course I already had my *Starship Enterprise*, my '67 Cadillac with leather seats, genuine chrome, and custom-made, pale-ale paint job, one intended to please a wife with pale-ale eyes. And one wife at a time seemed to be all I could handle. If handle was the word.

Still, I was a bit jealous. In eleven years of marriage... I have to discount the four months Bluejean was pregnant with Teapot before we married in July of '62, adding five months to get Teapot's birth on Christmas Day of '62 plus eleven months accrued since Teapot's tenth birthday. Close to twelve years. So, in close to twelve years of marriage, Bluejean must have split on us a couple of dozen times. Just up and disappeared. For weeks, maybe a month or more. Without warning. Shacking up somewhere with Woolpack in Europe or the United States. Leaving Teapot, but that was all right with me. While I pulled duty at the base wherever it happened to be—we were in Kaiserslautern, West Germany, before I shipped for Fort Carson—I'd get a friend's wife, one of *my* friends, to babysit, but off duty I'd have Teapot to myself. There was nothing I didn't know about disposable diapers, joyless recipes from one of those *Joy Of* books, and reading aloud the crucial histories of Peter Rabbit and Mrs. Tiggy-Winkle and the *Just So* story of the Great Grey-Green Greasy Limpopo River. Sometimes I told Teapot stories of my native land and the great grey-green greasy Danube River. It was a magical place for her. For me the magic was her falling asleep in my arms after story talking. Bluejean split so often she became a sort of fiction herself.

"Where's Mommy?"

"Oh," I'd say, "saving the whales, I guess."

Teapot would ponder and say from her floor mattress, "Is someone hurting the whales?"

"Yes," I'd say. "That's why she has to save them. Whales are like people. Better than, probably. They breathe air and sing songs as we do. Someone has to care for them."

"How does she save them?"

"Sings to them, I guess."

"Mommy can't sing," Teapot would say in a tone of slightly flirtatious incredulity. "She smokes reefers. Yuck." *Reefers*. And Teapot would say, "Why don't you sing to the whales, Daddy?"

"Well," I'd say, "Daddy's English isn't very good, and whales don't understand Hungarian."

"What a load of codswallop!"

"Tea! Where did you pick up such a vulgar expression?"

Wrinkling her brow like Shirley Temple, she would say with a deadpan expression, "From Mr. Woolpack."

She could flummox me, that kid. She didn't know Woolpack at the time. I mean, she *couldn't*. Bluejean had never taken Teapot on those *trips* before. That's what I wanted to believe, but I was probably wrong. I told myself, Teapot must have heard Bluejean talking about Woolpack, using his crummy English slang. Teapot knew, somewhere in her little woman's blood, how to get a rise out of me with Woolpack's name for bait. A born actress.

"Goodnight, Tea. I love you."

"I don't wanna go bed. Another kissie."

"One more and lights out."

Then from the dark: "Daddy?"

"What is it now?"

"Who's going to win this year?"

She and I used to bet matchsticks on football teams. She rooted for the Washington Redskins. I rooted for the Oakland Raiders.

"Raiders," I said.

"Redskins," she said. "Daddy?"

"Yes?"

"I love you, too, Daddy."

About Karl Marx and other strays. Karl Marx was Bluejean's black tomcat with the cut-off tail. At least you could call for him, "Here, Karl Marx, here Marxie baby," without being surrounded by secret agents sniffing for sedition. Trotsky was another matter, Trotsky the three-legged stray mongrel, sort of a cross between a Dachshund and a Doberman, that Bluejean found starving and named when we lived on base in Kaiserslautern. Back then, I had grown negligent about secret agents. It was "Here, Trotsky, come here, boy" without a second thought. Until one night. I'd been awake on a 48-hour NATO Alert, came home uptight, found Bluejean gone, fed and bathed Teapot and put her to bed, and then slogged into the drizzle of Germany to find Trotsky. Couldn't find him of course, and I was bellowing "Trotsky! Trotsky!" from the barracks to the motor pools to the officers' quarters. Somehow without realizing it I arrived outside the Commanding General's house.

"Trotskiiii! Trotsky, Trotsky!" I called, varying the cadence. No Trotsky. The street was brightly lit with mercury vapor lamps that sizzled bugs.

A tall man with a general's insignia strode out of the darkness and studied me with significantly squinty eyes. "What in the goddam hell are you doing here, soldier?"

I snapped shit. "Sir, Sergeant Szabo. Sir!"

"Did you say *Trotsky*, soldier?"

"Yessir! I said Trotsky. Sir!"

There was a silence like that which follows an avalanche.

"*Leon* Trotsky?"

I knew a court-martial voice when I heard one. I gulped and said, "No, sir!"

"Do you know who Leon Trotsky was?"

"No, sir!" I lied.

"Leon Trotsky was a goddam commie, that's who."

"Trotsky's my dog, sir. I mean, my wife's dog. Sir!" A sweat broke out on my face, became clammy in wet air.

"A dog? Who in hell would call a dog Trotsky?"

I started to say Bluejean would call a dog Trotsky. I thought again and requested permission to explain with my hands.

"At ease," said the CG. "Explain."

I walked two fingers across the palm of my hand. "He *trots*, sir. Trots. Trotsky. That's how he got named, sir. Because he can't run, sir. He has only three legs, sir. So he trots, sir. You should see him, sir."

"What's your name again, soldier?"

I told him.

"Where are your quarters, Sergeant Czar Bo?"

I told him.

"Stand at attention," the CG commanded and went on when I was braced, "because I have some advice for you. If you don't change that dog's name, I'm going to have your ass kicked so hard you'll be spitting teeth like goat turds. Is that clear?"

"Yessir! Thank you, sir!"

"Dismissed!"

I snapped shit, a great salute, and trotted off hoping my knees wouldn't buckle. The more I thought of what the CG had said, the more I realized the matter would not be closed. And the more I thought of the compromising materials that agents, should they happen to search my quarters, would find there, the more quickly I trotted. Ran in fact. Bluejean's Che Guevara poster alone would be worth six months in the stockade, not to mention her drug paraphernalia and do-it-yourself terrorist manuals!

Back home and stinking like a goat, I set to work at once. Che, that murderous rogue, was ripped from the bedroom wall, though I left the framed picture of The Feet. I also left the framed reproduction of Masaccio's fresco of Adam and Eve. I never asked Bluejean when and where she developed interest in early Renaissance Florentine art or in early human disrepute. The shoebox of drug paraphernalia was fetched from under Bluejean's side of the bed. Periodicals and books in the pine-plank shelves came next, the *International Socialist Review*, anything by Marx, Lenin, and Trotsky (right there), then the fellow travelers Bertolt Brecht, Pablo Neruda, and Jean-Paul Sartre. As I warmed to the work, I tried to think what else might intercept me in the end zone, howsoever congenial to my own play of mind. I trashed Bertrand Russell and Gandhi and Martin Luther King. Germaine Greer's *The Female Eunuch*, which Bluejean had practically memorized, had to go. On the cover: "The ultimate word on sexual freedom." Then there were the dictionaries. Because the most commonly used verb in English did not appear in standard dictionaries, I left the Shorter Oxford and Webster's on the shelf, but, as I knew, Wentworth and Flexner's *Dictionary of American Slang* printed the word as *fxxk*. I flung it on the heap. The censorship mania over, the question was where to put these treasures. At once the answer came: put them in the empty refrigerator. I did that. Agents searching your house will look in your closets, in your bureau, up the chimney, under the bed and under the toilet seat—but not inside your refrigerator. This is a peculiar aspect of culture. Poking your nose into the fridge violates decorum. Like hinting at an invitation to dinner.

Sure enough, the agents came just as I closed the refrigerator. They rang the bell, flashed ID and sauntered in, the two of them looking morally clean. One of them carried a walkie-talkie that said *erk psst blat*. He huddled with it, calling the next play. I walked them around the house diffidently, like a Realtor. "Look all you want, gentlemen. No problem. You guys have a tough job. You can't be careful enough, with all the weirdos and junkies... Do you see that picture of The Feet? My wife's an amputee, you see. She inked her footprints on paper before the operation. The little feet on the same paper belong to my daughter Teapot, I mean Christina. Cute as a bug's ear..."

Now, that picture of The Feet was all right to look at but not to think about. Behind the picture frame was pasted Bluejean's copy of a document: *Nonrelinquishment of Parental Rights*, that affidavit was called. Bluejean and Woolpack had signed it and had Woolpack's original copy notarized in the maternity hospital in Atlanta the day after Teapot was born. I'd married Bluejean so that I could take care of Teapot as soon as she was born, and the son of a cowboy who had abandoned Bluejean caught a jet from London and had the cheek *not* to waive his rights but to insist upon them. Bluejean signed too. In those days there were a lot of things deep down inside that an Army lifer named Paul didn't like to think about.

I shushed the agents before they searched Teapot's

room. She lay zonked out on her mattress, mouth open, wee hands clutching the soiled doll I had given her. She had twisted off one of its legs.

"I hope you found everything in order, gentlemen," I essayed a few minutes later as they were leaving. The agent with the walkie-talkie came and studied my face as if memorizing it. Then he sighed and placed a book in my hand. It was *Little Red Riding Hood*. I looked from it to him. He glared at me as an interior lineman does waiting for the snap of the ball. Suddenly his mouth twitched into a leer. Fxxk you, the leer said.

Just then, Trotsky slunk gimpily through the door and to the bathroom where he slurped water from the toilet bowl. "My dog Adolf," I explained to the agents. "Have a nice day."

So when Bluejean called, Karl Marx waited in ambush on top of the refrigerator in the kitchen. I held an empty can of Coors in my hand and decided not to remove my sunglasses as I watched Pike's Peak from the picture window of the empty family room. I felt exposed in the light.

"Hello?"

"Señor Pablo Thawbo por favor."

I made an instant data-retrieval for my Military Occupation Specialty, language. *"Aquí."*

"Acceder lung deestance de señora McQueen de Ciudad de Pacífica?"

Bluejean had not taken my name. Ms. Bluejean McQueen and Sgt. Paul Szabo cordially invite you for Molotov cocktails. *"Claro está,"* I said. Someone scored a touchdown during the ensuing pause. No CIA involvement was reported.

"Hi, Paul! Guess what? I'm in South America." She mentioned the name of the country that was on the news and that I am calling Pacífica.

"Great," I said without heart.

"So you got home all right."

It wasn't a question. "I'm stressed out but I made it," I said. I didn't like the sound of my voice.

"Whatcha doing, man?"

"Watching the ball game. Drinking."

"Double martini with a prune in it, huh?"

"I'm not in a nursing home yet," I replied to that old joke. "What are you doing there if you don't mind my asking?"

"I'm in the archbishop's office."

"*Why* are you in his office?"

"Oh, things," she said. "They have this Vicar, Vicar—I can't say it." She giggled. "Vicaree-rate of Solidarity. Whew! They are trying to keep records of missing people." She sounded nervous. "God. It's like, man, it's, you know, spring and the purple jacaranda are bursting along the avenues and there's limes and lemons in every garden, and burros with knitted caps, and... You know what? I saw this crowd gathered to hear a kid in jeans who, someone told me, talks with the Virgin Mary. He was telling everyone over the microphone to welcome Mary by waving handkerchiefs toward heaven and taking snapshots of the sun. The archbish here thinks the government is just using the kid to discredit the image of the Church. *Far* out... How's Karl Marx?"

"Karl Marx?" I checked out the refrigerator. Karl Marx leapt to the floor, avoiding Kentucky Fried Chicken bones, came and rubbed his back on my polished boot. "He and I make a fine couple," I said.

"Oh, I'm sorry," she pouted. "I know I'm a pain in the ass."

"I didn't say you were—"

"But I'm a *nice* pain in the ass. I can't help—"

"Wait," I interrupted. "Now, let's just talk very calmly

and get the facts straight. Okay? Now. Where's Teapot?"

"She flew down with me."

I said nothing.

"Did you hear?"

"Loud and clear."

"She's all *right*. Don't *worry*."

"She's all I have, Bluejean. You know that. What are you trying to do to me?" I asked on the rising inflection of a tantrum.

"I said she's all right."

"Look," I said. I was crunching the can in my fist. "Aren't they having a revolution?"

"You bet your buggybumpers."

"I want you and Teapot to fly home at once. Got that?"

"No way," Bluejean said. "There's only one flight a week and half the country's trying to get on it."

"So find a ship. But get out of there."

"No ships. The archbishop says the government has seized the ships and is using them to haul bodies out to sea, to dump them. So they'll never be found or identified. This is fascist revolution, kiddo."

By now I was breathing heavily. "Bluejean. Listen. I *know* about revolutions. The Soviet tanks came. Kids, just kids, threw rocks at the tanks. Potatoes. Molotov cocktails. People got killed, lots of people got killed. Maybe revolution *is* something that has to happen and is better than giving up your freedom without a fight, but not sentimental revolution. It's not a game anymore when one side makes the rules. Stay out of it, whatever you do!"

"Don't shout at me, Paul. Don't you dare shout at me. Don't give me that sergeant crap, and don't tell me you were a freedom fighter in Budapest. You were only twelve. You told me yourself you never made a commitment except to shoot your father's persecutor, and you screwed it up. You're jealous, that's all. You want to control everything

I do. I want a divorce. You men are all assholes. God!"

I finished crunching the can. "So where's Teapot?"

There was a pause.

"With Jack," she said in a low voice.

"Who the hell is Jack?"

Bluejean half laughed. "Are you kidding me or something? And the ballbuster, Grace. We had dinner in her mansion last night. She was fat and dressed in pink: Pepto-Bismol on a Dairy Queen cone. She's still hot for your body. Come on down. We'll have an orgy."

"Right," I said. "Now we're getting somewhere. The Woolpacks are in Pacífica, and Teapot is staying with Jack. I suppose Woolpack is giving you the old BS about getting a divorce from Grace after a quarter of a century, and that's where you fit in. You always think of yourself first. That's why America goes to war, to keep the world safe for narcissism."

"Paul, are you listening?"

Tears were springing to my eyes. I couldn't see through my sunglasses. "I'm listening."

"I'm not trying to hurt anybody," she said. "But Jack has the right to have Teapot. You've been a great father to her, but you don't have his rights. And she inherits his bread on Christmas Day. I'm thinking of her future first. And what if you hadn't come back from Vietnam? Did you think of that?"

"I'm back," I said in a barely audible voice. "I miss her. I miss you. Come home... I want to talk to Teapot. How can I reach Woolpack?"

"Just call Earthco. So relax. Teapot's living in a penthouse that has a swimming pool."

"What about you? Don't you sense a slight contradiction between your ideals and your acts? Aren't the Woolpacks supposed to be pigs in your book?"

"They need me here," Bluejean said in a weird tone. "I'm

helping the Church to find missing people. They're sending me to the Andes to one of the copper-mining districts. It's important. It's the most important thing that ever happened to me."

"Bluejean, I love you..."

"Paul, you don't love me. You're just a lonely little boy with a big insecurity problem. You're always afraid the world will disappear. But it won't. So don't worry about it, *okay*?"

Karl Marx jumped on a chair, then on my shoulder, and purred. I took off my sunglasses. Pike's Peak gleamed against hard blue sky as in a picture postcard, not sacred then, not putting me down properly. I had a right to call Teapot my own in my little world of disappearing. *Luv to daddy from CHRISTINA.*

It didn't seem proper to hang up without saying goodbye, but I lowered the receiver and cradled it slowly. I picked it up again, dialed zero. When the operator answered, I asked her to connect me with Earthco in Pacific City. After a long wait she said, "I'm sorry, sir, but all lines are busy. Would you like me to try again later?"

"That's all right," I said on a heavy expiration of breath.

"Have a nice day, sir."

A few minutes later I decided to go to the high country in the morning. Maybe my buddy, Virgil Warbonnet, would go along. Maybe he *should* go along, I was thinking. I'm no cowboy in spite of dude attire, not someone like Woolpack, solid and separate and alone who can ride off into the sunset and feel free of connections. I began to stroke Karl Marx gently, then urgently, holding his furry throb against my ear to hear the heart.

PART TWO

1

THE only child of Attila and Terézia Szabó, I was born in Budapest after Easter in 1944 at the close of the Second World War and the dawn of the Atomic Age. According to my mother, my father was descended from Attila the Hun, the Scourge of God in the fifth century. Perhaps from the Hun have come my blond hair and seagreen eyes—but that is whimsical. *Anya*, mother, was darkhaired with a widow's peak, of small stature with big, old bones pleasantly proportioned. Her parents and their parents before them were paprika farmers near Szeged, but I never met my grandparents or other family on either side: all by the time of my birth had been deported and enslaved by the fascists under Regent Horthy, the land later confiscated by the communists and any deeds or other records destroyed. My father, it was said, came of middle-class background in the city of Szeged. He was a poet and musician and, just before Hitler marched into Austria, matriculated at the University of Szeged where he took a passing interest in the *Szegedi Fiatalok Müvészeti Kollégiuma*, a progressive group. It was this intellectual and political activity, I suppose, that eventually brought him to the attention of the fascists. He married Terézia; they moved to Budapest where he continued his studies in music. In 1943 he was deported to a slave-labor camp in the Yugoslavian mines at Bor and later transported to Abda in the northwestern section of Hungary where, with Jewish slaves, according to false reports prepared by Soviet conquerors, he was clubbed to death by the fascists and dumped in a mass grave. He, or what was left of him, reappeared in Budapest under an assumed name following torture and enslavement by the Soviets. There briefly I came under his influence, learning to distinguish between lies and reality, to recognize attributes of eternity in time, and to uphold the honor of living.

I lived in the sky. The sun was there, inaccessible, and the clouds were there, impalpable. When fog from the Danube curled about my loins, I felt sad and mewled like the wind. At its zenith the sun burned off fog and cut down shade.

Grey, gap-toothed women, men wearing faded berets, the tobacco of their Five Year Plan cigarettes shed through their lips, peered over the rim of my pram. Sometimes men in uniforms aglitter with medals leaned over and spoke to me as if I were an old friend. "*Szervusz.*" Hi.

After the sun went down, I hungered for his return.

Terézia gave me milk, called me *Angyalom*, her darling, and rocked the pram. I breathed my puke-sour rag, which had its own name—in English, Suck-Suck—until it was time to live in the sky again. "*Jo regelt, Angyalom.* Good morning," my mother would say. "Little Pál." Soon the sky moved. The sun found out the bullet holes in buildings. Willows and walnut trees, lampposts and bird-fumbled wires: the sky was filled with earthbound shapes. Boots tock-tocked, trams droned and clanged, children splashed in fountains, pigeons awk-awked in parks. By the river I could smell the wind in pulsing air. Only the wind could reach the sky where the sun was. The grass in the parks by the river rushed up. I fell on my face and ate sticks, snails, turds, cigarette butts and bullet casings. Terézia pried open my mouth.

My walking made her happy. *Angyalom.* We scattered bread for the ducks where the stumps of a blown-up bridge gnawed at river reflections. Gliding nonchalantly prissy out of eddies and up the mudbank, ducks pretended I was invisible. I screamed, clapped spiky hands, wet my pants, and watched steamboats crowded for Visograd plow the bright scent of distant waters. Sometimes paddlewheels churned against the current, sometimes a boat caught the strong flow of the river and steamed on a long journey to a vanishing point.

I cried for my father and imagined myself with the weight of the earth on my face. Then it seemed that the sun was my father and that he just went away and came back again—away and back. At night a hard threatening silence reigned. Then someone cried—it was I—and Terézia took me in bed with her so I would sleep. She smelled of fire and flowers. Rain slapped slowly on the windowpanes of our single room. Outside in the rain, tires of motorcars were long rips of adhesive. Feathers of snow plumed the cones of streetlamps. Snow turned black windows white. In the frigid room I sometimes coughed until strangling. My heart thumped in my ears, and I measured out breath against my nerves. *Angyalom*, she said, returning me to the wonder of love and belonging.

When a big bearded man in worn-out duck pants was in Terézia's bed, I wrapped my shivering and asthmatic skin and bones in Blankie-Blankie on the floor and buried my face in reeking shreds of Suck-Suck. If I needed to go to the toilet, I waited until morning when the man went away. The toilet was down a corridor and used by all the families on the fifth story of our Workers Housing Unit. The place was infested with rats so huge that Terézia had to poke around the toilet bowl to make sure I wouldn't be eaten alive.

I didn't know yet about the *Allamvédelmi Osztaly*. The AVO. Political police.

"No."

At first Terézia merely shook her head in disbelief. Then she said, "No... no," in a diminishing whimper until she covered her mouth as if someone else's hand were gagging her from behind.

Where I lay on the floor, still rubbing my eyes since the moment a few minutes earlier when pounding on the door wakened us and Terézia admitted three officers of the AVO who stabbed our faces with electric torches, I wondered why three of my father's friends would come at the same time. There was already a friend in Terézia's bed. He looked frightened as he covered his long johns with a fur-collared greatcoat and stumbled toward his Russian-style army uniform piled on the floor near the gasburner. The AVO officer who did the talking scrutinized Terézia's Red Book by torchlight. He had a mustache of the pushbroom, Stalin variety and weary eyes under a gloomy forehead. He returned the ID and rocked on his bootheels. He licked his lips thoughtfully. "Everything is arranged. He will be well cared for. His new home will be more suitable to his welfare than... this."

"He's only five." Terézia was not whimpering now but almost laughing on a mocking note.

The friend had picked up his uniform and shoes and was

tiptoeing barefoot to the door. The officers let him pass, then kicked his buttocks. "*Menya polkaba!* Go to the devil!" they roared good-humoredly. I started to laugh. I didn't really like the friends who came at night, the workers from Csepel wearing oil-stained clothing, the clerks in leather coats, the soldiers in uniform, even though, after night visitors, we had bread, smoked and dried sausage, dill pickles, strudel, coffee and once in a while a tin of Chinese fruit. My father, before he disappeared at Abda, had had a lot of friends. I let them fondle me but hated them in my heart, knowing the sun would undo them. This AVO officer, though, this Comrade Mustache had control of the sun in the dark—a vast magic.

"You have saved me from a demon!" Terézia exclaimed and tossed her long hair from bare shoulders. "He used to be my husband. When I found out he was a *fasiszta*, I wouldn't let him hang around. But he comes and takes his clothes off, pretending he can get it... Now. A little paprikosh, a little wine... Pál?" She had not changed her voice. She came and hugged me into her warm bosom. "Angyalom, dress quickly, go to toilet for do-do's, and don't come back till I call. Off we go, or no chicken, you understand?"

I didn't want to face rats alone in the dark, but we hadn't eaten paprikosh in months. I put on sweater, lederhosen, and Boot-Boots.

"Wait," said Comrade Mustache, blocking the door. His eyes fixed mine with a strange sort of sorrow. He reminded me of the statue of Stalin that towered over us when we walked to the Municipal Woods. Terézia fidgeted with her nightgown. "Of course," she smiled on a nervously rising inflection. "Poor lad. He has asthma, he'll catch a chill... Look! He likes you, sir. He lost his father—a Soviet captain—during the liberation of the city. See his eyes shine? Isn't he handsome, Pál? Wouldn't you like to have a handsome comrade for a new friend?"

Comrade Mustache kneeled and put hands on my shoulders. "Would you like to see your father?" he asked me quietly.

Childhood surged through my developing bones, and the habit of mourning lifted from my heart. Comrade Mustache repeated his question. I nodded in a sort of enchantment. "Good," he said, lifting me in his arms. "If you're a good boy we shall go now to see your father."

"Is Anya coming too?"

"She shall come tomorrow."

I followed his gaze. At first Terézia looked as if she would say something, but she sat on the bed, limply, and murmured, "He's only five. He is all I have."

One of the other officers, who during this time had transfixed her with a torch, remarked that I belonged to the people now.

"We go," said Comrade Mustache.

"Good-bye," I waved. "Good-bye, Anya." I kept on waving as Comrade Mustache carried me from home and down the flights of concrete stairs. I began to wonder if my father would like me after all the bad things I'd done. Of course it was Terézia's fault for having lied to me about Attila! If I had known he was alive and would send for me one night, I would have gone to mass every Sunday, would have thanked the Latin inscriptions in gold letters and the mosaic pictures of prophets circling the base of the church's dome, would not have made a monkey face at nuns sputtering along on mopeds, their caps starched and fluted like the wings of gulls.

In those days it was not uncommon for war orphans and the children of political prisoners to be taken to an institution where, under false names, they would be given years of intensive training for socialism. Their real names, officially despised, became part of the government's secret records.

As a fog-fingered dawn silhouetted the great spires of the city, I was taken in a rattling Russian car to a secluded estate on the outskirts of Buda, on a hill overlooking the river through thick groves of oak, pine, and lime trees. The estate was surrounded by a high stone wall on top of which were shards of broken glass and several tiers of rusted barbed wire. Outside a wrought-iron gate our driver beeped the horn until a stoop-shouldered old man came and unlocked the gate. We drove in. A sprawling stone mansion with iron-barred windows came into view. We halted before an oaken door beside which were chipped, fungus-blotched stone pillars. There was an eerie murmur of sad winds in trees. When the old man ushered Comrade Mustache and me into the house, I realized that my father must be rich and important.

Down a marble-floored corridor Comrade Mustache's boots went tock tock tock and likewise down another long corridor at the end of which the sun, through those high iron-barred windows, cast grid patterns upon cracked plaster walls. Finally we arrived in a sort of vestibule: at the side was a wide, worn stone stairway, in the middle was a dry pool and sculptured fountain in the bowl of which knelt a marble nude, and in a recessed corner was a small oaken door with a pitted bronze knocker. Comrade Mustache rattatted the knocker, commanded me to wait, and tock-tocked away.

I was alone, my heart wildly beating. Was my father behind the door? Did I dare to open the door by myself? I looked at the nude statue. Slender arms, hands relaxed on thighs near a perpetually tight delta smudged by pencils. Her oval face was lifted to reveal dreaming, half-closed eyes. Her hair swept back from the brow to cascade down serenely curving buttocks. I heard a creaking sound and wheeled about. The door was opening but no one stood there to greet me. Taking deep breaths, I went in.

I found myself in an enormous room rather like a high-ceilinged, crossbeamed library of a monastery or ancient university. Slowly my eyes accustomed themselves. There were three walls of bookshelves some seven meters high and recessed behind metal screens. In the center of the room was a kind of amphitheater: a semicircle of wooden desks facing a high dais from which was draped a colossal poster portrait of a jovial József Stalin.

"Here," a man's voice squeaked. I gasped. But saw no one. "*Here*, you silly twit."

Like a buzzard popping its head up from offal for a bit of ruminative swallowing, a thin man peered over wire-rim spectacles from the dais above Stalin's portrait. He wore a black gown which, for want of shoulders to support it, seemed to plunge from his elongated neck. I approached the dais and looked up. The man's adam's apple pumped up and down. His red nose, jutting cheekbones, and balding scalp with loose hanks of yoghurt-white hair were jerking about as he munched a hunk of salami, ravenously, with a Stonehenge of teeth.

"Are you my father?"

He pondered as he chewed. A morsel of salami worked its way down his throat as a mouse through a snake. He licked the ends of skeletal fingers and said, "Good heavens! Why should I want to be your father?"

"They said."

"Who said?"

"The AVO."

"Stupid," he said.

"Are you?"

The man peered over the dais.

"Do you realize," he piped in a sort of conspiratorial tone, "that the abortion rate is extremely high? Is it possible that the answer to Scientific Exactitude is to provide no children for the future? How logical is that? Who would want to be anyone's father—let alone *yours*—if, after the prodigious effort required for mating, one's bipedal immortality is to be wrapped in newspaper and surreptitiously tossed in a dustbin? Answer me *that!* And who would want to be a child? The trouble with you and your lot is, you have this absurd notion that you're going to grow up and have your turn at mucking things about. But you're wrong! The only grownups now permitted are dwarfs, you silly twit. Truman, Stalin, Horthy: all dwarfs. Why are you so determined to be a dwarf?... Do I look like your father?" He paused and chewed salami.

I had never heard such bewildering discourse before. I was glad to shake my head, negatively.

"So," he resumed after swallowing. "They've spoiled you. You've been eating real butter and using toilet paper and singing folk songs. Yet here you are in Hell believing in your own existence. How can you be my son when you don't exist? Answer me that."

"I don't know, sir," I ventured.

"Comrade," he said.

"Sir?"

He ducked his head, then reappeared standing on the dais, wiping chalky lips on the black gown. "How would you like it if I called you *sir*?... I am Comrade Supervisor Oszkár. You may call me Comrade Oszkár. You *are* a communist, I presume?"

I hesitated and said I didn't know. I wanted to cry.

"*What*?" screeched Oszkár. He dropped to his knees and fixed me with a bird-like gaze. He had lustreless green eyes. "This is incredible. You have to be a communist. If you're not a communist, then you must *not* be dead. Logic, simple logic. Would you like some chocolate?" he asked suddenly.

I told him I was very hungry.

"Yes or no?"

"Yes, Comrade Oszkár."

"Well," he said with a scowl, "let's have it."

I said nothing.

"Do you mean to tell me you have no chocolate?"

I shook my head.

"If you haven't brought chocolate with you, how do you expect to eat chocolate? Answer me that."

"I don't know, Comrade Oszkár."

"Logic, simple logic," he declared with a sigh of disappointment. "If you don't bring chocolate, you don't eat any. The next thing you'll be wanting is to go home, am I correct, little comrade?"

"I would like to go home," I said.

"Tautological. That's what they all say. But," Oszkár continued, standing up and waving batlike arms toward the room, "you *are* home. Who are you?"

I swallowed hard and told him.

"Pál Szabó. Hm." Oszkár stroked his chin, then shook his buzzard's head decisively. "You'll need a name, that's the long and short of it." He elevated his finger as if testing for weather. "Come," he beckoned. When I mounted steps, Oszkár was seated and poring over a leatherbound ledger on his desk, mumbling names. "Balázs, Boldizsár, Domokos, Elek, Emil, Ferenc, Gábor, Gellért, György, Henrik, Ignác, Imre... There! Ince!" He peered over his spectacles. "Comrade Ince. I thought you were dead. What miracles cannot be performed in the Age of Dwarfs! You died, you know. Pity."

Now, I knew, he was playing. "I didn't die. Don't be ridiculous," I said.

"*Sic probit?*" he declared in mock surprise, bloodless lips like puckered mushrooms. "See here. Your name has been crossed out in red ink. I, N, C, E, Ince, *kaput*. Yet here you are again."

"You're funny," I said.

He lifted his finger. "I'm so good-looking, it frightens me... Now. Last week, mark you, Comrade Ince, *aetatis* eight, tried to escape our home by climbing over the garden wall. He impaled himself on glass, thus creating a vacancy. But I warn you, now you are reborn as Ince. If you try to escape again, you can expect no mercy from the Party. First, it is unhistorical to imagine that one would want to escape after one has been set free. If you leave home, you are an unhistorical person. It follows that an unhistorical person is an enemy of the people. Therefore, the Party, spontaneously acting on behalf of the proletariat, cannot permit said unhistorical person to have been consciously in search of freedom, especially if the Party's consciousness is spontaneity itself. Simple logic. Isn't the dialectic illuminating? Besides, if you escape, I shall be tortured and shot."

I giggled in spite of myself. "Logic, simple logic," I said.

"Ho ho." Again the uplifted finger. "They've sent me a bright one at last, a true Hungarian who can distinguish between lies and reality!... Now, let's pretend that I am your father... What is my name?"

"Comrade Supervisor Oszkár."

"No, no. Pretend name. Give us one, that's the lad."

"Attila," I said.

He glanced away. When he peered at me again, his glassy green orbs breathed a silent flame. "Very well," he said. "I'll play Attila. Tell me about Attila."

I told him that Attila was a musician born in Szeged who was killed by the fascists. He nodded slowly and said, "Permit me to continue the story of Attila. He was, as you say, arrested by the fascists. He was sent to the mines. He did his work so well that the Soviets, after liberating him, pretended he had been murdered with Jews and retained his services for years. Dressed in rags, their toes and fingers frozen, ankles swollen from malnutrition, their teeth rattling like dice, he and his fellows survived as best they could. There were tortures: one winter night Attila was stripped naked and sloshed with water so that he had to jump in order to avoid the sleep wherein he would have frozen to death. His cries were not always human. Oddly, however, he and his fellows firmly believed that they would be freed, not at some vague future time but the next day—the next hour! They had to struggle against the desire to give up. In all those years they heard not a single word of recognition or encouragement. They became obsessed with visions of food and vengeance. Still, he, Attila, remained human. What delight he found in the companionship of spiders! What joy it was for him to have rats receiving the crumbs he offered them! He had something to give.

"About a year ago the communists transferred Attila from the mines to a collective farm. He groomed and watered the horses. And he loved horses, you understand. Attila's father had maintained a stable of horses in—where was it?—Szeged. Now, compared to his previous employment, this job of groom was heaven. He could see the sky. He could hear finches make their summer music. However, the task of drawing water from a well should not be underestimated. Poor Attila! In the winter the water turned to ice beneath his fingernails and cracked them open. To correct this misfortune, his masters pulled out his fingernails with pliers. How stupid was this? Now he could not work on the farm at all. And so Attila was sent to Budapest for intensive study of the works of Marx, Lenin, and Stalin, which in his youth had seemed noble but were now revealed as the mendacious gibberish of lunatics. And that is all I know about your father... Care for a bite of salami, Comrade Ince?"

"I didn't bring any," I replied quickly.

Oszkár threw back his head and wheezed an obbligato of squeaky hee-haws. "You didn't bring salami. That's a good one! Therefore, like a good communist, you must share some of mine." So saying, he removed his gnawed salami roll from a drawer of the desk and presented it to me. Then, as I was eating, he produced from yet another drawer a half-empty bottle of red wine and pulled the cork with raw fingertips. "Once upon a time a Hungarian hero fought so bravely that his conqueror wished to drink his blood, that such courage might come into his own possession. But the people, rather than execute the hero, served the conqueror bull's blood instead... To your health. *Egészségedre.*" Oszkár drank deeply and passed the bottle to me. When he opened a desk drawer, I saw a pistol next to a book. He removed the book, opened it at a marker, and began to read to himself, pausing every now and then to chuckle. Finally he placed his ruined hand upon the book and said with satisfaction, "Every morning for breakfast I read passages from this book. It is Tolstoy's *War and Peace...* So many *dead* Russians! It gives me hope... Now to business."

After Oszkár had explained that I had been enrolled in an institution for orphans, I asked him if Terézia were coming to visit.

"Terézia?"

"Anya."

"Impossible!" he exclaimed. "How can you be an orphan and also have a mother? Your father is officially deceased, and the Party does not recognize your mother's existence. Ergo, you are an orphan. Logic, simple logic. Come," he said, and rose and took me by the hand, "we might as well make the best of a bad job. You're lucky, you know. The other boys were turned out before dawn in order to march in the May Day parade... You'll need a uniform and a bed. But, first, I shall show you the only object in the world that has no use."

He led me to the vestibule. "Here she is," he said, pointing to the statue in the sterile fountain. "Soul. The fascists stripped this splendid old house of most of its treasures, and the Soviets stole the rest, but no one thought to remove Soul. She was of no use, you see. They couldn't recognize her. You must have a soul to recognize her. What do you see, my dear Ince?"

"A girl, I guess."

"Barbarian! What do you *feel*?"

I felt nothing except dizziness and the desire to lie down and cry, but Oszkár, tightly clutching my hand, circled the statue and said, "Now, my dear Ince, you have felt Soul. But unawares of how... Observe. Soul is not part of slab or mountain. Soul is free, in space alone. Thus, first, we know that the artist, who has given her all the degrees of circumference, understood the spirituality of the individual. Second, the artist has so shaped the figure that, from whatever vantage point you perceive it, what you see is perfectly proportioned. Every angle contributes to the symmetry of the whole. In short, Soul is not a representation of a girl; Soul is ideal, abstract, like a musical composition. Although sensuality may form the initial attraction, you move beyond desire to feel with your mind. At this moment recognition occurs. Freedom and proportion, attributes of eternity, have been arrested in the world of time.

"Cherish the soul within you, my son. When you become a man, you shall meet Soul in living flesh. Come."

I followed Oszkár up the stone stairway to a long, low-ceilinged dormitory room. Two rows of identical bunks were aligned against plaster walls, though one wall had windows, all with iron bars. The room smelled of dirty clothes and urine.

"This is your bed." Oszkár tapped a mattress discolored by what seemed wine and paprika. "Your predecessor, here, believed that a six-meter-high stone wall topped with broken bottles and barbed wire could be scaled without injury to the vital organs, a deficiency in logic for which I would have been shot had I not contrived to fetch his corpse back to this bed and to arrange the official version of death from causes unknown. At least your uniform is new."

He ordered me to remove my clothes and Boot-Boots, and I did so even though Terézia had tucked away forints for months in order to afford their purchase. I liked the new uniform: red flannel shirt, red trousers with white suspenders, heavy black boots. Oszkár seemed to admire the effects. "You're free," he told me, "until the boys return tonight for dinner. Me, you will see only in the classroom in the future. Stay in bed, eat plenty of chocolate, and enjoy the view of the stone wall from your window. And... one thing more, Comrade Ince."

Swiftly he lifted me into his spidery arms and kissed me, then put me down, about-faced, straightened himself like one of Terézia's night visitors, and marched from the room, his footfall ghosting on the stairs. I gazed out the window, wondering why the political police had lied to me about my father. Beyond a playing field with grassless patches by soccer nets, beyond an oak grove and the sun-dappled wall, beyond distant tiled rooftops—the river gleamed as with rippled panels of cathedral glass.

2

THAT night several dozen boys burst into the dormitory. Sunburned and blowsy faces, intense, almost demonic faces. Some big boys carried guidons and marched down the aisle between bunks as if drums and cheers still animated their goosestepping.

The suddenness of this onslaught set my nerves on edge, and an asthmatic attack sent me into spasms of coughing.

"'Ello 'ello," a hoarse adolescent voice mocked in a Hungarian dialect for which Cockney is a reasonable equivalent. The room grew silent save for my coughing. "Any a' you coves smell summat queer?"

Hot bodies crowded around my bed. Above me, a fat boy of about thirteen was pretending to sniff as if he were a rat emerging from a toilet. He croaked "Who cut the cheese?" in a falsely desperate way. There was an appreciative chorus of giggles. "It do stink like a Jewboy's fart, don't it?" Then, loudly: "Arse'ole, stinky poo, I'm a blindman, 'elpless until I bugger you..." Through misted eyes I saw the fat boy giving a good imitation of a blindman's groping. "Got... find... arse'ole," he groaned. Then: "Got it!"

The fat boy had swooped and pinned me by the arms. I could feel other boys piling on, their shrieks of laughter muffled as I squirmed for air. Someone pulled off my new trousers. I felt disrepute in my throat.

"Bugger 'im!"

"Piss in 'is mouth!"

"Screw the Jew!"

"Lay off, Zoltan."

"You're chickenshit, Günter."

"You're chickenshit yourself, Zoltan."

"Jew-lover!"

"He can't breathe."

"Yeah, Zoltan, leave 'im alone. 'E's only a fuckin' baby."

The hot bodies went away, and I found my breath. As I was putting on my trousers, the fat boy named Zoltan shoved a blond boy of about eight. "You're a Jew-lovin' Kraut, Günter." Zoltan hawked phlegm as if to spit in Günter's face, but he didn't spit, and Günter crouched, a wary smile taunting the other.

An alarm bell clanged. Boys whooped and ran out of the room and downstairs. Günter, relaxing his guard, came and looked at me. He had a steady blue gaze. "You all right?"

I nodded.

"Well," he said, "we better go eat the garbage. My name's Günter. What's yours?"

I told him and added that Oszkár had named me Ince.

"The school is very stupid," said Günter with an expression of disgust. "Here, they call me Tamás. My father is German. I am going to escape and find my father." His smile was cool. I liked Günter. "The food gives you gasses," he said as we went downstairs together. Passing the strange statue of Soul, I was about to ask about Oszkár when Günter divined my thought. "Oszkár's a bit—you know." Günter tapped his forehead knowingly. "But he's all right. He has to teach us politics. He tries to make you listen so that you understand that he means the opposite of what he says. It gets boring. But the man to watch out for is Venzel, a creep from Czechoslovakia. You don't want *him* to get your pants off... Do you realize, Ince, if I live to be eighty, I've only lived one-tenth of my life?"

When we came to the corridor that would lead to the front door, Günter didn't turn; instead we approached a bedlam of shouting boys, of clink-clashing plates. "Gas City," said Günter. Indeed, upon entering the dining room, we were met by such an odor of grease and sweat that I lost my appetite. We sat on a bench fronting a long table. A serving woman with an overbite like a chipmunk's—Mrs. Pribéky her name, as I would later learn—brought us plates in the middle of which were dumped mounds of noodles and gravy. Günter ate.

I looked up from my plate and there seated on the opposite bench was my persecutor, Zoltan. After carefully considering what Attila the Hun would have done in this embarrassing situation, I rose, picked up my plate, and with a single motion pushed it into Zoltan's face so hard that he fell backwards onto the floor, the plate shattering. There was a quietening in Gas City. The chipmunk, Pribéky, stood above me, arms akimbo. "The food is terrible," I declared with indignation. "It gives you gasses." I pointed at Zoltan, still spraddled on the floor and picking noodles from his red shirt. "That boy is full of gasses," I said. "I think you must not give us garbage to eat or you will be shot." I sat down.

Someone giggled, then someone else. Günter shouted, "Three cheers for Ince! Hip, hip—hooray!"

"Hooray!" chorused the boys, three times. "Ince!"

I went to Zoltan. "Terézia says you can't tell if a broom is good until it sweeps the floor. I'm willing to be friends if you are."

Zoltan rose and made a noise in his throat like that of a dog by a spent fire. He was twice my size. I crouched the way Günter had done and balled my fists. Fortunately, he pretended to be afraid. "Don't 'it me. 'E's a bloody giant, 'e is. I'n' at right?" He grinned and looked around.

I hunched my shoulders, clawed the air, fanged my teeth and also looked around.

Everyone started to laugh. Even Zoltan, who had called me a Jew. I had never been called that before and imagined myself disappearing in a mass grave.

After that evening, I had no more trouble with the boys.

I was to spend years at the school. It would be tedious to relate how I passed them and erroneous to assert that we all led lives of brutality and unrelieved desperation. True, a sense of abandonment made a hollow place in my viscera, but I quickly learned to work my life around it. The world beyond the walls seemed a fantasy even on those occasions when, under armed guard, we were paraded across the Danube to Parliament Square and up Lajos Kossuth Avenue. We made a good impression on government officials clapping on their reviewing stand, and had no reason or capacity to know that they were gangsters. We took pride in presenting the eyes-right salute as we goosestepped. We were an elite corps of Lilliputian patriots with automatized conviction of our superiority. Superficially, we shared the same emotions. We loved the fatherland and our allies, the Soviets, who had liberated it. We hated Jews, fascists, capitalist warmongers, *kulaks* and women.

Oszkár, however, saved some of us from lies and stimulus starvation while we inhaled the alpine air of logic and deductive reasoning. How could we possibly have known that people deprived of creativity were indoctrinated to wrap the whole planet in a shroud? Intuitively, of course, because there is something in the mind, especially in the minds of children, that resists identification with conscious thinking. And Oszkár, as I regard him in retrospect, understood exactly the problem of the modern individual, whose habits of thinking are so deeply ingrained in scientific and rational process that the higher powers of feeling and imagination and intuition are relegated to an underworld, separate and evil. Yet Oszkár could not lead us directly to hope. He was, in some way unclear to us, a political prisoner restricted to the school's premises. Although he seemed impregnable to official criticism, I later understood that he lived in perpetual fear and expected at any moment to be arrested and executed. We knew he was indiscreet, for he did not disguise dangerous opinions behind the veil of Party propaganda. How he hoodwinked the authorities into believing the school was orthodox and pure, I can only guess. Doubtless, he filled in forms with approved jargon and signified dignity; his lesson plans, I'm sure, complied with regulations deemed suitable for converting children into turnips. Then, too, he must have been the slave to whom he attributed the fate of my father, though this particular penny did not drop in my brain for some years. Probably the authorities considered him a broken, harmless fool. Probably the school's staff was itself so preoccupied with strategies for survival that it remained silent about our preceptor. There were six staff members: an old groundskeeper, the Gas City crew of three women, Comrade Ernö who was in charge of sports and military drill, and Comrade Venzel, a surly young maintenance man and notorious pederast. Finally, Oszkár's long avoidance of official displeasure can be explained as a result of his having a savior in high places, a fixer: none other than Comrade

Mustache. More about that later.

So we had some enthusiasm for the school, and we loved Oszkár whether we knew it or not. Nevertheless, not a day passed when we did not yearn to be free, and those of us who had been separated from a family and who nurtured under false names a sense of personal identity dreamed incessantly of escape. Even those boys truly orphaned or of unknown origins felt no gratitude to the system that provided for their welfare. They also dreamed, and their fantasies about mothers and fathers flourished even more wildly than my own.

Günter, my best friend, was such an orphan. Of his parents, he knew what officialdom recorded: that his father was German and his mother Polish, and that the Germans had liquidated her in a death camp. Günter had been raised by gypsies, then abandoned at an orphanage; like me, he had been transferred to the school at the age of five. Yet he persuaded himself that his father was alive. He had seen him in a dream, he said. In the dream his father was living in Argentina. Günter planned to escape to Argentina as soon as he grew old and big enough to scale the wall bloody with rust from its tiered barbed wire. Once over the wall, he would go to Argentina and find his father who—the fantasy expanding—was a prosperous rancher. So gravely did Günter confide to me his dreams, I refrained from questioning their validity and began to share them.

Rain or shine, frost or snow, we boys were jarred awake by the bell every morning at five. Naked save for shorts, we ran onto the soccer field for half an hour of calisthenics with Comrade Ernö. Our collective hands shook, our collective feet danced on ice, our collective teeth chattered like runaway telegraph transmitters. My asthma ceased. I strengthened my body for the ever-approaching year and day of escape. After calisthenics, it was back to the dormitory to scrub ourselves with lye soap and cold water, to squat in the Bog, a Turkish latrine, and to dress in uniform; then it was downstairs for breakfast of milk and larded bread. Then to the classroom—and Oszkár. Mornings we studied reading, writing and arithmetic according to individual age and ability. Following a lunch of sausages and black coffee, and a period of sports or military drill, we returned to the classroom for science, politics, philosophy and foreign languages. Dinner was at seven, usually *gyulas* or a heavy soup flavored with paprika. After dinner, and again according to age and ability, we had books to read, essays to write, formulae to resolve, dates and vocabularies to memorize. At Lights Out, Venzel the Czechoslovakian creep often appeared, like a sleek and voluptuous sultan, to select a wretched favorite for the night. And then we slept, plotting treason.

About philosophy. It was called that, and I suppose it was that part of the curriculum intended as instruction in dialectical materialism. But we were taught how to think for ourselves. It was all "logic, simple logic," as Oszkár would say. First, he would give us an absurd proposition to ponder. Then it was our responsibility to defend that proposition with all the reasons at our command, except for reasons based upon evidence *ex contrarius* or derived from common horse-sense, these being playfully ruled out as inconsistent with socialist reality. This exercise was called debate. At no time during debate were we to admit to the absurdity of the proposition. To do so would have spoiled the game, which required painfully disciplined restraint of the Prometheus a few of us were learning to love with all our hearts—Truth. At the end of debate we rose and applauded one another, thus preserving that sanctimonious decorum so esteemed by Party congresses.

Oszkár would initiate proceedings. "Today's debate concerns the proposition that the Earth is flat. Comrade Imre, cogitate and regurgitate."

IMRE(rising solemnly and bowing toward the dais): Comrade Oszkár, your proposition is absolutely true. The Earth is flat.

OSZKÁR (magisterially): State your reasons.

IMRE: If the Earth were not flat, we would fall off.

OSZKÁR: Good point. More?

IMRE: Maps are flat. Furthermore, feet are flat, proving that one level plane deserves another.

OSZKÁR: Excellent. You may sit down. Today's debate now concerns the proposition that dictatorship is democracy. Any volunteers? Comrade Róbert.

RÓBERT: Comrade Oszkár, your proposition is absolutely true. Dictatorship is democracy. Reason number one: in a true democracy the people are represented by a party which dictates in their behalf. Reason number two: in a true democracy, everyone has equal rights, and these, to be truly equalized, must be surrendered via social contract to a dictator. Reason number three: in a true democracy, the people have no property, so there is no crime because the dictatorship has the property and commits all the crimes in the name of the people. Finally, reason number four: if all the individuals within a democracy were allowed to think for themselves, there would be chaos because illusions are the basis of social order and too many illusions in contention undermine authority. Consequently, the dictatorship establishes the correct illusions, thus preserving true democracy in the same form it has enjoyed since Neanderthal Man worshipped bears 30,000 years before Christ.

OSZKÁR: Splendid. In proving the proposition, you have also correctly surmised that Marxist-Leninism had its precursor in the democracies of early Paleolithic hunters. You may sit down. Today's debate now concerns the proposition that the United States is evil...

So it would go. The proposition about *Egyesült Allamok*,

the United States, opened fields of incongruity. In proving that nation's vileness, we established its idealism and freedom. Which we didn't have. We had to argue that the American continent was property belonging to Indians from whom European imperialists stole it, and this was no tendentious argument but, rather, one faulty in its major moral premise. We had to argue that the Americans had conquered or controlled many areas of the earth, but we were not allowed to mention that these areas were usually occupied for brief periods and then returned to their own sovereignty. Which we, as part of the Soviet empire, didn't have. We had to argue that this American imperialism was based upon exploitation of the masses as in the European fashion. We were not allowed to argue that the basis of American wealth lay in the fecundity of the land, in the vast store of natural resources, in the industry of the people, and in the relative freedom of the United States from class, ethnic, racial and nationalistic constraints. Which we in the police state certainly had. By these and similar arguments we were secretly persuaded that a major source of creativity and morality in the modern world was this same, evil United States, a nation with grievous faults but one that made room for everyone and upheld the honor of living. By the same token we learned to laugh in our hearts at the oppressors of our native land, knowing those rascals for what they were.

Nevertheless we were children. I felt entombed in self, seldom fully realizing that I, not the world, was responsible for my own happiness or the lack of it. We were a dreary lot. In that enormous room with the obscenely jovial portrait of Stalin, we hunched over desks scarred and stained from generations of use by other pupils in other rooms. The past lived on, and the present seemed doomed never to yield to change.

One bright spring morning in 1953 Mrs. Pribéky scurried into the classroom and presented Oszkár with a note. His expression, though always cadaverous and sickly pale, became wooden. Presently he fumbled out of a desk drawer an object that made a metallic sound. He stood, clasping his gown as if to deliver a lecture, and cleared his throat.

"Gentlemen," he said calmly without a squeak. He had never before addressed us as gentlemen. We gave him our full attention. "Gentlemen, the AVO are coming. There is no need to be alarmed. As soon as they arrive, I must ask you to avert your eyes. Meanwhile, I have a story upon which I wish you to reflect in future."

The room grew absolutely still as Oszkár's voice drifted as a feather in the breeze, lightly yet magically see-sawing.

"Once upon a time over 2,000 years ago there lived a stonemason who was ugly and poor and who went about in bare feet and a filthy robe. He lived in Athens, and his name was Socrates. It is possible that he could have passed his days pleasantly plying his craft. However, he could not be happy unless he wandered through the city stopping people, young and old, rich and powerful, and posing to them questions. Quite an odd sort, you see, inquisitive, pawky, most annoying. And perhaps the oddest thing about this fellow, Socrates, who was forever posing what seemed to be simple questions, was that he was not satisfied with simple answers. He himself claimed ignorance, and his interlocutors felt flattered when he told them he knew nothing and merely sought enlightenment from them. Naturally, being powerful, they believed they knew everything. Here was this poor ugly fool so brainless that he didn't give lectures, as intelligent men were supposed to do, and so impractical he neither demanded nor received payment for whatever wisdom he might accidentally impart. They could have pushed Socrates aside, but... well, he *did* have an ingratiating and persistent manner and unfailing good humor. To indulge him, they opened up their storehouse of received ideas. *This*, they said, is the nature of justice, *this* of morality, *that* of spiritual truth. Come, old man, you have your answers now. Be content. Oh, excellent! exclaimed Socrates. Truly you are wise, and I am eternally grateful to you. Except that I am still curious to know this, to learn that. If, my lords, things are indeed as you say, as for example that might makes right, then it must be wrong for a young man to marry against his father's wishes, is that correct? Or for a young prince to avenge himself upon his mother, the queen, even though she has committed adultery, murdered his father, and usurped the power of the state, is that correct?

"Relentlessly, Socrates raised questions. People called him a gadfly. He stung them into thought—and thought is tolerable not for the many but for the few. Those rich and powerful men to whom Socrates directed questions became uneasy. What if they also knew nothing? Exasperated, they lost their tempers. Their judgments could not stand the test of honest inquiry. Of course some of Socrates's pupils—Plato among them—realized that here was a method of teaching superior to any other. Socrates taught through the power of implication, so that his pupils would learn to think for themselves and eventually to arrive at positive beliefs upon which a truly human set of values could be erected.

"Now, gentlemen, it is curious, but human nature has been trapped in a circle for millions of years. Only the most remarkable of persons, Socrates being one, call our attention to this circle and by means of self-sacrifice release the human spirit into hopes of fulfillment. That circle is called *Causa Effectus*. The beneficent aspect of *Causa Effectus* is to do unto others as you would have them do unto you. The malignant aspect of *Causa Effectus* is to do unto others what others forced you to endure passively, what one was forced to suffer or what was forbidden. Defeated children overcome defeat by perpetuating abuse. Slaves overcome masters in order to perpetuate slavery. The simple logic of *Causa Effectus* is based on power but polarized to fear or to love: either you act to gain power over others, torturing and persecuting them because the pain of fear is intolerable, or you satisfy your need for power by effecting the response of love in others and toward all life which requires nurturing. That is the choice you must face. It is the choice I have faced. I leave it for you to decide whether Socrates made the destructive or constructive choice..."

Outside the mansion, car doors were being slammed.

"Pay no attention to the sound of the dwarfs," Oszkár resumed. "Unfortunately, Socrates made enemies among those who could not tolerate their own powerlessness. One day those enemies intimidated the people of Athens and had Socrates condemned to death by suicide. Socrates gathered his beloved pupils around him, made his farewells, and cheerfully drank hemlock and died..."

Tocka tocka tocka. Boots in the corridor.

"Gentlemen, I salute you from the grave. Don't disgrace me. Kindly avert your eyes."

The door of the room burst open and uniformed men poured through, leveling machine pistols at us even as two of their number dashed toward Oszkár.

Then we saw a pistol in Oszkár's scarecrow hand, saw him raise the pistol swiftly to his head.

"In the name of love, avert the eyes!"

Often in nightmares I am visited by an image of Oszkár from that supreme moment. The image is motionless. He is emaciated. His gown droops as if attached to a peg. His spectacles have slipped below the bridge of his red nose. I cannot see eyes in his sockets. In my nightmare he does not squeeze the trigger of the pistol he has pressed against his head. I do not hear the report of the pistol. I do not see blood spurting in diminishing arcs. Yet just before I wake gasping, I see blood dripping down Stalin's face. Stalin seems to be relishing a strange kind of wine.

We never doubted that Venzel was he who betrayed our master. It was rumored that one of Venzel's boys had, after the first rape, reported the matter to Oszkár, who had evidently been ignorant of the maintenance man's depravity. Whether Oszkár could have dismissed Venzel, we didn't know. But Venzel, to save himself, must have reported Oszkár to the police. And Venzel thereby gained a promotion.

Not a minute had elapsed since Oszkár's suicide before Venzel strolled into the half-stifled screams and convulsive sobs of the room. He was dressed in a two-piece suit with the white shirt, winged collar and black bow tie of a parvenu. As Oszkár's ragdoll form was being dragged away, Venzel briskly mounted the dais. "I am the comrade supervisor now. You there, stand up."

He pointed at one of us. I looked around to see who it was. Faces were stunned, mouths agape.

"I said, stand up. You. Blond hair."

For a moment I thought he meant me. But Günter stood up.

"Wipe that stupid look off your face. How long have you been in this school?"

Günter did not speak. The acrid odor of gunsmoke floated to me. The soldiers slammed the door. Drops of blood dripped from Stalin's portrait to a pool at Günter's feet.

Venzel had a fat round face and frizzy hair. He tapped fingers on the desk like an arthritic pianist.

Drip. Tap.

"I don't know," Günter muttered and added, "Comrade Supervisor Venzel."

"You don't know."

"No."

Drip. Tap.

"Seven years, Tamás. Seven years," Venzel repeated like a judge. "And how old are you now?"

"Twelve."

Venzel stopped tapping and pressed his palms down hard against the desk. "Think of that. Seven of your twelve years have been at the expense of the people. Why? Why should we care about fascist bastards like you? My sister was raped by your SS troops and her belly slit open with bayonets. She died a lingering, horrible death. Yet here you are, a contemptible German bastard in our midst. Why? Why? I ask myself why. What is the purpose of this school?"

Günter said nothing. There was furtive whispering.

"Silence!" Venzel barked. "What is the purpose? Come, tell me. It's an examination." Venzel seemed to think that word examination was amusing. Günter said nothing.

"I'll tell you," said Venzel. "The student is to be instilled with respect for the working man, appreciation of socialist morality, and desire to protect the fatherland. Tell me, Tamás, what I just said."

Günter said nothing.

"Seven years, Tamás, and we've given you everything. Food. I hear you don't like our food. How could anyone with a trace of human feeling complain about something as precious as food? Shelter, education, privileges... You think your name is Günter. But it is not. We have even given you a name. But we can't make you human. We seem to have failed..." Venzel began to tap the desk again, at first slowly, then violently. When he spoke again, he seemed almost breathless. "Lenin said, quote, 'Oppressed peoples are especially susceptible to the principles of equality and cannot endure any affront to those principles, particularly when the authors of it are their own proletarian comrades.' End quote. I shall teach you not to affront our principles. Stand up!"

Günter stood, his head no higher than Stalin's streaky mouth.

"If you move, Tamás, if you so much as shift your feet, I shall have you whipped. Now, comrades, we have lessons, do we not?"

Some of the little boys were crying, but no one moved. That morning we were required to repeat after Venzel a litany of political rubbish. After a while Günter swayed, trying to shift his weight from one foot to the other without actually moving. He made no sound. When we were finally dismissed for lunch, Günter remained standing, Venzel above him leafing through Oszkár's *War and Peace* with an air of enlightened approval. When we returned to the room, Günter lay unconscious on the floor and Venzel was urinating on his face.

A few of the oldest boys (Zoltan, I should mention, had left school for indoctrination elsewhere) were ordered by Venzel to remove Günter's boots and socks and to tie Günter to the back of the statue of Soul. There Günter dangled, arms secured by belts to Soul's neck, bare feet in midair. We were forced to form a queue and to take turns striking the soles of Günter's feet with a paddle, one with holes in it like a Swiss cheese. If any boy failed to strike hard, we were warned, he also would be whipped. Before it came my turn, Günter's feet turned purple. He was taken down, bleeding from the ears.

Venzel lit a cigarette, extinguished the match with an abrupt flick of wrist, and dismissed us for the day. I helped to carry Günter's semiconscious body upstairs and stretch him on the bed. A consoling rush of hatred made me whisper to Günter, "I shall kill him."

"*Macht nichts.* Makes no difference," Günter said. It was one of two German idioms he had appropriated for his special utterance. The other idiom was *Sie können mich alle gern haben*, meaning, "They can all go to hell."

That very night something happened that was to bring our plans for escape into the realm of possibility.

"Ince."

Out of the moon-silvery bedroom loomed a boy's head. I recognized Róbert, a bright one.

"I've brought some lard for Günter." Róbert opened his hands. There were lumps of grease in them. "For Günter's feet."

We woke Günter and smeared lard on his feet. "Where did you find the lard?" Günter asked Róbert.

"In the pantry."

"Gas City?"

"Of course. I go there when everyone is asleep."

"It is forbidden," I said.

Róbert made a face. So what, it said. "Zoltan showed me. Why do you think he was so fat? He feasted in the pantry. Oszkár too. Oszkár did not get salami rolls at the butcher shop."

The story came out. The pantry was padlocked. Oszkár had two keys and gave the second key to Zoltan. Before Zoltan left school, he passed this key on to Róbert.

Günter and I exchanged looks. "Show me," I said to Róbert. "I must get more lard for Günter's feet. We won't tell anybody."

Some while later Róbert and I tiptoed down the corridor and into the dining room. From there to the kitchen and a padlocked door. Róbert unlocked it, and we entered a damp pantry reeking of bread mold and sour milk. There was moonlight through a small window. But no iron bars on the other side of the window. About this discovery, I said nothing to Róbert. He picked up a butcher knife and cut me some salami. He showed me a tin of lard, and I scooped some into my hand. Then we returned the way we had come.

As I passed Soul, I vaulted into her fountain and kissed her unyielding lips.

3

ANOTHER year passed before we could escape. Günter recovered from his injuries and grew into a strong, tall boy. His voice changed and so did his demeanor toward Venzel. He became one of Venzel's boy lovers and one of the bullies if someone were to be whipped. In fact, Günter's apparent avidity to adopt the features of a mirage personality earned him the hatred of many in the school, nor did it help matters that he started boasting about his parents and about the superiority of the German race. His father, he told us, had been a member of Hitler's general staff; his mother, Polish no longer, had been none other than Countess von Albensleben or some such fantastic appellation. The Third Reich would have ruled the world with atomic bombs. Even in the classroom he expressed himself along these lines as if daring Venzel to punish him for boorish and slanderous opinions. Venzel, however, was amused by them, a response that seemed all the more remarkable because SS troopers had committed a ghastly atrocity in

Venzel's own family. But a bond had developed between Venzel and Günter, that of master and slave. Even I, though still in my tenth and eleventh years, had understood Oszkár's gallows speech about *Causa Effectus* and could now understand the power game. Still, I considered Günter's conduct the subterfuge of the opportunist.

The installation of a military obstacle course on the school's playing field proved to be what Günter had been waiting for. At one place three-meter ropes dangled from a log over a ditch. Günter had volunteered to assist Comrade Ernö in erecting this particular obstacle; he knew exactly the length of the ropes and what sort of hitch had been taken to secure them to the log. By his calculation, as he confided to me one night, five of these ropes tied together would provide what we needed for ascending and descending the garden wall. By throwing one end of the rope over the wall, we could secure it from the opposite side to a padlocked iron-grille entryway at one corner of the wall. Here, then, was a device that might work. Previously we had been dismayed. Should we manage to climb the wall by means of small toeholds in tile and stone, we still had to contend with shards of glass at the top as well as with a metric tier of barbed wire; and, if we somehow avoided serious injury at the top of the wall, we would still have to risk a prodigious leap to clear its other side.

Then what to do? Here again, Günter had a plan. He had observed during parade marches to the city that there was a small quay on our side of the river and at the quay were some rowboats. If we could steal a boat, the floodwaters of the Danube would propel it swiftly past Budapest and into open country where we could hide by day. We could reach Istanbul in no time. And Argentina practically the next stop. I raised several objections to this plan. Neither of us knew how to row a boat or to swim. We would need food, drinking water, money, clothing other than school uniform, and sensible impedimenta. Günter dismissed my objections one night in a way that stopped my mouth—and heart.

"Pál," he whispered, using my old name as if to place distance between us, "you are not strong enough yet. I can't promise that my father will welcome you at the ranch in Argentina."

I asked him what he meant.

"My father might not understand."

I repeated my question.

"Very well, if you must know, my father's culture, his high rank and important position, might be compromised by association with a Jew, good as you are. Of course," Günter went on, looking nervously about the dormitory room, "we will find you employment suitable to your station. Would you like to be a cowboy? Yes, I think you will be a cowboy."

I was dumbfounded. For the second time in years I had been called a Jew, first by Zoltan and now by my best friend. Having learned from Oszkár how gifted and courageous Jewish peoples had been throughout history, I had never participated in any thought or language insulting them; indeed I admired them and wished I would come to know them. Was I, unknown to myself, a Jew? Was Attila? Terézia?

One chill April night in 1954 just before what I reckoned as my tenth birthday Günter wakened me by shaking my ankle. He was dressed in uniform and boots and held Róbert's pantry key in a fist. "Pál." His whisper was vibrant. "I am going to my father."

I nodded, sprang from bed, and began to pull on trousers.

"No," he said. "You stay. You're a Jew and your mother's a *meggyaláz*."

"You say that again and you die," I retorted hotly after

a pause. "She's not a whore and I'm not a Jew."

"Oszkár said so. So there."

"He did not."

"Did."

"Did not."

"The day before you arrived here, Oszkár told us all about you. He said your father was taken to be executed with the Jews at Abda. He said your mother was a prostitute, and that was why the political police were bringing you to the school. I've decided it is best for you to stay. Good-bye."

He was gone, and I sank back, disconsolate. Though I but dimly remembered her, Terézia had loved me—not my father's friends, the night visitors—and Oszkár would not have told the boys stories behind my back, would he? Now my best friend was trying to insult me so I wouldn't get killed as the other Ince had been... Well, why should I care anymore? I rose and went to the barred window.

Far-off rooftops glistened in moon-drowsy mists, inert as sleeping seals.

Then, a movement on the playing field like that of a stork learning to fly: Günter was shimmying up ropes, sawing them off with a kind of gleaming object, collecting them, knotting them together. He went with them to deep shadows by the wall. Minutes passed. I heard a faint *tink* of broken glass. A shape moved up the wall, crouched briefly and vanished from sight. He had done it!

I dressed quickly. Heedless of the noise, I ran down the stairs and corridor to the kitchen pantry, which was unlocked. The butcher knife was missing, and I realized that Günter had been using it to sever the ropes. But despite the many times I had planned for this moment and for calmly collecting provisions, now I acted on surges of adrenaline: dropped from the open pantry window, dashed across wet grass, found the rope, climbed it beyond the broken bottles that resembled translucent sailboats, and completed a finger-slashing roll over the barbed wire. I descended into a murky alley that smelled of dry rot and of something dead: a rat. Fog-slick empty streets echoed the slap-click, slap-click of my boots.

The shrouded river ran.

I found the stone quay where Günter's boots had made holes in the mud, dark pools now. There were flat-bottomed dinghies moored there, and I saw a slashed mooring rope, oars and oarlocks in the bilge of one of the dinghies. I was moving as though moved by an unseen and foreknowing force. I fitted oarlocks, readied oars. Untied and cast off the mooring rope. Pushed off into swirling dark popple.

Oarlocks scrawked, oars stabbed and answered to my heave.

"Gün-terrr! Gün-terrr!" My voice was swallowed in fog, in the tug of cold and powerful waters.

I rowed—I could row!—and still I rowed. My hands became numb and raw, my shoulders ached. I experienced a kind of ecstasy of significant pain as I rowed against the current. Heave! Pull with the right-hand oar, skim the left-hand oar rotating its blade. Reverse the procedure. Heave with both oars. Steady. From sounds and undulations, I believed I was gaining against the current. Although I wanted to find and join forces with Günter, who would be drifting with the current, I was also angered at him for impugning the honor of my family. I had to figure things for myself. Perhaps if I could cross to Pest above Petöfi Square, I could hide in one of the many bomb sites that remained from the Soviet bombardment of Budapest a decade before. Perhaps I could find Terézia if she were not under surveillance. Perhaps we could escape across the border to Austria where American and British troops would protect us... And so I rowed, thinking I made headway though in fact not even treadmilling but beginning to hurtle downriver.

An ominous sound grew louder as it approached me: first a hollow rushing sound as when one presses a conch shell to one's ear, and then a roiling, roaring sound that did not communicate *bridge* until my dinghy was thumping and scraping against moss-slimed ramparts and, as in an underground cavern with white-water rapids, thunderous tumult reverberated to all sides. The dinghy, having passed under the bridge, spun around. An oar tipped up like a suddenly abandoned seesaw. The hand that gripped the other oar struck me in the teeth. I almost fell into the fish-foul slosh of gunwales but regained control of both oars, rowing furiously against the current but now aware of being catapulted by that unknown force that had earlier seemed beneficent.

City lights blistered through fog. With all my remaining strength I managed to row toward them. The lights became enlarged. Trees were etched against a faint glow of sky. A drayhorse and cart materialized above the floodwall. I glimpsed the fashionable hotel district... And then a cramp took possession of my right hand, the one lacerated by barbed wire. Finger by finger the cramp spread. The hand was a useless claw. I released the right-hand oar in order to flail my hand against the gunwale, but the fingers would not unfold. Thunking, the oar slipped from its lock and was gone. Then, just as I backpaddled with the other oar, my left hand twisted into a cramp. Then my whole body was cramped as though squeezed by a serpent. The left oar also slipped from its lock and disappeared. Writhing now in agony, I fell into bilge, and fog closed around me as the dinghy plunged on.

First dawn light flayed the sky. Birds swooped and stitched cries into clouds. I bobbed in swells of passing barges, pitched and rolled beneath bridges. The sun rose and I was disgraced.

I heard a power boat baROOM. Heard it throttled back

to a pud pud pud. Smelled petrol exhaust. Heard voices of men above me as the dinghy thumped a hull. Clang clang. Ship's bell.

Sailors peered down at me. One of the sailors was holding a machine pistol. A man in a black rubber suit lowered himself into the dinghy, lifted me into the outstretched arms of sailors. Who pushed me to deck.

"That's the lot, then," said a commanding voice.

The boat cleared its power nostrils.

A man came and nudged me with his boot. At first I didn't recognize Comrade Mustache because the mustache was gone. But the uniform of the political police was familiar; also familiar were the weary eyes under the prominent forehead.

Comrade Mustache barked an order. Someone came and wrapped me in a blanket.

"Where's Günter?" I asked through chattering teeth.

Comrade Mustache looked at me for a long time before replying in a tone of calm satisfaction. "He was lucky. His boat was capsized. He would have drowned. He was taken to my villa."

"What will happen to him?"

"I haven't decided."

"What are you going to do with me?"

"Well," he said after leaning forward confidentially, "we'll have to ask your mother, won't we?"

His name was Roman Malakov. He thought of himself as a righteous man entitled to feel contempt for the world and to do whatever he pleased. It had pleased him for years to have Terézia as his housekeeper, cook and mistress. He thought of himself as a savior of situations.

Eldest of four children born to a prosperous Ukrainian landowner and his pious wife, Malakov was a child when

Lenin's government confiscated the family property and set fire to their dacha. The father protested to authorities. One day he went for a stroll and was never seen or heard from again. The mother took the children to the Crimea where she had a wooden Black Sea villa with sloping tile roof and a ground floor of stone to protect against fire in the aubergine season. The mother dedicated young Malakov to the priesthood. When he turned fifteen, an accident occurred for which he blamed himself. It was summer. Malakov had invited his three sisters for an afternoon's sailing near the beach. They trusted him as he trusted himself. They all set out together under favorable auspices, skies blue, breeze gentle, the small boat flitting over sparkling waves with lambent ease. About a kilometer from shore, the sailboat was overturned by a sudden squall even though Malakov had scudded before the storm, striking jib, slackening topsail, and tacking toward the beach where, as in an old-fashioned color-tinted postcard, antlike bathers dotted a stage of peppermint-striped tents and spiderwebbed fishing nets. The girls, swept beyond Malakov's reach, were drowned. One moment everything had been so jolly, the next, so appalling; and the sensitive youth, soon to be rescued by a passing coal barge, sank beneath waves of melancholy, forever thereafter the lugubrious castaway. Had he forgiven himself for failing to save his sisters, he might have been reconciled to the world, but no one punished him.

"Be good to yourself," his mother would coax him. "The Lord giveth and the Lord taketh away." Her gaze would lift toward distances. His flesh prickled. "The Lord is for peasants," he retorted. He wanted to return to the Ukraine. There was an old schoolmaster there who, whenever Malakov had arrived late for school, caned his backside until it turned into braids of blue-black. When he was eighteen, Malakov's mother died of tuberculosis. He felt nothing.

Soon the lines of his mouth curled rigidly at corners and he grew a thick black pushbroom mustache.

More, presently, about how I came to live in Malakov's luxurious apartment with my mother. For now, let me tell of the extraordinary confessional visit Malakov paid to me, a boy not yet thirteen, on an evening in October, 1956, when all of Hungary was in revolt against Soviet occupation.

From the very beginning of the revolution the wrath of Hungarians had been visited upon the hated AVO. According to Radio Budapest, hundreds of the political police had been slaughtered; many were hanged from lampposts and their bodies mutilated.

Malakov was nervous, very nervous. He dressed himself as a worker in duckpants and beret and chainsmoked Five Year Plan fags while he was seated on the window ledge of my room four stories above the street. We heard from afar the chatter of rifle fire, the gaflumping shudder of artillery. Malakov scrinched up his face against acrid cigarette smoke and began his story abruptly, his voice sepulchral.

"After my mother's death, I was sent to study at the Odessa Institute of Fine Art, going to Moscow at the age of twenty as a set-designer for the theatre of the Komsomol. Having no artistic talent save for sculpturing papier-mâché, I was not required to produce art expressive of genuine feeling. I was quite successful at portraying what the Party wanted: heroic leaders, muscular engineers, lyrical peasants. Life took a predictable course. I joined the Party." Malakov flicked one cigarette out of the window, lit another, and went on, "One evening I attended an after-theatre gathering for Party bohemians. I met a beautiful ballerina."

"Was she really a ballerina?"

Malakov almost smiled. "She was really a ballerina. Her art did not demand the suppression of the one theme with any validity in those days—death. She was slender, graceful, golden-haired, rosycheeked. Fire opal eyes! A classic beauty whom Degas could have painted. And there was I, cold as the Ice Age, infatuated and inflamed with that passion that rides the brain as a storm tosses a boat. Biology, of course. You cannot persuade a young man that beauty is an illusion; it is the illusion he desires. You cannot tell a young man that the woman with the illusory beauty is also prisoner of her beauty; he seeks for private possession that love she feels destined to give to lovers. All biology, all stupid. In short, I pursued her, and she consented to be my wife. The Party bohemians had neglected to propose such a conventional solution to the customary glandular problem.

"There were obstacles. These fed our passion, made us slaves to the illusion of freedom. The Party must not discover our marriage, nor my ballerina's parents. We married secretly. She became pregnant. I was soon tired of her company, but another obstacle came between us and seemed to rekindle the fire: the war.

"I served in the Red Army from 1940 to 1945. I saw little of the fighting, for I had been prudent enough to realize that there were two enemies, the Germans and the police, and the police better suited my gifts. Accordingly, I secured assignment as a political officer and performed my duties so well that, at the end of a year, I returned to Moscow on furlough and with certain... powers... to find our ballerina living with another man, also a dancer, one quite famous in those closed worlds of art in which they flitted like Paolo and Francesca. I don't know why I became so infuriated with them. One telephone call and I could have had my wife's lover dancing his steps on the steppes of Siberia. But my fury cooled down. They could drown in Swan Lake by themselves. But my son, my little blond and blue-eyed son, could not be left in the care of devils. I took him away, far away to the Crimea. One day, as I was driving in a car over a country road, scattering flocks of ducks and geese pasturing freely on the verges, I passed a dark wood with gypsy wagons rear-ended to a blazing fire. I stopped, got out, drew my pistol. I approached the fire. I could see many stolen items hidden in the trees. A gypsy woman screamed, 'I no stealee! I no takee anything!' I understood her sentiment perfectly. I asked her where the caravan was going. They were going their usual route up the Danube to Hungary. 'Good,' I said. 'Take my son far from the Soviet Union. Take him to Budapest. I will pay you handsomely.' She agreed. I returned to Moscow, requested and received permission to return to duty. After the war, I received assignment to the new democracy in Czechoslovakia.

"I was sent to Prague. There was to be an international youth festival there in the summer of 1947 with thousands of young people from the West coming to sing songs and see folk dances. I confess, I had hoped to be charmed by these children who believed what we told them about peace. Instead, I was bitterly disappointed to discover the secret weakness of the West—an aversion to history. The Americans especially believe that youth is eternal, maturation a disposable product like their chewing gum. The West is to be undermined by a belief inconsistent with reality, her people doomed to the womb. First that doom, then the failure of nerve, then the squandering of riches, increased greed, decreased sense of public service, seductive and enervating exploitation of the arts, then selfishness on an unparalleled scale, crime on an unparalleled scale, ignorance on an unparalleled scale, and finally infantilism, apathy, and collapse."

Malakov sighed and lit another cigarette. Off in the city,

guns... "It is said," he resumed, "that revolution is a test of our capacity to love. However, my boy, nothing will change. The revolution will be crushed the precise moment when your people believe themselves victorious. Today... perhaps tomorrow the Soviet armored divisions will return. Nobody will stop them, because freedom is too frightening in the Atomic Age. Premier Nagy, who has foolishly proclaimed Hungarian independence, will be murdered. Poland is quiet. Yugoslavia is neutralized. The British are bogged down in Egypt, the French in Algeria and Indochina. The Americans are chewing gum." Malakov tossed his head in a derisory motion.

There was a pause. He squinted as if threading a needle in bad light.

"After the Prague Youth Festival, I was assigned to Budapest as what might be called a truancy officer. Then in 1950 my wife and her troupe were performing in Vienna. She and her lover made a clumsy attempt to defect to the West. They had arranged to meet an agent at the Ferris wheel in Praterstern, then the Soviet sector. They were arrested. She was found to be married to a certain officer in Budapest. She was escorted here. I was given responsibility for her fate. I had no choice."

"What did you do?"

Malakov rubbed smoke-reddened eyes with his knuckles. "We were given an hour together in a villa of mine near your former school. I'm afraid she did not care for my company even though I saved our son by giving him to gypsies. Her opaline eyes flashed when I proposed a reconciliation under humane terms. We could share the villa while she underwent a period of house arrest. Considering the harshness of other alternatives, I hoped that she would be reasonable. However, she refused to let me save her. She was taken to prison... It is for the best. Because now, my friend, I have the annulment papers from Moscow. Do you see now why, instead of returning you to school, I brought you home to live with Terézia and me?"

I didn't see why and said so. Malakov half laughed and tousled my hair. "Soon," he said, "I shall be free to marry your mother."

He stood to leave. I knew he wanted me to smile. I smiled with a sickening kind of eagerness but said nothing, fearful of betraying what my heart held in store for him.

4

ON the first of May, 1949, Terézia went to the Kilián Barracks and left a message for one of her acquaintances in the *Honvédség*, the Hungarian regular army. That night, when the parades were over and the streets cleared, he met her at the entrance to the Municipal Woods by the colossal statue of Stalin. She told him what had happened to me, described the AVO officer who had taken me from her, and offered this soldier the rather large sum of ten forints to trace the officer's identity. The soldier refused her money, saying, "*Alegislegmeg-esztegethetetleng*," an expression which, roughly translated, means "I am a person who cannot be bribed." But he did as Terézia wished and the following night met her at the same place.

"His name is Roman Malakov," he said. "One of the good Russians, they say."

"How do you know if a broom is good until it sweeps the floor?" Terézia thanked the soldier. She removed an envelope from her purse. "Will you see that Malakov gets this letter?"

He would try, the soldier said.

One must suppose that Malakov received the letter and fully understood its purpose. It read:

I am all yours.

Malakov visited Terézia alone in her apartment a week later. The room was hot, no breeze fluttering the artificial fog of curtains. Malakov was perspiring but did not loosen his collar. He sat stiffly at the small dining table, lit a cigarette, and brooded for a long time. Terézia brought a bottle of Slieberwitz and poured two glasses full.

"*Egészségedre,*" Malakov saluted with a whimsical smile.

"*Egészségedre.* Is he well?"

Malakov said I was well. His informer at the school, Mrs. Pribéky, could be relied upon to keep an eye out for my welfare.

"You understand," Terézia said, "that I must also have this information at all times."

"Agreed," said Malakov after a pause. "But you must understand the sacrifice I am making. If you abide by the rules—"

"I know the rules," Terézia interrupted.

"Yes," said Malakov, "of course. Then it's settled. You will speak to no one about the arrangements, now or in future. There must be no children."

"Can you make any?"

Malakov cracked a smile. One must suppose that he admired Terézia for her impudence and that, in rescuing her from a rat-infested slum and in providing her with some of the luxuries of life, he paid a debt to conscience. Of course, Terézia herself never knew until I told her seven years later about sisters drowning, a mother in the Crimea pleading, a wife betraying.

He downed his brandy at one gulp.

"I am going for a holiday at Lake Balaton," he announced, standing up and tugging his tunic straight over the bulge of shoulder holster and revolver. "Your dress must be elegant and à la mode. Your hair must be shortened and curled. There's a coiffeuse who is said to be excellent, in Bajza Street near the Soviet embassy. My driver will pick you up the day after tomorrow. Noon," said Malakov and went, pausing only to drop a packet of banknotes on the table.

Terézia went to Lake Balaton with Malakov. When they returned, he installed her in an apartment suite in Pest complete with Biedermeier furnishings and marble-mounted ormolu mirrors from the last century. There were times when Malakov stayed in his villa across the river. Those, for Terézia, were the good times. Although Malakov was good to her, never striking her or raising his voice in anger, and, true to his word, kept her informed of my health and progress at school, he had robbed her of far more than she had anticipated his doing. Indeed, had he been brutal, she would have found reason to play her role without suffering feelings of self-abasement. As it was, her hatred of Malakov seemed to lack a basis in morality other than the conventional. They were using one another according to agreement. There was even a kind of commitment, as in marriage, between them. Yet she abhorred his touch, his detached and dilettantish demeanor, the odor of tobacco on his breath—in short, his very presence humiliated her. She didn't know why. It was all as though she had surrendered to him something so precious that it went deeper than pride, something so elemental that the inherently moral action of self-sacrifice could not suffice to fill the void and heal the wounds of loss.

Meanwhile, Malakov thrived on the relationship, relaxing in her company and confiding quite openly his paltry affairs and dreams. If he were beginning to resemble a contented and witless husband, it had to be because his vanity was expanding of its own accord, like a cancer. There was no other source of love to be identified. Certainly not Terézia's. She had given her love to Attila and to me. Her love was exactly as strong as life, a splendor in essence, inseparable in its loyalties, and not for sale.

"I have had a dream," Malakov said pleasantly one night after consuming Terézia's chicken paprikosh and marzipan cake along with a bottle of red wine. He was drunk. "Shall I tell you about my dream?"

"Of course," Terézia said. "It is always so interesting to hear a pig talk."

One may suppose that Malakov was not offended. "In my dream," he began, "there is an emperor who lives on a beautiful island. It is like a shield afloat on bright sea. With utmost urgency I realize that I must send a reply to the emperor, even though I am not aware of any inquiry. But, *faute de mieux*, I cannot send the reply. Strange creatures are swarming about me and telling lies. Some say the emperor has received my message but cannot be found. *C'est tout à fait banal.* What message have I sent? None. Why do the creatures tell me these absurd lies? *Alors. Tout s'arrange.* The empress herself appears by my side."

"The empress?"

"The empress. She is lovely as a ballerina."

"What does she look like?"

"To describe is to despair. Her presence is all. She is very kind. She promises to give the emperor my reply. That is the end of my dream."

"That's very interesting," said Terézia with a frozen smile.

"Yes." Malakov was nodding with impressive solemnity. "I am reminded of the surrealistic art that the Party forbids. We must not be *trop sérieux*... All the same, I have considered the matter and have arrived at an altogether remarkable conclusion! God is aware of my desire to be united with Him. There is the intercession of a radiant female personality. *Voilà!* What persiflage! Remind me to say my prayers tonight. Thank you, Father. Thank you, József and Mária. Happy birthday, Jézus. Amen."

"It is good to see you in such a fine mood," said Terézia.

"You see how devout I have become!" Malakov exclaimed. "Thank you, Father, and so forth."

"The woman does all the work, and it is a man you are thanking," Terézia remarked.

"Ah, but *you* will thank me nonetheless," Malakov cut in abruptly and patted his stomach with both hands. It was a gesture of more than usual satisfaction and meant, as Terézia later told me, that he must have consumed something more than dinner and was ready to spill it on a rush of buffoonery. She was right. But caught by surprise.

"Pál has escaped from school," Malakov declared as if reading aloud from a newspaper. "My men have him in custody. Shall we return him to a juvenile reform school or shall we have him live here as part of the family? I'm giving you the choice."

While Terézia sat and listened to the beating of her heart, Malakov told her all that had happened, how Pribéky had arrived before dawn to warm the ovens, found the pantry unlocked and its window open, and scurried upstairs to the dormitory where the bunks of Tamás and Ince were empty, and how she returned to the kitchen and telephoned Malakov at the villa. How he himself not twenty minutes later drove to the school, found the rope at the wall, put the rope in his sedan, and searched the area between school and river. How he discovered boats missing from the quay. How he had personally saved the boys from drowning—and Supervisor Venzel from official displeasure.

"Now," Malakov concluded, "I have Venzel in my pocket. Pál and his friend will continue to be enrolled at the school even though they will never again *be* at the school. When I telephoned Venzel and explained this arrangement, the stupid fellow was quite beside himself with gratitude, thinking I am his friend and protector. On the other hand—what he fails to realize—if for any reason I should decide in future to have the fellow brought in for interrogation, it will be amusing to watch him try to save himself. Two boys missing? Come now, Venzel, explain this situation. No lies. We shall know if you are lying." Malakov tsk-tsked. "Do you understand, Terézia, all that I have done for you? It is not what people do that matters. It is what the records *say* they do that matters. I have access to the records. Even to yours, I might add. We are rooted in paper, *feuilleton d'un cadavre exquise.*"

It was at this moment that Terézia understood why she loathed this man. He was flesh and blood, all right. His pulse ticked and his fingernails grew. But he and his kind were like locusts, swarms of them clouding the sky and busily devouring the roots of the tree of life, converting these to pulp. And the pulp to paper.

Now that she understood, she felt as if a stone were lifted from her heart. She reviled this insect, but she was grateful for the acceptance she felt.

But she still did not understand what it was that she had surrendered to Malakov. Was she not entrusting to him not only her own future but her son's?

A year and a half drifted by. Just as I had given up hope, there was hope, and everything was turning out for the best. Not that I liked Malakov, especially after what Terézia told me about him, but he seemed preferable to Venzel. Moreover, in my simplicity I considered the trick that Malakov had played on Venzel to be quite clever, for Venzel had an invisible noose around his neck whereas I was scot-free and living in the lap of luxury. On arrival at Malakov's apartment, I had looked in the ormolu mirror and recognized a pale and savage little boy with eyes that seemed flash-frozen in anticipation of torture. Soon, however, my mother's pampered darling grew and became quite a big boy for his age.

That was a good summer. Terézia and I often strolled the parks and boulevards together. Once in a while we saw Soviet troops being transported in square vehicles with badly painted metal number plates. The troops waved to us and whistled at Terézia. She blushed and lowered her gaze and I waved back. Everyone seemed so friendly. One could even enjoy the sight of the Soviet Hero on Mount Gellért illuminated by thirty intersecting beams of searchlights. Gypsy music was played violently over radios as workers came home in shirtsleeves after their fourteen-hour workday. Boys cycled, satchels on their backs. Girls in blouses primped their hair, peeped out of mawkishly applied makeup. Young men in untwilled trousers swung off bright tramcars in rain puddles. Old men sipped espresso and read *Szabad Nép*, the Party newspaper, at cafés under green metal cover. Reality came in small doses.

But reality was about to be served up, intoxicating and ruinous.

The weather was fair, just a touch of chill in the air. At 1500 hours there was a meeting of students, professors, and Party leaders at the College of Higher Technical Studies in Béla Bartók Avenue, some 5,000 people in all. Suddenly in the midst of a typical political discussion they wakened to the fact that they had been deceiving themselves about communism: far from serving humanity, they had become accomplices in crimes. Why was Hungary not free to govern itself? Why were workers earning starvation wages?

After some hours of passionate discussion, the people drew up a list of demands, and a delegation of students set out to have the list included in the radio station's evening broadcast. The same list was printed and distributed on foot or by bicycle throughout Budapest. A peaceful demonstration was announced for the next afternoon. The radio station did not broadcast the list of demands. But suddenly people everywhere seemed to realize that a few well-indoctrinated students represented the aspirations of an entire nation.

That was on Monday, October 22, 1956.

The next day the million-and-a-half citizens woke to clear sunny skies. Classes were cancelled at the universities, their gates guarded by young men wearing tricolor armbands. Thousands of young people converged on Petöfi Square, then marched up Lajos Kossuth Avenue singing the Marseillaise. Workers joined in. Hungarian flags, the Soviet emblem cut out, were raised or hung from windows. At the General Bem monument the marchers gathered to sing the national song that ends,

> *By the God of the Hungarians, we swear, we swear,*
> *No more shall we be slaves—no more!*

By 1800 hours a quarter of a million people were converging on Parliament Square. More were coming.

Then fighting broke out. The AVO opened fire upon unarmed students demonstrating at the radio station. Word of this atrocity spread. Workers and students commandeered trucks in the streets, drove to arsenals of the Hungarian regular army, and armed themselves with the help of their countrymen. The offices of *Szabad Nép* were stormed, books and furniture burned. Streetcars were overturned, set on fire. The statue of Stalin was pulled down; next day it would be carved up and children would inscribe W. C. on his head. Youths threw up barricades at Moricz Zsigmond Square and Szena Square in Buda, at Baross and Boraros Square in the narrow streets of Pest. At a checkpoint on Margit Bridge, an AVO officer was dragged from his car, beaten, and thrown in the Danube. Other AVO were hanged from lampposts, sometimes by the feet, the body soaked in kerosene and set on fire. Live men had their hands chopped off, their hearts cut out. Mobs spat upon the disfigured corpses.

Wednesday, October 24, 1956. In the early hours 600 tanks of the Soviet Second and Seventeenth mechanized divisions rumbled into the city. The leading tanks were burned out by young men and women hurling Molotov cocktails. Children threw rocks, potatoes—anything. Crews were shot scrambling from tanks. Some bewildered Russian boys surrendered their weapons in return for food and vodka.

Thursday, October 25, 1956. Fighting everywhere. The Soviets massacred a crowd of people in Parliament Square.

Friday, October 26, 1956. The entire nation was in revolt. The blood of slain girls was daubed upon motor cars to read *Ruszki Haza*: "Russians go home!" A general strike. Insurgents took the AVO barracks by storm, broke into an AVO prison, and liberated hundreds of political prisoners. During the cold twilight, Budapest was a deserted city, most of it without electricity.

Between October 27 and 31 there continued to be fierce fighting. Then Soviet forces were withdrawn, and Hungary formed a new government. By All Souls Day candles by the tens of thousands were flickering in windows and at road level at streetcorners, candles to commemorate ancestors and the newly dead. Between November 1 and November 3 the new government under Imre Nagy proclaimed neutrality and appealed to the United Nations to protect the country. The Soviets pretended to negotiate complete withdrawal.

Hungarian independence was proclaimed!

November 4: we were betrayed. The Soviets invaded Hungary in force. Premier Nagy took refuge in the Yugoslav embassy. Military, government, and union leaders were executed. The mass flight of a quarter of a million refugees began. The United Nations did nothing. Although fighting continued in waning pockets of resistance, the true revolution of an entire nation was gradually suppressed. On November 23 Nagy was abducted upon leaving the Yugoslav embassy. That day the people of Budapest refused to go on the streets between 1400 and 1500 hours: the eloquence of a haunted city spoke louder than gunfire. Mass arrests of refugees and workers began the next day.

Thus ended spontaneously activated idealism. Thus, however, was rekindled the faith of our fathers. Humanity did not vanish, in spiritual truth.

I remember a day in the streets. I remember being swept along by marchers who waved deSovietized national flags, chanted slogans, smashed windows with cobblestones, sang, drank, ran and thronged in boisterous and awesome riot. I remember seeing a tramcar being rocked back and forth like a toy boat tossed on a pool's violent tide until, with a shower of high-voltage blue sparks and a final totter, the car was overturned. The impact of shattering glass and twisted steel was greeted by thunderous cheering. From Bem Square arose the sound of tens of thousands of voices that drew me irresistibly there on an undertow of the excited heart's lifting.

No more shall we be slaves—no more!

The sun glowed red. Gusts of hot air and sweating bodies. Clenched fists hammered the sky, a forest of arms, an undulant sea.

"Pál! *Halljuk!* Hear me, Pál!"

I swam my gaze to a high granite pedestal upon which some Hungarian soldiers were waving machine pistols aloft in jubilation. Among these soldiers was a teenager armed but not in uniform, and he was shouting at me and holding his machine pistol in one hand, a wine bottle in the other. He was blond.

"Günter!"

Presently I had squirmed through the crowd and had clambered to the pedestal where Günter embraced me with many expressions of delight. What a sight we beheld beneath and all around us! An ocean of people delirious with a single energy, a single mind of pride and defiance, a single passion of love for one another. We could not hear ourselves above the din, but we could drink together, Günter and I, and so we did, and we were comrades with one another and with the people, an inseparable part of the world's noble dreaming.

After a while we left the crowd and walked arm in arm through many narrow streets and, little by little, listened as stories sprang from concealment. Finally we arrived at a bridge that spans the Small Danube in the northwestern part of the city. There was a park with benches facing the water and a cinder path running through shadows of tall walnut trees and weeping willows. Humid air held the scent of mosses and lime. We crossed the park and halted where some buildings with blackened façades leaned precariously upon bomb-battered joints and over a crater aglitter with stagnant pools, strewn with garbage, and cordoned off with barbed wire. It was a bombsite from the old war. Wooden beams had collapsed over stone foundations and been covered with rubble abloom with poppies, but a cellar remained and Günter had been living in it. We went there. It was cool and quiet.

In the two days since Günter had been released from the juvenile reform school where Malakov had sent him, he had managed to assemble a collection of weapons and ammunition, including two machine pistols, a box of hand grenades, and a revolver. "Here," he said, giving me the revolver after loading its chamber with bullets. "Do you know how to shoot?"

He showed me how to slip off that gun's safety with my thumb, how to aim at a target, bringing my arm down to a level position, and how to prepare my body to absorb recoil. "Remember," he repeated, "squeeze the trigger, don't pull it. The gun is yours."

I didn't think I wanted to kill anybody. I shook my head and told him that Terézia would not approve of my owning such a thing.

Günter spat. "*Macht nichts.* If you show me where you live, I'll shoot the bastard myself."

"Malakov?" I asked incredulously.

"Malakov," he repeated in a flat tone. "Are you going to do it or shall I? He tormented your father, a cat tormenting a mouse, then devoured him. I think you should do it."

Quiet as dust a ghostly presence gathered.

"Give me the gun," I said.

"Good," he smiled. "I am sorry about things I said at school. I was crazy and did not know that Oszkár was lying to keep us from ever learning about Malakov. And then Malakov told me everything himself when he saved me from drowning and locked me in his villa. Out of the blue. As if by telling me that Oszkár was Attila Szabó, he added your father to the list of persons whom he believes he has saved... Saved so he can destroy them later, whenever he feels like it. As if he has already destroyed them. They don't exist. Except as names. The real names, the names in the records that Malakov keeps, are turned into fake names, and finally the fake names *seem* real to him. He can dispose of people as if they were ... his cigarettes. I don't know. Why else would he tell me about your father while I am being held prisoner in his villa? Because you and I are friends. Because we have succeeded in escaping. That made us into opponents whom he can consider worthy. To whom he can offer glimpses of the truth, the more pleasure to be derived from loosening the noose before he decides to choke us, slowly... *Sie können mich alle gern haben!*"

After a while Günter and I set out to roam the streets and came to a circle where four narrow streets intersected. Just before we would have entered the circle, we heard the grinding and screeching of badly oiled sprockets: a tank! Backed against a yellow wall, I saw the duncolored, mud-died, cobble-spewing dinosaur, engines raving and grunting with a painful hunger, burst into view and come to a halt in the middle of the circle. Its gunmuzzle wobbled, was swiveled on the turret mount. The hatch was opened. Two Ghirghiz Mongolians crawled from the monster's belly, lit cigarettes and sat smoking like morose, catatonic sheiks.

Günter readied his machine pistol, checked the hand grenade fastened to his belt.

"Are we going to kill anybody?" I whispered. "I don't want to kill anybody. I don't think I do."

But Günter was not listening and sprang forward and there were shattering muzzle bursts filling the air and the Ghirghiz Mongolians crumpling into instantly motionless lumps, one of them fizzing like a Roman candle. Günter took and armed the hand grenade and ran to the tank and tossed the grenade down the hatch and ran back to me. He flung himself to the street as a coil of greasy smoke rose followed by a flare of light fierce as a welder's torch. Then BLAM, a swollen brightening, and everything was illuminated by a diminishing incandescence as the monster exploded in sheets of flame.

I heard a long, involuntary wail in my throat and felt my heart breaking open in secret places.

A few hours later I lay restlessly in bed in the home of my friend, a devil, no longer pretending to myself that I was uninvolved with Hell. Susceptible though I was to grief, I might yet harden my heart and give my soul to violence. There was a hard object under the mattress, my revolver.

I did not see Günter again in Budapest nor become inured to the laws of retribution in the land. I stayed home and waited for events to relieve me of duty. One word from me to Günter, and Malakov was as good as executed. But I had not accepted the revolver on a pretense, either. I intended to do my duty. The odd thing was, I could have prompted anyone to perform it for me. I could have betrayed Malakov's hiding place to the mob, could have passed along the word to people in the streets or telephoned for help from insurgents—much as one might call public health officials to remove a rodent from the drinking water. Still, I did nothing. Where others would kill Malakov out of hatred for a political officer and all he stood for, I felt especially elected to squeeze the trigger. On the other hand, my reason tainted thought. It was as though, once I squeezed the trigger, I would no longer belong to myself but, paradoxically, to—Malakov! And then I would never know my proper elegance.

Another odd thing was, I had the impression that Malakov had divined my intention. How, I couldn't conceive. The information about his enslavement of and prolonged mental torture of my father had come from Günter, and Malakov surely could not have known or guessed about that accidental reunion. Had my revolver been discovered? No, for I remained in the room feigning illness and Malakov was elsewhere in the apartment all the time, save once, so he surely could not have known or guessed about the revolver. Nevertheless, somehow, he suspected things—was even provoking me. He had come to my room for the surprising confessional. He had said, in effect, "I am guilty and have sought punishment all my life." But he was *not* guilty of the death of his sisters by drowning! By a kind of presumptuous self-abasement and insinuation, he was accusing himself of that for which he was innocent in order to absolve himself, by a twisted power of inference, from guilt for the enormous crimes that he had in fact committed, thus severing his connection to the weal and woe of ordinary humanity.

Relief seemed to come on November the fourth. Malakov was right: the Soviet invasion had been planned for the very moment in history when Hungary believed itself free. Terézia, who had been listening to the news on the radio, came to my room. We had a long discussion. Although I could not bring myself to reveal what Günter had told me—how Attila's disappearance at Abda had been faked so the Soviets could further enslave him, and how Malakov had come across Attila's records and reanimated him as school supervisor and later elaborated upon the game by sending me to my father's school and by accepting Terézia's unexpected offer of herself—I *did* tell her about Malakov's confession several days earlier.

"Then," she sighed with a rueful expression, "he is more human than I thought. He has a conscience. He is, after all, righteous in his own way."

"Yes," I said without heart.

Terézia clasped me in her arms and kissed my brow and tousled my hair. "Pál," she said, "he will help us to leave Hungary. I'm sure of it now."

I asked her when we were to leave.

"Tomorrow," she said, "we will go to the station. Many are already leaving. The *Honvédség* are permitting people to go as far as Mosonmagyarovar. We must get to the border before the Soviets close it... Now," she went on, taking a deep breath, "we will tell Malakov of our decision. Come along. I'll need your support."

We found Malakov at an ornate table in the drawing room perusing a pile of documents with the usual concentration. He was dressed in uniform for the first time in days, but his tunic was unbuttoned and the shoulder harness in which he usually holstered a pistol did not come into view. We stood at a polite distance and waited for him to grant us his attention. "Ah," he said finally, shoving back his chair and blinking as if surfacing. "Is there something you wish to tell me?"

Terézia's lips trembled. "We wish to make a request."

"A request?"

"We wish to go to Austria," she said after a tremulous pause.

Malakov cracked a smile. "You'll need money."

"Oh. No, thank you. You've done so much for us. I have a little money saved. We'll manage."

"But I insist," said Malakov. He opened a drawer of the table, extracted an envelope stuffed with forints, and placed it on the table. "There," he beamed. "Enough for tickets and bribes. Enough to begin your new life in Austria."

Terézia hesitated, took the envelope. She did not look inside it or count the money. "That is very kind of you, Roman." I had never heard her call him by his first name before nor seen her crawl to him before. "We have your permission to go?"

"Of course," he said and turned to me. "And how does Pál feel about this... exile? Eh?"

I said nothing. He went on: "We mustn't act irrationally.

We mustn't forget what I told you about the decadence of the West. Life will be dog-eat-dog for you there. Here, here in your fatherland, life will prove immeasurably better after all this *coquinerie* and folly... Whatever happened to your friend what's-his-name?" Malakov snapped his fingers.

"Sir?"

"The one with the German name?"

"Günter?"

"Exactly! One gets confused about identities."

"I don't know." I shrugged elaborately.

"You don't know?"

"No."

"I thought you'd seen him recently."

My heart thumped in my throat. "No, sir," I said.

"That's very strange," Malakov murmured as if to himself. "I was sure someone told me you were walking with, er... Günter. Just the other day... What did he tell you?"

"I haven't seen him," I said out of the panic in my throat.

"Ah. It must have been someone else?"

"Yes, sir."

Malakov fumbled a cigarette from his tunic and lit it, flicking the wooden match out with a slow motion of wrist that reminded me of Venzel. He left the cigarette in his lips and narrowed his eyes against the smoke. "We had," he said, "this Günter under arrest. There seemed to be nothing we could do to save him... Now, alas, you are leaving us after all I have done to save your friend. Do you understand what I am saying?"

I said nothing. He went on: "He was taken to be executed. But I told him you were exchanging your life for his. We arranged to have him released and deported at the Austrian border. We shall execute Supervisor Venzel for this, er, escape. Of course, you and your mother now owe it to conscience to remain here. Think it over, Pál... It isn't often one has an opportunity to sacrifice oneself to save the life of one's best friend. You may go."

I went to my room. When I pulled the mattress of my bed aside and reached for the revolver, my hand was shaking with a tremor all its own and I was gasping for breath as in the old days of asthma. *It must be now,* I said to myself, and the hand steadied so that I could grip the revolver and slip off its safety with my thumb. I don't remember how it was that I returned to the drawing room, raised the revolver, aimed it from ten paces at Malakov—he was rising, the cigarette still dangled from his lips, a look of faint enjoyment on his gloomy forehead—and squeezed the trigger, save that it all happened very quickly, and I was still amazed that the recoil from the explosion could almost jerk my arm from its socket even while Malakov fell backwards and was left sprawling as if a rug had been suddenly pulled from under him.

Terézia let out a sharp cry of pain. And was steadying herself against the table as the gunshot reverberated in my head. It seemed a long time before she spoke. "Have you killed him?"

It did not seem a particularly mistimed question. I took a few steps forward and peered at Malakov, half expecting him to jump to his feet and patiently resume study of his documents. He breathed. His eyes focused intelligently upon me. He seemed to be smiling at a hidden joke. Suddenly he guffawed with chilling mirth, his head thrown back and his hand over his mouth as if he were about to devour a communion wafer. There was no blood. My shot had missed him entirely.

"Give me the gun," Terézia demanded nearby.

"Your Günter is," Malakov gasped after laughter, "is already deported. You are spoiling everything."

I gave Terézia the revolver. Malakov's laughter ceased, his mouth quivered. "Don't be a fool," he said. "Don't you know? Günter is my own son."

Terézia fired two shots at pointblank range. Malakov's body jerked and went still as blood spurted from his chest.

Terézia stared at the corpse, came and rocked me in her arms, speaking vehemently through tears: "Angyalom, you have not done this! You must always remember you have not done this! It is I who have done this, it is I! I did not understand what I had surrendered to him that was so precious. And now I know, I know! I have my freedom back, Angyalom!" She lifted me in her arms and repeated in a kind of hysterical exaltation: "My freedom!"

She drew away and held her face in her hands. "We will take his money," she murmured as if speaking her thought aloud.

Then for the first time I saw a dark patch of blood staining her dress at the thigh. My bullet had been deflected off something, striking Terézia's thigh but not, it seemed, sinking deeply. She dressed the wound. We both put on winter clothing and left the apartment without a backward glance. An icy wind clawed at our faces. She walked with a limp. We shrank into shadows when tank columns waggled thunderously past. Where there had been fighting, there were now black shapes of women bending and turning over the dead. At the train station there were masses of people frantically trying to secure passage to the border.

We waited twenty hours to board a steam train. Gusts of snow blew across the undulating countryside of Transdanubia. We arrived at a border town just as the snow was blotting out visibility, and there we were followed by a woman with long red hair and freckled face who said to Terézia, "I'd like to talk to you." She took us to a farmhouse and demanded 2000 forints to have us guided across the border. But the woman's father, an unshaven old man with piercing eyes and a bloodstained bandage on his head, intervened. "500 forints," he declared with finality.

Terézia paid him at once. The old man fetched a bottle of wine and glasses. "We leave after midnight. I will show you the way through minefields. The Russian sentries will be drunk and standing carelessly around fires. The *Honvédség* will not do this and will look the other way," the old man explained. He poured four glasses full of a thickish red wine. "*Egészségedre.*" After we drank the wine, Terézia and I huddled by a fireplace and fell asleep.

"Come," said the old man many hours later. "Much snow falls. But there is moonlight on the fields. When we leave the forest, we will use haystacks for cover. At the frontier, keep your head low."

We followed the old man. Geese squonked. Snow scrunched beneath our feet. Firs lolled their shrouded tongues. Against the ungoverned shapes of night the wind, whitefingered, swirled and screamed like a devouring feline phantom.

The old man paused every now and then to listen to the night. Then waved us on.

A faraway owroo owroo: dog fanging moon.

Several times Terézia stumbled and had difficulty getting up. I supposed that her wound had stiffened, but she made a shooing motion of hand at me. We plodded on. Gulps of frigid air brought a taste of bloodsalt.

We came to the edge of a forest. In front of us, a field about 400 meters across. The old man crouched and signalled for us to do the same when we approached. He spat and said, "Many soldiers." He pointed and I saw in a distant part of the field by a blazing fire the jerky movement of little figures, heard the night-muffled noise of crude guffaws. "Now," said the old man. He set off at a crouching half-run, pausing by haystacks covered with snow like Christmas cakes. Halfway across the field I paused and glanced back.

Terézia was rising, stumbling, sprawling. I was about to

run to her assistance when a rough arm grabbed me about the waist. The old man was muttering, "Too late now. First you, then your mother." Half carrying, half dragging me, he took me across the field where we entered a patch of obscure sylva. He stood up and blew steam from his mouth. "You are in Austria now," he said. "I must go before it's too late." He started back for Terézia, then froze in his tracks. For it had happened—the hissing, the wop-wop, pow-pow of magnesium flares, the incandescent glazing of field and sky. Terézia was floundering in the middle of the field, floundering and pulling herself forward on her arms.

The old man gripped my arm. "We cannot go to her."

There would be more flares. Men shouting, soldiers running, weapons unslung. There would be the cautious movements toward Terézia. Harsh words in Russian. A falling of white light to the vagaries of moonlight. There would be one agonized scream—*Aiii!*—that has followed me all the days of my life.

I turned and buried my face against the old man's chest. He stroked my hair. "There is nothing we can do. Now. Listen to me. There is a patrol station about a thousand meters from here. They will give you hot soup. The God of the Hungarians go with you."

And so I was separated from my mother forever. I left the old man and walked into a dark forest alone.

PART THREE

1

IN those days an hour's trolleycar ride would take you from the Ring near the Imperial Palace in Vienna to the refugee camp at Traiskirchen. The camp consisted of a few barracks used by the Austrian Army from the First World War until the end of the Second, when they were occupied by the Soviets. Before leaving Austria in the early fifties Red Army soldiers removed from the camp all the doorknobs and windowpanes. When I arrived there in November of '56 the walls were shored up with rotten timber, the windows were covered with newspapers, and doors swung and banged. I was assigned to a small room in which forty Hungarian refugees slept in tiers of unvarnished troughs. Tickings of straw and American Army surplus blankets had been furnished by Quaker volunteers from England and the United States. The center aisle of the room was clogged with wet clothes, crying children, impedimenta of exile such as albums, dolls, framed pictures of saints, and bags of special candies wrapped in fluted tissue paper.

Because my knowledge of English was, thanks to my father's teaching, passably good, and because the Kommandant of the camp was overwhelmed by the sudden influx of Hungarians caused by our revolution against the Soviets, he sent me shortly after my arrival to offer assistance to an English lady who had been exhausting herself as a cook in the mess hall. Her name was Grace Woolpack. From the moment I met her, I believed no falsity could ever cheat the constant angel at her lips.

I crossed the snow-packed compound where young men played soccer with a child's rubber ball. I opened the makeshift latch of the mess hall door and was met by the delicious aroma of baking bread. And by a woman's calmly inflected voice from the kitchen: "*On ne peut pas manger devant cinq heures...* Hellow." She saw me, dried hands on an apron, and came forward. "*Pardon,*" she said in a hesitant but friendly manner, "*je n'ai pas parlé français depuis longtemps. Comment...* O dear." She did an eye roll of exasperation. "My French is hopeless. We will have to speak English... There we are."

"I am speaking a little English," I said. I could not take my eyes off her. She was about thirty and had a kind face and cornsilk sheen to her hair.

"Super." She pronounced it *sue-pah* with a hushed and radiant intonation. "And what is your name?" When I told her, she extended her hand, shook mine and held it. Her hand was cold. "My name is Grace. Shall we be friends?"

"Yes," I said.

"Super. You'll be a good friend, I can tell. What can I do for you?"

"Herr Kommandant said to help Fräulein Woolpack."

"He said that? He's such a dear, I'm afraid I'm an old married woman, not a *fräulein.*"

She looked no older than Terézia, my recently, probably murdered mother. "You're not old."

She squeezed my hand before she released it. "You *are* a friend," she said. "We'll have a jolly good time, you and I."

"Yes," I said. "We are having good time." Now, the Kommandant had told me that the English lady would be going to Vienna in the morning and might be willing to show me where to go to apply for emigration visas. When, as best I could, I explained this possibility to Grace, she was immediately enthusiastic. "Super!" she clapped her hands. "We'll go Christmas shopping and have a proper tea at a lovely hotel on the Mariahilfestrasse and go to the Kino... O dear, I do natter so," she sighed and half smiled as if distracted. "You'll need to queue up for a visa, poor lamb... I'm afraid all these revolutions and politics are far over my head. Those dreadful Russians, why can't they be *sensible*?... Are you with your family or by yourself, Paul?"

"I am alone now."

"Poor poppet," she murmured, eyes glistening, but went on in a brightening voice. "Not to worry, then. Come along with you. Work to do. Mind you, not on an empty stomach."

I followed her to the kitchen where an aluminum pot was steaming on the wrought-iron stove. Grace stirred the pot, ladled from it a bowl of soup. I went and pressed my face against her cashmere sweater.

"Get on with you now," she said gently. "Drink your soup, there's a fine fellow." I sat at a table and spooned mouthfuls of soup hungrily—a thick potato soup laced with carrots and leeks and flavored with paprika and with something else, wild, that I couldn't identify. "Sage and onion," Grace replied to my look of puzzlement. "It reminds me of walks on a heath after rain, the skylarks hovering above their nests and braving it all out so splendidly... Is the soup good? Just the job, eh? Well, I should hope. Before the war, when I was a little girl, the family had servants. My father was a doctor, you see. He was posted to India at the outbreak of war, and Mums and I were evacuated from London to the Yorkshire dales. No servants, then, *be gomb!* We ate boiled nettles and horrid porridge. Learned *nowt* about cooking, as they say in the North Country... When I married John, he was horrified to discover that I couldn't cook working-class food, bangers and mash and gooseberry tart... My word, I do go on. I must be tired. Excuse me." Her voice had trailed off. She massaged her temples. Although I had not understood all of her words—they come to me now as her manner of speech—she was the sort of grand lady whose magnificence one instinctively worships and protects in hopes of some intercession by the powers of light.

"You sleep now, please."

She smiled without parting her lips. "I don't know what's come over me. I do apologize. Perhaps I'll just pop off to sleep for twenty minutes. Wake me up... Mind the bread. You'll need to remove the bread from the oven. Cover with the damp teacloths. You are. So kind." Resting her head on her arms, Grace fell asleep. I stood behind her, breathing her golden hair, and she sighed as though dreaming. Then I went to the door and peeped out. Snow sifted through the cones of light shed from naked bulbs. The young men were still kicking the ball. A trolleycar from Vienna, brightly lit, was discharging passengers who trudged without animation toward the barracks. I had no intention of waking Grace. I wondered what it would be like to have her for my mother.

After a while I went to the kitchen to remove the bread from the oven and to prepare for Grace a little surprise out of my knowledge of mess hall management in Mrs. Pribéky's Gas City.

I don't know
but I believe
I'll be home
by Christmas Eve

Sound off
ONE TWO
Bring it on down
THREE FOUR

Chowhounds—halt!

Boots were stamped outside. The door blew open and in sauntered tall, unshaven young men in jeans and jackets who rubbed their hands, sniffed the air, and talked too loud. My first Americans.

"Hey, baby, what's for chow?"

One of the Americans with a Society of Friends patch on his jacket had shaken Grace awake, an imbecile grin on his face, a startled look on hers as she discovered my masterpiece: mess trays stacked, buckets for hot rinse and waste disposal lined up, bread prepared for slicing, aluminum soup pot on line and ready to be ladled into metal cups. I had tied a white apron about my waist.

Grace came, started to say something, and hugged me in her arms.

"Thank you, precious lamb."

The Americans did not wait for me to serve them but grabbed their food. Their jaws moved mechanically as those of oxen. For Grace's sake I was mortified, but she was already busy serving the long queue of my countrymen that shuffled quietly along my line. She had words for everyone: "I'm *so* glad to see you" and "what frightful weather" and "*les yeux de votre garçon, madame, sont tout à fait adorable.*" My people's faces brightened from the glow of these more or less unintelligible words. Some of my people essayed the courtesies of our new environment: "Zank you" and "goot" and "we remember you in prayers."

An old man fumbled in his baggy trousers, pulled out a brooch set in gold, and gave it to Grace with a speech that I translated. "He says the brooch belonged to his grandmother. He wishes for you to be having it. You are an angel." Grace shook her head and was going to protest when I addressed the old man in excellent Hungarian terms: "The English angel wishes me to convey to you the greetings from the Queen of England. On behalf of those who worship in the spirit of St. Stephen and recognize the divine mission of Hungary to sacrifice herself for the salvation of Christendom, she will wear your gift next to her heart and remember always your grandmother who is close to God in Heaven."

The old man bowed his head. "It is necessary," I explained to Grace, "to give the most valuable possession from the old country. He has said the good-bye. You give him the happiness."

"And what is your most valuable possession, pet lamb?"

I remembered my father's teaching and said, "It is my soul. I cannot give it away."

An hour later I had the mess hall tidied up, everything in its place, floors wet-mopped, coffee brewed. Anxious to impress Grace and the Kommandant with my *savoir-faire,* I poured out three canteen cups of chicory-flavored coffee, placed them on a tray, and tip-toed quietly to their table. They were talking in whispers. On the table lay a packet of banknotes wrapped in a rubber band.

"Now for my next trick—coffee," I said. "*Voilà*!"

Grace spun around so violently I almost dropped the tray, and in the same instant the Kommandant swept the banknotes into his tunic. He spoke first. "Goot, goot... Ve vere saying, Red Cross until Christmas Eve not commen." He sighed and winked at me. "Ja ja. Red Cross commen, vork done already. Vill be Swedish aristocrat voman in white trousers, carry riding crop, stay at big hotel in Wien, singing to me *Der Rosenkavalier* over telephone. Greta Garbo, she is. So."

I put the tray on the table, distributed the canteen cups, and waited for Grace to drink from her cup first.

"The Red Cross are wonderful—" Grace protested and stopped. "Surely you jest."

"Is so? Maybe so. Quaker voman all vork, no play. Old Cherman saying, what expect from ox only the beef."

"You're impossible, Herr Kommandant. *And* you work twenty hours a day. *And* you don't care for yourself properly. Cheese omelette with sausages?" She rose.

"Sitting down," he motioned insincerely with a twitch of a smile in my direction. "Something I tell you, young man." The Kommandant lowered his voice to a conspiratorial whisper that Grace could hear. "This Fräulein Voolpick has always money. From England commen vork for nothing. She is terrible."

"Rubbish!" Grace paused before going to the kitchen. "We couldn't cope without you. You shall have an omelette, *and* you'll go home for a proper rest, *and*, if I catch you working all night in your office, I'll give you my cold tongue so you'll never forget!"

The Kommandant chuckled in his throat. "You see? Terrible, this voman. No goot. For me is Red Cross *führer* like Greta Garbo."

A few minutes later Grace brought plates of omelettes and sausages for me as well as for him. When we had eaten, she hugged me to her. "Tell me about this one, Herr Kommandant. What is his chance for obtaining a visa?"

The Kommandant waggled his hand. Meaning so-so. The quotas for many countries, he said, were being filled with freedom fighters and with families with money and skills. "His mother was taken by the Russians at the border. We are trying through the diplomatic discover what has happen. Not goot. No relative, no money, no skill. What you vant, young man?" He had turned to me.

"A home," I said.

"Ja, ja." He paused and did not look at Grace. "Of course, with the sponsor, he will have the visa. Perhaps there is the family without *kinder*? And tomorrow you take boy to Wien?"

"We shall have hours of entertainment. Shall we not, Paul?" She caressed my hair and smiled, then exchanged a glance with the Kommandant and said, "Perhaps it will not be necessary to visit the embassies tomorrow."

Next morning we took the trolley to Vienna, pausing in Praterstern by the Ferris wheel once in the Soviet zone of occupation. The feeling of recent enslavement lingered. People scurried furtively into doorways, leaving streets deserted. Buildings were still pockmarked by gunfire. Not a shop or automobile in sight.

How different the atmosphere of the former Allied zone of occupation! As we alighted from the trolley near the Imperial Palace, the streets were bustling with traffic and the pavements were crowded with people. As Grace and I strolled, I looked everywhere with amazement. Flash and zoom of sports cars, pungencies of benzine. Shops with mouth-watering aromas of bread and cheese, with displays of pink capons and strungup sausages, enamel trays of tripes and liver pâté. Churchbells sonorously peeling and a boys' choir shrilling *Stille Nacht* through throats of loud-speakers. Near the Opera some baggy-suited young men, possibly freedom fighters, warmed their hands by a fire in the street. But not a policeman or a soldier to be seen!

"Gorgy. Absolutely gorgeous!" Grace would later be exclaiming after a visit to one of those Limited shops specializing as outfitters to gentlemen. There I was—quite a fantastic dude in grey gabardine trousers, Harris tweed jacket, wonderfully squeaky hand-stitched leather shoes, a white shirt from Paris, a polka-dot bow tie and a Chesterfield with velvet collar! While the proprietor deposited something called traveler's checks, Grace had stood back and admired my transformation. The proprietor, with a slightly supercilious look, presented me with a box containing my old Five Year Plan rags and brogans. I waved him away. Out in the enchanted street, Grace exclaimed in approval and opened her arms to me and I flew to them and kissed her cheek and thanked her. I felt a strange dizziness as if the pavement had disappeared beneath my new shoes.

"There's an old saying, Paul: if the sky should fall, we shall catch larks. Let's have a bang-up meal. Would you do me the honor, sir, of escorting me to your finest hotel?"

Presently there we were—seated in a glittering dining room of a luxurious hotel on the Mariahilfestrasse, a maître d' hovering over us, snapping fingers at masses of uniformed waiters.

"Herr Ober," Grace said imperially to a waiter, "we shall have cocktails. Pimm's Number One with three cherries."

"Very good, madame. And you, sir?"

"Champagne," I said. "What do you recommend?"

"Perhaps the Piper Heidsieck, sir?"

"Excellent," I said.

"The bottle of course?"

"The bottle, naturally."

"Thank you, sir."

The waiter went. Grace leaned over the damask tablecloth, placed her hand over mine. She wore a large diamond ring. "You," she half giggled, "are absolutely to the manner born. 'The bottle, naturally.' He almost wet his pants in disbelief."

I sat up proudly. "I have much ancestors, Grace. I am descended from Attila the Hun."

The waiter returned with Grace's fruity cocktail and a bottle of champagne, my first in almost thirteen years. I gave approval to the label, and he poured. "Hm," I murmured to the exquisitely burning taste. "*Egészségedre.*"

"Cheers, love," she said.

An hour passed as in a dream. My first raw oysters, my first *canard rôti à l'orange*. Turkish coffee with Cointreau.

I don't remember all the questions Grace asked me about my life, but I told the truth, mostly. She caressed my hand. "Thank you for telling me, Paul... I also lost my father in the war and not long ago my dearest friend, my American father-in-law. I've been left quite comfortably off, and I'm married to a super fellow. Our only regret is that we don't have any children." She looked at me thoughtfully. Then smiled. "Perhaps you'll visit us if you come to England. We have a large house in Frognall, near Hampstead Heath. Just bags of room. You can see the city for miles. We have a lovely garden. You can take jolly good walks... We're having such a lovely time, you and I."

I was suddenly overcome by the realization that I would be losing Grace in a few weeks' time.

"What is it, love? Did I say something that hurt your feelings?"

I shook my head, unable to speak.

"Tell me, love. I can't bear it."

"*Macht nichts.*"

"What does that mean?"

"It means nothing matters anymore."

"What doesn't matter anymore? Are you angry with me?"

Again I shook my head. I pretended to wipe my mouth

with the damask serviette but dabbed my eyes and glanced away. In truth, I didn't know what to make of my emotions.

"The trolley leaves at three," Grace said. "Time to go."

Outside, a light snow was falling. Grace hugged me as we walked to the trolley stop.

"Are you feeling better now?"

I was going to stop the words in my mouth but ran and flung my arms around her and moaned the words into her fur coat: "I love you."

She caressed my hair. "Pet lamb," she said, "I love you, too."

Just then a bus splashed slowly past us. Leaning from its open windows were happy young men. I heard one of them shout, "Pál! Pál!" I looked and recognized Günter. He was waving and saying in Hungarian, "I go now to South America! You saved me from that bastard Malakov! Come to South America... !" He continued to wave until the bus turned a corner and was gone. My heart thumped in my throat. Did he know that he had commanded me to kill his own father?

The double-decker red bus with *Drink a Pinta* and *Guinness is Good For You* and *Players Navy Cut* ads glued to its sides lurched to a stop at Marble Arch, and a maturely developed girl of fifteen stepped into a drizzle of bonechilling December rain. She waved to the Jamaican ticket collector, who always held up the bus a few extra seconds for her and lifted her to the pavement so she could steady herself. He ding-dinged the bell and waved back as the bus roared toward the Bayswater Road. He was what the girl called a good bloke.

An obvious prostitute, little older than she, was leaning against a mercury vapor lamppost and smoking a cigarette. The usual black outfit from stockings to umbrella and the usual cheek rouge like suddenly smashed cherries.

The girl, too, wore black—an expensive zipup leather jacket—though her jeans and blue suede shoes suggested the mode of calculated sloth. She wore no makeup and nothing to protect her long dark hair from London weather. She fumbled inside her shoulder bag, extracted one of her reefers, and swore an oath. Then at a hobbling gait she approached the prostitute.

"Mind if I borrow a light?" she asked in an American accent. The prostitute looked at her with a kind of smirking vacuity, took out a box of Swan Vestas, and lit the girl's reefer by cupping the match in polished hands while the girl leaned in. "Fancy," said the prostitute. She pronounced it *fawncee.* "Have a drag," said the American girl. The prostitute took the reefer and inhaled deeply before returning it. "Ta," she said. "Working up our nerve, eh?"

"Kiss off," said the American girl with a nervous grin. She pivoted and walked down Oxford Street, shielding the reefer from the rain and sucking smoke at frequent intervals, finally crushing the butt end beneath her artificial foot. Opposite Selfridge's, she turned toward Grosvenor Square, presently entering it and being met by the noise of jackhammers where a new American embassy was being erected. She attended school there at Number Thirteen, a private school for American kids whose parents were, in her parlance, into oil or the Strategic Air Command with its so-called nuclear deterrent. She herself had been shipped abroad by divorced parents. Now that it was the Christmas holidays the Georgian brick buildings were emptied of Americans and made her feel homesick. An occasional black hackney cab circled the square and left shiny trails on wet asphalt through which poked cobblestones of another era. As if the past were trying to disrupt the present—good. She believed that the world suffered from social and emotional constipation.

She was glad to see the sleek black Jaguar parked near her school and an American man in an overcoat pacing near the Roosevelt monument. He watched her approaching but, as she expected, pretended not to notice her until she stopped and stood before him, scanning his face for the recognition that she knew, one day, he was bound to give her. But it was difficult to gaze at him too long without trepidation. He was "incredibly" old—about thirty-five—and looked "devastatingly" distinguished with that silvery streaking of groomed black hair, that thin mustache above full cupid's-bow lips, those deepset blue eyes like the reflection of a summer sky on tin, of that depthless hue, and that aquiline though slightly puggish nose of one acquainted with brawling. She knew he was, just as she knew that the hard muscles of his back, invisible beneath his toff's attire, could be scratched toward painful pleasure.

"Hi," she said with a quick toss of hair. "I painted a water color for you. Would you like to see it?"

He had seemed to be scowling. She hoped that his mood would not be so black that her gift would not lighten it. She took the picture from her bag and held it up to keep the rain from spoiling it.

"My word," he murmured as if taken aback, "you're in rare form, Bluejean."

"Do you like it?"

There was a pause. Then he crinkled his eyes and smiled with slightly parted lips, like Clark Gable in *Gone With the Wind*. He made a polite cough behind his hand, but he was amused, she could tell. She came and pressed herself against his overcoat. Took its damp lapel between her teeth and made a growling noise in her throat. And tried to study her picture through his eyes.

It was a picture such as one finds on any lavatory wall though not altogether lacking in art. The penis rose like a reddish purple crocus against a black sky pricked with stars.

At last the man chuckled in spite of himself. "What a marvelous cock!"

"You ought to know," said Bluejean. "It's yours."

"The picture or the cock?"

"Both."

"I'll have to charge you corkage."

"So you like it okay? I mean, like... I mean, God, I'm not into obscenity. I paint what I feel. Okay? I mean, when you look at it, I want you to think of me. Have you missed me? I've missed you so much... Can we go to your house now? Please, Jack?"

He made a bruffing sound in his throat and consulted his wristwatch. "I asked you to meet me here because something has come up. Shall we talk in the car?"

The Jaguar smelled of oiled leather and Jack's aftershave. She pressed the cigarette lighter, but he held her hand away from the panel and said, "No fags. I want everything tidy." She noticed that the ashtray had been emptied of her old stubs. He turned on the ignition. Warm air was clouding the windscreen as he spoke. "Grace cabled from Vienna. She's arriving at Victoria Station tonight. Christmas Eve, of all bloody nuisances!"

"Which means?"

"It means we'll have to pack it in... But not to worry. I'll give you a tinkle now and then."

She fought back tears, sobbed on an intake of breath. "I thought you cared for me. Oh, shit."

"Well," he said after heaving a sigh, "of course I care for you, darling. You're all I have to live for."

"I've heard that one before," she snorted.

"Grace means nothing to me save the money."

"Don't go back to her! I'll do anything you want! Jack! I don't want anyone but you, ever!"

"Well, darling, it's not quite as simple as all that. It seems

I'm to be foster father to some Hungarian orphan boy she's secured through bribes. Grace wants an heir and wants me to swear he's my flesh and blood."

"I'll give you children, Jack! I swear I will! Only don't leave me!"

"Stop it!" he hissed at her and moved to slap her, but took her face in his hands instead and crushed his lips to hers. With one hand he then unzipped her jacket and fondled her breasts until the t-shirt rubbed the nipples raw. She gasped and kissed the salt of her tears on his bristly, burning cheeks.

"Not here. But quickly! I love you so much, Jack."

He engaged the gears, frantically wiped the screen with his hand, and pressed the fury from his clenched jaw into the accelerator while she slipped off her jacket and loosened her jeans. It seemed five minutes had passed before he braked the car in a thicket of tall trees with leaves sweating raindrops. The engine went dead. She heard the rain splattering in gusty bursts upon the car. She closed her eyes, turned a knob that placed her seat into a reclining position.

After it was over she felt as if every cell of her body had been fused in brilliant relaxation.

"Wow," she said.

"I can't get enough of you," he breathed heavily into her ear.

She cleared the window. Just then, like an omen, a woman in black riding habit and black pipestem jodhpurs galloped past the window on a pale horse.

They were in Hyde Park.

In another place and time Bluejean would tell these matters to her husband—me, Paul—down to the last detail. She would even show me the picture John Woolpack had praised as akin to the fresco of Priapus so long buried in the ruins of Pompeii. Bluejean's husband was habituated to the fact that she had been only fifteen when swept away by the undertow of desire and to the fact that she had grown to womanhood still prolonging the passion.

True to Herr Kommandant's prediction, the field commander of the International Red Cross arrived in Traiskirchen, though earlier than expected, wearing a white uniform, waving a riding crop at her minions, and resembling Greta Garbo. Herr Kommandant helped me to secure documents necessary for emigration. I missed him as he waved from the concrete platform in Vienna at our departing, electrified train.

First class to London via Munich and Paris: with every hoot and whistle, every chime for dining car or wagon-lit, apprehensions eased. Beside me, Grace. Before me, freedom.

"What does Mr. Woolpack do?" I remember asking her. She did not remove her gaze from the window. "He works for world peace," she replied.

Now it is 1960 and tea and treacle tart prepared and served by maids, and Huntley and Palmer's sweet biscuits, ordered from Fortnum and Mason's, are waiting for Paul Woolpack's return from the Hurtfield grammar school on the Golders Green side of Hampstead Heath, his head swimming in classical and Romance languages but at least thinking in English and speaking it with a diminishing trace of accent: a youth ruddy-cheeked, strong, ten stone and five-nine by his sixteenth birthday: a youth running after completion of the last class with Mr. Simonini, the language teacher, running each day, rain or shine, through thicket and bramble of the heath, past a duck pond, past Galsworthy House, down shady streets, arriving as a freight train declined its only noun in the tunnel of Frognall

Station—tu whoot! tu whoot!—arriving breathlessly home at Frognall Gardens for tea with Grace whom he called Mum: his home on a green hill surrounded by red brick wall, on a hill with a view of oaks thick with nesting rooks beyond which shifted the diaphanous lights of London; on a hill where long-winged swifts, gliding to eaves above his third-story bedroom window, went snapping at insects in midair, and swallows clamored.

Grace I called Mum. I adopted the Woolpack name to please her and to satisfy school officials in awe of that name, and there were hugs and kisses awaiting me after school. After tea, there were strolls around her walled garden—perfected by two full-time gardeners—among the violets and daffodils, the roses and, each May, the bridal lace of pear trees, and primrose and Sweet William. Then, after I had finished my homework, we might sit by a fire and listen to recorded music or read poetry aloud to one another.

I seem to hear her now, practicing that French of hers that had been lingua franca at Traiskirchen:

"'*Quand vous serez bien vieille, au soir, à la chandelle, Assise auprès du feu...*'"

"Rubbish, Mum."

"Really?"

"Ronsard was an egotistical old fart when he wrote that."

"He was, was he? Mr. Simonini seems to lack appreciation of the finer things in life."

"Oh, *Mum.* Why do you have to spoil everything by reading morbid, sentimental nonsense? You want to know what I think? You're married to that grotty American blackguard who lives with that American girl who's not much older than I... I say, divorce the blighter."

"Don't," Grace admonished, "teach your grandmother to suck eggs."

School breaks and holidays were our best times together. She who could have afforded a stable of Rolls Royces drove a Princess saloon, and we drove everywhere. Once, when I was fifteen, we went camping on the Gower peninsula in Wales where the Atlantic goes ramping up a long white beach, the wave-lapped sands blown by winds, seagulls canting sideways. We pitched our tent in salt grass, changed into bathing costumes, and strolled hand-in-hand to the beach. Where, suddenly, I began to run. Barefooted at surf's edge, mindless of shell and shingle and braids of seaweed, I ran, ran with an energy I had not known I possessed, an energy streaming from the sun. When I returned to Grace, who was sunbathing, I raised my arms in a sort of primal exaltation.

"Fantastic!"

"I was watching you," she said, shading her eyes. "You run well. Head up, arms relaxed. Springing from the toes... Paul, what *are* you doing?"

"Come along, Mum." I was pulling her to her feet. She had shaved her legs and under the armpits and glistened with oil. "Come run with me."

"Paul, for heaven's sake, let go."

"Come on. It's super."

"Super for you. I waddle, like a duck with a Victorian bustle."

"Oh, *Mum*."

"All right... Race to the water. Last one in's a clot."

"Cheek!"

She had a head start and was diving into the curl of a wave before I spreadeagled in icy waters. Something had been coyly prophesied in the fat of her thighs. I tried not to think about it.

That night in the tent, after a fry-up of sausages and eggs, after drinking pints of Watney's Red Wallop—the stars near, crickets chirpy—I tried not to see her undressing, half in, half out of her sleeping bag. The sheen, though, of her hair aflow over pale shoulders and down to apple-breasts: my body's thought was mercifully inurned by the sweet rush of sleep.

Once, when I was sixteen, we drove to Cambridge and stayed in separate rooms at a British Raj-style hotel on Parker's Piece. At first as we strolled down St. Andrew's Street I thought Cambridge would be just another defeated English marketing and industrial city, but then we turned down Petty Cury and suddenly saw King's Parade and the soaring buttresses of Henry VI's chapel. And then the façade of Clare, a great lawn sloping toward the Cam, and the bridges over the Cam, the snowdrops and crocuses and aconite ablaze, the plane trees and chestnuts, the tennis courts of the Fellows Gardens, the slowly weathering Portland stone of the great colleges of the Backs reflected in the river where gaily be-scarved young men and women were punting in flat-bottomed boats and coxes yelled. And students with tattered black gowns aflutter, as in nineteenth-century etchings, balanced on bicycles, and people of all ages crowded the bookshops. And Trinity College where Lord Byron kept a bear and Sir Isaac Newton breasted the seas of thought. On and on we strolled, and never in my life had I seen, or even imagined, such a university as this of Cambridge—a place for clear thinking and decent feeling, a place that upheld the honor of living, a place to erect positive beliefs.

We sat on the banks of the Cam by Garrett Hostel Bridge.

"I say, Mum, do you think I would ever have the least little chance to come here?"

"If you set your heart on it," Grace said.

"I've set my heart on it already. But I'm afraid I'm not brainy enough."

"Tosh!"

"Well," I conceded, "I did all right on O-levels. But A-levels will separate the sheep from the goats. I'm not top of the form, you know."

"Just second," Grace remarked with a droll remonstrance.

"All right, I'll *be* first!" I said. "Anyway, I'll have a go. And next year I'm asking Mr. Simonini to coach my running. Could help."

"Super," she said. "Perhaps I can help. I'm an old Girton girl, after all. And John has connections at Cat's."

"No," I said after a pause, feeling the tension in her voice. "I don't want any favors from Woolpack, thank you very much and have a shrimp. After the way he has treated you."

Grace looked at sluggish waters and emerged from her inner life with a smile.

"What's so amusing? You know, your face is very beautiful when it lights up..."

She looked at me and stroked my hair. "Your hair is like an unmade bed... Paul? I think we should have an understanding about John. He's a good man. He's just a bit, well, unworldly. My late, beloved father-in-law always said one must keep John toeing the mark."

"With a Jag and a teenaged mistress?" I snorted. "He's no saint, if you ask me—"

"—I didn't ask you," Grace interrupted harshly. "I didn't ask you," she repeated in a quiet tone. "I respect your opinion, and I can see how one might arrive at it. But I must tell you, one should learn to abjure an opinion found to be untenable. You see," she spread her hands with their glittering jewels, "when you are young, you wish to pass moral judgments on people, and, when you are British, you are predestined to exercise moral influence upon others. *That*," she continued with a sudden clap of hands, "is why John's father wrote the Woolpack Will, leaving everything from the Trust Fund to me instead of to John. I exercise the proper moral influence over John... Naturally, one should not overrate one's moral influence over others. On the other hand, the income from the Trust Fund would have ruined a man with John's weakness and prevented him from fulfilling himself. Don't you see, pet lamb? John Woolpack the Third is an extraordinary person deserving respect for his ideals and tolerance for his peccadilloes... I shouldn't, if I were you, worry about me. As for John, he will tire sooner or later of this poor crippled girl with whom he's infatuated. He shall come back to me, and I shall get the best out of him yet!" Grace clasped her hands in a kind of rapture.

I was learning at Hurtfield that people who talked about money were not the right sort of people with whom to be associated. One could, however, talk about *American* money in a special category—namely, if one were clever enough and aristocratic enough to find a rich American in need of moral uplifting. Grace had done splendidly in that regard, but it saddened me to think of her life as loveless.

"Do you really love him so much, Mum?"

"Of course, darling."

"Does he love you?"

"We're very good friends, John and I."

"I don't understand."

"What don't you understand?" She placed a hand on my knee and left it there in apparent ignorance of the spasm touching its tongue into quiescent loins. "Come off it, Mum!" I exploded. "You haven't seen him in four years."

She removed her hand. "On the contrary, Paul, I see John at least once a week. Sometimes we meet at his flat on Cheyne Walk, when his, er, little tart is at school... John, poor thing, hasn't a threepenny bit to his name." She looked me in the eye, blinked, and said flatly, "To give her credit, she has an income of her own until the age of twenty-one. But I pay for everything else. Do you see now?"

"I thought he worked for world peace," I said in some bewilderment.

"Dear me," Grace sighed. "He's *against* the British and American governments. They make nuclear weapons, and John couldn't compromise his anti-nuclear position... Besides, he has been persecuted. Beaten pretty badly when they interned him during the war."

"So," I asked, "what does he *do*? A moment ago you stated that one shouldn't overrate moral influence with others. Now you seem to be saying that his moral convictions are more worthwhile than anyone else's..."

She started to say something and stopped. Again she put her hand on my knee, rested chin on hand, and purred, "I've upset you, darling. Let's talk another time."

"Let's talk now," I said. "What does he *do*?"

She had a dreamy look on her face. "He's writing a book. He goes regularly to the Reading Room of the British Museum. Years of labor, and now the fruit is about to be picked. It's what we've struggled for." The dreamy look was held on this vibrant note, but her mouth was drawn with a kind of bitterness that I'd never seen there before. She seemed older than at any time in our years of constant companionship. My heart stewed with emotions which found relief in the detachment of chitchat.

"What's the book about, Mum?"

"Well," she said, "it's dreadfully important, but far over my head. I believe he has discerned the causes of war in ancient and modern cultures. So that we can abolish nuclear bombs before the world is destroyed... I understand that Bertrand Russell himself may write the foreword. John's quite chuffed at the prospect."

"Bertrand Russell? That's impressive. Does he have a publisher?"

"Dear me, no. We mustn't allow the establishment to

make profits from our book. We are publishing the book privately and donating the proceeds to the Campaign for Nuclear Disarmament."

"What did he read when he was up at Cambridge?" I asked, changing the conversation and sitting up so that Grace had to relinquish command of my kneecap.

"His tutors considered him absolutely brilliant," Grace said. Her non sequiturs were something to watch for. At that time in my life I had not learned to interpret them as a sign of mental illness. "I had a devil of a time getting John to propose to me before graduation. He was twenty-seven, I but a silly twit of twenty-one."

"Really, Mum? What did you do?"

"Oh," she giggled. "Shall I tell a naughty secret?"

"I love your naughty secrets," I said without enthusiasm.

"Well, darling, John escorted me to the May Ball. We danced all night and for breakfast had champagne and strawberries with cream. Yummy scrim-jams! And... you won't believe this."

"I promise to believe it," I said.

"All night while we danced, I held in my gloved hand a small edition of *The Psychology of Sex*, by Havelock Ellis... John proposed over the champagne."

"Have you ever read it?"

"Read what, darling? Oh. *The Psychology of Sex*. Of course not."

Grace and I arrived at Victoria Station on Christmas Eve, 1956.

A porter took our luggage. We followed the crowd along the platform under the sooty, vaulted ceilings where pigeons gossiped in plumes of steam. The station echoed from the tread of many feet, the thumping of carriage doors, and the sigh of resting locomotives. There was an odor of decay.

"There's John," Grace exclaimed and waved. A broad-shouldered man dressed in tuxedo and black cape and sporting a straw boater stood at the ticket-collector's gate looking like a bon vivant at Toulouse-Lautrec's Moulin Rouge. The crowd parted around him. Women glanced at him over their shoulders. He knuckled his mustache and gazed about with a bemused air. He made a stop sign with his gloved right hand, like a bobby. When we passed through the gate, he took off his boater and kissed Grace on the cheek. "You look in top form," she said. "Are we going to a party?"

He consulted his wristwatch. "As a matter of fact, darling, one of Princess Margaret's friends is having a little bash. I thought I'd fall to the occasion."

"Here's our very own son." Grace beckoned me forward. "Paul, this is Mr. Woolpack."

I looked up to blue eyes. Woolpack smiled stiffly. "Well, my boy, pleased I'm sure. We'll make a rugger player out of the lad, eh? Or do you prefer footers?" He patted my shoulder without looking at me. "Hang on," he said and directed the porter toward a black car parked in a cab rank inside the station. A bobby with a truncheon stood by the car without seeming to notice it, though drivers shook fists in annoyance, their cabs splashing through puddles.

"I wonder, darling," said Woolpack, guiding Grace toward a Left Luggage area, "if we may speak in private."

"Paul? Wait for us here." Grace bent over and whispered, "He's a super fellow. You'll like him enormously when you get to know him."

"I don't think he is liking me," I whispered back.

"Nonsense. He's just—theatrical. Aren't we all?"

They went. I could see Woolpack pacing back and forth, pausing to rock on his heels with hands clasped in the small of his back, occasionally one of them raised and fluttered as if to say No, No. Grace seated herself on a bench, took out a handkerchief, and dabbed her eyes.

Also seated on the bench was a man who wore a muddy suit and workman's cap. He cuddled a boy of about my age.

"Hi. Are you the Hungarian?" said a voice behind me.

I spun around. A girl with a young woman's face and figure blossomed where she stood in a beam of fluorescent lighting. She was wearing an off-shoulder, pale organdy evening gown with a bright sash at the waist. Her dark hair was held by champagne-yellow ribbon, exposing earrings and a slender, creamy neck asparkle with pearls. Her eyes flared with a kind of feverish insurgency.

"Yes," I said. "Thank you."

"Say something in English." She giggled in a blushing way.

I placed my hand on my head. The thinker.

"Go on."

I removed my hand. "I think," I said, "you are very pretty."

She bit her thumb. Her eyes flashed about. "Not bad," she said. "The nicest thing anybody ever said to me. What's your name? Mine's Bluejean. Well, it isn't really. My American handle's about a mile long. Beatrice Jay Biddegood McQueen," she said in foghorn baritone. "*Rawthuh* puritan and respectable."

"Pál Szabó. I am pleasing to make your acquaintance." I bowed Hungarian-style.

"You're funny," she giggled. "Like to be friends?"

I had almost never spoken with a girl before and was surprised and flattered by this one's sincerity and friendliness. Whoever she was, she seemed almost as much of a dislocated person as I was. "I like to be your friend. Mrs. Woolpack is my friend. All my old friends are gone. Now I have two friends."

"Well," she said, rolling her eyes, "I don't think Mrs.

Woolpack and I—" she stopped and took a deep breath. "Here they come. I'm all rattled up. My God! What am I *do*ing?"

Grace came and nodded to Bluejean but did not extend her hand. It rested, diamondy, on her bosom. "I don't believe we've met. My husband tells me you're going to a party together. I'm sure you'll be the talk of the town." Grace fluttered her eyes. "Pray, what do you do in our country?"

"I'm in the prune business," said Bluejean.

"He's old enough to be your father," said Grace.

"I don't sneak around, Mrs. Woolpack."

"Evidently not, Miss McQueen. Your consideration of others is quite remarkable."

"I'm not interested in finding the best wife for your husband," said Bluejean. "I'm interested in finding the best husband for me."

"Then," said Grace, "there's nothing more to be said. You've made your bed, and you can lie in it."

"I do, Mrs. Woolpack, I do."

Woolpack cleared his throat. "Shall we go? This place smells like decomposed cabbage."

Bluejean pivoted and began to walk with puppet-like stiffness. There was a creaking noise.

"Why," Grace said in stage whisper to Woolpack, "the poor child is crippled."

When Bluejean pivoted again, her face blazed. "You blew it!" she hissed. "I'm not a crip! Nobody calls me a crip, or I—" Her voice faded on a petulant suck of breath.

"Well, now that's over," said Woolpack, clasping his hands as if to pronounce a benediction, "did you have pleasant weather in Austria?"

A few minutes later Grace and I were seated in a taxi. She was clenching her hands. "The cheek of the man! What absolute cheek!"

I said nothing. I was still trying to understand the meaning of the scene I had just witnessed.

Grace heaved a sigh, half smiled at me. "Not to worry, dear. He's just in a bad mood. There's time enough for him to adopt you."

2

WHEN Bluejean was pregnant and I was doing basic training at Fort Benning, we were married strangers. She was twenty-one years old, I eighteen. We tried to close the gaps by talking about ourselves. Sometimes, that year of '62, we tape-recorded the talk. Then we had instant replay that enabled us to laugh. During this period before Teapot was born, Bluejean tried to forget Woolpack. That was all right with me.

She was born Beatrice Jay Biddegood McQueen in 1941. From Beatrice to "Bea" to "B. J." was the family's idea, from "B. J." to Bluejean, Bluejean's. Having worn blue jeans, plural, as a child, she felt she wore jean, singular, after amputation of her leg below the knee, for cancer. So much for the name Bluejean. The name Biddegood belonged to the family's mills, Biddegood Brothers, in a town a few miles from Hartford, Connecticut. The name McQueen was her father's, Barry McQueen.

In the last century Biddegood Brothers had been manufacturers of silk, but a series of misfortunes plagued the family just as a dynasty seemed in the making. Although there were twelve Biddegood brothers at the height of the mills' prosperity, all Harvard-educated, Protestant-Work-Ethic patriarchs with genteel wives never seen in dishabille, there was no male issue. The wives produced daughters, and these daughters grew up without practical education other than that provided by a starched procession of witless governesses. It was deemed sufficient for Biddegood women that they learn to sign their names on dividend checks from a gross institution called a bank. The family business soon came to be managed in far-off New York City by minority stockholders. With the Wall Street Crash of 1929, stock plummeted, the family lost control, and operation of the mills was turned over to the very immigrants whose cheap labor had in balmy days seemed in inexhaustible supply. Biddegood women began to sell what stock remained amidst what they considered to be a plague of ingratitude: those splendid Irish, Polish, and God-knows-where-they've-been's struck to demand wages beyond their customary station. Anticipating the company's liquidation, the Biddegood women had the remainder of their stock sold, just as the entry of the United States into the Second World War in 1941 brought a sudden demand for silk parachutes. By the end of the war some of the grandchildren of poor immigrants boasted bigger houses and incomes than those remaining to members of the founding family.

From the beginnings of the family in New England in the seventeenth century there was evident a curious admixture of lofty idealism and cold equivocation. Biddegoods supported religious liberty as long as they didn't have to tolerate anyone else's belief. By the nineteenth century they tolerated all religion as long as they didn't have to believe in anything. Also in that century they ardently favored the abolition of slavery as long as they didn't have to rub elbows with dark-skinned peoples, and the abolition of poverty as long as they didn't have to pay for it. By the twentieth century such a staunch advocacy of abolitions underwent, with the withering away of dynastic hopes, a change. Now some Biddegood women wanted abolitions without equivocation—alcohol, Franklin Delano Roosevelt, and sex. In their quaint abhorrence for the popular they succeeded so well that, had it not been for the clickity-clack of the usurped and newly prosperous hosiery and parachute mills, the town might have been given over to the caterwauling of spinsters.

Christina Biddegood, however, married the grandson of an Irish immigrant, McQueen. He had been to college—though, as it wasn't Harvard, it didn't count. He was an inventor—though, as he invented a trash compacter, it didn't count either. Biddegood women averted their eyes whenever one of Barry McQueen's trash compacters lumbered through town with its logo, "Satisfaction Guaranteed or Double Your Trash Back." It was rumored that McQueen would dump his wife according to the same principle. She was well-bred, fastidious, duchess-faced and dumb, whereas he was bluff, boisterous, good-looking and clever. But given to drink, to binges away from home. The day after the birth of Beatrice Jay, Barry went off on a binge that lasted for weeks. When he returned home sober he found his infant daughter in a crib and his wife in bed transfixed by a migraine. Intimacy ceased from that day forward, and war was soon declared in more ways than one. To the one in Europe, Barry went as an airplane mechanic; to the one at home he returned in 1944, now thoroughly addicted to the alcohol that would take his life in 1960. His solace was "B. J.," whom he loved to fondle. Bluejean adored him. Years later she was to remember that her mother had never petted her or expressed any affection for her. Their one-sided conversations consisted of a litany of complaint from Christina McQueen's bed in a room curtained off from light. If the problem wasn't an agonizing headache, it was The Curse, if not The Curse, then colitis, constipation, a seemingly infinite variety of abdominal gases, and the epic abolition of them by means of stewed prunes.

When she was six, Bluejean was being fondled by her father before bedtime. That night he started a painful kind of game that left some blood on her nightie. When she was nine, she was found to have cancer of the bone marrow. Because a biopsy indicated no malignancy, doctors in Hartford ruled against surgery for several years, but by her twelfth year the disease had spread and amputation of a limb was called for. By then, menstruation had begun. Recuperating in the hospital but bleeding on a sheet, Bluejean naively asked the surgeon whether her father had been sleeping with her during the operation. The surgeon asked a few questions and answered a few. She was relieved to learn that Barry McQueen's secret game had nothing to do with cancer and cramps. But the secret was out. During physical therapy and rehabilitation, Bluejean was subjected to a barrage of inquiries from social workers, lawyers, and psychiatrists; was accused of being a liar, a vamp, and a whore; was encouraged to speak the truth and threatened when she told it; and was finally made a ward of court while her parents were getting divorced. Still aged twelve, and learning to walk with a prosthesis, Bluejean was discharged from hospital to find a new life awaiting her. One of Barry's wartime acquaintances, a Major Sipe stationed at a Royal Air Force base in England, himself a US Air Force fighter pilot, had agreed to take Bluejean into his family provided that Mrs. Christina McQueen—whose divorce settlement left Barry a pauper—paid all expenses of travel, board, lodging and schools until Bluejean was twenty-one.

Bluejean set sail, never to see her parents again. She tried to effect reconciliation with her mother by naming our baby Christina and sending to Connecticut a letter with snapshots from Georgia. There was no reply.

"My foster parents were four-square friendly Americans with perfect teeth and Jesus Saves bumper-stickers. The major was a big, easy-going bloke from Texas who talked about 'driving' airplanes, and major's wife once won a beauty contest, Miss Community Chest. They had wall-to-wall 100-watt smiles. Their dialogue was a blend of Hallmark cards and comic-book bubbles. But I liked them.

"The bloody Brits were something else.

"We were at this RAF base in Oxfordshire surrounded by lovely green hills with little thatch-roofed stone houses. I had to go to a local Church of England school in a village just a couple miles from the runway. The kids were as friendly as a bed of nettles. They called me 'that Merrycan.' Putting people down: they were into that. So was this teacher, Miss Cunliffe. She always waited for me to do something stupid. Like leaving the 'u' out in spelling 'favour' or putting an 'i' in 'tyre.' Miss Cunliffe would get this little smirk on her lips and fuck me over in her chirpy voice: 'I see the Colonies are still *hyar* today.' Everyone giggled, but I couldn't tell her to stuff it because Major and Mrs. Sipe had warned me I had to be a good ambassador.

"Anyway, their country and welcome to it. So I laid low. But I had to wear this school uniform: blue skirt, dinky cap, black shoes, cropped hair. You didn't have to be a genius to see the trend: be a good little girl, then be a good little mother and housewife so that men can fuck over your life...

"I was a good girl for two years. Then came the 'hollies,' meaning holidays. Living with the major and all, I had PX privileges. I bought me some American jeans and T-shirts, and one of them had printed on it a nude chick straddling a motorcycle and the words, DO IT IN THE STREET. Well, I thought, I'll wear what I bloody well please. I wowed 'em at school with the jeans and printed t-shirt. Instant leprosy. Old Cuntlips drug me before the headmaster who said I was 'veddy nawty.' This headmaster was an old baldheaded vicar of the Church of England. His name was Pigge. The Reverend Pigge, I shit you not. You should have seen him in his ecclesiastical drag with a black dress and a silver chain around his beefy neck. He was hot for giving us sermons about English cities being built on proceeds from the slave trade, but the guilt trip didn't stop him from stuffing his face with cucumber sandwiches or beating the pluperfect piss out of kids with his cane. We had a joke. We'd say, 'Did you hear that Pigge is going to Africa? He says he's going to *cane-ya*.' Anyway, Pigge made me drop my panties. He caned my ass into a bloody pulp and called the Royal Air Force and they called the whole United States *and* America and Major Sipe arrived in his station wagon and the headmaster said I was a disaster area or something and I sure as shit wasn't passing inspection at Buckingham Fuckingham Palace.

"He was a tall man, the major. He asked old Pigge very politely, 'What's the problem, sir?' 'Well,' said old Pigge, 'terwibly sorwy but we've had a wahthuh nasty to-do hyar. Saucy wench. I've given her ten o' the best. She'll learn a lesson she'll naught be forgetting.' The major looked from me to Pigge. 'Are you referring to my *daughter*, sir?' Major'd never called me that before. It was great. Pigge said with a kind of sneer, 'If you claim her as your daughter, may I suggest that you keep a *veddy* sharp eye on her in future.' The major smiled, nice as pie. 'Thanks for the suggestion, sir,' he said. Suddenly his arms shot out. He grabbed Pigge by the collar. 'Sir,' he said, 'I have a suggestion for you. If you beat my daughter again, I'm going to drive you so far into the ground that you'll be sucking air through your asshole. Good day, sir.' The major and me went off in the station wagon and the major didn't chew me out or anything, just told me to wear my uniform to school and anything I wanted at home. God, he was great! I mean, like, he was *great*, man.

"He died, the major. He was so easygoing, you forgot what his job was, to drive jet fighter planes so that the English could drink their pinta and turn on the telly and get preggies without having to worry about a third world war, in which they would all get buggered in ten seconds... The major bought the farm. Routine flight. Took off. Engine cut out on him. Had cleared the runway. Would have crashed into the playground of our school. Would have killed children. Had one second to decide. Decided. Nosed her down. Plane exploded in a pasture just a hundred yards from school. The major was burned to a cinder. All that remained after the wreck was removed was a charred tree, black accusing fingers. Oh, the English papers were nice, saying the major died a hero. 'Deed he was.

"Well, I dropped out of school to help Mrs. Sipe get packed to return to the States, and she arranged for the Connecticut lawyers to have me sent my child support direct to a London bank. That arrangement didn't bother my mother or father or the lawyers one bit. All those Right People from Newport to Pasadena have enough skeletons in the closet without Bluejean McQueen around to open hers. Oh, my dear Mrs. Puke-a-Duke, materialism is dreadfully out of fashion these days. Have you tried incest? Whatever, fifteen going on sixteen, I went up, as they say, to London, got me a quid-a-week bed-sitter in a coldwater flat off King's Road, and enrolled in an American school in Grosvenor Square."

To Bluejean that fall of '56 the money from home was not child support but blackmail. It wasn't even sufficient blackmail. She did not seek more. She had survival rations and school tuitions, but she also had what she called a "life style" to maintain, clothes, pop music, and pot. She decided to work on weekends, and, for a foreign teenager in England, that meant being an *au pair* girl, a sort of live-in babysitter and factotum.

She *au pair*ed for the Bodger-Jones family, Australians, in a mouldy two-story flat near Paddington Station. Because Bodger-Jones was a dental surgeon, he insisted on being titled "Mister" instead of "Doctor," one of those oddities of tradition that elevates the parvenu to a position midway between the dustman and the Queen. Mr. Bodger-Jones agreed to pay Bluejean five pounds fortnightly in exchange for babysitting Tonikins, aged five, and for tidying up the lodgings with wet-mop and broom. On Saturday nights Bluejean was to sleep on a couch in the ground-floor surgery among the flaking plaster, the mingled odors of dry rot and antiseptic, and the instruments of the trade such as the upholstered dental stool above which dangled a spider-armed high-speed drill. On a surgery table was a bleached human skull with a perpetual grin. In the skull's cranial cavity Mr. Bodger-Jones kept his petty-cash ledger. A gas installation in a Victorian fireplace provided heat; however, one had to insert a shilling in the meter once an hour in order to survive the fog and chill.

Mr. & Mrs. Bodger-Jones led lives of ritualized banality and paralyzing dullness. Tonikins, weather, and Royal Family exhausted the topics for conversation, even though the arrival of Bluejean on weekends added the spice of remarks about The Colonies. Saturday afternoons, Mr. Bodger-Jones dressed in white flannels and other cricketer's attire, Mrs. Bodger-Jones dressed in Marks & Sparks' frumpery, and the two of them set off in their Morris, he to play for his club, she to knit for Tonikins and clap her hands without making any real sound, exclaiming "Well done" and "Jolly good" whenever there was anything resembling human motion on the field. After a few suspenseful innings came tea; after tea, more cricket; after that, the pub; after the pub, faces blowsy from pints of bitter ale, Mr. & Mrs. Bodger-Jones toddled home in the mini to imbibe a nice cuppa or hot Horlick's and watch telly until beddy-byes. On Sunday mornings Mr. & Mrs. Bodger-Jones permitted themselves the luxury of a hot bath—threepence worth on the gas meter. And a jolly good read of *News of the World*.

One foggy October morning the pupils of the American school were assembled to hear a talk on the subject, "Nonviolence or Nuclear Annihilation." The headmaster introduced the speaker, John Woolpack III, as the Arizona-born, English-educated grandson of one of the West's great "pioneers," J. Byron Woolpack, founder of Earthco, participant in the building of Hoover Dam, etc., and the son of John Woolpack Jr., who until his recent death had directed Earthco's mining operations in South Africa, South America, and the United States, etc. Jack ("May I call you Jack?") had been interned in Scotland for his pacifist views during World War II, held a first-class honors degree from Cambridge, where he studied in the new field of human ecology and was also noted for his acting in productions of Shakespeare's plays, had entirely devoted his life to the cause of world peace, etc. The subject matter was certainly significant and timely, the speaker distinguished, and the school was especially grateful to accept a check for $25,000 from Jack's wife, who unfortunately could not be present.

Bluejean sat spellbound while Woolpack spoke. Here was an authentic gentlemen dressed in a Savile Row pinstriped suit, custom-made French-cuffed shirt, and a dark necktie sporting a heraldic design. He was of medium height, broad-shouldered and dark-haired. His blue eyes penetrated to the depths of her soul with the look of someone who had wandered the world, suffered its contumely, yet fixed a steady gaze upon another world. He spoke softly yet with mellifluous intensity punctuated by impatience. And what a mind! Sailing with grandeur and panache over the history of mankind, Woolpack traced ideas to their root in order to expose either their pertinence to or monstrous folly for a planet on the brink of self-destruction.

Woolpack's peculiar magnetism still enthralled her years later. Bluejean tape-recorded her recollection of Woolpack's lecture, apparently having received a direct imprinting of its argument. He had persuaded her of his nobility from the very beginning, and nothing thereafter could shake her faith. Indeed, as her second-hand summary closely reflects the published book, the lecture retains some intellectual force.

He had begun by showing that the basic idea of practically every war is that the enemy is a monster and that in killing him one is protecting the only truly valuable order of human life on earth, which is that of one's own people. With brutal examples from both ancient Greek literature and the Old Testament, he illustrated the principle of holy massacre. He then extended his argument by exposing the fallacy of the Apocalypse. If there were to be a series of wars followed by the end of historical time and the subsequent restoration of the right people to a universal reign of peace under a King of Kings, *who* were the elect survivors if *not* those of a closed society believing that it was the only good, that beyond its bounds were the enemies of God, and that they were called upon to project the principle of hatred outward upon the world while cultivating love within, toward those whose system of belief was of God? In the

Atomic Age the extinction of the Earth's life could not, save by a perversion of religion, be attributed to God's will when humanity itself possessed the means to unleash annihilation. This would not be a Day of Judgment in which God destroys the world but raises the dead and metes out perfect justice to everyone who has ever lived, because the complete destruction of mankind and other living creatures by men would be an apocalyptic premise without apocalyptic promise. Face to face with the death of Earth, we had no choice but to recognize that we no longer belonged to a tribal cluster but to a single world culture; and that the way to peace was to allow love to expand, like the ever-widening ripples on a pond, to include the mutual humanity of all peoples here and now and to come. Here, the practice of nonviolence, so wonderfully evinced in the life of Mahatma Gandhi, and an ancient idea that could be traced as far back as the Chhandogya Upanishad and the Tao Te Ching, came to the fore. Nonviolence involved the nonviolent person's capacity to absorb violence without retaliating. "One must redeem the enemy," Woolpack had concluded.

After the lecture Bluejean followed Woolpack out of school and into Grosvenor Square and hailed him where he stood by a black Jaguar.

"That," she declared breathlessly, "was neat, Mr. Woolpack."

His face lit up. "How very kind of you to say so. Rather esoteric, I'm afraid."

"No, no. You're right *on*," she protested. "I mean, my family back in the States thinks they're so superior to everybody but they're useless as tits on a boar. And the English, too. Excuse me."

"Quite all right. Go on."

"What I mean is. I mean, the English can be terrible—"

"—Snobs? I'm not English, in spite of my lost American

accent."

"But you're different, Mr. Woolpack. You care."

His eyes hypnotized her. He smiled and said, "Really, one does hear and read so much rubbish nowadays. It's refreshing to have a younger colleague concerned about the most appalling situation in history. American, I believe you said... ?"

She nodded, looked in his eyes, bit her lower lip.

"I didn't catch your name."

"Bluejean."

"Splendid! Bluejean. Well." He extended his hands and held hers in them. "I do hope we shall meet again, Bluejean." He released her hands and consulted his wristwatch. "I must pop along."

"Can I ask a question?"

"By all means."

She shifted her gaze to the pavement and swiftly returned to his gaze, mortified lest he notice her artificial foot inside a shoe. "You said we have to redeem our enemies. How do you *do* that?"

"A very interesting question." Woolpack stroked mustache with index finger. "Let me see, Bluejean... I'll put it this way. Defiance must be freed of contempt or arrogance. This is not to say that one must not employ a modicum of violence if it reduces the total of violence that would occur if the outcome were produced in this way rather than through protracted conflict in which nonviolence is outmatched by ruthless armed force. Do you follow me?"

Bluejean had only half listened to this speech. If she said anything, she feared that Woolpack would laugh at her ignorance, but if she said nothing, she would not exist for him. "Yes," she ventured desperately, "I see what you mean. Everything being relative to a given situation, you make the commitment to the idea or act that includes your enemy's best interest. What makes the Atomic Age different from any other in history is that your enemy's best interest lies in abolition of nuclear weapons. Then we can all go back to throwing stones and kicking ass."

Woolpack frowned. "I guess I blew it," Bluejean said. But his face relaxed as if charmed. "Why, this is absolutely bang on!" he exclaimed. "A Daniel come to judgment!"

"I like to hear *you* talk, Mr. Woolpack."

"Jack. Call me Jack. Hang on." Woolpack drew an engraved card from his tooled leather wallet. "Give me a tinkle on the blower some afternoon. We could chat over tea. Perhaps this Saturday afternoon?"

Bluejean accepted the engraved card without reading it and sighed dramatically. "I have to work weekends. *Au pair* girl. It's like living under a stone. Know what I mean?"

Woolpack tossed back his head and laughed in his throat, "Here, here! Couldn't agree with you more."

"I'd like a raincheck, Jack. Like, after school."

There was a pause. "My word," Woolpack muttered. "Well," he went on briskly, "it's a fixture. Tomorrow at four?"

"*Today* would be okay," said Bluejean. She gave him a sidelong glance.

"My word... Very well. I'll park down the street. Near Claridge's. Cheerio."

He went. If he'd noticed her foot or stiff gait, he was too much of a gentleman to say so. Bluejean did not move until the Jaguar had gone.

When he met her that afternoon and drove her to a little French café in the Soho district, he had changed attire in deference to her own. He too wore jeans and leather jacket. A Liberty scarf loosely knotted at his neck added a touch of impudence. He was in his mid-thirties, she estimated, just a flicker of grey at the temples to perfect his distinction. He seemed young at heart and actually timid for a man in the company of a girl less than half his age. Now and then he stammered as though the façade of self-assurance shielded a shy and lonely schoolboy. She saw he was unhappy, as Barry McQueen had been.

"You look smashing," she said when the waiter had seated them in a secluded nook. "Does your wife like you dressed this way?"

"Oh, uh uh, Grace? Uh uh, dear me, no. That is, uh, she doesn't *see* me at all. Hang it, I mean, she's too upper, too 'U' to understand a failure like me."

She lowered her gaze, then brought it up with teeth-clenching indignation. "You're not a failure, Jack. You're a beautiful man! Don't *ever* talk to me like that again!"

"Oh. Dear me. I—" he glanced away as if seeking escape. "I, I'm not an easy person to know. I, I feel I have so much to give, uh uh if I were only *allowed* to give it. I, I can't explain."

"Explain to me," Bluejean said. She placed her hand over his. He did not take her hand at first but stared at it as if it would bite. Then he held her hand. "It's so bloody difficult to speak of one's intimate, uh, business," he began. His lower lip quivered.

"I can listen."

"Very well. Sex," he blurted. "In a word."

"Grace?"

"Not her fault, really," he sighed with a despairing gesture. "They take the sex out of girls in school. Lots of field hockey and cold showers. What a load of codswallop!"

"Call me a bitch!" Bluejean suddenly cried. He released her hand.

"Gracious me, whatever for?"

"If you stay with that woman, I'm a bitch."

"Well," he said with a breaking smile, "Grace *is* of a holy, cold, and still conversation." He nodded wistfully. "I, I have thought about it. Leaving Grace and all that."

"Well? Where's your survival instinct? Look at me. Are

you looking at me?"

He wouldn't look at her. "Really, Bluejean, I'm a hopeless case."

"No, Jack, no, you're not! You just need to get warmth on a regular basis. Pussy. Man, I've had cancer and... some other problems. I tell you this: I'm going to *live* my life." He was looking at her now as if beseeching her. She wanted to cry. She again reached for his hand. "Can I help you, Jack?"

He shook his head. "Warmth, you say. Warmth! What if *I* am the one without warmth? What if *I* am the one incapable of loving? Do you know what they used to call me at the public school here where my father packed me off when I was seven, the bully boys? Ice-pack! I repudiated my father, you see. I cut him from my heart. In the process I steeled myself against pain and pleasure and shaped my life as an instrument for historical justice."

"We were talking about sex," Bluejean cut in sharply. "What's the big deal? Tell me. Please, Jack."

The waiter came with tea and caramel flan. Bluejean excused herself. As a test of Woolpack's sincerity, she dragged her artificial foot past red-checkered tables to the WC where she confronted herself in a mirror. "Hey, Bluejean," she was saying half out loud, "you're falling in love with this bloke. Cool it." She noticed that someone had written in lipstick on a stall: EXTERMINATE ALL MEN. She returned to table in a humor to force life to a crisis. Woolpack was using a knife to mash custard on the back of a fork. Bluejean surrendered to the undertow of feelings. Tears watered her eyes. She swam their gaze to his harbor. "I'm in love with you," she declared with unabashed misery.

"Bluejean." He sighed from a depth of his own.

There were to be many afternoon teas followed by drives in the Jaguar. He took her home to the coldwater flat off King's Road, escorted her to the door, consulted his watch and departed. That damned watch! Just when Woolpack seemed ready to accept the love she freely offered, the watch pulled him to another world away from her. There was nothing for her to do save wait for that world to yield its secret. If anyone else had spoken of being an instrument for historical justice, she would have dismissed him as a stuffed shirt. But not Woolpack. He saw something that he had to do, something so strange that he was embarrassed to be burdened with it, yet something so necessary that it was as inevitable as the ticking of time. When she saw the world through his eyes, her lameness would cease to be of consequence in that new world of his soul's dreaming—whatever it was and required, wherever the path to it led.

She began a diary in order to pull together the Woolpack story and also to commit to memory those touchstones from Shakespeare which he dropped into conversation. By snooping around the office of the school in Grosvenor Square she was able to peek at the notes the headmaster had used in introducing John Woolpack III. She jotted down headings in the diary: family, education, money, marriage, goals, work, Shakespeare. Soon she had notes under the headings, and from the notes as well as from Woolpack's piecemeal confessions emerged the profile of a life that in certain startling respects resembled her own.

Woolpack's English great-grandfather had owned mines in South Africa and in South America. J. Byron Woolpack, the grandfather, having inherited those mines, emigrated to Arizona Territory at the beginning of the century and founded the mining and construction company that was now known as Earthco. John Woolpack, Jr., usually called "John Junior," was a chip off the old block, emulating J. Byron in all ways but with a single important exception—he served in the American Expeditionary Forces in the First World War and was permanently afflicted by the effects of mustard gas. After hospitalization in England, John Junior married an English nurse, and the result of this union was the birth of John Woolpack, III, in Flagstaff, Arizona, in 1921. Then in 1928 something extraordinary happened to little Jack. Although Bluejean could not get Jack to talk about the occurrence, it resulted in the expulsion of a seven-year-old boy and his mother back to England and in Jack's forced continuance at a public school, alone in a foreign land, after the death of his mother. In 1939 Jack matriculated at Cambridge. When England entered the Second World War, Jack declared himself a pacifist and was sent to a hard-labor camp in Scotland. After the war, he returned to Cambridge on a government grant, played rugby, specialized in human ecology ("the human use of the human environment," Bluejean noted in the diary), and married Grace Littlehale upon their graduation. Then for the first time John Junior showed an interest in a reconciliation and summoned Jack and Grace to a meeting at Earthco headquarters in New York. Again, something extraordinary must have happened. Perhaps Jack argued with his father whose mining operations had expanded to include uranium, the fissionable element needed for production of atomic weapons. Perhaps John Junior formed an understanding with his daughter-in-law, Grace. But whatever it was that happened, John Junior at his death in 1954 had left a will under terms of which Jack inherited only a ranch near Flagstaff and Grace was given the income from a trust fund. Thus Grace became Jack's source of financial support. Moreover—and Bluejean underlined the entry in her diary—Grace threatened to commit suicide if Jack were ever to divorce her. Jack believed that Grace would carry out the threat.

One afternoon at the French café Bluejean decided to press Woolpack for more information under the heading of money. Beatrice Jay Biddegood McQueen had been educated in that subject.

"Did you ever consider flying to the States to hire a lawyer and negotiate with your dad?" she asked.

Woolpack's eyes smouldered.

"By Jove, what a corking good idea that would have been, once! If I'd had you, I'd now have means to my ends. I *do* have a sporting chance, actually. But..." His face fell, abruptly drained of energy.

"What is it, Jack?"

"Grace," he said.

"Who cares about her?"

"She'll commit suicide."

"I'll buy her the razor," Bluejean said.

"You don't know what you're saying."

"I love you, Jack... All right... Tell me flat. Who in the goddam hell do you think I am? I may not look like a lady. I may not act like a lady. But I'm a damn sight more of a lady than the ballbuster you married. And I'm an American. You've forgotten what it means to be an American."

"Very well," he said after a pause. "I'll tell you what American means. It means indulgence of personal liberty in a land which can only survive by means of social cooperation... Have you any idea how much money my father was worth when he died?"

"I don't care about his money," Bluejean said.

"Billions! That's *billions*. B as in Bomb. Those billions will probably double in ten years or so."

"Who needs it, Jack?"

"I do," he said evenly. "My billions will help to abolish the Bomb my father's uranium mines have built."

"Explain."

"Very well," he said.

Out it came in detail. John Junior's trust fund was irrevocably bound up with his estate. From the trust fund, Grace received income and paid Woolpack an allowance. If she died, the capital of the trust fund would go to charities. If, on the other hand, Jack were to father a child or children, said child or children became heirs at the age of eleven, heirs not only to the capital of the trust fund but also to the Woolpack estate, which would pour over into the trust fund and come under its regulations. There were several rules of consequence: first, when his child inherited the fortune at the age of ten, Woolpack had to prove to Grace that the child was legally his. Then Woolpack would be appointed guardian with powers to expend the capital as he wished, and, second, given these circumstances, Woolpack became Director of Earthco itself. Thus his father had left a loophole for Woolpack to come to power—but the loophole would be closed if Grace died or if there were no heir.

"When I get the money, if I do, I'll break my staff, bury it certain fathoms in the earth, and deeper than did ever plummet sound, I'll drown the Atomic Age." Woolpack spoke passionately. He had revealed his world.

"*The Tempest*," Bluejean said and went on in another voice, "Jack. Let Grace have everything. Leave her. You can start a new life."

"A new life?" Woolpack said with a quizzical expression. "You're a lady. You're right about that. And I don't intend to ask you to breed me an heir when I haven't a thing to offer you in return."

"Ask me," said Bluejean.

Back in Georgia when Bluejean and I had recently been married and were talking so candidly together, I questioned, as I recall, Woolpack's belief in his father's incredible wealth. Bluejean shrugged. The Woolpack wealth was of no interest to her. I was interested, though. During my years with Grace, when I was Paul Woolpack, I had been filled full of hot air and great, vague expectations about inheritance. So I went to the Fort Benning Library and did some research, and what I discovered was this: Earthco on balance was broke and only protected by means of government loans from going into receivership. Clearly, the only fortune lay in the trust fund as it was. Clearly, I concluded, Woolpack knew nothing about money or the business world. But could anybody tell him? Could Bluejean, if I were to set the record straight?

How I wish, now, that someone had told him!

The fourth weekend in October, the year of '56, Bluejean had finished her chores and was waiting in the surgery for Mr. and Mrs. Bodger-Jones to toddle home from the pub. It was cold. They'd left her no shillings for the gas heater. Nor did she have more than a few pennies herself. Mr. Bodger-Jones owed her a fortnight's wages. Locomotives from nearby Paddington Station chugged and clanked, turning the last screws on the lid of night. Bluejean snuggled in the comforter on the couch. Suddenly lights were flicked on and Mr. & Mrs. Bodger-Jones were peering at her. He was wearing his cricketer's whites.

"Ish me l'il Tonikins shleep?" asked Mrs. Bodger-Jones, making an effort to steady herself. "Crikey, I do believe I'm a bit tiddly, I do. Goo' night. Riddy, Ridge?"

His name was Reginald, Mr. Reginald Bodger-Jones, his wife called him Ridge, and he was riddy. Upstairs they went, neglecting to flick off the lights. Bluejean got up, closed the door, darkened the room, stripped shivering to her underwear, unstrapped her prosthesis, cocooned herself on the couch and fell asleep.

"I was having the weirdest dream," Bluejean would one day be telling me. "I was lying at the bottom of a lake. The weight of black water was pressing me down. The water turned to ice. The ice made a high-pitched drilling sound, like a metallic mosquito. I woke up too late."

Mr. Bodger-Jones held the high-speed drill near her

throat with one hand. Icy water sprayed her throat, trickled between her breasts. Mr. Bodger-Jones whispered as if coaxing a foal into harness. "There's a good girl. Easy, girl. We don't want commotion now, do we." She felt paralyzed with shame, momentarily, so insidious was the power of the insect's intention; then she reached for her prosthesis and pushed it in his face until he stood up and turned off the drill. "I can have you deported," he said through clenched teeth.

"You owe me five pounds," said Bluejean.

He turned on the lights, extracted a slip of paper from the cranial cavity of the skull, and read aloud. "Bed and breakfast twice at seven and six. Fifteen bob. Gas meter, forty bob. Twice forty, eighty. That makes four pounds, fifteen shillings you owe me. I owe you five bob. Here are two half-crowns. Settled." He placed the coins on the dental stool and tiptoed back upstairs. She lay still, listening to her blood.

Half an hour later she was at a cab rank near Paddington Station. Mercury vapor lamps glowed like orange tumors through fog. She found a driver reading a Fleet Street newspaper. ELVIS THE PELVIS, said the headline.

"Can you take me to King's Road for five bob?"

"Four and six, miss, I should say." He pronounced it *sigh*. A good bloke.

About one in the morning the driver dropped her off at a telephone kiosk on King's Road. She paid him the four and six and took coppers in change. "Ta, miss. Aw royt?"

She said nothing. He U-turned and parked across the road, dimming his lights. He was being protective. She concentrated upon the tasks of telephoning and of holding back engulfing shame. She took Jack's engraved card from her purse. She inserted coppers in a slot. When Jack's voice answered, she pushed Button 'A.'

"Can I talk to you?"

He said that Grace had left the country to do volunteer work for the Quakers in Austria. They could talk.

Next afternoon a Jaguar drove up to the curb by a dentist's office in Paddington. A man and a girl stepped out. The man rang the bell. When Mrs. Bodger-Jones cracked open the door, the man charged through, followed by the girl. They found Mr. Bodger-Jones in the surgery. There was a patient on the dental stool. The girl pointed at Mr. Bodger-Jones. He, at sight of her, held a whining, spitting drill outward, like a proboscis. The man did not wait to say anything but rugby-tackled the strange insect and swung his fists repeatedly into its pasty face, breaking the nose so severely that the girl would later say she heard the bones crack just before blood poured from lip and nostrils. The man rose, kicked the insect in the groin. The girl and the man ran from the office. They climbed into the Jaguar and sped toward a house in Hampstead.

3

ONCE a year Grace and I drove to Northampton to pay a visit to her mother there in a mental hospital. Mother Littlehale, hospitalized since the death of her husband in India in the Second World War, showed no sign of recognition when Grace appeared with flowers and sat in silence by the bedside. Afterwards, Grace would confer with the medical staff and make her annual contribution of 10,000 pounds while I roamed about the corridors in hopes of finding a beautiful young nurse with whom to fall in love and to rid myself of my confounded virginity. I fell in love with scores of young nurses but could never pluck up courage to speak to them. I experienced a sense of kinship with the patients who, dressed in National Health Service pajamas and robes, also roamed the corridors. Some patients picked invisible nits off walls, others stared into space, their eyeballs bulging like pickled eggs and their mouths contorted as if perpetually awaiting a dentist's drill.

In the spring of '62, not long after my eighteenth birthday, Grace and I were driving back to London following a visit to Northampton. The subject uppermost on my mind was raised by Grace. "I've been thinking, darling," she said, concentrating her attention on driving the van in traffic. "How are you doing at Hurtfield?"

I told her that Mr. Simonini thought I was ready for A-level exams.

"Super," Grace said, "but I mean your social life. Girlfriends. That sort of thing."

"It's a single-sex school, Mum," I said after a pause.

"Oh dear," she sighed, "there are so many homosexuals."

"Mum," I said, "I'm not queer, if that's what you want to know."

"Of course not! All the same... They say that young men of your age and women of my age, as it were, mid-thirtyish, are the most sexually active. What do you think?"

"I don't think about it," I said.

"It's so bloody unfair. Don't you agree?" She swerved to overtake a lorry, then half-smiled at me. She reached over and patted my thigh. "There, darling. You have your studies and your running, and soon you'll be going up to university. The world's your oyster. *And* you have a gorgeous body. Don't think I haven't noticed when we visit the hospital or go shopping. The girls are simply drooling over you."

"Name one," I snorted and looked out the window, thinking: *They practically push your face in them. You come up the escalator from the Underground and there they are coming closer and closer, no heads, just daintily diapered crotch ads.* Grace went on talking as England's green land received caressing rain from the sky: "Did I tell you I was visiting with John the other day at his charming little love nest on Cheyne Walk? It seems that his mistress with the funny name... ?"

"Bluejean," I said. *Closer and closer the knickers come, black silk with a wingspread like an enormous bat's, the model's navel caved in like a crater left by a meteor on the moon.*

"Bluejean, it seems, is preggies. I think we should have a party. Are you listening, darling?"

Then the escalator spews you into the street... "You said something about Bluejean's knickers?"

"Paul! I *said* she's pregnant. I *said* we should have a party."

"Party?"

"It's just the thing. My old dear friend Princess Del Drago is arriving from Rome, and we must give a party, and—"

"*Princess* Del Drago? I didn't know we knew royalty, Mum."

"Well," said Grace, "she's absolutely the most gorgy creature on earth. She married into the Black Aristocracy."

"What's the Black Aristocracy?"

"They're descended from popes."

"Oh."

"We'll have the Princess Del Drago. You'll fall head over heels in love the moment you set eyes on her. We'll ask John and his Bluejean. Yes."

Grace had finally gotten my full attention. "You're asking *them*? You must be daft, Mum."

She laughed on a tense note. "Why not? Now that the baggage is obliging John with an heir, I rather fancy we should behave as civilized human beings and take a charitable view... Oh dear. It's raining like billy-o." She switched on the windscreen wipers, and for a few minutes we both strained to see the road ahead. But I was really thinking now, stunned as I hadn't been since Grace and I were in Vienna and chasms seemed to open before my tread, and not the chasms promised by the ubiquitous underwear advertisements of Underground tube stations, either. For these were my old never-quite-covered chasms for disappearing into the abyss. I took a deep breath. "Mum?" I took another deep breath.

"Mum, am I your heir?"

"Of *course*, darling," she declared and again laid a hand on my thigh momentarily before grasping the gear stick and shifting down for a steep grade. "Didn't I give you a thousand pounds for your birthday? Shall I tell you a surprise? No. I shall spoil you."

"Spoil me," I said.

"What's your absolutely favorite color?"

"The mildewed fangs of a vampire sucking a virgin's blood."

"You must be joking... Say black."

"Black."

"Black it is then," she said.

"It?"

"I'm giving you a black Jaguar for your graduation... *There*! Won't it be smashing, darling, just the two of us going on Long Vacs together? You'll be the driver... Bugger this rain!" Grace accelerated, shifting to top gear.

Grace had lavished gifts upon me for years. I wanted for nothing. Even a thousand pounds in banknotes seemed a paltry instalment on a future life as a pig. I had tucked the notes in my dresser drawer next to a box of condoms purchased at a barbershop ("Is there anything *else*, sir?"). Now that Grace was giving me a car like Woolpack's, however, a sort of hatred passed through my heart. "Thank you very much," I said in an even tone.

"Splendid," said Grace with a smile that turned up a corner of her mouth. "You see, darling," she resumed without looking at me, "you're more precious to me than a mere heir. Blood relations are a cross we have to bear:

look at my own poor mother, a vegetable, no more. But you—you are *la crême de la crême*. You're handsome. I can spoil you to your heart's content... Let's pull over to that lay-by. I want to breathe! I want to feel rain on my skin!"

It was a soft spring rain as we stopped the car and got out. Grace took off her raincoat and stretched herself inside blouse and tweed skirt. Suddenly she clambered up an embankment to the edge of a tall forest thickened with misty leaves and with the sharp scent of nettles. "Oh," she sighed deeply with a kind of girlish ecstasy. "Come, darling. Walk with me. Come quickly. This is absolute heaven."

Presently we walked hand in hand into the forest away from the rip of motorcars—away where raindrops bit the heat of my face and small birds gathered leftover silence. Grace stopped. Mushrooms poked from a glade of moss. She rolled up sleeves, massaged her arms. She came and put her arm around my waist. When I put my arm around her waist, she came closer. I breathed the wetness in her hair. I closed my eyes. She kissed me in the ear and let the moisture linger. I removed my arm from Grace. I tried to turn so that she wouldn't see my trousers. "What have you got down there?" she whispered. She slipped her hand inside my trousers, grabbed my stalk and moved her cold hand up and down, up and down, until the mushrooms at my feet moaned and went out of focus.

"Do you feel better now?" she murmured.

"As a matter of fact," I lied, "I do."

The hand was still there. "What are these naughty things, darling?"

"My balls, Mum?"

"Don't call me Mum anymore, darling. I'm not your mother."

I said nothing.

She removed the hand. Birds twittered. I mashed mushrooms beneath my foot. I looked at Grace. Her gaze awaited me. Rain trickled from her brow. For a flicker of an instant, I wanted to throw her on the moss. The instant passed.

After we returned to the car, Grace hitched up her skirt. I could see where a stocking met the pale flesh of inner thigh. I tried to glue my eyes to the road. Soon she was prattling of this and that, jumping from one subject to another in what, later in life, I would learn to identify in mentally ill soldiers as schizophrenic thinking. She became coherent when the subject was money.

"That American girlfriend of John's is twenty-one now. She is no longer receiving support from the United States. Has no work permit. Is a dreadful housekeeper. Sits about all day while John is in the Museum. Reads rubbish. Probably a communist. Though, to do her credit, she has been assisting John with the Campaign for Nuclear Disarmament. Organizing rallies so that John can give his speeches on banning the Bomb. But *really*! The cheek of that girl! Why... Who cleans up the love nest once a week? *I* hire the scrubwomen. And sees to John's laundry? *I* hire the washerwomen. And supplies them with food from Fortnum and Mason's? *I* do. Who is their sole source of support? *I* am! And I've had it up to *here*!" Grace drew a diamondy finger across her brow just as I turned my head in spite of myself. I could see her bra through the rain-soaked blouse. Her thigh muscles twitched as she pressed the accelerator. "Oh dear," she said after a heavy sigh. "It will all end in tears."

"Do you see Bluejean?" I asked.

"I've avoided seeing her for years," Grace replied, "but now that she's helpless..."

"So you see her?"

Grace seemed to give the question thought. "Yes... Now that she's bearing John's child... Yes, I see her. She has her price."

"What do you mean by price, Mum? I mean Grace."

"For the child, of course."

"As your heir," I said, catching her drift.

"If I should die," Grace said. "Without John's child."

"The money goes—"

"—to charity. Precisely."

"Leaving John—"

"—buggered," Grace said.

"So you want Bluejean—"

"To surrender John's child at birth... I've offered the slut enough money to cobble dogs."

"Has she agreed?"

"She has no alternative."

"So she has agreed," I said. "I feel sorry for her."

"You're sweet, Paul," Grace said. She patted my thigh. "But I shouldn't waste my sympathy on a tramp."

"*I* was a tramp," I said.

She caught her breath, then relaxed her voice. "But, darling, we love each other."

"What about them? They've lived together for six years. Bluejean's twenty-one, you say. There must be *something*."

"There's always something else," Grace said.

"Money?"

"Yes," she said. "Money."

"What if Bluejean decides to keep her baby?"

"A possibility," Grace admitted. "We haven't come to a final agreement. John, bless him, does what I jolly well tell him to do... He's persuading her to see reason. He can't marry her. He can't support her without my help. Whereas we can give her a tidy sum and raise John's child with every advantage."

"You didn't quite answer my question," I cut in. "If Bluejean keeps her baby."

"I should hope not," Grace said. "John will throw her out on the street... What a super party we're going to have!"

she cried with one of her sudden changes of mood. "So much to celebrate. Your graduation. Your new motorcar. The Woolpack heir. The Princess Del Drago will boggle your mind!"

Mr. Simonini was a stockily built man with the leonine visage of a Roman emperor and round-rimmed National Health Service glasses. In addition to teaching Latin and Romance languages, he coached athletics at Hurtfield. Early that year of '62, after Latin class, I asked him if I could run for the school's club in a meet to be held with North London clubs the next Saturday afternoon. He lit his pipe, shook his head. "One must train, Woolpack. *Tanta est animi beatitudo*," he said, blowing out the Swan Vestas match.

"The more of it the better?"

"Very good, Woolpack." He removed the pipe and squinted at me, then puffed again.

"I can run, sir. I feel it."

"How fast are you, Woolpack?"

I told him I didn't know.

"Can't put the clock on you before Saturday. Still," he nodded to himself. "We need someone for the 800 meters. Just follow the pack. Forget about winning."

"I intend to win, sir."

He squinted, puffed. "*Marcus condidit imperator*, Woolpack."

"I didn't mean to be ostentatious, sir."

Simonini cracked a smile. "Very *good*, Woolpack. Do give my regards to your lovely mother, there's a good chap. She's one of the school's great benefactors. Here." He went to a closet, removed a box full of muddied track shoes. "Find a pair that fits. Remember. *Festaene lente*."

"I'll make haste slowly, sir. Thank you, sir," I said. He

left the classroom while I sorted through shoes.

Saturday afternoon arrived, grey with gusts of rain, a few puddles on the cinder track. A hundred or so of the school's boarders had turned up for the occasion wearing blazers and scarfs. Dozens of runners were warming up or competing in their events. I went behind the bleachers in order to prepare myself mentally.

For I had learned to play tricks with my mind. I seemed to have two minds, one that reasoned about things and one that related them according to a sense of wholeness. By concentrating thought upon a power outside myself, I partook of that power, albeit fleetingly. Thus it happened on the occasion of my first—also my last—competitive race. Opening my mind, while physically present in one of the great benighted cities of the world, I found myself by the strand of a sun-bright sea, by the uncoiling crash and sough of surf where seagulls screeched out of the immeasurable silence. I would run upon that coast. My legs would sing of the sun and the wind and the sea.

The 800 meters was announced. Soon the starter's pistol cracked. My legs sprang forward of their own accord. The sound of scuffed cinder receded. I was free and the invisible sun fueled my body and the invisible ocean echoed my breathing.

At the three-quarter turn of the first lap I glanced back and laughed in my heart, the nearest runner about 100 meters behind me... A sound of applause rippled like waves. A face leaned from the track: Simonini. "Fifty-six," he said. "Mind the headwind, save the kick!" Words, meaningless words! I was free in the song of the sun, the wind and the sea! What did the creature say? Headwind. I could feel it now separating me from the rhythm of my will. Not the wind my undoing, I thought and picked up the beat of my legs and lengthened their stride until I rounded the one-quarter turn of the second lap and had the wind behind me...

With half a lap to go, thighs were on fire, legs loosening. The seascape of my dream had dissolved into the ever-closer pounding of feet behind me. A sensation akin to terror grazed my heart. Heavy breathing ever closer, then one runner, then another could be felt beside me, overtaking, and my legs churned on beneath me, their song all but spent, and my head spun as Terézia screamed in snowy blur, incandescent flares bursting like disks in my eyes, and suddenly—suddenly on a far-off surf returning—the statue of Soul lifted her gaze to me from the seaweed of her hair. The pain was gone.

I kicked. My legs sang once more. Like a bird in flight on the wind soaring to the sun, I lifted from my heart. First one runner overtaken, then another. The last wave over, I breasted the tape, slowed for 100 meters, wobbled to a wire fence, and vomited until tears streamed from my eyes. I didn't need another race, ever.

In the grey distance, some women pushed prams, a couple embraced on the grass.

Bluejean didn't look particularly pregnant, but she did look defenseless and frail in spite of her me-against-the-world appearance. She wore jeans and a cotton singlet that exposed the cleavage of her full, unsupported breasts. A leather pouch for pot was slung from a glass-bead necklace. She had no makeup, no polished fingernails. A poppy was clasped in her loosely flowing, clean dark hair. Her appearance could not have been better calculated to put people off. In fact, while scores of fashion-plate ladies and Moss Bros. gents had been wandering about the garden and the house in various stages of intoxication, she was simply left alone.

I found her sitting under the Chinese lanterns that festooned the gazebo in the garden.

"Come with me, Bluejean," I was saying in a voice so peremptory that it left no room for scruples. "Let's get the hell out of here and never look back."

Her eyes studied me from out of their own injury. "Now?" Her voice did not sound particularly reluctant.

"Now," I said.

"Man," she said, biting her lower lip. "You're tough as cougar meat and twice as nasty."

"I know what I'm doing," I said.

She tossed back her hair, smiled. "Okay," she said, rose stiffly with my hands in hers. "Let's blow this fly-trap... Where are we going?"

"We'll decide on the way. If we get married, that's what I want. If we go to America, that's what I want too."

"Sounds good," she said.

She entwined her fingers in mine. When we reached the street where I had parked the new Jaguar, I had already made up my mind about that, too. After removing my suitcase from the passenger seat, I left the keys in the ignition and slammed the door. "Slave trade," I said. "We'll take the tube."

I looked a last time at the house which had once been home. At Grace's second-story bedroom windows, still curtained off. At my third-story bedroom window, still lighted. The ground floor, the veranda, the garden: all glowed with artificial light, and angry rooks circled the great oaks silhouetted against the pandemoniac twilight of London in July.

That was later.

Woolpack and Bluejean had arrived at seven ahead of the others and were being served champagne by a caterer when I returned after an hour's drive in the Jag. They looked at me in my hired Moss Bros. outfit—white dinner jacket, black bow tie—and I assessed the situation at a glance. They were going to conclude the deal for the sale of Bluejean's baby.

Woolpack approached and shook my hand as if we were old friends. "Congratulations, old man," he said and snapped his fingers. "Waiter. Bring some champers for the graduate... Bluejean. Paul Woolpack. Grace's Hungarian protégé, you remember? Ah. Here's the bubbly."

"Hi," said Bluejean.

"Hi," I said. I saluted her with my champagne glass. "*Egészégedre.*"

"That's cool," she smiled. "Been a long time. You look great."

"So do you." We stood for some moments appraising one another. "You're having a baby, I hear."

"'Deed I am, man."

Woolpack cleared his throat and fingered the lapel of my dinner jacket. "I see your tailor has a sense of humor," he said with a little twitch of greying mustache. Bluejean cut in, "He's just kidding. Don't mind him, Paul. And is it Paul Woolpack? I thought it was Paul Szabo. Did you really change your name?"

"No," I said. "Call me Paul."

"She didn't adopt you?"

"No."

"Interesting," she said after another appraising look. She went on in a singsong, "Today is the day they give babies away—"

"Shut up," said Woolpack.

"—with half a pound of tea... Did you say something, ducky?"

"I said to shut up."

"Well," said Bluejean, "you can go fuck yourself. Excuse us... Good ole Jack. He's really hoping the ballbuster will give me more bread than Ex-Lax has pills. Know what,

Paul?"

"I told you to pack in the drugs," Woolpack said in a menacing tone.

"Know what, Paul?" Bluejean tilted her champagne glass, took a sip, then emptied the glass. "They think they've got it all figured out. Did the ballbuster tell you? Bluejean's baby is worth a hundred thou, cash on the barrel. Wanna know something else? They don't know shit from Shinola. No way they're gonna buy my baby. No-o-o-o way."

Woolpack consulted his watch, then rocked on his heels, tossed back his champagne, and sauntered off with the air of a man inspecting pictures in a gallery.

Bluejean's eyes followed him until he was gone. When she spoke again, she grimaced. "I love the guy. How stupid is that?"

"It's not stupid," I essayed, "but you can live your own life."

"Say that again."

I told her that I had only lately come to realize that the Woolpacks were playing a game. "They're cold, Bluejean."

"Funny you said that. He told me when I first met him that he was incapable of love, but I don't believe he's cold. Grace is something else... Do you mind my asking why you're hanging around with Grace? Is she fucking you over?"

There was a silence as the two of us came to an unspoken understanding.

"No way," I grinned.

She grinned too. There was another silence. I was feeling a familiar flame at the back of my neck.

"So you're leaving him?"

"Left," she said.

"Why come here?"

"No bread. Jack says he'll get some from Grace. I'm

going home to America."

"I've got some bread," I said. Her slang felt seductive in my throat. "I'll get it. It's yours. I won't take no for an answer. Go to America. Meet a decent fellow... You raise that baby. Look." I was pumping my hands. "I *know* what it's like, the hunger for parental affection. Do it for me. Don't go away. I'll be back."

"Okay," she said in a voice above a tearful whisper.

As I bounded upstairs, Grace intercepted me. "You're back, Paul. Enjoy your drive?"

"Smashing."

"How do I look, darling?"

She was dressed in sheer blue silk cut low over her bosom and tucked at the waist to accentuate the flare of hips. Hair permed, diamonds dangling, expensive perfume thickening the air.

"Smashing," I said and turned to go. "Woolpack's downstairs waiting for the dole."

"Aren't you forgetting something?"

"Huh?"

"Kiss me?"

"Oh. Sure." I pecked her on the cheek. She coiled her arms around my neck, pulled her lips to mine, drew dreamily back, eyes closed. Made a little sound in her throat. "That's better," she said. "Now come and meet Princess Del Drago. She's expecting you."

I started to protest, but Grace took command of my arm and led me down the long hallway to her bedroom.

"In there?"

"But of course, darling... She has a migraine. We've been having champagne. And talking. Mostly about you."

"Why me?"

"Secrets." Grace opened the door, closed it, and we

entered her large bedroom. The curtains had been drawn. Light came from a pair of candles on a teacart. On the teacart were buckets of ice from which poked the green snouts of champagne bottles. Behind the table, seated on a chaise longue with bare legs crossed, was a dark-haired woman in a black dressing gown.

"Come," she said in a purring voice. "Let me see this *bello bruto*... Ah." She flicked a glance toward Grace, then extended a delicate white arm toward me. "I am so jealous, my dear Grace. I comprehend this infatuation of yours. He is so charming. Come, Paolo. Come seat beside me." She again glanced at Grace, this time languidly, and nodded. "Leave us alone, my dear... Attila the Hun conquested Roman Empire."

An hour must have passed while I sat gulping champagne and listening to the musical drone of Princess Del Drago's voice. Candles made pillowy motions on giddy walls. Suddenly Princess Del Drago leaned over, undid my bow tie, and helped me off with my dinner jacket. She parted her dressing gown and slowly—slowly—drew my face down to her naked breasts. We began to breathe heavily.

"I want," she said from a nearby, muffled distance.

"Yes?" I said.

"To make *amore*," she said.

I pondered this idea and said, "Thank you."

I groaned when the black knickers were off. Black knickers right there! "God," I said.

She French-kissed me and stuck her tongue in my ear. "Take off your clothes," she whispered. "Blow out the candles. Wait in the bed. No lights."

She tiptoed from the room, closed the door after her. I lay on Grace's bed in pitch dark. I sensed a straining to perpetuate tumescence.

The door was opened and quickly closed.

Clothing rustled.

Silence.

A wee sound of feet on carpet.

A wee sound of boxsprings.

A cold hand on my leg.

Perfume coming closer and closer.

Then a body, surprisingly heavy, hunkered over mine, was lowered.

I eased into a supernal world.

She pushed, I pushed.

And the perfume came down.

Her mouth, a suction pump, found mine.

I swooned then the swoon of all lovers. Then I heard Grace's voice gasping, "I almost had a naughty one."

Grace!

I was still seething in a cauldron of rage twenty minutes later up in my room as I piled belongings into a suitcase. I had a thousand pounds in my pocket and one controlling idea in my head: "Another fixer like Malakov and you knew it. Idiot! Get cracking!" I was talking out loud to myself.

Was overheard.

"Paul. Darling. *Si peu de chose mais tant de plaisir...* Poppet. Please."

I didn't look at Grace. Violence was in my throat, and my head was aflame with wine and loathing. "How could you do a thing like that?" I blurted. "Does the princess turn your tricks for free, or have you fixed her a wage packet? When you look in the mirror, do you see a human being?"

"No gentleman speaks to a lady like that."

"Good point," I shot back.

Her voice was cold. "I wouldn't, if I were you, push my luck too far."

"Who's going to stop me?"

"Paul," she resumed in a coaxing voice. "This is absurd... I know what the trouble is. You've been jealous of John's baby ever since I stupidly referred to it as the Woolpack heir. But that's water under the bridge now. The girl refuses to give the baby up. *You* are the Woolpack heir! Don't you see?" Grace came and coiled her arms around me from behind. Her diamond bracelets clinked. "You're going up to university as a rich man. You'll be replacing John. Certainly you don't suppose we're under the slightest obligation to maintain him? It's all *yours*, darling... Now. I'm sorry... I shouldn't have listened to the princess. That... *that* business was all her idea. I was a fool. You know how I am when it comes to..." She chuckled against my shoulder. "Why, darling, I didn't know where babies came from when I was your age. Forgive me?"

"Good-bye," I said.

"What?"

"I said good-bye."

"Oh," she groaned with a stifled sob, releasing me and standing by the window. She was dressed as she had been earlier. Tears streaked her mascara. "I feel so depressed. I'll commit suicide. You can't leave me all *alone*... Tell me where you are going. Where I can get in touch with you if worse comes to worse. I *know* when I feel suicidal. I can't *bear* it alone."

I told Grace that I was thinking of asking Mr. Simonini for shelter until I learned whether any of the universities were accepting me. This, while I completed packing and closed the suitcase.

She drew herself up, folded her arms, and smiled from the corners of her mouth. "You've *forgotten* something, Paul," she said, drawing the words out in a singsong.

I said I would return the Jaguar as soon as I was settled.

"Not that," she said. "Keep the car. You're welcome to

come back any time. You will, after you return to your senses."

I shrugged. "So. I forgot something. I don't plan my life in advance. But I intend to, starting now."

"Bravo," she said. "But you've forgotten that I'm Hurtfield's largest benefactor. All I have to do is to inform Mr. Simonini of your disgraceful conduct tonight, and, Bob's your uncle, no university or college in the United Kingdom is going to accept you. You'll be permanently rusticated before you start. Even start your car." Grace's folded arms tightened over her bosom.

"Mr. Simonini wouldn't falsify documents," I protested without confidence.

"It's not a matter of falsification, Paul, darling. It's a matter of moral fibre. Your refusal, after your splendid victory in the 800 meters, to train yourself for a champion. You blotted your copybook there."

I must have gone red in the face. "Simonini told you that? It's a lie. I didn't refuse to train. I discovered that I could win. I don't need competition. The hell with it—" I paused to catch my breath. "You and Simonini know each other, do you?"

"Intimately."

"What is that supposed to mean?"

The corners of Grace's mouth dropped. "I spoke with him this morning over the telephone. I told him of your attempted rape in the woods. The dear man was apoplectic with outrage. But—"

"But what?"

"But he agreed to take no action with respect to the school's recommendations until you've had your last chance. There you are. I'm all yours!"

I stood for a moment stunned. *I'm all yours*. The words tumbled and swirled in a vortex of the mind until they were translated into a half-forgotten language and Terézia was writing them, sacrificing herself to Malakov that I might be saved. Now the words came again, and I felt as though I'd disappear unless I swerved. I grabbed the suitcase, ran downstairs, and placed it in the car. My head was sobered by a rush of revolt. I was going to be father to Bluejean's baby, if Bluejean would agree.

That night Bluejean and I registered as man and wife at a London hotel. The actual ceremony was performed a week later. We traveled by bus around England—a country mine no more—during the months while papers were being processed for my induction into the American army. When we made love, Bluejean's baby seemed to be mine.

PART FOUR

1

FLYING home after a year of combat duty I had dreamed we would all drive into the High Rockies for a camp-out until the silences up there opened our voices to talking, and talking became healing.

Then Bluejean called.

"Hi, Paul! Guess what?..."

"They need me here," she had said at last in a weird tone. "I'm helping the Church to find missing people. They're sending me to the Andes to one of the copper-mining districts. It's important. It's the most important thing that ever happened to me."

"Bluejean, I love you. . ."

"Paul, you don't love me. You're just a lonely little boy with a big insecurity problem. You're always afraid the world will disappear. But it won't. So don't worry about it, *okay*?"

Karl Marx jumped on a chair, then on my shoulder, and purred.

A few minutes later I decided to go to the high country in the morning. Maybe my buddy, Virgil Warbonnet, would go along. Maybe he *should* go along, I was thinking. I'm no cowboy in spite of dude attire, not someone like Woolpack, solid and separate and alone who can ride off into the sunset and feel free of connections. I began to stroke Karl Marx gently, then urgently, holding his furry throb against my ear to hear the heart.

2

VIRGIL Warbonnet and I were in the same outfit in Vietnam. He was a Navajo, the first Indian I'd ever met. Some men would make racist jokes to his face. Virgil was six-four, two-twenty, and could have sharpened all their heads and driven them in the ground. Instead, he would just tilt back and roar with high-pitched laughter—the most wonderful laughter anybody had ever heard. Other men liked to slap him on the back as if to establish the amplitude of their generosity. He was appreciated for bonhomie, seldom speaking a word, always laughing.

As sergeants, we shared quarters apart from other men. The first thing I noticed about him was his silence. Not shyness or secretiveness or dejection or the lack of amiable presence, his was the silence of simply being himself without the need or pressure to talk about himself or to solicit information about another. He seemed to be content to let hours pass without utterance. If I spoke to him, well and good, he would cease whatever he was doing—meditating, writing a letter, but usually reading—and reply cordially and without any sign of annoyance at having his time wasted.

When I first encountered Virgil's silence, I attributed it to arrogance or to a personal dislike for me. I pretended to ignore him by silently pursuing my own interests, also writing letters and reading, often dropping off to sleep for lack of diversion from the stupefying boredom of military life. But then, by and by, I don't know how it happened, our mutual silence started to become pleasurable, as if we were doing exactly what two human beings adrift on the planet, itself adrift amidst infinitudes, *ought* to be doing: listening for articulate infinity. Cavorting on the moon, one astronaut said, "What a neat place!" I'd rather have watched Virgil dancing wordlessly over rocks, to tom-toms—the language of space.

Out of silence, then, grew acceptance, and from acceptance, friendship.

The other thing I noticed about Virgil was his scholarship. Gradually we had come to reveal to one another little glimpses of our lives. I learned something of his family and education. Both his parents spoke a little English, his father Hosteen having served as a codetalker in the Marines in the Second World War (notably at Iwo Jima where the battle had been won because the Japanese could not decipher the radio messages being relayed in the Navajo tongue) and his mother, Sun's Forehead, having gone to the mission school in Ganado. Virgil himself had been to the white man's "away" school in Riverside, California; thereafter he had matriculated on a football scholarship for a year at Arizona and then transferred on full academic scholarship to Yale. However, midway through his sophomore year at Yale, he dropped out. He wandered for a period, returned to the Navajo Reservation where he married a lady named Txó, and then joined the army at the lowest possible rank, apparently having no ambition to make a success of his career in spite of opportunities to attend Officer Candidate School. His was, to appearances, a promise blighted. In reality, the scholar's curiosity began to bloom as soon as it was left unconfined by sterile curricula. Subject matter dismissed as esoteric or unscientific proved for Virgil an ever-widening field of inquiry. For instance, stashed in his dufflebag were, to name a few of his books, *The Tibetan Book of the Dead*, Hoyle's *Astronomy*, and P. D. Ouspensky's *In Search of the Miraculous*. From Virgil, as we conversed from our bunks, I first grasped the Eastern mysticism and the scientific basis for something known to Indians for thousands of years, namely, that humans are made of the same living stuff as everything else in the universe. Made of the same stuff as animals and trees, as water and earth. We are all composed of energy, though at varying levels of intensity, all composed of the one living universe—and with this we had to live in harmony if we were to live at all.

My Cadillac was in the garage and somehow operational in spite of bald tires, a crumpled fender, and an odometer to which Bluejean had added fifteen thousand miles in the year. Although the gas gauge read empty, I switched on the ignition, and the engine roared on a surge of energy composed of the one living universe; simultaneously, however, I felt like a pilot ejected from his cockpit. Bluejean had left the radio on full blast. When I turned off the radio, my hand was shaking with a kind of exquisite palsy and tears sprang into my eyes. In the back seat Karl Marx buried his head in mounds of mildewed towels and sour-smelling sheets that I was taking to the laundry. Him, I was taking to the Humane Society on South Eighth Street. "Sorry, buddy," I told him as we eased down the driveway, "we may be made of the same stuff, but I've got *more* of it. We've got to find you a good home before you start looking like Colonel Sanders." Then I braked, hard.

Across the street beside a red pickup stood Virgil. Amazing. I hadn't telephoned him that I was home, if home was the word. He had rotated back to Fort Carson the previous week, and, the way I figured it, he needed to be with his wife, Txó. Yet there was Virgil looking off in the distance nonchalantly as if he had just happened to stop by my place with no special purpose in mind.

I turned off the engine and waited. After a while, he took long steps toward me, a lord-of-the-earth tread. Out of uniform, he was one impressive-looking dude: skin-tight Levis with an extra-short crotch so that his carved belt circled his hips rather than his waist, a purple nylon shirt open at the neck, a string of turquoise nugget beads against the shirt and ending in a heavy *nacall* just above the silver-and-turquoise buckle on his belt, and turquoise-set silver bracelets on his powerful wrists. He had crewcut hair at this time, not the shoulder-length black hair tied with red headband he wears nowadays. Without greeting, Virgil spoke: "A man's wife asked if his friend would like supper of stewed mutton, dried corn, and squash. The man said, 'Yes, he would like it. He's been going to the mountains.'"

So he knew I was going to the mountains, too. After a pause during which I restrained the impulse to moan about the Queen of the Counterculture, I used the only Navajo phrase I had learned, "*Ake'he.*" Thank you. "What time?"

Virgil said nothing but pointed west toward Pike's Peak and went. Judging by the sun's declination, I had about two hours before sunset, three before supper, enough time to do the chores. For sure, Virgil and Txó were people who thought about things, even about my neurotic obsession with having time to kill on activities of little consequence such as delivering a tailless tomcat to the Humane Society, tanking up a car color-coordinated with Bluejean's fire-brewed eyes, and socking detergent to her Monkey Ward sheets. On the other hand... "Hey, Virgil!" I yelled frantically at his disappearing pickup.

He had neglected to tell me where he lived.

I found out the address by calling post headquarters. The house was a small imitation adobe with an acre of fenced-in backyard and corral in a canyon close to Manitou Springs, a small town west of Colorado Springs at the base of the Peak and an area of redstone formations long regarded as sacred by Utes and other Indian tribes. In the corral, a horse, out in the yard a tethered goat and a mess of clucking chickens and a couple of lidless garbage cans, long regarded as sacred by the grey, waddling old dog who guarded the place against evil spirits not by barking at them but by fooling them into thinking nobody was home: that's what I found as I approached it. Stepping out of the car in the cool thin air of November night, I relaxed. It felt good to be dressed again in starched Levis with the thick leather belt and Coors buckle, the doubleknit ski-sweater and shitkickers. My five-ten, one-eighty—hard lean pounds—were not moving with the weight of remembrance.

Bluejean, I half persuaded myself, was having but a last fling with Woolpack. For years Bluejean and Woolpack acted within the same frame of reference, both seeking power, he from Grace; Bluejean, in her powerlessness, from him. Woolpack, fifty by this time, had been married for about twenty-five years to Grace, mid-forties herself, and, even though they had no children, I believed they were unlikely ever to divorce. Whatever Bluejean had been scheming when she delivered Teapot to Woolpack, and however dangerous the Pacifican revolution, I would probably be seeing Bluejean and Teapot safely at home for Teapot's eleventh birthday on Christmas Day of that year of '73.

I looked now with wistful eyes upon the lovely home that Virgil's wife had kept for him, the white picket fence enclosing a garden that in summertime would have blazed with orange marigolds and masses of petunias, juniper bushes and sighing cottonwoods blanched by porchlight.

Virgil stood on the porch holding a bottle in his hand, grinning and chuckling and sneaking elaborately furtive glances over his shoulder. He tilted the bottle, gulped, and wiped his mouth with the back of his hand. "Ways of the white man have often been bitter on my tongue," he intoned with a guttural and magisterial solemnity, then burst out laughing. Handing me the bottle, he tossed his Samson's head toward the house. "No drinking on the res'." He was laughing again as I gulped from the bottle. My eyes seemed to pop from their sockets and snap back watering on invisible rubber bands. Scotch, good scotch. I took another swig. This time my head cleared, and fragrances came to my nostrils, the roasted, nut-like odor of piñon smoke, the tang of powdered dung from the corral, and the fat smell of simmering mutton. "How did you know I was fixing to go to the mountains? Would your wife mind if we went together? There's a hot spring in the Sangre de Cristo. . ."

Virgil placed a hand on my shoulder. "I know, my friend. You have spoken of this place often. We shall go together. As for your epistemological inquiry"—Virgil didn't learn words from *Reader's Digest*—"remember that I have acquired the big medicine of deductive logic at a number of institutions on the white reservation. When there was mail call, when did Sergeant Szabo receive letters from home? And why, when I drove by your house each day for a week, did I find no sign of habitation? I do not wish to insult you by pointing out the obvious. Tomorrow we shall speak of your troubles. Tonight, I shall speak of mine. It is not right for one man to have a store of troubles and another man to pretend to abundance. One more thing," Virgil said, breathing deeply the pine-scented air, and made a sweeping arc with his hand. "Do not ask me to explain the way of the spiritual powers. Myself, I have never questioned them. So that's *finish*," he grinned, resuming a style of Navajo English which may have made his wife more comfortable with him. "Think I going in."

"What about the scotch?"

"Maybe put in car. For tomorrow. More where that comes from."

A few minutes later we were seated cross-legged on rugs of rich colors before a blazing piñon fire. It was a small, sparsely furnished room with fire-shadows playing on plaster walls decorated here and there with baskets, rattles, and prayer fans. Against one wall was tacked a survey map. From a kitchen floated the most wonderful aromas of mutton and corn to blend with the piñon smoke. Txó had slipped in quietly from the kitchen while my attention had been distracted by the Navajo rugs. Their aniline dyes of reds, yellows, oranges, and black, all contrived into zigzags and squares and star-points and all somehow melding earth and sun at our feet, had withstood untold decades of constant treading. I heard a little giggle, and there stood a plump young matron with inverted pear-shape face and a heavy mane of black hair in pigtails. She was wearing a blue percale skirt and purple blanket shawl. Aware of my gaze, she ducked her head and grinned at moccasin feet.

Virgil rose and put his arm around her. She snuggled into the hollow beneath his arm. His head tilted protectively toward her. She grinned at him, again with a little giggle, and slipped back into the kitchen. Quick steps made the blue skirt shimmer in firelight. "Come," Virgil said softly to me, "let me show you this map before supper. After supper, I will tell you the story of a long walk... Txó, she must taking care those corn and squash. *Now*."

He pointed to the map. "Here is Arizona bordered by New Mexico, Colorado and Utah. Navajoland, *here*, is known by those sacred mountains, their English names being Mount Taylor to the east, Mount Hesperus and Navajo Mountain to the north, and San Francisco Peaks to the west near that city of Flagstaff. Over here, Grand Canyon. And here, surrounded by Navajos, are Hopis — the ancient ones. Hopis are those cliff dwellers up here in Mesa Verde, Colorado. They built the oldest continuously lived-in cities of the American continent *here* on the mesas. Those Hopis have big doings to bring rain and peace to their land. They do not raise sheep much, like Navajos out here in the sage and greasewood. Navajos do not come into the area until 600 years ago, many centuries after the Hopis. Navajos respect Hopis very much. We learn very much from Hopis. But we used to steal their horses and women. We didn't steal their land, but the Navajos are many, many thousands. Gradually we came upon Hopi lands and settled upon them so long that those are our lands too. Now."

His finger made circles on the map.

"Look here, my friend. Here, centered by Big Mountain, is an area of 1.8 million acres that Wash-*een*-ton has ruled to be owned jointly by the two tribes. This area is known as the Joint Use Area. That is fine. Maybe Hopis don't need their half of the range. The people continue to follow the old way of life. Except—*now*!" Virgil made a vehement period with his finger on the map at the area called Big Mountain in the JUA range. His adam's apple worked in his throat. But he resumed quietly, "Now, while you and I are serving Wash-*een*-ton in Vietnam, the district court in Arizona has ordered drastic Navajo livestock reduction to allow for Hopi use of half the JUA range. They have also barred Navajo construction in the JUA. You see, the government has learned to be subtle and patient."

I didn't see the point and said so.

"This area has billions of tons of coal and possibly some of the largest uranium deposits in the world. Right under the feet of our women. Now you will see where all this is leading. Already Hosteen and Sun's Forehead have been forced from their hogan on Black Mesa. The government talks of relocation, but to my people that is death. Moved from the land, the people will go crazy. Then the land will be destroyed by energy companies, forever."

I half smiled. "Liquor is talking," I said. "Where is your deductive logic now? I had a heavy dose of logic, myself, when I was growing up in Budapest, as vaccination against ideological nonsense. You are hinting at a dishonor that returns our country to genocidal policy."

"Precisely!" Virgil exclaimed with a vigorous nodding of head. "The forced removal of native peoples is an act of genocide. True, we are only witnessing the renewed preparations for genocide against Indians. In the late and supposedly enlightened twentieth century," Virgil added. "The final solution to a race killing that began with the arrival of Columbus in the fifteenth century."

"Come *on*," I protested, the flame of disrepute caressing my neck. "What is the connection between an order to butcher your livestock and this paranoia about the survival of your people? We're different now. Times have changed."

Virgil slowly shook his head. "We cannot hold back the wind. We may try, but it is always there, merely changed in velocity but not in direction. That is why I said the government has learned to be subtle and patient... It is rumored that the government plans to build houses for the people in places like Flagstaff and Gallup, on condition that the people cannot return to the reservation. Doubtless, some of the people will go, even though, until now, the Navajo have never collaborated with the enemy. So, there you are... A house with hot and cold water and flushing toilets is a ruse. Many of my people refuse to learn English. They have few skills to sell. They won't be able to pay mortgages. The houses will be repossessed. And the people won't be allowed to return to the res'. They will starve, freeze, drink themselves to death. But the worst is this." Virgil elevated his index finger, then slowly stabbed the air. "The land is sacred to the Indian. Earth is our religion. Remove us from our land, destroy our relationship with it, and we will die inside."

I pondered and said, "This... this removal, then... if it is about to take place, which I don't believe... is promoted not only for the sake of greed but also for religion. It is war to eliminate the one idea necessary for survival, the interrelationship of man and nature."

"It was never anything else." Virgil burst out with that wonderful laughter of his. "Come, come. We are spoiling our appetites. And we have a long walk ahead of us... But first, let me show you a surprise," he beckoned and led the way toward a small bedroom. "Maybe it is my son whom I met for the first time last week."

As my eyes grew accustomed to the room's dim light from the moon at a glass-paned window, I made out the figure of Txó seated on a bed and suckling a round-cheeked infant at her breast. She was saying, "Chi... chi... chi" in a soft singsong.

"She must taking care that baby," Virgil said. Txó ducked her head, giggled, and lifted it on a beatific smile.

"That was a long walk," Virgil concluded his story several hours later as the three of us, our bellies replete with good food, sat warming ourselves on the rugs before the fire. Txó's skirt shimmered, slight as a breath of air.

In the late winter of 1864, Kit Carson marched more than eight thousand Navajo men, women, and children hundreds of miles from the canyons where they had been hiding to Fort Sumner in eastern New Mexico Territory. Here the *Dineh*, The People, as Virgil called them, began to die from exposure, disease, and starvation. What provisions the government supplied were almost inedible. The People had no taste for flour, bacon, and coffee. The land was useless for crops, being salt desert; after the first crop failures, The People refused to plant seed. Floods, drought, hailstorms, plagues of insects. The People wept for return to their homeland—"where the sun is always shining." Finally after four years the government relented and granted to the Navajo a reservation on their homeland, each returning family to receive three sheep and goats. The surviving People left at once, westward to their mesas and canyons "where rays of many setting suns spread amber light over the bluest sky in the world."

The baby cried.

"Maybe get Little Horse," Virgil said to Txó. "My friend him liked it see them fingers." While she was out of the room, Virgil continued, "During pregnancy Txó lived with her family in a reservation area where low-level radiation from mining and power stations is already greater than that caused by the atomic bombs in Japan."

Txó returned with Little Horse and showed me one of his hands.

"Born without a thumb," said Virgil. "The People have always known that life began with the sun. Now the power of the sun has been usurped, it is no longer a question of the survival of a small tribe of Indians in a remote part of the American Southwest. It is a question of the survival of the world."

Next morning Virgil and I drove west alongside the winding flash of the Arkansas River to Salida, then south over Poncha Pass to the high wind-rippled grasslands of San Luis Valley, finally east and up to the hot spring at 9,000 feet elevation in the Sangre de Cristo. We pitched camp in a cluster of aspens near a half-frozen waterfall. We put on swim trunks and eased into steam-frantic springs, let the bright sun and chill air breathe on our faces the diastole and systole of the earthly pulse. I had told him about Teapot and Bluejean and the Woolpacks while we were driving, yet here where I was surrounded by the zigzag pyramids of the great Colorado plateau, a vision of Teapot's face rose like a dream on turquoise sky.

"I can't give her up, Virgil."

He seemed not to hear me. He clambered from the springs, toweled himself off, and walked to our tent on spring-step like a deer's. I was alone, remembering Teapot. How she had loved the spring one summer's afternoon when we came for a picnic and swim! At that time of year the place was crawling with tourists and nature-freaks, with nudists showing off their lack of puritanism: inhibited one moment, then born again. A college girl from Boulder, stoned, waddled from the springs, covered pubic hair with jeans, cupped peachy breasts, and proclaimed, "I did it!," then seated herself on a motorcycle behind a hipster and roared off to a life of predictable respectability. Masaccio's Eve, anodyne life style. About that time a bullsnake came, black and bulging, slithering nonchalantly out of the aspens between styrofoam chests full of Pepsi and watermelon and into the water, like a magic dragon guarding gold. Such panic and shrieking! Naked men, women, and children were scrambling, some of them sprawling as if suddenly clotheslined. But not Teapot. Teapot, all peaches-and-cream complexion, her blue eyes wide, had befriended the monster. It coiled and uncoiled around her shoulders like a serpent in a primal myth. She laughed with pure pleasure and ran her tiny fingers over the seven-foot slimeball.

"Can I have him, Daddy?"

"Will Karl Marx like him?" I replied evasively.

"His name's Fred," she said.

"Oh," I said.

Teapot pondered. "Fred, you go and play now. Don't be naughty or Mommy will whip your ass."

Fred went, bless him. Teapot swam to my arms. She said she would like a peanut butter sandwich and RC Cola.

Wrapped in fur-trimmed parka like an eskimo, Virgil brought me a paper cup full of scotch on the rocks—stalactitic cones. "From the waterfall," he chuckled. He also had a cup and we drank.

"No way," I declared to hear my own bravado. "Something tells me that I ought to fly down to Pacífica. That sounds right to you, doesn't it?"

Virgil said nothing.

"I watched that kid being born. Virgil, I really wanted that kid. I wanted to be her father so I married. That's why I signed on with this man's army at the embassy in London. So I could support a family. When I was going through basic at Fort Benning, the word came, and I got a Christmas Day pass to make it to the hospital in Atlanta. Made it, too. I swore that the baby was going to be loved and happy!" I struck that womb of a hot spring violently, thinking, *Woolpack came next day when I had gone, claiming his heir, not for love.*

"Time for number two," Virgil said quietly, pouring scotch in my cup.

Hours later, we sizzled steaks over a piñon and mesquite fire, ate them, and were sipping black coffee, the moon pulsing radiantly through pillows of steam from the spring. Virgil settled his bifocals and said matter-of-factly, "I do not speak of myself often. I shall do so now."

He paused to place yellow wood on the fire. "When I

was sent away to the white man's school, I left the reservation eagerly. Indians are not where it's at, man: that's what I believed. I wanted to become an individual, a white man. I considered going into the ministry. But I found myself sorely troubled by your namesake."

"*My* namesake?"

Virgil nodded to my comically surprised look. "Saint Paul, like you, places highest value on the act of atonement. Unlike you, if I guess correctly, he regards the sacrifice of Jesus as a ransom to Satan, one that redeems mankind from sin. Jesus, I believed, was teaching something more psychological than that—that another person's life is your own life, in the sense that God is not separated from man but exists in all persons."

He paused to sip his coffee, adjust the glasses on his nose. Then went on. "When you perceive the mystery that another person's life is your own life in fact, you arrive at a point where time and eternity intersect. You're not a separate individual anymore, someone with only that kind of standing, for you look through that level of existence and discover your relationship to other levels, to humanity, to nature, to the universe. You discover that life is whole and that the great teachers like Jesus and Buddha saw us joined together in the presence of compassion.

"In Matthew it says, 'For he makes his sun to rise on the evil and the good, and sends rain on the just and unjust.' So atonement, it seemed to me, is affirmation of the mystery that is in us, here on earth... Waken to the mystery, and you are prepared to put your life in peril for the sake of another person.

"You may also discover that you've been an Indian all along!" Virgil threw back his head and laughed his great laugh.

I had lots to think about when Virgil and I zipped into our sleeping bags that night by the spring. Bluejean and Teapot in Pacífica. The disappearance of Virgil's people from the land. Perhaps the disappearance of all life. And Virgil's words, evidently intended to guide a friend toward inner balance. I wanted to think clearly, but I sank into sleep as if poleaxed.

In predawn stillness I woke feeling cold, disconsolate, and lost. Virgil was gone from the tent. I reached for my rifle. I didn't have my rifle... I was close to flipping out. That close. Peering through tent-flap, though, sobering on frigid air, I saw freshly fallen snow shining with the silence of a full moon, spring waters steaming, and heard, as if for the first time, the waterfall's hushed rampage. Then I heard, or thought I heard, something else. Not a noise, but a perturbation at the soft spot or "open door" of my head, the *kópavi* or Thousand-Petalled Lotus about which Virgil had taught me in Vietnam.

Across and upslope from the spring, a shadow ghosted: a doe. She had the rounded, dream-laden eyes of Bluejean McQueen.

It seems I vanished into nonrational consciousness. It was as if I had been shot through with spears of the sun and inwardly whirled on interstellar winds to the drumming of waterfalls. Into a world of light I was falling, head aflame as if bolts of lightning had entered its door to the thunderous drumming of the falls, and the falls within became incandescently rivers of molten blood. Then I heard a sound so familiar, so instantaneous, so deafening that I wondered why I had not recognized it in one-millionth of a second—the crack of a pistol! In a time-lapse that was no time I felt the bullet moving nonchalantly amongst innumerable nerve fibers, like a spaceship's delirious probing of the Milky Way. Then I saw *it*. It was the body of a woman in a cave. I recognized Bluejean. She lay dead as an arc of blood gushed from a hole in her head...

Then I was cold, breathing snow. When I recovered rational consciousness, nothing had changed. Weightless as a dream, the doe was ghosting upslope beyond pillows of moonblanched steam. The waterfall murmured. Smoke from the black snowcovered fire inscribed S-shapes through aspens.

Not a shot had been fired, but snow was crunched, the deer, spooked, leapt into darkness, and there before me stood Virgil, his arms laden with tree branches antlered in silhouette against the steam. I watched him while he knelt and rekindled the fire. How mysterious this man in writhing light and crackling sparks! And yet how equally mysterious had I, but a few moments before, become to myself! I had come to an inward place where he had gone before.

I still lay half-tranced in the abyss I had seen. I cleared my throat and called Virgil. He came and knelt by the tent and peered at me over the dim orbs of bifocals. I asked him if he'd heard a pistol shot. "No," he said, studying me now. I asked him if he had experienced any ill effects from what we had been drinking and eating. Again he replied in the negative.

I told him about my vision. "I heard and saw everything as if it were actually happening!"

He did not resettle his bifocals. I could tell that he believed in my vision more than I believed in it myself. Yet I believed in it, too.

"Am I going nuts?"

He glanced away. "Maybe have breakfast, break camp early," he said.

3

I DROPPED Virgil off in Manitou, went home, and booked a flight to Ciudad de Pacífica via Miami. The flight would be leaving in two days. On impulse I booked a return flight for me, Bluejean, and Teapot for Christmas Day. The travel agent also booked me a room at the Sheraton in Ciudad de Pacífica. She said that the military government welcomed American tourists; that Pacífica's people were beautiful and wines incomparable; that the revolution had been exaggerated in the media; and that the 300 percent rate of inflation down there favored the dollar. I called my bank manager and asked for $7000 in traveler's checks readied for pickup. Having built up some momentum, I asked the international operator to get me Earthco, Pacific City. She got it.

"Uthco. May I hep yawl?" came an American lady's thick southern accent.

"Yes, ma'am," I drawled, having learned in the Army that Americans like people who sound folksy. "I'm callin' from Amurica to speak tuh Mistuh Woolpack. I'm Paul Woolpack."

She turned me over to the mercy of Muzak. A golden oldie, something with cascading strings. I held the receiver away from my ear.

"Yawl go ahead now, hear."

"Thanks, honey... Hello? Is this Woolpack?"

"Paul, is it? Bloody long time. Kind of you to give us a tinkle. How have you been?" He pronounced it *bean*. He was Woolpack all right, though I'd scarcely ever known him. It was Grace who had adopted me, unofficially.

I told Woolpack I'd returned from Vietnam and heard that Christina was visiting with him. "I'd like to know if she's okay. That's all. And give her my love. And love to Grace, too."

There was a silence.

Woolpack broke it with a backed-away solicitous tone, as if he were talking to a lunatic. "I'm frightfully sorry, old man, but I haven't the slightest clue what you're getting at."

"Christina. My daughter. I mean, *your* daughter. Bluejean's baby."

"Oh," he said, "how *is* Bluejean? Haven't seen her in donkey's years. Is she still that wild American we used to know in London? You married her, if I'm not mistaken... Look, old man," Woolpack went on in lowered voice, "we can't chat over the blower. I'll be leaving here for New York on Christmas Day. We could arrange to get together then. A few more weeks and we'll all be laughing... Hello?"

"I'm still here," I said. "Bluejean called to say she was in Pacífica. She left Christina with you at your penthouse."

"When was that?" Woolpack asked sharply.

"Three days ago."

"Well," Woolpack said, "Grace and Bluejean have never been on speaking terms. It's most unlikely... She's not here, do you understand me? Good-bye! I shall give your regards to Grace."

Click.

I clicked off and anxiously dialed Virgil's number, one he had given me. "Virgil," I said as soon as he answered, "it's the fourth quarter, I'm losing by three points, I've got one time-out remaining, and I'm in my own end zone with 99 yards to go with just thirty seconds on the clock. What would Coach Landry do?"

"Quick draw, call time, throw the bomb, get out of bounds, and kick the field goal," he replied.

"Thanks," I said and hung up.

Then I called the international operator and asked for the Vicariate of Solidarity, Archbishopric of Pacífica. I had to spell it out: *Vicaría de la Solidaridad, Arzobispado de Pacífica*. "Try the yellow pages under God. Anything. I've got only one time-out left."

There was some unintentional electronic whale music, I mean those eerie yearnings from the deep as recorded by Bluejean during her Save the Whales period, then an awk awk awk sound, and somebody answered. It was my day on the hot line.

He called himself Reverendo Juanito. He agreed to speak English. Archbishop Mendoza, he said, was ill. Would I please state my name and business? The church was under surveillance from General Scarpio's government. The church did not wish to have anything to do with *la política*.

"*Claro*. Of course," I stalled, trying to think of some lies in case the line were tapped. I told reverendo Juanito that my name was Tom Landry of the Dallas Cowboys and that I was interested in poetry—*la poesía tradicional pacificana*. I was doing research on seventeenth-century book shipments from Spain to the colonies. Might I have permission to peruse the books in the archbishop's private library?

"We have no collection of seventeenth-century poetry

here. Only theology, señor Landry."

"*¡Estupendo, reverendo!* Already what you tell me is fundamental to my thesis. If no books of Spanish poetry were shipped to the New World three hundred years ago, it follows that the great Pacifican poetry of our time has its roots in popular culture."

"Roods? What is?"

"Root? *Momentito.*" I ran to the bookshelf, flipped through my Spanish-English dictionary, and returned to the line. "*Raíz,*" I said.

"*De acuerdo,*" he said. "It is good that the Dallas Cowboy coach is interested in our popular culture."

"Well," I began and stopped. It seemed as if he knew about American football. He was reading my signals. I had to throw the bomb. "*Otra cosa,* reverendo. I believe you are acquainted with a friend of mind. Bluejean McQueen. *Bajo el nombre de* Bluejean."

"Boo yeen?" There was a pause. "We do not know this person."

"La señora McQueen. She is fundamental to my thesis. She is in the Andes collecting poems for me. La señora McQueen has an artificial leg. *Enferma.*"

"One mo-*ment,*" said reverendo Juanito. He was gone a long time. I had thrown the bomb, stepped out of bounds on his thirty-yard line, and stopped the clock. Juanito returned to the line. He spoke slowly. "There is possibility we know this woman. You are *un amigo*?"

"Sí, sí. A friend. There is great urgency. She does not know Spanish. I am flying down to help her sing the songs."

"It is good to say nothing at this mo-*ment.*"

"Then it is not good?"

The snap from center was down, the imaginary kicker's leg swung toward the ball.

"The archbishop and I look forward to your visit. Where do you stay upon arrival?"

"Sheraton. The day after tomorrow I am leaving. I can visit the following day."

He told me to expect a message at the hotel. "Adiós, señor Landry."

"Muchas gracias. Adiós."

Click.

We were going into overtime, play to resume in three days.

It took eighteen hours to fly from Denver to Miami to Ciudad de Pacífica. The plane was crowded with Americans in a festive mood, though there seemed to be an unusual number of long-faced businessmen with attaché cases and of those morally clean, secret-agent types. Perhaps, I surmised, the American government *was* involved in the Pacifican revolution. I had been wise to make no telephone calls to the Department of State. Only Virgil knew where I was going and why. I had taken the precaution to inform him, should I end up among *los desaparecidos*, "the disappeared" of whom we were hearing so much on the TV broadcasts. Myself, I was wearing shitkickers and Levis, open-collar shirt, Palm Beach jacket, and sunglasses. My blond hair, growing out since Vietnam, was shampooed and blow-dried. Jet set.

We arrived at the airport at eight o'clock on a hot smoggy morning. The first thing I saw in the customs shed were battle-dressed, sunburned soldiers with American automatic weapons unslung, horizontal, waving slightly from the waist like tillers for rudderless boats. An area had been cordoned off. Behind it waited an anxious throng of families who seemed to be heading into exile. Elegant-looking women in silk blouses, black alpaca skirts, knee-length boots. Mustachioed men in three-piece suits, their luggage bound with rope. Schoolgirls in white shirts, navy-blue skirts, and white socks. A few young men sported Beatle haircuts and smoked cigarettes as if blowing kisses. I felt an instant tightening of the viscera. The sun visited the echoing marble floors through unwashed windows.

I have not been a stranger to exile, to the fall of cities, the ruination of the heart's country.

A young Latino whom I'd noticed on the airplane was led out of customs by three armed police in chlorine-yellow uniforms. The police had confiscated his guitar. In a corner of the shed, they smashed it on the floor. We Americans, after inspection of passports, were waved along to the passenger loading area, where there was a *cambio* and I could change a small amount of currency into pesos. A number of black limousines with little American flags on the hoods picked up some of my fellow passengers. *Carabineros* cleared traffic, and the limousines burned rubber. A longhaired young man with smiling dark eyes grabbed my PX suitcase and guided me toward his yellow Datsun taxicab. I felt for the wads of currency and traveler's checks in my Palm Beach jacket, then studied the cabbie closely. Not the mugging type, I decided. I settled into the back seat while the cabbie started the meter, then the engine.

"You going to hotel?" he asked in English. When I told him the Sheraton, he flashed a crooked grin through the rearview mirror and exclaimed, "*¡Fantástico!* It is the best... Do you like Frank Sinatra? *¡Fantástico!*" He waved his arms as if conducting an orchestra, then clutched down and accelerated as though coming out of the pits at Indianapolis.

"What do you think of the new government?" I asked.

He shrugged. "*Tranquilidad.*"

"In the United States it is reported that President Moreno Báez committed suicide in the palace. Is that true or General Scarpio's propaganda?"

The cabbie eyed me in the mirror. "Who knows?" he shrugged again and fell silent. We were entering the outskirts of the city. From the look of things, Pacífica was where big old-model American cars came to die. Continentals, Galaxies, Imperials and Furies were lurching about, drivers' faces halved by high dashboards into Kilroy Was Here graffiti, the monster cars honking along dusty side-streets where barefooted *campesinos* played soccer, dribbling the *pelota* on forehead and toe. A sharkfinned paintless doorless windowless Cadillac hunkered down on springless coils scattering blooms of sparks as from an oxyacetylene torch. There seemed to be something incorrigibly happy about Pacificans.

"*Mi hermano*," the cabbie suddenly offered.

"Your brother?"

"*Sí*. My brother saw an officer pointing a pistol at the head of President Moreno Báez. Like this." The cabbie pointed index finger at the temple and pulled the trigger.

He was beginning to be an interesting cabbie. "*¿Es verdad?*"

"*Sí, sí.*" A story, half in English, half in Spanish, began to pour out. It seemed to me that he had been waiting to tell it to someone for a long time, like the Ancient Mariner.

His family was respectable but poor. When the people began to demonstrate against the socialist regime of Moreno Báez, the cabbie's brother had been conscripted into Scarpio's own regiment. At first no one believed there would be civil war. Moreno Báez was an idealist who had ruined the economy and was threatening to nationalize Earthco, the foreign-owned copper-mining industry; it was stupid of him, but Moreno Báez was a good man and a true patriot. Perhaps it was the American banks who precipitated the war by refusing to lend their capital to Moreno Báez. Perhaps Earthco secretly funded General Scarpio. One heard rumors. Who would know? Still, women came to regimental headquarters and threw wheat at the soldiers, meaning they were *gallinas*—chickens. Then early one morning about a week ago the soldiers were marched to parade grounds and told that the presidential palace was to be stormed, following its bombing by the Air Force. Those who did not wish to participate in the military overthrow were invited by their officers to break ranks. The cabbie's brother hesitated. His friends who broke ranks were executed on the spot. Then the soldiers were given gunpowder to swallow with milk. Later the soldiers seized the palace, suffering many casualties. Later still, the cabbie's brother happened to glance through a large oaken door and see an officer pointing a pistol at Moreno Báez, who was wearing a blue suit. About an hour after that, he saw a body in a blue suit being dragged to a van outside the palace. He did not positively identify the face. "My brother's eyes make the conclusion." The cabbie tapped his forehead.

By now we were driving down spacious tree-lined boulevards bordered by high-walled, wooded estates. "There," the cabbie pointed at a granite mansion. "The Soviet Embassy. A week ago, hundreds of functionaries come and go. Now it is closed. What do you think of my country?" the cabbie went on in a bright tone. "*¡Qué lindo! ¡Qué precioso!*"

I saw green Mercedes buses packed with denim-jacketed industrial workers. I saw rubber-tired carts drawn by drayhorses. On a corner, an old man was vending steaming oysters from a pushcart. We passed the blackened ruins of the Presidential Palace. Looming up from palm-shaded gardens was the boarded-up building that the cabby identified as the Congress of the Republic. Yet people strolled about looking contented. Shops were open, selling records, stereos, scotch and cameras. Well-dressed men gesticulated excitedly in espresso bars open to the broad avenue. An armed guard looked bored in front of the revolving doorway to a steel and glass skyscraper. The cabby pointed to it with pride: "*Rascacielos*. Fantastic!"

"What building is that?"

"Edificio Earthco."

Right there. Bluejean and Teapot could be there, safe in an incorrigibly happy country.

We drove another mile in silence.

"A few days ago the death-police came to my district looking for *extremistas*," the cabby announced matter-of-factly. "Every man has to stand in the street. The death-police executed every number-ten man... Here is the Sheraton. *Tranquilidad.*"

Fountains splashed over verdigrised sculptures. Tropical gardens rioted. Behind a high chain fence was a swimming pool a-shriek with bikini-clad nymphs.

After stepping from the cab and securing my suitcase, I gave the cabbie a roll of pesos worth about twenty dollars. If that was a month's wages for him, he had earned it. Yet he accepted the money with that blank refusal to say thank-you which seems the birthright of the poor. Too late, I realized that I had offended him. I asked him if he were for hire for the rest of the day. He nodded gravely. "I wait until 2300. After that, no." He grinned with crooked teeth and made a choking gesture to the throat.

"Curfew?"

"*Sí, sí.*" He made his hand into a pistol and pulled the trigger. "After that mo-*ment*, you disappear."

How could I possibly have known that the impulse to hire that young cabbie—Enrique by name—would prove one of the luckiest of my life? *¿Quién sabe?*

I picked up a message for "Sr. Landree" at Registration. Reverendo Juanito's invitation for tea at the Vicariate of Solidarity was for 1800. A steward escorted me to a luxurious room on the eighteenth floor from which I had a view of the city, vast and sprawling at the base of the Andean cordillera. Cloud reflections scudded across the cool brilliance of the Earthco Building, from the top of which a beacon flashed red, on and off, as if to signal safe harbor. I showered, shaved, and went to sleep until five. When I emerged from the hotel, I found my cabbie gazing like a woebegone lover at the girls in the swimming pool. He placed his hand over his heart and rolled his eyes. As we drove toward the cathedral, I could not help thinking of the conflicting impressions I had already received about Pacífica. Everyone in the country seemed to be performing preassigned roles in a dance of death disguised as a comic opera. Bluejean, herself something of an actress, had stumbled onto this stage. Instead of weighing the dangers of a situation in which thousands of people were falling victim to terror, she had entertained herself by watching crowds taking snapshots of the sun because a teenager had allegedly seen the Virgin Mary among shifting cloud formations.

We found the cathedral in a poor district where white bungalows clung together like overcrowded baby teeth. A statue of María Macarena had been splashed with red paint, a building adjacent to the cathedral gutted by fire. Yet, all around, the lights of the city were disarmingly lovely in twilight. Cypress trees, like upright pythons digesting small pigs, were tucking themselves into sheets of fog. I asked Enrique to wait for me. He shrugged, lit a cigarette, and began to read a tattered copy of *Playboy*.

Upon entering the cathedral, I was met at once by a young sleek priest in wire-rimmed spectacles who asked if I were señor Landry of the Dallas Cowboys.

"Paul Szabo of the United States Army, but I have come as a private citizen about a private matter, not about *la política*... You are reverendo Juanito? I thought your telephone might be tapped."

"I see," he nodded after a pause and shook my hand without vigor. "Archbishop Mendoza awaits us in our bureau of Solidarity."

I followed Juanito's swishy soutane down an aisle and up a worn stone stairwell to a private chamber from which we looked down through fenestrated stone to the candle-flickered countenance of Our Lady whose marble effigy was enthroned in a modest chapel below. I was reminded of sights seen during a week's tour of Spain when I was stationed in Germany. "So like the chamber in the Escorial where Felipe II de España dreamed of eternity, don't you agree?"

Juanito arched an eyebrow. "Ours is a poor country, señor Szabo... If I may say so, we do not often meet Americans who have your appreciation of Hispanic culture and tradition. Excuse me."

Swishing about, he rapped on a polished door, then motioned for me to follow. On the door were the freshly painted words, "Vicaría de la Solidaridad." As Juanito opened the door, I was met by an odor of stale cigarettes and of something medicinal, like moth balls. The room itself, high-ceilinged and bare-walled, was illuminated by a single lightbulb dangling from a cord. On a mahogany desk and piled on the floor were stacks of documents. Behind the desk sat an old man resplendent in *estola*, *túnica*, and *crucifijo,* distracting the eye from the room's ruin. It was here that the struggle to identify missing persons had begun. Perhaps a losing battle: Bluejean's cup of tea.

"*Eminencia*," Juanito gestured, "*el amigo norte-americano de la señora McQueen.*" The archbishop rose, shook my hand. His grasp was weaker than Juanito's. His rings were too large for the blotched and bony fingers. His birdlike eyes were rheumy. A kettle of camphor-scented steam rested on a hot plate at his feet. Perhaps Mendoza awaited the final embolus, the relentless tumor, the spasm of sputum. Or perhaps the secret police, torture, martyrdom. I bowed my head to him, gave a go-with-God salute of two fingers to forehead.

Juanito fetched an unlabeled bottle and tumblers from a filing cabinet. "*Pichuncho*. A brandy of the people." He poured the tumblers full of a brown liquor. "It is good for His Eminence's digestion. *Salud*."

Lifting the tumbler with both his trembling hands, Mendoza swallowed the brandy at a single gulp and sank back in his swivel chair. Juanito sipped. A sort of mocking alertness played behind his spectacles. "In His Eminence's youth," he began and stopped. "In my youth," Mendoza began in English and also stopped, fluttering bejewelled hand and exploding into a racking cough. "In His Eminence's youth," Juanito continued as if on cue, "he drank pichuncho like water, is that not true, Eminencia?" He brushed the air as if whisking away a fly. "Now that we are tranquil, we speak of *los desaparecidos*. At this mo-*ment*, thousands have disappeared. *¿Eminencia?*"

Mendoza cleared his throat and fixed watery eyes on me. "The position of the church is delicate," he declared, again in English. "We are not involved in *la política*. The people come to us, the families of the missing. Where are their loved ones gone? *¿Dónde están? ¿Dónde están?* Where is my Roberto? Where is my María Valentina? What can we say? The government washes its hands like Pilato. Mass graves already are found with mutilated corpses. Bodies are washed up on the beaches. We are too few at the Solidarity. Seldom is there opportunity to identify the dead, to administer the sacrament." He paused and opened trembling hands and went on, "We collect the information only. The photograph. Who has seen the person for the last time? What is the name? The government is not pleased with us." Mendoza sighed and dropped his liver-spotted hands with an audible thump upon the desk, so hard that the telephone, there, jingled.

Bluejean's telephone. From this very room she had called me.

"The church has been desecrated," Juanito said in a flat tone. "Several of our priests have been tortured. Nor has His Eminence been spared, although he comes from one of our oldest families. His parents' gravestones have been smeared with excrement. In our culture, that is a terrible thing." He looked at me quizzically. "Forgive us, señor Szabo. You are tired from your trip. We should talk, perhaps, of the traditional poetry—?"

I gave Juanito the cold eye but lifted my tumbler of brandy and saluted, "*Egészségedre.*" That brandy would have killed cockroaches. The archbishop and Juanito were exchanging glances when my head stopped its spin.

"*¿Húngaro?*" archbishop to reverendo.

I explained I was Hungarian by birth, but a naturalized American.

Again Juanito studied me quizzically. "I have a schoolfriend who emigrated from Hungary. Perhaps you know him—*el coronel* von Albensleben?"

"That's German, not Hungarian."

"*Claro.* Nevertheless, he came to Pacífica from Hungary, oh, sixteen years ago."

"It is true, reverendo, hundreds of thousands of Hungarians fled the communists at that time," I said. "I was one of them. This Albensleben is a colonel, you say?"

Juanito and the archbishop exchanged one of their glances. "El coronel von Albensleben," Juanito said to me in lowered voice, "is one of the most feared men in the military government. An officer of the secret police, PRED—*Partido Revolucionario Educacional Democrático.*"

"Never heard of him," I said. I was glad to be able to say this honestly. The name, though, sounded vaguely familiar.

A sort of sigh of relief was exchanged between the priest and prelate before Juanito resumed, "I think perhaps you help us by acting the liaison with PRED. With the strong bond of former Freedom Fighters."

"I told you, I'm not interested in politics."

Looking disappointed, Juanito shrugged and managed to crack a smile. "*Bueno*... I think perhaps, now, you are *simpático* with la señora McQueen."

There it was, manipulative skill. Had he conned Bluejean into doing his bidding at the risk of her life?

"She is my wife," I said.

"*¡Pobrecito!*" they said at once.

Juanito sipped his brandy. He no longer smiled. "You must forgive us for being careful, señor Szabo. Of course we know who you are. Your wife telephoned you from this office a week ago. We have her passport in safekeeping. First, tea... Excuse me." He went and pressed a buzzer. As if on cue, a woman glided into the room, placed a tea tray on the desk, and retreated, closing the door behind her. There were pastries, buttered toast, a tea called *mate* sipped through a silver *bombilla*, and a weird orange sea-urchin like the tongues of birds. "*Erizos*," Juanito beamed, tucking in heartily, "a delicacy of the country. Perhaps you would prefer *cochayuyo*?"

"What's that?"

"Seaweed," he said, and suppressed a cough.

The archbishop drank his tea from a cup. It trembled in his hands. He polished off most of the buttered toast and licked his fingers afterwards.

Twenty minutes later the woman came and cleared away the tea things. Juanito drew his chair up close to mine and began, "Now that we are tranquil, I must inform you that your wife has disappeared."

No one had seen her enter the cathedral that morning. Of course she had been with the crowd in the plaza where the honor of the church was being assaulted by a teenaged hireling who claimed over a microphone to be talking with the Holy Virgin. Possibly the American woman had been swept along by the tide of people seeking comfort and sanctuary. There was the confusion of street fighting, the chatter of machine guns, tanks and armored vehicles grinding into action. A number of young men and women from the University of Pacífica had been carried into the church badly wounded or dying. While nuns attended them, Juanito strolled among the people and helped to dispense bread and water. In the late morning Archbishop Mendoza conducted a special mass. Black-shawled women knelt and prayed at the candlelit antechapels. The varicose-veined marble walls, like sugary decorations on a wedding cake, echoed with a cacophony of the keening and credulous poor.

Suddenly some people were shouting, "A miracle! A miracle!" They pressed toward an antechapel of the Virgin. On the altar stood a razor-sharp star of tin at the center of which was painted, in the style of Cuzco, a scarlet and blue image of the Virgin. "*¡Milagro!*"

Juanito came running. He had heard sheet metal rippling. He parted the crowd and entered the antechapel; he found the star where it had fallen from the altar; but as he returned the star to the altar, he saw blood dripping from the Virgin's eyes. Nevertheless, close inspection revealed blood on the tip of a star-point. Someone, clearly, had been stabbed by it, a fact that Juanito thought best to withhold from the crowd while he searched for the source of the commotion. His eyes found her. She was leaning against the wall in a dark corner of the chancel, that American woman who was wrapping a bloodied handkerchief about her forearm, tightening the knot with her teeth. Juanito rushed to her and offered in English to lend assistance. She said nothing until she was satisfied with the knot. Then she straightened herself. A look of wild amusement passed over her face.

"Sorry about that," she said. "I'm always stumbling into things."

"Perhaps, señora, the Virgin is trying to tell you something."

"Yeah," she said, "like beat it. Hi. I'm Bluejean. Bluejean McQueen. You wouldn't happen to have a cigarette, would you?"

"You come," Juanito beckoned. When she followed, he noticed for the first time that one of her feet was artificial. A prosthesis creaked. She walked quite rapidly, head high. Juanito guided her upstairs to the office which that very day had become headquarters for Solidarity. He offered her an English cigarette from the archbishop's silver case and lit it for her with the archbishop's silver lighter.

"That's cool," she said, inhaling deeply. "It's great to talk English."

Truly, she was most unusual, this American lady! Of course, he liked North Americans. They had permitted him to study for a year at the Loyola University in New Orleans. The señora McQueen seemed to bring memories back to him, the carnival atmosphere of the French Quarter, the sound of a calliope on a hot afternoon in Jackson Square in front of the St. Louis Cathedral, the taste of fried shrimp on the Poor Boy bread, yet amidst all this boisterous energy there seemed to be a terrible sadness, a soul of the land as haunted and lost and outrageous as a leper colony in the bayous. The señora reminded him of that too. She was lost—not helpless, not without that peculiarly North American trait of encountering the world with the manners of an occupying force, but lost and adrift in her mind, unanchored in the surge, a piece of flotsam snagged from aimless passage for Our Lady's purposes. Snagged indeed! Could the episode of the Virgin's star be chance merely? Such a simple child, this señora, and simplicity would be a factor in the choice she would make, as it had been when she was chosen.

Juanito closed his eyes, then opened them suddenly upon me. "She chose Atamoro in the copper-mining district."

The air of the office felt lifeless and damp as if enclosed by a wet blanket. I was thinking, *Trusted a priest for the first time in her life and she disappears*, as I heard my own voice filling with rage. "Chose? Bluejean has been drowning in other people's choices most of her life."

Juanito frowned and pressed a finger to his lips, nodding toward Archbishop Mendoza, who was snoozing upright in his chair. "Very well," I said in lowered voice, "tell me what happened. But first, before you forget, I want her passport. Why she would do a dumb thing like leaving it here, I don't know..."

He rose and went to a filing cabinet. Presently he came with a green passport. It was Bluejean's all right, Teapot's too. There they both were in the photograph. At the sight of them whom I had not seen for a year and whom I might possibly never see again, I dared not cry. "Was my—was Christina Szabo—she has my name—and that explains how you knew me—was she with my wife? Was she mentioned at all? Do you know where she is?"

"No," replied Juanito, tapping fingers lightly, "your daughter did not attend with your wife. However, your wife did disclose that the girl is staying with a friend in the city. The señora requested permission to telephone you in the United States so that you understand the situation. I'm sure the girl is quite safe. As for la señora McQueen, she was destined to fulfill her life in her own way. She was aware of the possible consequences of undertaking work for the Solidarity. She chose Atamoro. We were surprised that she was not unfamiliar with the name of this village. Something to do with the American mining there. She was determined to go to help us in Atamoro."

In this country I call Pacífica, and at that time, it was easier for an American than a Pacifican to be informed about the overthrow of President Moreno Báez and the immediate, brutal repression of the people. The newspapers there were under control of the military government and busy spreading such obvious disinformation as the story of Moreno Báez's suicide and the deportation of "disappeared" persons, whereas I myself, while still in Colorado, had been reading reliable reports and commentaries. At least they seemed reliable then and now, years later, have so proven, the situation down there having gone from bad to worse under the continuing dictatorship of President Scarpio.

Not the least informative of the commentaries I had read was one that placed the Pacifican revolution within the context of international mining operations. Thus I had been impressed with Enrique the cab driver. Although his reading material was limited to girlie magazines, he had through the agency of plain horse sense sniffed out the connection between Earthco and the events of November 1973. When President Moreno Báez threatened to nationalize Earthco, he effectively sealed his own doom. Conglomerates such as the Woolpack family's Earthco—the almost bankrupt but subsidized octopus which sank one of its tentacles into Pacifican copper more than a century ago—regained control almost lost to the socialist government of Moreno Báez.

That was how Atamoro entered the picture: it is one of Earthco's primary centers of operation. I had learned that fact from the newspapers. It was in Atamoro that several hundreds of Indian peasants and mineworkers were systematically hauled away on the first morning of the revolution. There, to Atamoro, Bluejean came, speaking no Spanish, having few skills, a partially disabled woman at large in a land where a woman can be raped and murdered for no greater provocation than wearing shorts or chewing gum, or could be arrested for humanitarian work construed as political.

I had to restrain anger at reverendo Juanito, for fear of losing any piece of crucial information. Also, in the final analysis, I considered him and Archbishop Mendoza honorable men.

As for that slangy dialogue between Bluejean and Juanito in the cathedral, one may wonder whether Juanito understood and remembered well enough to pass it along to me. He didn't. I have another source for that dialogue—Bluejean herself, in a letter.

She never disappeared, in spiritual truth.

"Are there Marxists in your organization?" I was asking Juanito. He shrugged and said, "Frankly, I don't know. The only thing we ask when someone wants to work for us is whether they can do the job, their professional and technical background, and whether they accept the ideals of the Church in the field of human rights, with preferential option for the poor."

I was wringing my hands with a kind of despair. "Look. Either you failed to ask Bluejean the proper questions, or you are a poor judge of character. For Bluejean, life is a game, an end in itself. She trifles with people and ideas. In a game, if you grow up, you have the option of not playing. But Bluejean doesn't opt out, for that would be a choice, and she feels most free when she is most in thrall to other people's choices. She needs to be protected from herself.

Yet here you give her a flaming box of dynamite and conveniently call it a message from the Virgin Mary..." I stopped. I was speaking of Bluejean in the present tense. I looked down at the floor, at the pile of documents stacked there as remembrance for the damned. "Tell me. Is she dead?"

"*¡Por la Madre!*" exclaimed the archbishop, waking up and blinking his bird-like eyes. "The position of the Church is most delicate, most delicate. Juanito, have you expressed our deepest sympathy?"

"Presently, Eminencia," Juanito said gently. "Sr. Szabo is under the impression that la señora McQueen did not make a conscious and wholehearted choice when she went to Atamoro. Exactly the contrary is true. She found her vocation. She understood her mission. She was filled with compassion. She was a saint."

There was a silence in spite of the hissing of the steam-kettle. "Then she's dead," I said.

And Juanito: "She disappeared shortly after arrival in Atamoro. We had just been informed of her disappearance on the day you called."

"How do you know she is dead?"

And Juanito: "The body has been found."

"In a cave," I said to myself. "Where?" out loud.

"In the mountains of Atamoro. In an abandoned mine."

"Did she fall?"

"According to our information, there was a bullet wound in the head."

"Who informed you?"

"An old woman telephoned from the church in Atamoro."

"Has she seen the body?"

"It was an Indian boy. He saw birds in the sky and discovered the old mine. He entered and found the body of a woman. A foreign woman. A woman with one leg. He ran to Atamoro to our priest, padre José."

"Why the priest?"

"One does not report to the government at this mo-*ment*. The boy's family has disappeared. The father worked in the mines."

"Did the boy recognize my wife?"

"*Es verdad*. La señora was helping our priest with—*el orfanato*. An orphanage? The boy recognized her as the foreign woman of this orphanage."

"Then why didn't the priest confirm the identification?"

Juanito and archbishop exchanged a glance. "We have not heard from padre José for days. It is a possibility—"

"*¡Pobrecito!*" the archbishop was shaking his head.

"Another question, Little John: are you reporting my wife's death to the government?"

"Not at this mo-*ment*. We would place the old woman's and the boy's lifes in the danger. We would give the government the opportunity to remove the evidence permanently. Now do you understand? In all cases, the government does not wish for the disappeared to be identified, but in this case *especially*, when relations between our country and the United States are extremely strained."

He had spoken truly. I had been right to avoid the American authorities, at least until I could make positive identification of Bluejean's body and get Teapot safely out of the country before running the risk of a high-level dismissal of the "case." Suddenly I had an idea. "Will you write me a letter of safe conduct? I am going to Atamoro in the morning."

A few minutes later I had the archbishop's signed letter of safe conduct and was prepared to leave. Juanito touched my arm. I almost jumped. "This is the work of God, señor. You have our deepest sympathy."

I would say that the look I gave reverendo Juanito was a military occupation specialty of a veteran American sergeant: the hard chew-out look. "And you have your saint." I slammed the door behind me. I left the cathedral quickly, in turmoil. But an image arose of Virgil and Txó and Little Horse with his birth defect, then another image of Virgil and the deer at the hot spring, and I knew that my prevision of Bluejean's death had been understood and respected: *you are another person's life.*

In the plaza outside the cathedral the air was cool and damp, freshened by fog. Twilight streaked with the clamor of swallows touched the city. Workers alighted from buses. Small, hunch-shouldered old women in black scurried here and there with little bags of comestibles. On a bench, a teenaged couple were hugging with a kind of breathless timidity. Everywhere the presence of insignificant death.

Enrique motioned me toward his yellow Datsun. No harm in asking. Give him jump pay, hazardous duty. "Will you take me to Atamoro in the morning?"

"*Peligroso*," he murmured, shaking his head.

"I know it's dangerous. I will pay two hundred dollars."

"*¡Doscientos dólares!*" he exclaimed. "*No es nada.*"

"It is nothing? Do you want more money?"

"No, don Pablo, sufficient. *¡Doscientos dólares!* Fantastic!"

"*Momentito,*" I said. "Questions." I asked him the distance to Atamoro, would there be roadblocks, that sort of thing. He said to Atamoro would be 100 kilometers. Yes, the *carabineros* would stop the cars. The countryside would be pretty. The road would take us to the top of the world.

"I want you to buy some things," I said, giving him a wad of pesos. "A cigarette lighter. That's for you. Two stereo cassette players, six bottles of scotch whiskey, and a shovel. Got that?"

Enrique seemed beside himself with delight and with his hands made scooping motions in the air. "*¡Máquina* *excavadora!"*

"Not a steam shovel, Enrique. A spade."

"Sí, sí. *Una pala*. Shuh-bell... Six whiskey! *¡Hola!* You?" He tilted an imaginary bottle to his lips.

"Five for the *carabineros*, one for me."

"Two stereo. The *salsa*. We dance with girls!"

"No. The stereos also are for the *carabineros*. They will want to confiscate property to make themselves feel very important... Let me see your wallet. Your *cartera*."

We sat in the cab under interior light and together sorted through the contents of his wallet. His ID said Enrique Rico de las Golondrinas—Henry Rich of the Swallows. There was a black-and-white snapshot of a family of seven, six of them with frozen smiles, the seventh a white-haired man with a scowling, glittering eye. Enrique identified everyone: Willy, not yet a conscript, there, *Mamá y Papá*. The cousin, José Manuel, a dentist, with his wife... there. And there—there!—the beautiful young lady with flowing dark hair and bright, dark eyes. "My sister, Teresa. *¡Muy muy inteligente!* She is now doctor from university." And Enrique himself who appeared to be whistling at girls through his fingers.

I made two hundred dollars in traveler's checks payable to his order and told him to leave the money, the photograph, and all other effects save the ID at home, for security. He was to meet me at the Sheraton at 0600 hours next morning.

"You have family, don Pablo?"

There was a fist in my gut. But I did not wish to offend this young man to whom I was entrusting my life in the morning. "My wife is dead. We must find her body in Atamoro. My daughter is in danger here. My father was enslaved by the fascists, then made to disappear by the Soviets. My mother... Mi Mamá was captured by the Soviets on the Austrian border. I may never know whether she is alive or dead. Her name also was Terézia."

Enrique nodded his head, then brightened, "It is necessary for you to meet Teresa. My sister is very beautiful."

"Are you always this happy, Enrique?"

"In my coun-tree, life is big yoke."

4

PAPÁ'S rooster brings dawn through the iron bars of her bedroom's single window. Already Mamá is astir in the kitchen boiling the black coffee, toasting the *pan*, and washing the sun-ripened peaches that José Manuel has accepted in lieu of other payment from an old farmer with an abscessed molar. Mornings are filled with sameness as far back as Teresa can remember from her twenty-six years in the same cramped house, the same city, the same country. First Mamá will prepare the breakfast and then Papá will make his grand entrance upon the *teatro del mundo*, shirtsleeves rolled up, collar buttoned without a tie, whiskers unshaven, the one good eye, the hawk's eye, pointed as a gimlet toward Mamá and shining in anticipation of a good, cruel, long day's quarrel. The quarrel will begin presently. Who is the favorite son? Willy or Enrique? It is Willy for this great man, don Augusto. Willy is the first-born son, like his father a craftsman, like his father a lover, each having begotten bastards upon impoverished girls, but, unlike his father, Willy the brave soldier now, even though Papá boasts that he himself would have taken the presidential palace unassisted but for the fact that cataracts have transformed one eye to milk and mooted the question of extravagant valor. Papá's hero rides tall, loves to fight with his fists, never misses a shot and shoots Mexicans, Indians, outlaws and Orientals depending upon which John Wayne movie is showing on Pacifican television. Whereas Mamá's favorite son is Enrique, full of fun. Enrique is Teresa's favorite, too, though he should be going to the university, as she has done, instead of driving a cab in order to bring money to the family. Teresa herself is not the subject of quarrels. Her fate is supposed to be fixed; her entirely self-motivated and unsupported achievement to the level of a doctoral degree is regarded as a sort of temporary aberration in God's sublime plan. Only when she marries and, like Mamá, destroys her body with childbearing and abortions, will Teresa become acceptable in that eye of God that is so like her father's. She wants a baby, of course. She would love to have a wee damp face pressed to her nipple right now in bed, would love to raise a big family. But not with John Wayne. And not with anyone resembling don Augusto. There is the family joke that Papá would have been Hitler's best friend.

Teresa smiles to herself about the old joke. She does not wish to surrender to hatred, that is so easily done, but hatred of Papá has accumulated from remembered cruelties, like pinches of poison. His *machismo* is merely mulish. His intelligence is a fact. Even though his judgment can sometimes be as clouded as the bad eye, it is with the hawk's eye he penetrates to the core of character, some people's anyway. There is much about don Augusto that is good and forgivable. His own father, a banker, squandered away the family's substance, died young and a pauper, so Augusto quit school and developed quite a remarkable skill for making bronze beds and doorknockers and ornamental condors. When first Teresa, then Enrique earned scholarships enabling them to attend the English School, Pacífica's finest, it was Mamá who gave permission, and Papá rewarded her by not speaking to her for a year. Still, Papá did not intervene, and he takes credit now for Teresa's graduation from the Universidad de Pacífica and subsequent, though interrupted, postdoctoral studies in psychology there. These ridiculous studies so wasted on a woman are prophesied to collapse of their own accord, and Teresa will get down to the real business of making babies. Never having contributed a peso toward her education, he believes he has sacrificed himself for it. He is a famous self-sacrificer. He has sacrificed himself to the degree that self-sacrifice is a function of his self-esteem. He has sacrificed himself to frequent bouts of drunkenness and to desultory seductions of barrio girls. He attributes the seductions to irresistible good looks. Nowadays, sacrificing himself for the sake of humanity, he forges passports. Lately, what with the sudden demand for fake passports, don Augusto has been flush with pesos and, better, flattery. It has not been an uncommon sight to have two or three cars, once in a while a Mercedes-Benz, parked late at night beneath the eucalyptus trees, their owners glancing nervously about while Papá practices the art that will take them to Havana, Mexico City, or Paris.

She hates her father for long-remembered acts of humiliation and unkindness. When she was fifteen, a rich girlfriend from the English School had given Teresa on her *cumpleaños*, her usually wretched birthday, a portable radio. For the first time in her life she possessed the magic portal to the world of music, to Mozart's C-minor Mass, to Beethoven's Ninth, to Debussy's string quartet, to the dreamy sorrowing passions of Mahler's *Das Lied von der Erde*, and to Frank Sinatra and the Beatles too. And one night in the fog and chill of Pacifican winter as she lay shivering in bed in the house without heating or insulation, the radio tuned low on the pillow beside her, and her spirits soaring toward another world of bright and ineffable beauty, don Augusto stormed in, smashed the radio beneath his boots in a frenzy of truculent rage, and departed the room, wordlessly. The same with her books: *Don Quijote, Madame Bovary, Hamlet,* the *Tristana* of Galdós, a precious American edition of Neumann's *The Great Mother*, and other treasures were found shredded on her stone floor one evening when she returned from school. And then the cosmetics. Mamá had been showing her how to apply perfume and lipstick and to primp her hair with a curling iron. Papá, home reeking of sweat and drink, took one withering hawkeyed look, pinned Teresa to the floor, and clipped her hair with metal-working shears until her nearly bald scalp was festooned with white scars, like worms. Her hatred then scorched away the twin impulses to guilty submissiveness and to self-pity, but she refused to eat for a week and woke in hospital, force-fed by Mamá and her brothers.

"¡Bruta! ¡Animal! ¡Infeliz! ¡Desgraciada!"

The quarrel has begun. Yesterday he said his coffee was lukewarm and smashed the cup against the plaster wall. A week ago, when Mamá brought him his false teeth from the washroom, he bent them with his fist—knowing of course that José Manuel, who is indebted for free lodging, would repair them. Today it will be something else. He hasn't slept with Mamá for months. He has taken to sleeping outdoors in the garden among the chickens, saying he will kill with his bare fists any thief who scales the three-meter wall to steal his lemons and olives.

Another voice, Enrique's, can be heard greeting Mamá and Papá, and she remembers that he is leaving early this morning to drive a rich American into the Andes. Last night, over a late supper Enrique had been showing off newly purchased trinkets and money, quite a lot of money in fact. Two hundred American dollars and a fistful of pesos. These he has given to Mamá. The stereos and whiskey are bribes for *carabineros*, he insists. Tonight there must be a big party. Ask Willy to bring his guitar. Ask Tio Carlos to bring his harp. And Enrique had taken Teresa aside, his handsome face quivering with mirth. His good friend, don Pablo the American, is, he whispers, *un hombre muy atento, muy inteligente, muy simpático*, very highly regarded by Archbishop Mendoza, no less. *¡Qué precioso! ¡Fantástico! ¡Estupendo!* Too bad his wife is dead, you understand? Teresa did not and does not take seriously Enrique's outbursts of enthusiasm about prospective mates. Still, as she lies half awake, she tries to imagine what the gringo looks like. Seeing John Wayne, she rests dreaming thought upon the sensitive and distinguished features of Ángel López Schneider, who had directed her thesis on new neuropsychological perspectives on closed and hierarchical systems of society. Ángel López Schneider has been in love with her but has a wife and grown children. And he is... dead. Taken to the Estadio Nacional on the first day of the revolution, tortured, executed; this unspeakable fate had been observed by a friend of Willy's, one of the soldiers who witnessed the activities of PRED in the stadium.

There are tears in Teresa's eyes as she falls into light sleep. She wakes to sounds of children. They pass her bedroom window chanting an old song on their way to school:

Tres chanchitas desobedientes
se fueron a pasear
sin permiso de su Mamá
tomaditos de la mano
y el lobo se los comió...

How beautiful it all is! It is the same song she chants for Ximenita, the three-year-old daughter of her cousin José Manuel and of his wife, Carmen, whom don Augusto calls The Peasant. So what should so disturb Teresa this morning about a cautionary tale, that of three disobedient little pigs who leave their mother without permission and are eaten by El Lobo, the wolf?

It is useless to tell Papá that he is a sick man, a schizophrenic. His withdrawal from reality and his violent expressions of mental and behavioral disturbance are mirrored throughout Pacífica. He represents the norm. Pacífica is a Purgatorio, she reflects, a place alternating between darkness and light, between the medieval and modern worlds, between the culture of patriarchal authority and the new worldwide culture of experience made known within, unconventional, numinous, creative and free. Dear Ángel López Schneider, he who had the wisdom to make her see the destiny of nations in the enlargement of consciousness! How bright, how harmonious his vision! Yet still the children sing the old song of obedience, and still El Lobo is waiting to devour them. Like Papá.

Fully morning now. Tonight she will wear the new clothes purchased from the tutoring fees at the English School where she has been employed during her postgraduate and now postdoctoral years. The black taffeta skirt, the high-heeled *botas*, the red knitted cotton blouse that displays her pale neck and the swell of her full bosom. Not tonight the *piedras del incas*, lapis lazuli set in silver, but the imitation pearl necklace, the single-pearl earrings. Lipstick, a touch, and a touch of Givenchy. Oh, the hair, the hair! But there will be time, after the meals, after the long day's tutoring, time to wash her long dark hair... A flame of excitement passes through her heart to and fro, to and fro, a warm ocean current wild and inviolate as the roots of sleep.

That night when we returned safely from Atamoro and were received for festivities at the Casa de Rico de las Golondrinas, what I didn't know about Enrique's capacity for talking flabbergasting nonsense would one day, in future, be told me by Teresa. I sipped scotch in the garden under the eucalyptus trees. Old Hawkeye was stalking me, while Enrique, out of my sight and hearing, was in the house talking, had I but known it, to Teresa.

He is a great man, this don Pablo de Szabo. He has done me, Enrique, the honor to reveal his history. Born to a noble family of Hungary, he lost his family in the wars with the fascists and Soviets and escaped alone to Western Europe. There he was adopted by Lady Wolfpack and educated in the great school of London. First he came, always, in examinations, and the great University of Oxford had invited him or possibly the great University of Cambridge had invited him—no matter... *¡Ay!*, a terrible misfortune befell this man of exile and sorrow, Lady Wolfpack has become infatuated with this man who has adored her in the purity of affections as his mother and protectress. He turns the back of his hand to her and is cut off without a peso. What to do? Always, always, like the great Quijote, he will serve honor. As for the crippled American lady who has befriended him in the hour of dispossession, she, too, is homeless, and she is bearing another man's child. Out of honor and pity, don Pablo offers to wed this crippled woman and raise her child as his own. *¡Mi vida!* It comes to pass, and the great army of the United States invites him to be their leader. But no. He disdains to be exalted above the common folk. Now he has done battle with the evil forces of Vietnam, fighting with the gun, fighting with the knife, with *los manos*—but there is much sorrow for him at his homecoming. His wife is not there nor is the precious *gua gua*, the baby who is his heart! *¿Dónde están? Aquí*, here in Pacífica. La señora has come to Atamoro at the request of Archbishop Mendoza and gives help to the new orphanage... She has disappeared. The death police have put the bullet in the head and thrown her body in the mine. *¡Ay!* We drove through the roadblocks. The carabineros saw this don Pablo. They dared not stop us. We arrived in Atamoro. We walked a kilometer into the mountains. We found the body—*¡horrible!* the acrid odor, the waxy face—and gave this lady the honor of burial. Then out we emerged from the great cave. We found ourselves surrounded by *indios* and *obreros* with the guns! It was time to die! But *momentito*. Don Pablo looked the evil people in the eye. He turned his back and walked away. Now he plots revenge upon the death police. *¡Fantástico!*

Teresa scolds Enrique in a teasing way. "If half of what you have told is true about this man, I would still have no interest in him. Already I have seen him from this window. That frog will never make a prince. Of course, it is remarkable how these North Americans hide their feelings. You say he has just buried his wife? Then he has no heart. Off with you!"

Enrique is crestfallen but brightens. "Papá is very impressed with this man."

"Truly? Papá is impressed by no man but himself."

But Teresa has missed nothing of the scene in the garden. Willy in uniform. He has brought the guitar. José Manuel in starched gown, having come hastily from the hospital. Carmen: too much weight, too much rouge. Ximenita like a doll, red ribbons in her hair. Tío Carlos has brought the harp. Neighbors in work clothes, wives in dresses that are worn as if still on hangers in a closet. Papá, unshaven and wearing a stained white shirt, pouring wine with a sort of magnanimous diffidence, Mamá meanwhile in the kitchen cooking, as ever. Suddenly in the garden, where the eucalyptus trees edge long shadows across flowers and century plants and up trellised, calcinate walls aflutter with pigeons, comes the beep beep of Enrique's Datsun arriving. Don Augusto unlocks the iron gate and opens it wide in a gesture of divine dispensation, and the floodlights on the garden catch the American stepping wearily from the car, catch the fair hair, the anxious mien. He shields his eyes from the glare, a hesitant smile on his lips, but he seems confused and does not shake the hands extended to him. Instead, he touches two fingers to his forehead in strained salute and looks about in a daze. Teresa, watching from the eight-paned window of the dining room with stone floor, is startled when the American's gaze lifts in her direction, vaguely pulled there, but he does not see her, his gaze finally coming to rest upon Ximenita who is throwing breadcrumbs to chickens and squealing in delight. The American walks slowly past Papá, past everyone, and squats beside Ximenita. His gestures are small and deliberate as those of a man who talks to animals. His smile has opened. He lifts Ximenita in his arms, strokes her hair, suddenly puts her down and glances away, biting a knuckle. Perhaps no one else understands—but Teresa's swift heart understands—that this strange man is weeping, inwardly. She is glad that the family and guests are shrugging, picking up their chatter, preparing to start the music, feeling offended by the stranger but leaving him alone, though Papá, arms folded, is staring in disbelief that the guest of honor is not expressing animated gratitude for having the sacred one-eyed countenance shone upon him. Then Enrique rushes from the car with a bottle of whiskey, pours a full glass, and presents it to the American. Who nods thanks before Enrique enters the house.

"No, Enriquito. He is not a man who is plotting revenge. Does he speak Spanish?"

"*Mal*," Enrique replies with an expression of blue funk.

"It is rude to leave him alone in his grief. I shall go to him."

She smoothes her hands over her breasts and fluffs her skirt.

She knows whom she will marry.

"Over there is the Estadio Nacional," Enrique pointed from the car's window. "The death-police bring the people for interrogation and ... *¡Horrible!*"

It resembled any large American football stadium, an oval amphitheatre of girders and concrete. Already at a few minutes past 0600 hours the parking lot adjacent to the stadium bustled with the coming and going of military vehicles, and there were the usual clumps of soldiers, weapons at the ready. I had learned in the American papers about atrocities committed in the stadium, tortures, executions. Thousands of people interrogated had been deported, and the Pacifican government was claiming that only terrorists had been eliminated. "I read about it," I said.

"My brother, his friend was in the stadium as the soldier. For three days and nights a lady, an aristocrat, refused drink and food. Finally my brother, his friend went to her, tears in the face. 'Lady,' he said, 'you are so beautiful. I love you. But if you do not eat the food, I must shoot you. Please, *por favor*, for my sake,' he said. And this lady eats the food."

I told Enrique not to tell me any more stories. He lapsed into silence as we sped past miles of squalid barrios, the bungalows sprouting TV antennae like metallic crosses in a cemetery. My eyes burned. I had slept at best fitfully the night before, having stayed up late drinking scotch to dissolve the fist in my stomach, trying to say good-bye to Bluejean, sobbing unabashedly until her ghost released me to continuance of my quest for honor and harmony. It had been finished between us, the marriage, long ago, yet there was the harvest of regret sown over the years with seeds of pity—pity that failed to flower into the mutual acceptance of love.

We took a coastal road for forty kilometers, on the one side the towering, snowcapped cordillera, on the other fog banks unraveling from the chilly Humboldt Current. Giant eucalyptus trees bared pink flesh to salt-scented air. Daedal peaks rising 5,000 meters quite abruptly from the littoral loomed closer and closer, then we lost them on switchback dirt roads until, at about 0850 hours, at approximately 2,300 meters elevation we arrived in high, sparsely-vegetated desert country, a broad dry valley at the end of which was Atamoro, its tin rooftops like broken pieces of mirror, its grey hills pockmarked with mineshafts spewing yellow tailings like flung doubloons. Not far from the village was a large, ramshackle processing mill with cathedral-like smokestacks. We passed a road sign: EARTHCO.

Our encounters with soldiers had proved less of a hassle than I had anticipated. The Officers-in-Charge at each of three roadblocks wore braided caps and yellow summer tunics and behaved in a military manner, save for thefts. When we were halted, Enrique explained what an important person I was and showed the archbishop's safe conduct letter. The officer, disregarding me, commanded Enrique to show his own papers and to unlock the trunk of the car. The first OIC confiscated two bottles of whiskey, explaining that six were not permitted because the Indians might drink them. The second OIC confiscated two more bottles, explaining that four were not permitted, and so forth. The third OIC confiscated a cassette player, explaining that terrorists might use it to conceal a bomb. He did not explain why we were permitted to keep the other stereo, but I was glad to have one in reserve for the return trip, together with two bottles of whiskey. Though I confess my adrenaline pumped overtime during these formalities, it was Enrique who shook visibly during them and jabbered incessantly after them. About The Peasant's beautiful little girl: *¡Qué lindá! ¡Qué preciosa! ¡Qué bonita!* Or about the weather or the scenery. What a lovely day. The lake is eight kilometers long. Good for fishing. *¡Qué lindo!* After one inspection his trembling hand kept trying to turn the ignition on until he realized he had left the key in the trunklock. When he started the car, he was in reverse without realizing it and almost ran over a pig rooting by the side of the road. When we reached Atamoro, Enrique had his favorite exclamation well pointed: "*¡Qué precioso!*"

It was a bright morning in barren high country. From the appearance of Atamoro it was difficult to imagine that something so calamitous as the disappearance of hundreds of Indians and workers had been accomplished the past week. Smoke plumes from Earthco's distant mill proclaimed business as usual. In the village plaza, life went on as if it were a movie set without a script. Indian women, their expressions detached and demure, wound raw cotton from knapsacks on their backs, adroitly turning cotton into thread by passing it between thumb and forefinger. The women wore knee-length vests of purple, black fedoras, and rubber boots. I saw peasants with flat rounded faces, pale brown skin, jetblack hair cut into bangs, and narrow, intensely dark eyes. I saw a legless beggar with a leather-shod stump like an elephant's hoof. I saw canvasses flopping in gusts of raw breeze, an open café with families at tables. I saw blankets in the street or on shelves of wobbly stalls, dusty items for sale: lapis lazuli, ponchos, pocket combs, and skewered pigs for flies to feast on. Here came the salesman for paraffin gas beating a tire iron on the metal cylinder of his pushcart. And there was a conjuror advertising messages from the dead. He had a box about two by two by three feet in size, lined inside with aluminum foil and revealing the head of a boy wearing a turban and suspended on a tin candelabra. The conjuror was placing a piece of paper in the boy's mouth, then bending near to listen, then saying something that seemed to be satisfying the cluster of women nearby.

Cruising slowly, we came to a small church just off the plaza. I told Enrique to stop. Here, perhaps, would be padre José who might report on Bluejean's death. Enrique parked. I went in.

Beneath adze-scuffed beams, an old woman—was this Juanito's old woman?—murmured over her rosary before candles. I shook her shoulder, gently. Where was the priest? She squinted raisin-wrinkly eyesockets and shook her head. Where was the orphanage, the orfanato? I slipped 500 pesos into her hand, which looked like a mummified foot. She flashed a graveyard of teeth, clutched her prayer shawl at her throat. She went out a side door. I followed. We stood in an empty courtyard enclosing a large shed of windweathered boards and rusted sheets of tin. "*Orfanato*," she pointed.

"*Mil gracias.*" After a pause, I asked again where I could find padre José.

"*Desaparecido*," she said and waddled back to church. "Where are the children?" I shouted after her. She paid no further attention to me. I had spoken in English.

The shed door creaked eerily as I pushed it open. Inside the shed, slants of sun pencilled *Forlorn* upon an earthen floor. There were signs of recent occupation: a few crumpled quilts, wool blankets, doll figures scissored from newspapers, a deflated rubber ball. I saw nothing that might have belonged to Bluejean, no clothing, no knapsack—nothing. Perhaps padre José had her things. Perhaps the children who must have played and slept here, until her disappearance, had taken them. Or the old woman. Or agents of PRED, that grotesque acronym. The place looked tidy, too tidy. No signs of violence, only a dark stain on the earthen floor, which, when I knelt and smeared it with my finger and whiffed it, yielded the odor of urine. Where were the children? *¿Dónde están?* I seemed to hear Archbishop Mendoza's shaky voice amplifying in the silence.

I returned to the church prepared to give another 500 pesos to the old woman, but the church was empty. I returned to the street squinting eyes against the terrible light until my sunglasses were fumbled on. Enrique stood talking with a hollow-cheeked man in blue coveralls, a cart with paraffin cylinders beside them. I saluted the paraffin salesman with two fingers to the forehead. "Discovered anything?" I asked Enrique.

Enrique nodded excitedly. "*Sí.* The church is more than 300 years old. *¡Qué preciosa!*"

"Ask him what he knows about the people here."

After a rapid-fire verbal exchange, Enrique turned to me. "He does not live here. He comes once a week. He says, '*todo el mundo es más apretado que un traje de torero.*' These people are tighter than a matador's trousers. The business, *mal.*"

"Ask him if he would like to earn 5,000 pesos."

"*Sin problema,*" Enrique said after translating to the paraffin salesman what I wanted done. A few minutes later an exceedingly eager paraffin salesman was almost running around the plaza, beating his tire iron against a cylinder, shouting in Spanish, "One thousand pesos for the boy who knows the whereabouts of the American lady with one leg! One thousand pesos!," while Enrique and I observed from a distance.

"Everyone will know," Enrique groaned.

"I want everyone to know."

"It's okay," Enrique shrugged.

Presently the paraffin salesman beckoned to us. My stomach tightened. We crossed the plaza to the spot where the conjuror was standing beside his magic box.

Negotiations began at once. Was it the boy in the box who had found the body? Yes. Where was his father? Killed by the death police. Was the father employed by Earthco? In the mines, yes. Did the boy know padre José? Yes. When did he last see padre José? The first day of the *orfanato*. What did he tell the old woman? He told the old woman he was playing near a mine and saw evil birds and found the body of the American woman from the orphanage, the woman with one leg. Did he look closely at the body? Yes. What did he see? A wound in the head.

"Ask him if this is the woman." I gave Bluejean's passport, open to the photograph, to Enrique, who translated to the conjuror as he had throughout. The conjuror placed the passport in the boy's mouth and waited. "*Sí*," said the conjuror after what seemed an interminable pause and returned the passport.

"Will he lead us to the mine at once?"

It would depend.

One thousand pesos.

Ten thousand, said the conjuror.

I held up four fingers.

He held up six.

I held up five.

It became a deal: 3,000 pesos to the boy upon proof of his story, 2,000 to the conjuror, and another 3,000 to the paraffin salesman to guard Enrique's car with his tire iron. We all returned to the church, the conjuror and the salesman evidently deciding who would buy the first drink, a little Indian boy in rags and a turban trailing behind, kicking stones. I took the shovel from the trunk of the car. Then Enrique and I followed the boy through dusty streets and out of Atamoro.

As the village dropped from sight below us, the air cooled and a few hardy wild flowers trembled in patches of snow. After following a boulder-strewn shelf road for about a quarter of an hour, the Indian boy stopped. He was pointing to some old tailings above the road. I could barely make out a small, half-concealed mine shaft entrance framed by rotting timbers. The dirt incline showed evidence of trampling. I approached the shaft.

A tiny lizard with its tail in its mouth lay curled on a timber. I crawled into the mine. The air was cold as one of Bluejean's empty refrigerators. Darkness rushed out in a kind of palpable kiss to my laboring breath. I took off my sunglasses. I stood, slowly, and flicked Enrique's cigarette lighter. There, flung in a hollow to the side of the walkway, she lay Egypt-eyed, serene save for the wound in her head and for the prosthesis bent at a gruesome angle beneath her. She was dressed in jeans and a ski parka. I went and straightened the prosthesis, then I crawled out of the mine and sucked fresh air.

A hummingbird darted outrageous iridescence.

The Indian boy studied me without expression. I turned to Enrique. "Ask him how much for the turban."

"He doesn't know," Enrique presently declared.

"Tell him 10,000 pesos."

"*¿Cómo?*"

"Tell him to go to the city. To get the hell out of Atamoro."

"*¡Estupendo!*"

I went to the boy, removed his turban, and tousled his jet-black hair. When I had counted out the big notes, he took them, ran.

"Enrique?"

"¿Señor?"

"I want you for a witness. Bring the shovel."

We returned to the mine. I collected splinters of powder-dry wood, lit a small fire beside the body, and pondered what to do.

Bluejean's wedding ring caught my eye. I tried to pull it off, but the finger was swollen. I raised the shovel intending to sever the finger and retrieve the ring as evidence of Bluejean's existence, but icy perspiration broke out on my face and I lowered the shovel.

"*¡Horrible!*" Enrique muttered.

"Help me with the parka. Try not to leave fingerprints. Here, use this." I showed Enrique how to use the turban as a glove.

It took us five minutes to remove that parka. A forearm scar revealed the Virgin's stab. When we had finished the job, the fist in my stomach wanted to explode. I looked about. Close to the body, the mine shaft was collapsed upon the walkway. One rotten timber still restrained the wall. I unraveled the turban, tied it in a band around the parka, and told Enrique to go outside, carrying the parka by the band. Then I heaved and dragged the body to a narrow place beneath the sagging wall. I scooped up the fire with the shovel. Soon flames licked lizard tongues into rotten timber and tongues became serpents and smoke gushed from crackling consummation. I stumbled up the walkway and emerged in an acrid and choking world of light just as the wall collapsed with a thunderous *crump* followed by the commemorative silence of implosion until the hummingbird could be heard squeal-darting in streaks.

As smoke and dust were clearing, I became aware of being surrounded and watched by armed men in rubber boots and at the same time heard a man's voice, loud, gruff, and guttural:

"*¡Usted!, señor Woolpack. ¿Quiere que le devuelva su plata?*" The man barked a laugh.

Flat rounded faces. Intensely dark eyes. Soiled denim work clothes. Rifles. In the movies these men would have been cutthroats with greasy sombreros and bandoleers. In reality the occupation may have been the same. The dust had cleared from the appalling earth. In the moment that these suddenly interesting acquaintances of John Woolpack realized they had mistaken my identity, I saluted with two fingers to forehead, turned my back, and walked away. The fist in my stomach had exploded into words.

You, Woolpack! Want your money back?

Now the carefully sandbagged feelings of years were giving way to flood. The hand that clutched a tumbler of scotch was trembling. I could hardly bear the sound of happy voices and the lilting thrum of guitar and harp.

Once, in the war orphan's school in Budapest, when I was five, there was that nude sculpture of a girl kneeling, lifting her gaze, her long hair blowing back. My master told me the girl's name was Soul. He said I would one day meet her incarnate. In my innocence I believed him. Experience seemed to teach otherwise. There was no mystic soul incarnate in girls, though some were kind. Suddenly before my disavowing eyes I knew my master had been right. Lovely through the garden she came.

"My name is Teresa."

"Huh?"

"Teresa."

"Oh. Hi."

"Enrique has told me so much about you. Enrique is my brother."

"Have we met before?"

She cocked her head. "I don't think so."

"When I was a boy, you were the girl I dreamed about."

"You are being whimsical."

"Forgive me," I said. And met her gaze a long time before she lowered hers.

"No," she said in an even tone, "forgive *me*. It is possible we have met before. In dreams, as you say. You are crying."

I waited for the reflexive gush to ebb. "It's going away. Excuse me."

"I understand," she said gently, then brightened. "I hope we don't have to apologize to each other all evening, Mr. Szabo."

"Paul."

"Paul."

"No more apologies... You are very beautiful, Teresa."

Her bright dark eyes danced to mine. "Thank you. Was she beautiful, your wife?"

"Teresa?"

"Yes?"

"I need to talk with someone."

"I'm here, Paul."

I must have been gazing at her a long time when I heard myself saying in a sort of murmurous rapture, "I believe you are."

"When would you like to talk?"

"We couldn't have chosen a better time to start," I said.

That is how we began, Teresa and I, with the predilection of the eyes.

I don't remember all that we talked about. We sat side by side on a bench in an evening perfumed by eucalyptus and distantly stirred by harp and guitar and by the clapping of people dancing the *cueca*. But eventually, as I recall, I spoke of Woolpack. Bluejean had called to tell me that Teapot was staying with Woolpack. Why had Woolpack denied having seen either Bluejean or Teapot? From whom, if not Woolpack, had Bluejean learned about Atamoro and perhaps been made to feel secure in going there? Had he gone there the day after her arrival? Had she gone walking with him into the mountains? Who were those men who spoke of getting money back from Woolpack, and why did they assume that the only gringo at the site of the murder would be Woolpack? At one point in all this airing of suspicion, Teresa rested her hand warmly on mine and asked, "What does your little girl look like?"

"Well," I said, "she has cornflower-blue eyes and peaches-and-cream complexion and the most marvelous—really the most marvelous—poise for someone her age I've ever seen... You know what? She was in this hot spring and let this big bullsnake crawl all over her, and she just called him Fred, and... Here, I've got a picture of her." I showed Teresa the passport picture of Bluejean and Teapot.

"Is this Christina?"

"Yeah, yeah, it's she. See that little cowlick?"

Teresa rose and studied the picture by floodlight and returned to the bench. Old Hawkeye laser-beamed her moves.

"Paul," she said after a swift glance over her shoulder, "I believe I can help you."

"I don't want you mixed up in this, Teresa."

"You don't understand. I know this little girl."

"You what?"

"I know her. She's the new little girl at the English School where I work."

"You mean—?"

"Her father enrolled her in the school a few days ago."

"Her father?"

"Señor Woolpack. He had some papers that proved he is the father, in addition to adoption papers dated the same day. Strange... The headmaster, who told me these things, hesitated to admit Christina. But Señor Woolpack said her mother was dead. It was important for the sad little girl's peace of mind that she come to school for a few days before the Christmas holidays when he is taking her to New York. Señor Woolpack had to pay an entire term's tuition. The girl's name is Christina Woolpack."

5

WHEN Teresa told me in the garden that Teapot was now Christina Woolpack, my initial reaction was—*I always knew his intention.* The old son of a cowboy had adopted his own daughter and legalized her existence by giving her his name. He had exercised his rights under the terms of that American affidavit about nonrelinquishment of parental rights. Perhaps Woolpack had lured Bluejean to Pacífica, her murder a mere statistic in the sum total of disappearances to be attributed to the military government. Perhaps Woolpack had lured Bluejean to Atamoro. It was an Earthco fiefdom where either Woolpack or those hired workmen could have carried out the murder. Perhaps Woolpack had friends in the Pacifican government to cover up his crime, and perhaps he had friends in the American government, too, and if the American government were covertly supporting General Scarpio through the agency of Earthco, where might that leave me in any attempt to rescue Teapot? In the football stadium, that was where.

As I've said, there are deep-down feelings about which I didn't like to think. In the garden with Teresa I resisted dragging those feelings into the light, though one of them was this: I respected the man whom Bluejean had loved. They belonged to each other, married or unmarried.

Teresa and I formed a plan for me to see Teapot next day at lunch break at the English School. I would let Teapot know I loved her always.

With but an hour remaining before curfew, the party was breaking up, the men were no longer waving handkerchiefs in the air pretending to be roosters, Mamá's meat pies had been consumed, and everyone was hugging and embracing after the style of the country. When Old Hawkeye's attention had been distracted, I summoned up nerve to squeeze Teresa's hand, gently. She squeezed back.

Szabo was in love and loved!

Then I dashed, casting many backward glances at Teresa and wondering what fate held in store for us now that the sculpture of Soul had taken human form. Enrique gunned the motor. There was little time left for him to make the roundtrip to the Sheraton without falling prey to the dreaded *Partido Revolucionario Educacional Democrático*.

Late that night I wandered through the lobby of the Sheraton in full view of some officers who were drinking toasts with some of those clean Americans. The officers might have been agents of PRED. Dangling from a rag of a boy's turban in my hand was a blood-soaked ski parka. I was collecting evidence toward a day of corpus delicti when the dead could be raised and Bluejean's killer or killers brought to justice.

I went to my room on the eighteenth floor and was stuffing the parka in a plastic laundry bag when I heard a noise of crinkled paper. Upon unzipping a pocket, I found a sealed, unstamped Vicaría de la Solidaridad envelope in Bluejean's handwriting, addressed to me. Inside the envelope on the same stationery was the longest letter she had ever written to me.

As I read Bluejean's letter now after many years, I am again struck by its revelation of another side to her character. She remained the lost and feckless child of her times, playing with fire, finally consumed. That side of innocence still makes its impression: she seems unaware of what a person might have realized was a trap. Yet, reading between the lines, I get another impression that she well recognized the danger of playing games and had decided to take the risks. I had been right to warn her over the telephone about playing a game in which one power makes all the rules. But I misjudged her determination to risk everything on a conclusion to such a game. That, I'm convinced, is what she had always wanted from Woolpack—a conclusion to his game. Whereas his and Grace's rules had in the past required that warm personal relationships be excluded from life, Bluejean's rules required that Woolpack recognize her natural power and be forced to accept a role in relation to it. Bluejean perpetuated her existence in Christina, reached at last beyond pain and pleasure, and at the supreme hour discovered time and eternity as two aspects of the same experience.

As I say, there was another side to her character. It was the side recognized immediately by reverendo Juanito, that good man whom, to my dismay, I had scorned when I thought he was fabricating saints. He had discerned in Bluejean a desire to be purged of egocentricity and the concomitant desire to sacrifice herself for others, whereas I, so long without communication from her, had not taken seriously her exaltation over the telephone: *They're sending me to the Andes to one of the copper-mining districts. It's important. It's the most important thing that ever happened to me...* Now, reading her letter again, I understand what she was trying to say. I dare to believe that, even as someone put a bullet through her head, she had come through her storm to the calm of transfiguration.

DEAR PAUL, she begins,

I'm high in the mountains in a village called Atamoro. It's a mining and mill village controlled by Jack's family since the last century. It's a little like the mill town where I was born in Connecticut, the place where my mother's family, the Biddegoods, built red-brick silk mills, lived in patriarchal splendor, and employed emigrant workers at near-starvation wages. Well, one reason I'm in Atamoro is that Jack is going to introduce reforms in all of the Earthco operations. He becomes director of Earthco after Christmas, when we go to New York. The other reason I'm in Atamoro is to start an orphanage. The fascists came before dawn yesterday and left dozens of children with no place to go, nothing to eat. I have some of these children here with me. Father Joe rustled up some grub for them. I know you won't believe this, but I cooked it! Now the children are asleep on the ground. Teapot's here, too, sleeping. She asked where's Daddy. I told her you have come home from the war. She cried. She has been very anxious about you all year. When can I see Daddy, she asked. I told her soon as we go to New York after her birthday, we'll then head for Arizona and be seeing you. I care about you, Paul. I care about you so much I could cry.

God, god, I wanted so badly to talk with you early this afternoon back at the Solidarity office. I just felt so goddam nervous. The words wouldn't come out right. I didn't mean the things I said.

About you, that is. I meant it about a divorce, though. You need a good woman. You'll find her and deserve her, too.

I've been a long time in my development. I owe a lot to you. You picked me up almost literally—note fancy words used by Bluejean—and tried to make things work for us. But I couldn't change. When you were in Nam, and you would be coming home expecting to make things work for us, I panicked. Like sick panic, man. I went to a shrink. I told him that my father abused me, which is true as you know, and that my mother kicked me not just out of the house but out of my country. The shrink didn't believe me. Hysterical, he said. Lots of women like you have fantasies about their fathers. Well, I said, it doesn't matter a hill of beans what you believe. You could check it out with the shrinks in Hartford or with my mom, but my dad died of alcoholism thirteen years ago. So the hell with it. But, I told him, I've loved a man since I was fifteen years old and I still love him in spite of trying to forget him. And, I told him, Jack wants to marry me. He's free. I'm going to marry him. The shrink said Whatever. He had a live one. He wanted to interpret my dreams. Look, I said, haven't you ever heard of morality?... remorse? Look, I said, you're going to tell me that my repressed feelings are the cause of my concern about oppressed people. Man, I said, you're the hysterical one. I have to hurt somebody who's important to me and to my daughter. I have to give a good man pain. That's my panic. Well, said the shrink, you just graduated.

Paul, I'm going to marry Jack. He and Grace are divorced. They'd been married ever since the invention of frogspit, on account of the Woolpack Will.

But this summer Jack couldn't wait any longer. Now he has only to wait for his father's money to come to him indirectly through Teapot instead of always going to Grace. Personally I don't care about the money. Jack, though, can't fulfill his dreams without it. So we flew on down here where Grace is now living in the old Woolpack mansion called Casa Roja. Under the terms of the Will, Jack has to establish Teapot's identity legally before Grace. Am I sorry for Grace? She keeps the mansion. She has her house in London. Oh, I almost forgot: Grace has remarried. We don't know who he is except that he's some colonel in the army here. We'll probably meet him on Christmas Day—Teapot's eleventh birthday! God, god, I can't believe it! Eleven years old Christmas. She's going to be so beautiful, I can't believe she's really my child. Anyway, Jack and I will be living at Paradise Ranch. You'll see plenty of Teapot. Jack really likes you...

It was now clear to me that Bluejean, Teapot, and Woolpack had flown to Pacífica together for the purpose of meeting Grace. The meeting had taken place at La Casa Roja on the night of Bluejean's arrival in Ciudad de Pacífica, the eve of the revolution.

Her letter continued...

The last time I had seen Grace was in London over eleven years ago. I'll always remember it: you looked so handsome in your tux, and you proposed to me like you wouldn't take no for an answer, and we blew that fly-trap. Grace, that time, was your typical stiff-uppers-and-thank-you-very-much la-de-da English upper-class bitch, but she wasn't bad-looking, sort of a plastic Botticellian Venus. She still has the diamonds. Looks, no way. She's fat and has hair like a blue-rinsed Medusa and wears loud pink.

We had dinner at her house night before last. I was bummed out, but Grace insisted we all come over. She wanted Jack to drive to this village of Atamoro and attend to some Earthco business. So we were going to come here yesterday morning. Then, yesterday morning, we woke up and everybody's saying it's revolution time, barricades of rubber tires and stones going up. Look, Jack, I said, I'm going for it...

It was late on the morning of the outbreak of revolution. Bluejean left Teapot with Woolpack and went wandering into the city as though street-to-street fighting and people hurling their bodies under tanks were a theatre benefit. About the time in early afternoon when she was caught up in a crowd taking snapshots of the sun, the stump of her leg had been rubbed raw by the prosthesis. She stumbled—"literally"—into the cathedral.

The letter never mentions her leaving the passport with reverendo Juanito, yet I believe she wanted him to secure her ID against the possibility of something happening to her in Atamoro. Juanito had insisted to me that she fully understood the risks. Her leaving the passport with him was a hedge against disappearance. She established credentials, so to say, for going to Atamoro. Not a joyride anymore, the journey came under the auspices of the Church and left a tentative network of persons aware of her whereabouts. I infer from the fact that she telephoned me from the archbishop's office, not from the Earthco Building, that she was setting up a connection between me and Solidarity, an Ariadne's thread with which, if she disappeared, I might find my way out of the labyrinth of insignificant death. She used Solidarity stationery, I infer, with the purpose of writing me immediately upon arrival in Atamoro. So, bone-weary, she had stumbled against the star of the Virgin, and still further exhausted from the journey to Atamoro and from responsibilities for bitter and bewildered orphans, she nonetheless chose to stay up all night and write me the longest letter of her life. The conclusion was plain: urgent, conscious awareness of high stakes.

The letter concludes...

> *Juanito couldn't believe I was ready to go to Atamoro immediately. After you hung up—I don't blame you, I really was a pain in the ass—I called Jack at Earthco and asked if the trip to Atamoro was still on. He said no problem. He said he admired my idealism in going to help orphans for a few weeks until Christmas, and, coming from him, that was pretty swell. He and Teapot picked me up from near the cathedral in a brand-new Mercedes with Earthco markings, loaned to us by Grace for our stay here. All hell was breaking loose, but nobody hassled us in an Earthco car. Jack slowed for blockades, got the salutes, and off we went. We got to Atamoro about five yesterday. Wow! What a fantastic experience it has been for me! Jack had to leave me and Teapot with Father Joe, to see to his business at the mill. He promised to be back by sunrise. Which it is. So, hey, guy, everything's going to be just great. Jack will take Teapot back to the city, and I'll stay here. I've made a commitment! I love it!*
> *BLUEJEAN*

I couldn't sleep. I lay sweating as pieces of the Woolpack

puzzle surfaced from depths to which, years before, I had tried to consign them. *The Will of the Woolpacks*, that was the key: one of those strange, legal bequests that enable rich fathers to persecute beyond the grave. If I now remembered correctly, Woolpack's father had established a Trust Fund, income from which was distributed to Grace for life, with two provisos. First, if Woolpack fathered a child, that child at the age of eleven not only automatically replaced Grace as beneficiary of the Trust but in fact received the capital of the Trust. Second, if Woolpack had no child and Grace died, the capital would go to charity. That was the Will, and at the time of the death of Woolpack's father in the early fifties there had been no children. The marriage was barren. Enter Bluejean. Enter Bluejean's baby, Woolpack's baby approaching her eleventh birthday on Christmas Day. Now, if I surmised correctly, sleeping in the penthouse of the Earthco Building.

I went to the window and pondered that skyscraper. A checkerboard of lights pricked its lustrous sheen. Beneath the red beacon, Teapot lay. She was safe.

A chilling sensation slithered across the thin flesh of my heart. *Was* she safe? The sensation coiled in my throat and stopped my breathing. My eyes sought stars. There was a black abyss out of which Teapot's eyes stared, receding into illimitable void. Suddenly I became her eyes. We were looking down from insuperable height and seeing the vanishing Earth, a wee barren ball of ice with the brilliance of one of Grace's diamonds thrown in the air.

At three in the morning, I put on swim trunks and robe, locked my room, took the elevator to the basement, and was presently diving into the submerged light of the hotel's outdoor swimming pool. I floated on my back and looked at stars, Teapot's eyes now ineluctable in the firmament.

How they seemed serenely to smile at creatures small! About half an hour later, I returned to my room.

During my absence, it had been ransacked, the contents of suitcase and closet flung on the floor, and the mattress overturned. My first thought was, wallet and passport, but I found them where I left them, in the empty miniature refrigerator that is nowadays *de rigueur* for jet-setters; also in there were my last, half-finished bottle of scotch, Bluejean McQueen's and Christina Szabo's passport, the letter, and the unconfiscated stereo cassette player. *Bueno*—only the laundry bag with the blood-soaked parka inside it was missing from the mess on the floor. I removed swim trunks, crashed on the boxsprings, and fell instantly asleep.

Next morning, I shaved, showered, donned clean Levis, cowboy shirt, and bolo tie with the silver-set turquoise stone that Virgil had given me, went to the dining room, ate a huge breakfast, read a newspaper that said that General Scarpio was the savior of his country, returned to my room, secured my passport, and watched a TV rerun of a John Wayne movie until Enrique called from the lobby to say that Teresa and Christina would be waiting for us at noon in the garden of the English School. Soon we were on our way.

Far from being a foreign enclave, for a century and a half the English grammar school had been established for the bilingual education of Pacifican children of both sexes and all social classes and, as such, was a sort of recompense for all the wealth that foreigners had leeched out of the country. That Bluejean's baby—now Christina Woolpack—had been enrolled in one of the finest schools in the hemisphere was indeed a point in Woolpack's favor. Grace had gone to the expense of putting *me* through Hurtfield in London. She had even changed my name, at least informally, to Paul Woolpack. She had done things for me, an orphan and an exile, that were once beyond my dreams. So, now, I had to have a degree of confidence in what John Woolpack as guardian could give my Teapot: far more opportunities in life than a low-income, deracinated US Army lifer could hope to provide. One hug, one kiss of farewell, that was all I could give.

It came to pass that I met Teapot in the garden of the school that noon. It would be disingenuous of me to pretend that the brief reunion was anything less than a swoon of heartbreak. Outside the school's open, wrought-iron gates, two blocks away on a leafy street Enrique waited as ordered, while I vaulted a low brick wall into the humid, perfumed air of a garden rioting with tropical bushes and flowers. There I waited and watched as in the distance a flock of children was let out to play, followed, to one side, by Teresa, who was leading by the hand a sad little girl in pigtails, leading her slowly enough to give the impression that a kind of botany lesson was in progress but leading her ever nearer to our place of rendezvous—and then the release, like the wail of a seabird in flight, O *daddydaddydaddy* as she flung herself on my neck and I pressed sobbing kisses into the dear warmth of her hair and onto her hot salt cheeks, there in the dispossessing garden.

"You'll have to hurry," I heard Teresa saying in a stage whisper. "They only have ten minutes before lunch."

I looked long into Teapot's final eyes and said, "Mommy's dead. Did they tell you?"

"They said she disappeared."

"Do you know what that means?"

Teapot nodded gravely. "A soldier takes you away when everyone is *sleeping*," she said on a rising intonation of disgust.

"And were you sleeping when Mommy disappeared?"

"I slept *all* night. I didn't cry *one* bit. Those other kids pissed on the floor. Yuck."

"Did Mr. Woolpack come and take you away from the

orphanage?"

"He took Mr. Joe."

"Father José? the priest?"

"Yes."

"How did you leave the mountains?"

"That *big* truck." Teapot spread her arms and nodded as if to confirm a vague remembrance.

"Tea, sweetheart," I asked, gripping her shoulders, "was it like a big army truck—you know what they look like—or was it like a truck used for construction, a dump truck?"

Teapot puckered her mouth, brightening, and replied by shifting her gaze from side to side, "It was one of Mr. Woolpack's trucks."

"Earthco," I said to Teresa.

"Hurry," Teresa said. "I heard something from the street."

"And Mr. Woolpack has adopted you?"

Teapot nodded silently.

"Sweetheart," I resumed hurriedly, "did Mommy ever tell you that Mr. Woolpack is your father?"

She pondered and nodded silently.

"And do you understand that you can't live with Daddy for a while but Daddy will always love you?"

"Are you going to marry Miss Teresa?" Teapot asked.

"Do you like Miss Teresa?"

Teapot nodded with wide eyes.

"Miss Teresa and I are going to talk about it. Okay? Daddy has to go now. Okay? Is Mr. Woolpack being nice to you?"

Teapot lowered her gaze and nodded. "Good-bye, Daddy," she said.

"Good-bye, sweetheart. I love you."

When we hugged, her little bones had stiffened. She turned and ran without looking back. I watched her disappear between two lilac bushes and was about to wave my hand when a sound of violently rustled leaves distracted me and I saw, like images on a screen, passionless faces, those of Easter Island heads, popping from concealment, the chlorine-yellow uniforms, lustreless brass, and unpolished boots betraying a certain lack of military propriety in the proceedings.

"*¡Usted!*" one of these clowns beckoned me with forefinger. "*¡Usted!*" he barked at Teresa.

They pushed us inside a windowless police van without license plates and told us to exchange no words with one another or with the three other people. Opposite us on a bench sat a longhaired young man with effeminate features, and a muscular functionary in a business suit. There on the floor of the van sprawled the twitching body of the possible victim of torture: he was a young man, all skin and bones, his visage as chalky as a mime's, his teeth chattering. I wrapped my arms around Teresa, pulled her head to my chest, stroked her hair.

It was the football stadium all right. Arriving in the glare of sun we were hustled through a maze of concrete girders and finally to an interior mezzanine. Here we were told to wait in line—a file of men and women stretched fifty meters ahead of us—and to remain silent, though smoking was permitted. The nauseating odor of chain-smoked cigarettes thickened the air, but the silence—it was the silence that appalled me. It was not a natural silence but a kind of dull anticipation of the eardrums in between intervals of cushioned machine-gun fire. Not your ordinary machine gun's chattering staccato, but one so absurd... then I knew. Somewhere out on the playing field those clowns were executing people with the six-inch armor-piercing shells from an old, belt-fed .50 caliber, the kind that used to get so overheated in combat against tanks and human waves that the barrel would become molten red and explode.

I continued to hold Teresa tightly against me. I told her I loved her. She whispered she loved me too.

Slowly, the line shuffled forward. After a while, I saw that we were moving toward a table behind which sat an officer and several civilian functionaries. They were examining ID, consulting lists, whispering behind cupped hands, and deciding which of us was to join a queue, which to be dragged through a metal door that needed oiling. When it came my turn, the OIC studied me for a long time, then tongued a mustache like a raised eyebrow and said:

"Norteamericano."

"*Sí.*"

"Pasaporte."

"*Sí,*" I said, adding, "señor." I presented my passport. One look at it and he tossed his head in the direction of the queue. "*¿Amigo?*" he asked Teresa, indicating me.

"*Sí,*" she said.

The OIC again tossed his head in the direction of the queue.

He had not returned my passport. I saw it handed to a functionary who placed it in a carton marked Coca-Cola. Later I watched the functionary take the carton across the mezzanine and deliver it to another functionary at the entrance to an office door toward which our queue was moving.

Everything is happening at dream-speed.

We stand enchanted at that door. It is guarded by a soldier in a clean uniform. He opens the door for me. I am hugging Teresa tightly. He permits the two of us to enter. It is a small office manned by half a dozen junior-grade officers and a number of bored functionaries. One officer sits behind a desk and looks at my passport. He asks me to give my name. It is a stupid question. I give my name. He half smiles. He returns my passport.

*"One mo-*ment, *please," he says. He rises and knocks on the door to an inner office, enters it, closes the door, opens it and gestures for me to come. "El coronel von Albensleben," he says.*

I seem to hear Juanito's words. I have a schoolfriend who emigrated from Hungary. Perhaps you know him—el coronel von Albensleben? One of the most feared men... We enter the office and the picture freezes. I do not look surprised in this picture. Neither does the tall young officer with close-cropped blond hair and powder-blue eyes. A smile spreads back from his lips. His arms are opening for an embrace. How stupid it is, I am thinking, as fear and relief, shame and gratitude tumble together.

How stupid it is to be condemned by the son of the man whom he thinks I killed and whom I alone, perhaps, know was his father. How stupid and yet how sad it is for my schoolfriend to be living under a fictitious name because his real identity had suffered a disappearance.

"Günter," I pronounced in a voice above a whisper.

His own voice was vibrant with geniality. "Pál! Pál Szabó! Once you saved my life. Now I am at your service. Logic, simple logic!"

He had spoken in Hungarian. I pulled Teresa into my arms and stroked her hair. "It's all right, all right," I said over and over as her body shook violently and her heart beat next to mine.

PART FIVE

1

AS Christmas Day of 1973 drew near, La Casa Rico de las Golondrinas—"The Swallows"—became the scene of celebration. Word of Teresa's forthcoming marriage had spread rapidly through the city, and people from all walks of life came to shower her with affection, to consume Papá's wine and Mamá's meat pies, and to inspect someone known as The Good Gringo. That personage had never imagined, when he proposed marriage on the evening of the very day that Günter had saved him and Teresa from possible execution, that so much love was possible from so many. Uncles, aunts, cousins, nieces, nephews, neighbors, old chums, students, workers, soldiers, and even the barrio bastards begat by don Augusto came streaming in by noon each day and went reeling home before curfew each night. We ate and drank and laughed and danced. Pacificans formed one big family. I exulted in belonging to it.

Teapot was missing all the fun—and news of the surprise that awaited her on Christmas Day. I had three tickets for the flight to Miami then. One of them would be hers. Günter was going to bring Teapot to the airport. Günter would take Teapot away from Woolpack and deliver her to my custody. I trusted Günter.

We were there in Günter's office at the football stadium. He was coming forward to embrace me, exclaiming, "Pál! Pál Szabó! Once you saved my life. Now I am at your service. Logic, simple logic!," words of my father's adding a touch of nostalgia. Fear and relief, shame and gratitude tumbled together. My old school friend, now the dreaded Colonel Günter von Albensleben, had been told by Malakov that I was exchanging my life for his. Günter had already commanded me to execute Malakov. When Günter saw me from a bus window in Vienna, he must have concluded that I had first tricked Malakov, so that Günter was released at the Austrian border, and then killed him. In Günter's office at the football stadium I realized in a flash what my old friend was thinking. In the same flash I realized that I was guilty of the attempted murder of Günter's own father. By means of a curious reversal, it was not I who had a claim upon Günter's life, for I had never saved him, but Günter who had a claim upon mine. As a result of these instantaneous reflections, as we stood in Günter's office, I realized I must at all costs keep Günter believing that he owed his life to me.

After embracing me, Günter gripped my shoulders and beamed upon me with eyes that removed to charmed distance whatever duties he performed for General Scarpio's dictatorship. "Well, well, look at my Jewish cowboy," he said in Hungarian, "now destiny has brought us together again... Unfortunately, I was not informed until a few minutes ago of your presence in the country. Your file escaped my notice." Günter pointed to a manila folder on his desk. "You've been busy since your arrival. You've been to the Vicaría de la Solidaridad. Also to Atamoro on a safe conduct. I'm sure there is a simple explanation for the blood-stained jacket in your room at the Sheraton... Pál, I shall not ask questions. I shall issue a personal directive that you and the señorita are free to do anything you wish... No, no, don't thank me, I insist." Günter waved open hands in the air. "On my word of honor, the officer who ordered your arrest will be subjected to discipline. The matter is closed... *Sin problema*," he added with a nod to Teresa and went on in Spanish. "This is an old comrade of mine. To him I owe my life... I assume, Pál, that you took care of your father's persecutor?"

"Yes," I said. "Already you have asked me a question, Günter."

Günter's intense expression relaxed into a grin and a playful thump of hand against sun-burned forehead, cropped yellow hair. "*¡Por dios!* A bad habit one acquires... You have a foxy mind. Like your father's... We must become reacquainted in surroundings more conducive to interrogation. What did you say when you pushed the noodles in Zoltan's face? 'How do you know if the broom is good until it sweeps the floor?' And your father who said in squeaky voice, 'Logic, simple logic,' whenever two plus two did not equal four..." Günter threw back his head in an abrupt laugh. "Always some good times to remember... Now come and see the new Mercedes-Benz that my rich old wife has provided me. ¿Señorita?"

That afternoon Günter transformed himself from a terrorist to our personal chauffeur. At the English School he strode into the headmaster's office, apologized for the inconvenience caused by Teresa's absence, delivered an impromptu speech pledging the government's support for education, requested and got an invitation to speak to the children in the new year about his hobby, collecting semi-precious stones such as red *jaspe*, yellow *azufre*, and black *obsidiana*. I dreaded to meet Teapot and was glad the children had left school. Presently Günter accompanied us to where Enrique was parked, eyes glued to a girlie magazine. Soon he was demonstrating to Enrique the wonders of a Mercedes's engine and instrument panel. Later, as we drove toward "The Swallows," Günter waxed eloquent about such received ideas as the excellence of Pacifican wine and the benefits of social order. Arrived at Teresa's home, he leapt from the car, strolled to a eucalyptus tree, stripped off a piece of bark and inhaled it with an expression of delight.

Don Augusto, as can well be imagined, locked up the passports he had been forging, informed Mamá that she was a brute, an animal, and a disgrace, downed a tumbler of brandy at one gulp and strode toward Günter with the look of a man accustomed to greeting high-ranking officers in the manner of Hitler's best friend.

We went into the house for tea. I was dizzy from the volatility and ambiguity of events. I recall saying to myself: I've buried Bluejean, fallen in love, parted from Teapot, been arrested, faced possible execution by a .50 caliber machine gun, been rescued by an old friend and invited to tea by a man who forges passports and sleeps with chickens. Günter is a man who makes people disappear, collects stones, and savors the fragrance of eucalyptus. I shall propose to Teresa tonight.

In the days before festivities commenced, I saw much of Günter. Sometimes we dined at the Sheraton till midnight, most times at "The Swallows" with the family. I told him stories about myself and described how Woolpack and I contended for custody of a child. Günter listened carefully to my stories and told his own. He was the same old Günter. He still believed that his father had been an officer of Hitler's Third Reich and was somewhere in South America, ranching with the help of non-Jewish cowboys. It did not surprise me that he had created for himself a mirage personality. It still functioned according to a predetermined set of rules and could be discarded, like a pair of polished boots, when a day's work was done. He was married to a woman whom he described as "a rich, older woman who is crazy as hell and speaks little Spanish." He seemed genuinely fond of me. There were times when I caught him looking at me with an expression of secret sorrow. The look was, I supposed, inherited from Malakov. I kept the thought to myself.

He would do surprising things. Once as he was driving me back to the hotel after dinner with the family, he slammed on the brakes in a poor barrio of the city and exclaimed, "There's the man who runs after dinner!" Leaving the engine on, Günter dashed from the car and intercepted a man who was jogging together with five children along a badly lighted avenue of misty palms. Günter was tall and beefy in a tight-fitting uniform. Shaking his hand was a small, bearded, shabbily dressed man so emaciated he resembled a crudely carved New Mexican *santo*. The children—three boys, two girls—were clad only in shorts and shifts, and they too looked to be mere skin and bones. But happy children stifling giggles and darting mercurial glances at Günter, at me. Günter took some money from his billfold and gave it to the man; then the man showed the money to the children, and one by one they came forward and hugged Günter around the neck. Günter returned to the car beaming. As he engaged the gear, I looked over my shoulder to see silhouetted ragamuffins waving.

"Come now, Günter," I said in teasing voice, "you've been holding out on me. Don't tell me that the terrible Colonel von Albensleben has a gold heart."

Günter grinned with good teeth. "Oh," he said, "perhaps."

"What did you mean by 'the man who runs after dinner?'"

"He runs after dinner, Pál, because there is never enough dinner. What little there is, he gives to his children. Then, because they are still hungry, he says to them, 'Come along, children, we go to run until we are too tired to be hungry.' He used to have a job washing dishes at the military academy. He is out of work now... The children call me Tío Günter as if I am an old man."

I saw a chance, played a card. "Tell me about your wife, Günter. Do you have children?"

"No," he replied with a nervous chuckle. "We have money. No children." A smile twitched at the corner of his mouth. No more questions, the smile said. I took my pipe from my Palm Beach jacket, lit it, puffed, and spoke as if nothing of consequence were on my mind. "Teresa and I would like to take Teapot with us on Christmas Day. Teapot is already fond of Teresa, and Teresa will be a good mother."

Günter drove in silence. Just then we passed the cathedral. "You see," I resumed, "I haven't been able to find Bluejean's and Teapot's passport. But perhaps your government would issue Teapot a new one. Bluejean's passport would then vanish as a document proving she came to Pacífica and cease to complicate relations between Pacífica and the United States."

Günter shrugged. "She is now Christina Woolpack. She has been adopted in this country."

"Then you get her a visa. You have the power, old friend."

"Of *course*," Günter declared with guarded emphasis. "I will arrange the visa."

"Thank you, Günter. Thank you very much." I puffed the pipe, played another card. "You have my word of honor to remain silent about Bluejean's disappearance, until the proper time."

"What means this 'proper time?'"

"The proper time for your government to prosecute Woolpack for the murder. An American affair *solamente*. A chance for your government to improve relations with the United States."

"Pál, Pál," Günter chuckled without cracking a smile, "you are incredibly naive about international affairs. To prosecute señor Woolpack now or at any time in future is out of the question... General Scarpio has declared amnesty for anyone believed responsible for a disappearance. Therefore your wife's death is without legal remedy. We cannot prosecute because we cannot convict. Even if, for the sake of argument, the law of amnesty were not applied in this case, where is your evidence? Do you have a witness?"

"Perhaps—" I blurted.

"Perhaps, you think, this padre José of the village of Atamoro will identify the homicidal maniac you have created in your imagination. *You* don't know what has happened to this man... As for the so-called evidence which you have gathered so diligently, not a scrap of it—not your wife's letter, not your encounter with armed *obreros* at the alleged site of the crime, not the bloodstained jacket, and not the adoption of your little girl with the absurd name—none of this has validity... Wait! I know what you're going to say."

The body, I was saying to myself.

"The body, Pál. You were going to tell me that the body has been discovered. The body of an American woman—I regret having to be blunt—implies ipso facto that my government can be embarrassed, that the United States might break off diplomatic relations, that the World Bank will withhold loans from the country that has defeated communism, and so on, and so on. I must tell you, Pál, as my old friend, you must forget these fantasies... Listen carefully... If you mention the name of my country in a context of slander, your life and the lives of your loved ones, your family are in danger. Clear?"

I said nothing. Günter resumed after a pause, "I am not threatening you, I am protecting you... You mustn't think that PRED operates in isolation. Our agents operate throughout the world, often working for *other* agencies. Clear?" Günter fished a cigarette from his tunic and pushed the dashboard lighter. The lighter's glow touched a face that belied a cool voice. "Who has seen the body? A boy who wore a turban and who was bribed by you to run away. Enrique, a wonderful fellow but a fool. Señor Woolpack presumably and possibly some *obreros*. That leaves you. You executed Roman Malakov. Perhaps *you* are to be guilty of your wife's death?"

I said nothing.

"Pál, Pál, relax. You marry Doctor Teresa, have happiness, forget the game of power... You have buried your wife so well, you think, that one day her body can be exhumed, identified, and so on and so on... For a fact, I tell you the body has already been removed from Atamoro."

"You betrayed me," I said when I could speak.

He smoked for a while, crushed the cigarette in the ashtray. "Protected you, Pál, protected you... A moment ago you said you would keep silence about your wife's disappearance. But you have no power to make a deal. Nevertheless, I help you for old time's sake. On one condition. The condition is, you abide by the rules. The same condition for Woolpack."

"And what is this game?"

"I call it the Chalk Circle."

Günter attended festivities at "The Swallows." His

presence sent up my stock with don Augusto, and the story of my execution of a communist in Hungary helped to create my extraordinary reputation as "The Good Gringo."

One night at the crowded dinner table Günter exhibited new, spurious credentials of his own. Never one of the bright ones at school and a person without an intellectual's diffidence, he began to speak as if he were a philosopher. He was flushed with brandy and encouraged by Papá's obsequious chuckles. He fondled Ximenita on his knee and spoke in Spanish, Teresa translating any difficult parts by whispering in my ear.

"Once upon a time," he began in a "let's pretend" manner, "there was a penniless and beautiful Chinese girl named Haitang. She was loved by two men, the poor Prince Pao and the rich landowner, Ma. Now, Ma already had a wife, but she was barren, so he cast her aside and married Haitang. Prince Pao could not outbid such a powerful man. He returned broken-hearted to Peking where his father, the Emperor, held sway. Nine months later, Haitang bore Ma a son. Thus was aroused the hatred of Ma's barren first wife, who then poisoned her husband, threw suspicion for the murder on beautiful Haitang, and claimed the son as her own! Poor, poor Haitang... She was brought before a corrupt judge. He decided in favor of the first wife and ordered the execution of the girl. Oh, what to do? Well, in Klabund's version of *Der Kreidekreis*, a courier arrives announcing the death of the old Emperor and the accession of the new one, as well as bringing a command that all judgments be suspended and the litigants brought to Peking. There, the young Emperor (none other than Prince Pao!) decided the case by means of a chalk circle, in the center of which he placed the boy, asking each of the claimant mothers to pull him out. Haitang, the true mother, hesitated to use force on her own child, whereas the wicked first wife almost pulled his arms off, expecting, you see, to be declared the victor. Not so... Prince Pao awarded the child to Haitang because her refusal to use force proved her love. The wise young Emperor had based his judgment on the assumption that the true parent would refrain from handling a child roughly. Do you like the story, Ximenita?"

Ximenita smiled shyly.

"Other versions of the Chalk Circle come to the same conclusion," Günter continued, now addressing the rest of us at the dinner table. "There is a biblical version in which King Solomon commands that the child be cut in half, with the corpse divided between the natural mother and the child's nurse. The nurse, who loves the child, refuses this judgment, thereby becoming the victor... "

"Also in *Quijote* there is this story," Teresa broke in.

Günter waved his hand irritably. "Of course. Also in *Quijote*. I had forgotten... But the point is this: in every version there is a prior condition, namely the absolute authority of a kind-hearted judge. He is like God the Father always. That condition, my good friends, is stupid... We must erase fairy tales from our minds and consider reality. Do you agree with me, don Augusto?"

We all looked to see how The Greatest Man in the World would respond. There he was, sleeves of his white shirt rolled up, yellow stains under the armpits, his face unshaven. False teeth clicked in his mouth, and his Cyclopean eye, reddened by liquor, was drilling Mamá and Carmen, "The Peasant," to the cobwebbed wall. He flicked cigarette ash on the stone floor, cleared mucous from his throat, and pronounced the verdict. "*¡No seas gallina!* Don't be a coward!" All faces turned to Günter, who was lighting an English cigarette in impatience.

"In the position of reality," he began and stopped to remove a shred of tobacco from his tongue. "In the position of reality, which is the position of the world today, there is no authority. Only anarchy. Only the struggle for survival.

So, as my esteemed friend, don Augusto, has wisely implied, moral behavior is one thing in a system that provides predictable amounts and types of security, another thing where such security is lacking. In our story of the Chalk Circle, it is obvious that the state is secure and can indulge in judgments that give the illusion of justice founded upon gentle and loving behavior, that reject self-interested motives, and that rule against force as an element in disputes. When the state is not secure, however, the litigant who refrains from the use of force in order to win the dispute ignores his own survival. Exactly the opposite to the fairy tale of the Chalk Circle, you see? Force is not the outlawed element but the *necessary* element in disputes. One may even argue that loving kindness belongs to the litigant who uses force. Why? Because realism dictates a caring for one's possession—a child in our parable—that represents posterity. In short, children are the special care of those with the power to protect them, not of those who are too powerless to guarantee their future. If we now revise the story of the Chalk Circle according to realism, the parent who most loves the child *must* use force to become the victor... Doctor Teresa? Do I detect disagreement with this reasoning?"

Teresa, cheeks bright with rage, restrained her reply. "No, I don't disagree with your reasoning, given the premise of world anarchy. What you say is completely consistent with the struggle for power. But you are mistaken to believe that, as you expressed it, the position of the world today is identical with the position of reality."

"How so?" Günter asked guardedly.

"The struggle for power is obsolete," she replied. Her expression was determinate.

"Really? I'm sorry to disappoint the beautiful doctor, but perhaps I did not make myself entirely clear... You see, in our story of the Chalk Circle, we already observe the triumph of force: Prince Pao, who becomes emperor and judge, is predisposed to award the child to Haitang. A coalition existed prior to judgment. The Chalk Circle, therefore, is a pretext to disguise the reality of an alignment of self-interested power—"

"—You are being disingenuous, colonel," Teresa interrupted. "First, you refer to the child of the story as a possession. Second, you obscure the detail about two men who bid for Haitang's favors. Clearly she is a prostitute regarded also as property. Thus, you may be right to describe the story's meaning as a triumph of force, but the relationship of the man to the prostitute and her child is that of a master to slaves, not that of a strong man who secures a coalition for the sake of survival. In a true coalition in the world today, all powers have no choice but to limit force in order to avoid their mutual annihilation. That is why the original story of the Chalk Circle cannot be perverted. The true parent, loving the child for his own sake, symbolizes the only force for survival—psychological force, not political."

"Disgrace!" Papá exploded, sweeping chinaware and wine glasses onto the stone floor where they shattered. "Intellectual!"

"Schizophrenic!" Teresa shouted back. Mamá, Enrique, Willy, José Manuel, Ximenita, and assorted aunts and uncles began to laugh. The Greatest Man in the World staggered to his feet, hurled his chair against the wall, and stormed from the room. A violent squawking of chickens could be heard in the garden.

Günter rose from his chair and deposited Ximenita on the floor where she wouldn't be hurt by broken glass. He went into the garden and presently returned. "By order of General Scarpio," he declared with mock solemnity, "I have awarded the Medal of Valor to Augusto Rico de las Golondrinas for single-handedly capturing the Presidential Palace." Günter came sharply to attention and saluted. In came Papá, medal on his shirt, and surveyed the family with a smile of lofty disdain. "I have saved my country," he said.

"How modest!" Mamá giggled.

"You." Papá addressed Mamá. "You make too much noise washing dishes."

Enrique hooted.

"You," said Mamá to Papá, "make too much noise opening bottles."

Enrique kept hooting.

"Also," said Günter after relaxing his salute, "I have secured an appointment to *la Escuela Militar* for Willy and a commission in the Reserve for José Manuel so that he may work at the Military Hospital... Also—"

Everyone cheered.

Günter bowed and caught my eye. "Also for The Good Gringo, I have a surprise... By order of General Scarpio, a visa will be issued to a person named Christina Szabó... Well," he sighed pleasantly, "I must return Pál to the hotel before curfew. Otherwise I might disappear."

During the drive to the Sheraton, Günter was first to break silence. "This game of the Chalk Circle, do you comprehend, Pál?"

"Of course," I said. "We both learned about the *Causa Effectus* of power from my father."

"Good," Günter said. "Then you will be silent when the judgment of the Chalk Circle is effected on Christmas Day. Señor Woolpack will represent himself. I shall present your case. The judge will make her decision on the basis of an alignment of self-interested power."

"Her?" I queried.

"My wife."

"You said your wife is a rich, older woman who is crazy as hell and speaks little Spanish."

"Of course I said my wife is a rich, older woman who is crazy as hell and speaks little Spanish. But she is going to make me *president*!... Of course the people do not want a previously married and divorced woman to be the president's wife. But the people will forgive her... She has much influence with General Scarpio." Günter lowered his voice to a whisper. "My wife will get the visa for the absurd Teapot. My wife is a former acquaintance of yours... Grace Littlehale de Albensleben. You see?" Günter declared with a smirk. "It is all in the family. Now you comprehend the reality of the Chalk Circle."

After arriving at the hotel and collecting my room key from the desk clerk, I was handed a sealed envelope inscribed from the Vicaría de la Solidaridad. Inside was a penned note from reverendo Juanito, which read:

> *Coach Landree: Padre José wants meet*
> *with you tomorrow at 10:00 at Avenida*
> *Maximiliano O'Malley 1270, to discuss*
> *traditional poetry of Atamoro. Ask for*
> *Sr. Woolpack his apartamento at reception*
> *bureau. Also I come for the translation.*
> *Cordialmente, J.*

2

ABOUT three in the morning an earthquake snaked beneath Ciudad de Pacífica, enough to set the glass crystals of a mini-chandelier tinkling violently and to suck the water from the toilet bowl in a sort of deep-throated gobble. I caught the bottle of scotch as it fell from the bedside table. I poured myself two fingers of scotch and sipped slowly. The red beacon atop the Earthco Building went on blinking. I decided to call Teresa. She answered immediately.

"Hi. Sorry to call so late. You all right?"

"Hello, darling. I'm so glad you called. We're all right. The dogs are making a terrible racket. Papá is in the garden shaking his fist at the sky. Mamá and I are having a cup of coffee and laughing so much at Papá we could cry... I love you."

"I love you, too." I paused, plunged. "Does the Avenida Maximiliano O'Malley 1270 mean anything to you?"

"No... Wait. That's the Earthco Building. The bus passes by every day on the way to school... Wait. That's the address of Christina, the home address we have for her at the school. I meant to tell you but I forgot..."

"Don't worry about it. I have to go there tomorrow. Today, I mean. Don't you people ever go to sleep?"

"I'm going to keep you awake every night from now on."

"Who needs sleep? Look," I said, "a lot of things are happening. I'll tell you about them tomorrow. I mean tonight. Right now I want to tell the truth... I was a boy. I tried to carry out Günter's order to kill a man. I didn't kill him. My mother killed him. All the same, I have this horrible feeling that I am a criminal and that my honor is under a secret obligation to Günter. I despise him! But also... I want to be as strong as he is! He betrays my confidence, removing Bluejean's body, and I want to empty my soul to him... Another thing: he is married to Woolpack's former wife. I am under obligation to her, too. And she has betrayed me, too, in the old life! Our lives are in danger not only here but wherever we go... I'm madly in love with you. Excelsior!"

The handsome middle-aged American black woman at the reception desk of the Earthco Building was chatting with an armed Pacifican security guard when I sauntered into the marble-walled vestibule. She gave me the once-over with a deadpan expression.

"Hiya," I said. "Man name of Woolpack hangin' out here somewhere?"

She dialed a phone, tucking the receiver into chin, studying lacquered fingernails, and purred inaudible words. "Are you Paul?"

"If I have not love, I am nothing. Corinthians. Yup."

"Mr. Woolpack is expecting you. Top floor."

"Pre-chate it, ma'am."

The elevator was of the ultramodern kind that dings your arrival just as your stomach heaves itself into your throat. Doors parted. I stepped into tycoon heaven: white wall-to-wall carpet, air conditioning, vast plate-glass windows with claustrophobia on one side and vertigo on the other, paintings, potted palms, gleaming wooden antiques and foamy sofas like explosions of cottage cheese. There was a sound of splashing from a patio pool, and of men's voices.

"Come and have a drink, old man."

I whirled and there stood Woolpack. He wore a dressing gown that accentuated powerful shoulders and slim waist. His dark hair greying at the temples, his pencil-line mustache, his remarkable eyes and his tanned face made him seem younger than his fifty years. He clutched a highball.

"The others are in the pool. Two priests. That's an original Utrillo."

"Wha—?"

"On the wall."

"Oh." I saw a small oil painting of a street winding toward Sacré Coeur.

"My father bought it for $10,000. He once threw a dry martini on the canvas to prove what good *material* he had purchased." Woolpack cracked a wry smile. "I've considered stealing it, but my former wife owns everything you see. Temporarily, that is... I confine my kleptomania to unconsidered trifles—such as another man's wife." Woolpack's voice had shifted to a kind of groan.

"Wait," I said. "Let's deal with that right now."

"Please trust me, Paul, if you can." Woolpack moved close, and my heart filled with compassion. Next moment we were embracing. We were embracing with all the strength in our arms. "You didn't do it," I said.

"Thank you for believing in me." He drew back. "She always asks for her daddy."

"She's a good kid," I said.

"I've been thinking, Paul. I'm returning Christina to your custody as soon as financial arrangements are completed. I want you to have the ranch in Arizona. Perhaps you could live there. Perhaps you would be kind enough to allow me to visit Christina there once in a while... I'm ashamed to ask so much."

"Forget it," I said. "I don't want your ranch. I want what Christina wants... She can have two fathers. That's all right with me. Listen," I went on after a pause in which our gazes met. "There's a lot about you I've never understood, but we both knew Bluejean loved only one man. She was waiting for you to give up Grace. You finally did. I respect you for that. Why don't we just work together to make the kid happy? So, how about that drink?"

We went to the patio where Juanito and a bearded young man cavorted naked in the pool next to deck chairs and a cocktail trolley. A little girl's swimsuit was drying in the sun. Woolpack laid his hand on my shoulder. "That's Father Joe with the beard. He's convinced that the CIA and PRED are working together and terrified that one of us will go to the American embassy. Have you been to the embassy, Paul?"

"No way."

"Good," he said. "When I get to New York, I'll call the White House personally... Father Joe telephoned Juanito at Solidarity. We discovered that you came to Pacífica in spite of my lying to you. I was afraid you might go to the authorities and throw a spanner in the works."

"What's an American lady doing at the reception desk?" I asked.

"She's one of my father's former girlfriends. She hated him. She can be trusted." Woolpack patted my shoulder. "Let's get cracking. I have much to tell you before Christina's nanny brings her home from school."

It was hot. The sun had reached its zenith before Woolpack had concluded his explanation of the details of his father's will. I sat by the pool in the sun, drank gin and tonic, and listened—half listened. The Woolpack will had always seemed to me a remote and insidious instrument of manipulation differing in magnitude but not in kind from pieces of paper perused by Malakov. Still, I listened. Something rattle-brained was emerging from the bursts of Woolpack's voice. On Christmas Day, Teapot would inherit the Woolpack trust fund's capital. Woolpack would become director of Earthco and would have considerable control—he believed—of the uranium-mining market.

"I'm going to abolish the Atomic Age," Woolpack declared and popped fist into hand slowly. "If you had a billion dollars, some control over resources, and the solid basis of a definite intention, would *you* lift the curse of the Atomic Age?" He brought his deck chair close to mine. "You wonder how. I'll tell you how... Gradual slowing down of the production of yellowcake. Shutting down mines, blocking new operations. Then, through carefully distributed committees—all legal, mind you—we enable environmentalists of all parties to be elected to Congress. We pass laws. I am an American. I abide by the law. That is why I wanted—"

"Bluejean's baby," I offered.

Woolpack nodded. His eyes wandered without focus. "By law, the inheritor of the trust fund has to be my natural child and has to be legally recognized as such by Grace. That's why I'm here: to finalize the legal transition of the money. Grace wanted me to break the law. All those years when she was pretending to adopt you, she was waiting for me to sign fraudulent documents claiming you as my son. The fraud might have worked. I might have secured my father's power at any time. Grace took care to find a foreign child, an orphan already past the magical age of eleven... Perhaps I would have committed the fraud. But I met Bluejean. We produced my own heir, thank you. Grace, as you recall, wanted to purchase the child at birth. I agreed to the plan. It failed. But I could wait. I could wait."

I placed my empty glass beside the pool and studied Woolpack's vehement face. "Tell me about that," I said.

"Bluejean was a nonconformist, but she was a lady and wanted marriage. I couldn't risk divorcing Grace. She *might* kill herself—and then the money would go to charities. I could wait until the timetable permitted the transition of the trust fund from Grace to me via Christina. I have waited. I have succeeded. But you have borne the spurns that patient merit of the unworthy takes. And Bluejean has been murdered..." His voice trailed off.

"Tell me about that," I said.

"Father Joe saw the man. An officer of the secret police. A man named von Albensleben. Juanito knows him. Juanito says you don't know him. Is that correct?"

I squeezed my eyes tightly shut against the sun. Many things were clear to me now, and intuition told me that Woolpack was close to the vanishing point—and couldn't perceive it. I didn't have the heart to tell him the truth. I'd tell him at the airport after Teapot arrived. *If* Teapot arrived. "One person in fifty fled Hungary, including young agents trained by the *Allamvédelmi Osztaly*. I couldn't know them all... Fix me another drink, will you?"

He brought the drink and resumed. "You see, Paul, I intend to give Grace back her trust fund as soon as the original trust has been transferred to Christina. I want no ill feelings. Confound my father, sowing discord beyond the grave! I have to show Christina *and* proof of parentage *and* adoption papers on Christmas Day. Humiliating! If only Bluejean hadn't come with me, all could be well. I didn't want Bluejean with me here. Just Christina. But you know Bluejean. She feared the day of your returning."

"Yes," I said.

"She was fond of you, Paul. You gave her more than she asked. She took more than you gave. Her missing leg made her discourteous, and her lust for completeness made her insolent. But she feared facing you. Bluejean insisted upon coming with me.

"Well, I wrote a letter to the Casa Roja addressed to Grace Littlehale. I hadn't a clue what her new married name is. Still haven't. Some old colonel. I couldn't care less... I explained to Grace that I was flying down for Christmas to introduce her to Christina. Of course, just in case Grace were jealous—you know how women are—I mentioned the new trust fund I would be arranging for her benefit. Then, blow me down, I received the most charming letter from Grace inviting all of us down for a holiday. We could have this penthouse apartment and an Earthco limousine at our disposal. What's more, Grace sent me a check for $10,000. Just like old times. I was stony broke as usual..."

While Woolpack had been talking, Juanito had been listening attentively, his expression punctuated by grimaces. Padre José was trying to read our lips. Woolpack turned to the priests. "Did I dream last night that the world fell down? There has been a murder, has there not?"

"There have been many murders, señor Woolpack," said Juanito.

"Did the murder of Bluejean cause the earthquake?"

Juanito looked from me to Woolpack and frowned behind his spectacles. "I do not think so at this mo-*ment*, señor Woolpack."

"You think I am drunk, don't you? *¿Borracho?* A cauldron of unholy loves sings all about mine ears! Where was I, Paul?"

"Arriving in Pacífica."

Woolpack shook himself as from a dream. "I'm sorry. I'm so sorry, my boy... We arrived. Grace invited us for dinner at La Casa Roja."

The red-brick Tudor-style mansion called La Casa Roja had been built by Woolpack's English great-grandfather in the last century. In almost every room there was a fireplace with intricately carved mantlepiece with a coat-of-arms bearing the inscription, Ego Woolpack.

When it was built, La Casa Roja was situated among orchards and vineyards many kilometers from the small colonial city of Pacífica. Burgeoning population had brought the city to the mansion in waves of squalor necessitating the building of a high brick wall, soon ivy-twined and streaked with cries of tropical birds. Inside the wall there was a polo field; this was replaced by a deer park, but the deer were poached; the deer park became a nine-hole golf course and finally just a lawn pock-marked by sand traps near duck ponds. Woolpacks in tweeds and jodhpurs constantly twitched their necks to stare at the lawn as if it might suddenly vanish.

One soft spring morning in September of '73 a woman in her mid-forties might have been seen strolling on the lawn, stopping every now and then to throw breadcrumbs to ducks. With her were two officers of the Pacifican army, one of them her young husband, tall and Teutonic, the other a little man with pomaded grey hair, a mustache like a septic toothbrush, and a chlorine-yellow uniform complete with tasseled epaulettes and medals of valor.

The woman, who with her former beauty had lost inhibitions, was in a fury. The people in the nearby barrios had kept her up all night by banging spoons on empty pots. She drew a line across her brow: she'd had it. Something must be done.

Something must be done, General Scarpio.

"John, something must be done. And nothing happens. Nothing, nothing, nothing... Of course, darling, politics have always been over my head and, without you to advise me... But there we are. What a lovely daughter you have! Come here, dear. Come give Grace a hug and a kissie."

Christina shrank into Bluejean's arms.

"What do you want me to do?"

"John. Dear John. I knew I could rely upon you. Just a small favor? You know how much I've tried to get close to people. I'm simply too shy. Come to Grace, naughty girl... The devil take you! What was I saying? Oh. Atamoro. *Your* great-grandfather's mines. You'll want to inspect the property for yourself before... before the changing of the guard. Do it tomorrow! Why don't you *all* go for a spin? A jolly good drive in the country. What *is* wrong with that girl? Thinks she's the kipper's knickers, does she? The money will spoil her dreadfully. So you're getting married, are you? John, it's so bloody decent of you to let me stay here in Casa Roja."

"I haven't done a thing," John said.

"But you're the head of the family! John Woolpack the Third! If you have a son, I do hope you won't call him John the Fourth. What about a Shakespearean name for a change? Here's to Gloucester Woolpack, God bless 'im!" She lifted her wineglass, her diamonds a-sparkle in candlelight, drank deeply, and adjusted a tiara on dyed hair. "I've made the arrangements for tomorrow. It's an absolutely enchanting village, Miss McQueen. Lovely Indian jewelry in the market and the church is 300 years old and the people are so poor it breaks my heart and—John? Do you hear something? I thought I heard something. Out on the lawn... Never mind. We'll all end up in the poorhouse. One must get used to it. I do wish the Colonel could have been here."

Woolpack and Bluejean exchanged glances over the refectory table. Woolpack cleared his throat politely. "What exactly do you wish me to do in Atamoro?"

Grace batted her eyelids and fingered the puffed flounces of her pink silk evening dress. "Talk to the working classes," she replied. "Tell them the Woolpack family has not forgotten them, by Jove and little fishes! Tell them that you'll have food parcels distributed on Boxing Day. Capons! Strawberries and cream! I suppose they'll want seaweed and beans, the wretches. I'm sure I heard something out on the lawn."

"Christmas," Woolpack said in a tone measured for clarity, "is Christina's birthday. We're booked for the States that night. Still, what do you think, Bluejean? Shall we pop along to Atamoro? Grace is quite right: it's time I saw for myself what Earthco has been doing to people."

"Let's go for it," Bluejean said.

Padre José, Juanito translating:

The bearded young padre remembers that night well, how squads of men wearing ski-masks arrived in unmarked trucks, rounded up hundreds of workers, herded them into the trucks and roared away: the shouts, the gunbursts, the screams of women, then the silence that he himself broke with clang of bells after telephoning Juanito and discovering that civil war was erupting everywhere. Find out who is missing, Juanito ordered. Gather orphans to the church. Call back. He and the archbishop, having expected the worst for some time, had organized the Vicariate of Solidarity. The world must know.

The padre remembers the morning after, how trucks with Earthco markings droned into the plaza bearing not soldiers this time but armed workers from other villages, and there was silence in the village until a small pig, rooting by the side of the road, squealed as it was struck by a speeding Mercedes-Benz out of which stepped a blond officer who blew a whistle, the armed workers spreading out, knocking on every door proclaiming *tranquilidad*.

I could no longer contain myself. "For God's sake, get on with it! Colonel von Albensleben? Right?"

The young priest plucked his beard, spoke rapidly to Juanito, and folded his arms. "He thinks you are CIA," Juanito explained with a shrug. "Forgive him, señor Szabo. He has been hiding under protection of señor Woolpack ever since he witnessed the murder and I for him identified von Albensleben. He fears to return to his village because von Albensleben supervises the district and will recognize him."

"Holy shit! He *witnessed*? John, *you* tell me what happened. I already know why Bluejean went to Atamoro the day after the junta took over: to work with José at an orphanage. But why did *you* go? Grace's arrangements for you to deliver a jolly good speech to the *obreros*...? Wanting to see for yourself what Earthco has been doing to the people...? You must have suspected a collusion between Earthco and the military... You talk. I'll calm down."

"Same reason, old man," Woolpack murmured on a cough. "The Woolpack will. I spent the night at the processing plant explaining to surviving union leaders that in future we, that is I as director of Earthco, were going to plough profits back into the community, raise the standard of living, provide health and retirement benefits. That sort of thing."

Perhaps he had been carried away by the thrill of assuming leadership for the first time in his life and of finding his ideas expanding to a group of men who heard him as if he were a deus ex machina. There he was on the verge of power to ventilate the system, extirpate its basis in greed. Atamoro was a warm-up for the game of his life, lifting the curse of the Atomic Age. He had spoken all night.

"John," I said as gently as I could. "John, you left them there alone all night in a makeshift orphanage. Our friend Juanito will tell you she wanted to be a saint, but she just wanted an end to the games—"

"—*Sí*, a saint!" Juanito cut in. He had arranged the face behind his spectacles into something pontifical. "It is now fundamental to understand the martyrdom of la señora McQueen." He looked around, threw fingers in the air one by one. "El coronel von Albensleben came to the orphanage quite early in the morning, quite unexpectedly. He was alone and armed with the pistol. *Segundo*, he seized a child, a little boy. In front of everybody. José. La señora. He say to José, going for a walk. *Dar un paseo.*"

José affirmed the words with nods and clasped brick-red hands as Juanito went on. "La señora, she scream-ed from the *orfanato*, like 'Come back, you son of the *puta*,' but this coronel pay no attentions, go walking with child to the mountains. *Tercero*, she followed them. Also the padre follow at the distance... I will not describe abomination that von Albensleben he is doing with the child when la señora arrive on situation. But it is a terrible thing in our culture. *Cuarto*, she throw her body upon this coronel, she is a-screaming, she bites, she heats him in *testículo*. While she is doing this things, the boy escaped. There is a shot. One shot. Next mo-*ment* this coronel take the body in *una mina*. The padre has seen from distance. He runs before this coronel see him... *Último*: there at the orphanato when the padre is arriving is señor Woolpack with his daughter in the arms..."

Sun shimmered on bright pool water. A jet rent the sky over the Andes, leaving white dashes like maggots dissolving in indecipherable code. I was exposed to something in the hot air.

I stole a glance at Woolpack and wondered why he had aged so little. He was as solid as his definite intention. Men such as he—such as his ancestors, I supposed—were fueled by fervent imagination that laughed at obstacles and removed them, no mountain too high, no river too wild, and they harnessed that imagination to projects that reached to fill the sky's insuperable void. Woolpack's eyes flared in a kind of permanent rapture. They could weep, like the eyes of Masaccio's Adam, for shame and loss yet continue to fix their gaze on territory ahead as if the world only required a little fixing up in order for our own dreams to be moulded in the curvature of his hands. The world had not made him. He had made *it*, found the will to abrogate values that did not leave him free to lift us up. He rang a freedom bell all right. But there was something tragic in these reflections.

"Paul!" Woolpack's voice held an edge of admonishment. "Sorry about that," I said. "I'm not used to drinking in the morning."

"Cure for that." He rose, replenished my glass from the trolley bar, and returned the glass with a smile. He filled his own glass, hands swift and cocky as those of some gunslinger among the clicking of billiard balls, the jangling of a cash register, and men's low voices plotting wild justice. "I was listening," I said. It was half true. I had heard how Woolpack bundled José into the trunk of the Mercedes with Earthco markings, stopped at the mill and paid armed workers to bring Bluejean's body down from the mountain to the Atamoro police, and sent Teapot via company truck to the city. I had heard how, several days later, he bribed an official to fill out adoption papers, even the official being convinced that the affidavit called Nonrelinquishment of Parental Rights awarded Christina to Woolpack, and how he'd enrolled her at the English School in order to settle the heiress in the routine of her new estate.

"I was listening," I said. "The *obreros* never did the

job... But tell me about the affidavit. Is that why you flew to Atlanta the day after Christina was born, to make legally certain there would be no waiving of rights or eventual hassle with Grace? I had to return to Fort Benning to pull guard duty. Bluejean was spaced out... You must have offered her something."

"Marriage. I offered her marriage."

"On condition?"

"On condition. We would have to wait eleven years."

"You must have been counting the seconds. You *were* counting the seconds." I rubbed my neck. "Bluejean wanted you, and you offered marriage with installments of adultery amortized over eleven years. I'm not finished." I caught my breath. "I'm not finished because I've been an accomplice from the time I first saw a copy of your affidavit. I wanted Bluejean's baby. I wanted her to have the love and freedom that I didn't have. So I understand you now, John. We're much alike. We live for a child's future... But there's a difference between us. You're not paranoid enough. You're unacquainted with terror. You trust people as if you were still living in a time when men shook hands over a campfire in the middle of a wilderness and widows slept peacefully with millions of dollars stashed under the mattress and bearded patriarchs looked at a land larger than Europe and said, 'This is the place,' as though words took possession forever! Well, I have news for you." I swept an arm toward the city. "The world's a minefield now. You have to be careful where you walk."

"Was Bluejean careful where she walked?" Woolpack retorted. "Yet whenever I heard the creak of her, coming, she gave me hope."

A few minutes later I stood on the sidewalk of the Avenida Maximiliano O'Malley and wondered if I should go back to the penthouse apartment to warn Woolpack and the priests about Günter and Grace. I had just been trying to formulate the warning when I made a flimsy excuse about another appointment and fled to the elevator. There was now time to reconsider. But what was the use? Günter's threat to kill me and my loved ones, if I mentioned his country in a context of slander, was now so real that it fell from the sky like invisible, deadly particles. I began to walk, pausing at intervals to glance over my shoulder to see if anyone were following.

3

TERESA and I were married a week before Christmas of '73 and left immediately after the civil ceremony for a remote area of the Andes. After a four-hour journey by train, we hired burros to take us the rest of the way along a precipitous rocky ledge rising above a roaring river and mist-wispy glades to a blue lake. Following a creek that, spanned by fallen trees, snaked past talus, we came to a meadow where ferns grew in cool places. There above the meadow was a log cabin nestled against a backdrop of snow-capped peaks. That night we lay in one another's arms listening to the crackle of fire on a hearth, to the chiming of windbells, to the murmur of mountain water.

Teresa brought to our idyll in the Andes her doctoral thesis on neuropsychological perspectives on closed and hierarchical systems of society. On the eve of our departure we were sitting by the blue lake in the late afternoon with a bottle of wine, a hunk of cheese, and a clothbound dissertation. Teresa broke silence. "I promised myself to tell you about Ángel López Schneider." I made a face. "Oh, it's not *that*!" She was blushing. "He was an older man, married. My professor. He died a few weeks ago and left me with ideas that must not die."

Her expression was so sad that I kissed her cheek and told her I loved her. "I love you," she said with a warmly beautiful smile and began. "Ángel López Schneider was an aristocrat, a philosopher, a poet and a singer. At the university he was not only seeking to synthesize mind and brain—psychology and neurophysiology—but also exploring the implications of this research for social behavior and consequently for survival. Here I will read you from one passage. I will try to translate."

She flipped pages and began again. "'There are a number of ethical consequences to be inferred from study of the human brain. The first is that every human being is sacred. To arrive at this conclusion, we consider a number of such enormous magnitude that we are multiplying in trillions: the number of different states of a human brain is far greater than the total number of elementary particles in the entire universe. So great is the number of functionally different formations of a human brain, it is inconceivable that any two humans can ever be entirely or even very much alike. Each human being is rare and different. We must argue, then, for the sanctity of the human being.'

"'A second ethical consequence inheres in the brain's potential for creativity. Through millions of years of evolution we inherit genetically preprogramed behavior such as feeding and fighting, but in human beings the neocortex, which represents 85 percent of the brain, has the capacity for new learning. Thus we are not enslaved to genetically preprogrammed behavior. We have the power to adapt to new environmental circumstances and to transform ourselves and society. At the present time we have developed the power to destroy life. We summon the neocortex to our aid. We recognize that crisis in human evolution has been reached. We recognize that the cause of the crisis has been reliance upon overly rational, excessively masculine modes of thinking and of social organization. Perceiving the problem, we become aware of the solution: to engage the creative process in terms of the total planetary environment. Another ethical consequence then.'

"'Perhaps the most revolutionary ethical consequence of our new scientific knowledge of the human brain, though, lies in our emerging picture of its architecture. Now for the first time in a scientific way, not simply in the way of introspective and mystical philosophy, we begin to glimpse just how dynamic and democratic is the brain's system of command and control. It is not at all a system analogous to a master control center that enforces obedience from the trillions of neurons that compose the nervous systems and subsystems. To begin with, we have not one brain but two brains, two hemispheres, each playing a different, independent role in feeling and thinking. Therefore, the point of fusion between these hemispheres must be that which allows us to escape from the domination of self-preserving drives to a futuristic concern for others and an expanded view of space, time, and habitat. This point of fusion is the corpus callosum. It is a cabling system that integrates information and brings pressure to bear in favor of cooperative enterprise. The brain, as we now know, is an interconnected set of systems and subsystems that can pass control from one to another, undo past mistakes, forestall adverse contingencies, and, above all, insist upon harmony.'

"'Of course, one does not credit López Schneider with discoveries already generally known and accepted. He, however, has foreseen the next and indeed *immediate* stage in human evolution as the application of the dynamic of harmonious consciousness to a world culture composed of independent systems collaborating in unity of purpose. We *naturally* possess the power of harmony even though we persist in believing domination to be natural.'"

Teresa closed the book.

"He was arrested and murdered on the first day of the dictatorship."

"Tell me another time," I said.

"No," she said. "I continue... I *must* continue." I had never before heard her voice so charged with vehemence.

Her cousin, the dentist José Manuel, knew the doctor who performed the autopsy on Ángel López Schneider. Her brother Willy, the conscript, had an army friend who had witnessed events in the football stadium. The first morning of the overthrow of the government of President Moreno Báez, PRED had rounded up more than 15,000 citizens and herded them into the stadium. Men, women, and children sat huddled together, López Schneider among them.

"Suddenly he sprang to his feet," Teresa said. "Someone gave him a guitar. He shouted for everyone to be still and to listen. He would teach them a new song he had composed. When they had memorized the new song, they would sing together as one voice:

'Venceremos
y la gente volverá
con la pluma, una flor
y corazón.'

He taught them this song. At first hesitantly, then bravely such a chorus rose to the skies as would make possible to believe that the people will come back with the pen, a flower, and one pure heart.

"I want you to know that Günter von Albensleben has not been identified as one of the officers in the stadium. Another officer commanded Ángel to come to the center of the field. He went. Already he knew what lay in store for him. He went."

Teresa paused and resumed, "'Please,' says the officer, 'make the people to sing again. You direct them. From here.' Surrounded by many officers, all glaring at him with contempt and hatred in the eyes, Ángel did not hesitate but raised the arms to the people. 'Everybody sing,' he shouted. Then again:

> *'Venceremos*
> *y la gente volverá*
> *con la pluma, una flor*
> *y corazón.'*

It is said that when the song was finished, the people became absolutely quiet and still, the last syllable seeming to echo—*zón zón zón*.

"Then the soldiers pushed Ángel to the ground. With the butts of their rifles they smashed his hands and wrists to a pulp. Then an officer with a sword cut off Ángel's arms. He bled to death, slowly, over many hours... Always I will love him," Teresa said. She caressed my hand. "We must not be afraid."

That night the Teeth Mother came to me unsummoned in a dream.

I woke to a crack of thunder. Lightning chalked our little room. Rain pelted the windows. The burros screamed and stamped outside where I had corralled them. The room was cold as any tomb. I rose and kindled a fire, lit my pipe, shivered, and waited for the dream to go in thunder. After a while Teresa came and snuggled warmly in my arms. Spasms like hot grease from a frying pan flashed along my spine. She sat up, felt my neck. "You're trembling," she said. "What is it?"

"My corpus callosum isn't in working order," I said.

"Be serious."

"Well," I said, "I had another one of my dreams." I tried to laugh in my throat. "You'll think I'm nuts."

"*¿Como?*"

"Nuts. Crazy."

"Tell me."

"Forget it."

"If you don't tell me, I'll read my thesis."

"Well," I said, "that's different... Do you remember my telling you how Günter stopped one night to give money to a starving man whom he called The Man Who Runs After Dinner?"

"*El hombre que corre después de comida,*" Teresa said. "Was he in your dream?"

"The dream began with Runs After Dinner. I saw his face clearly. He had a black pointed beard, hollow cheeks, intensely dark eyes, and brown skin with a bluish tint as if earth and sky had gone into its composition. His expression was that of an effigy. He neither breathed nor perspired, although he was running and it was very hot. He was running so fast that trees and bungalows blurred, so fast that the candles that lined the unpaved road were flattened by his passage as though disturbed by a suddenly opened blast furnace. That fast... Do you want to hear the rest?"

"The neocortex represents eighty-five percent of the brain." Teresa looked at the ceiling.

"All right," I said, "I can take a hint... I forgot to tell you. It was Christmas. In the dream. In reality, of course, that's the day after tomorrow."

"Where was Runs After Dinner running on Christmas Day?"

"To La Casa Roja... Do you want to tell this dream or shall I?"

"I'm all ears."

"You have other attractions... *Bueno*. He came to a high brick wall braided with barbed wire. Runs After Dinner didn't climb the wall or go through it leaving behind the shape of a cut-out doll. He simply appeared on the wall's other side. Here he stopped running and lounged in the shade of an appletree. Hovering near his face, I saw him munching an apple, his jaws ruminative as a cow's. I noticed his large, pricked-alert, pointed ears, vestigial digits, like dewclaws, on the back of his hands, and hairy feet that were cloven like a goat's."

"Ah-ha," Teresa interrupted with a mirthful expression.

"Listen," I said and resumed after a pause. "We were at La Casa Roja assembled on the lawn—I, Woolpack, Günter, Christina and uniformed death police. I was invisible. There was a big chalk circle on the lawn, put there, I suppose, by one of those little trundle-carts that are used for liming tennis courts."

"You mean I wasn't in the dream," Teresa interrupted again.

"Very well," I responded with a sigh, "you are present indirectly. Runs After Dinner at one point speaks as if he had read your doctoral thesis and—I regret to say—saw little hope in evolution. Shall I go on?"

Teresa shrugged. I resumed. "In the dream, as I say, I was invisible. I was usually a camera with a lens that viewed proceedings from a middle distance and sometimes from close-in... For example, when Runs After Dinner and Grace were copulating on the lawn, I was at a discreet distance."

"*¡Por la madre!*" Teresa made a giggling noise in her throat and covered her mouth as if to stifle protest.

"Well," I said, "that's what happened. Runs After Dinner had just finished spitting out the apple core when Grace waddled from behind the tree. She was dressed in pink that flared from her hips at 45-degree angles. Her feet were set a meter apart, and her swollen ankles oozed over a pair of pink Cinderella slippers. Her skin was white as vanilla ice cream, her breasts were like enormous loaded slingshots, and her hair straggled like serpents. Next I knew, she was supine on the grass with Runs After Dinner vaguely lost in the mushroom clouds of her dress.

"Woolpack and Günter were there. Woolpack wore a black suit and bowler and carried a rolled English umbrella. He consulted his wristwatch. Finally he poked Grace's dress with the umbrella. Grace's dress shook violently as if beneath it were a geological fault during an earthquake. She said in the voice of an old hag, 'Don't teach your grandmother to suck eggs.'

"In the next instant Günter was pointing a pistol at Runs After Dinner's head and saying harshly, 'You took a longer time than usual. If you start getting pleasure from this job, I'll make you eat all day, every day.' Runs After Dinner shrank back."

Teresa pondered and asked, "But why does Günter threaten to feed a starving man?"

"What is your interpretation?"

"My interpretation," said Teresa, "is that famine and war are secretly allied with the old hag. In reality, Runs After Dinner overcomes the reptilian drive of hunger by running. He substitutes running for food. In the dream, however, he has grown so accustomed to deceiving hunger pangs, he no longer tolerates the possibility of relief. He *prefers* running to eating. His ego-consciousness has been freed of the dominance of the dark unconscious. He is at the forefront of human evolution. What do you think?"

"It's perfect," I said. "In the dream, Runs After Dinner is going to make a speech along those lines. Grace appoints him judge of the game of the Chalk Circle. He is the judge of all the claims of life because he has risen above life and death."

"What is the next scene?"

"The next scene was the judgment of the Chalk Circle. Christina, dressed all in white as if she were going to first communion, sat in the middle of the circle on the ground. Behind her, seated on a throne, was Grace, and on either side, standing, were Woolpack and Günter. Surrounding the circle's perimeter were the soldiers. At first, Runs After Dinner was nowhere to be seen. Suddenly he sprang out from beneath the folds of Grace's dress, ran, and took a commanding position with respect to the central figures in this tableau.

"Meanwhile, I was inside Günter's mouth. His teeth were snowcapped peaks. I was as small as a climber on Mount Everest. If I spoke the truth, I would be swallowed in an avalanche. For that matter, if Woolpack—he was on the lawn waiting to collect his booty—if *he* spoke the truth, I would be swallowed, he would disappear, and Teapot would disappear. Nevertheless, I could not remain silent. 'Günter,' I said, 'I didn't kill your father.' And Günter said, 'Someone had to kill my father so that I could become president.' And I said, 'You sent me to kill your father so that you could kill Bluejean.' And he said, 'Someone had to kill Bluejean so that Grace could kill Woolpack.'

"Next, I was outside Günter's mouth and again invisible.

"Grace's lips wrinkled back and she said, 'It's all John's fault. I warned him against the divorce. It's all his fault that Günter was assigned to Atamoro so that he could abuse a child and kill Bluejean. It's all his fault that Christina will be awarded to me by Runs After Dinner. It's all his fault if Christina has to be executed. Life is hard. I cannot experience orgasm. I have teeth in my vagina.' Grace's lips closed. She primped snake hair.

"Then Runs After Dinner declared, 'Life is hard. Life is bitter. Life is death. That's the judgment of the Chalk

Circle.'

"Woolpack then spoke. 'I have evidence to the contrary,' he said, 'plus the solid basis of a definite intention.' He flourished documents at Runs After Dinner. One document was the Woolpack will, another was the Nonrelinquishment of Parental Rights, another was Christina's adoption paper, and another was a reproduction of Masaccio's Adam and Eve. Runs After Dinner took the documents and stuffed them in Grace's mouth. Her mouth was like a volcano full of molten lava. The documents disappeared with a whooshing noise. Runs After Dinner's circular eye holes stared everyone into silence. His grim slit of a mouth made words. 'The child is awarded to Grace. She is committed to vengeance and the dark power of the unconscious mind. She has teeth in her vagina. Of course, there are those who believe in the brain's capacity to adapt and to protect Christina before her destruction. However, a characteristic period for the emergence of one advanced species from another is one hundred thousand years. How long do we wait for a burst of brain development to assert victory over reptilian drives?'

"'Forever!' cackled Grace.

"'I'm the judge here,' Runs After Dinner declared. 'I refuse to be intimidated by an archetypal woman. I run after dinner in order to assert a marginal victory of humanity over reptilian drives. Therefore, I have experienced brain development. Therefore, Christina is not condemned to vanish, and the judgment of the Chalk Circle is modified. *If Woolpack dies before Grace dies, Christina will be released unharmed*. Soldiers, take Woolpack to the airport. Grace, claim your hostage.'

"That was not the end of my dream. Grace descended from her throne. She was fat as an earth mother. She breathed fire from her open maw. Her facial skin was like lava streaming from an eruption. She approached Christina, reached to embrace her. And, just then, her pink dress fell away, her mountainous flesh dissolved—her body was revealed as a skeleton, her head but a grinning skull!

"Immediately the soldiers who surrounded the Chalk Circle broke out bottles of champagne and poured a round of the wine into magically materialized glasses. When Runs After Dinner received a glass, he lifted it in salute and shouted, '*¡Viva la muerte!*' The soldiers also echoed this toast: '*¡VIVA LA MUERTE!*'

"Meanwhile, Christina, in spite of being embraced by Grace's skeleton, hadn't moved or spoken a word. Now, however, she balled her fists and addressed Günter. 'You better not hurt me or let Grace die before Woolpack dies or my Mom will whip your ass!' Runs After Dinner lifted his glass in a new salute, this time to Christina.

"'*¡Viva la vida!*' Runs After Dinner shouted.

"And the soldiers chorused, '*¡Viva! ¡Viva! ¡Viva la vida!*'

"That was the end of my dream."

"It was a good dream," Teresa said after a long pause and stroked my face. It was as if she calmed the storm outside, for I heard no disturbance of the night.

"A *good* dream?"

"Oh, don't you see?" Teresa cried with a suppressed howl of dismay. "Until now in all your life you've seen yourself sinking helplessly back into the unconscious mind. But now you've brought its contents into the light. You've gained a calm that will strengthen your faith in life."

She was right about the calmness. I felt that. And feeling fulfilled as never before, feeling becalmed, not trapped in causality as my father had thought but centered in the eye of the hurricane, at last I saw the abyss for what it really was—an illusion. We were not forever swept by a river of life, lost and disappearing. Time was not a river. It was a now. And man was more than a here, a space enclosed, separated and alone. Man was also an everywhere. And the abyss did not exist, was not the bottomless pit of primeval chaos that I had dreaded, but was the veil of articulate infinity. And so what all of my life I had foolishly dreaded was but a universal order of participation, as distinct as speech if one but listened to the silence of eternal vivification.

We returned to the city on Christmas Eve. There was great rejoicing at "The Swallows." The Greatest Man in the World sacrificed chickens, which Mamá cooked and served up with seaweed like plump little goddesses, to a huge family, my family. Willy played the guitar and Tío Carlos the harp. There were presents. For Ximenita, a doll that wet its pants. For The Peasant, a cosmetic kit. For Papá, a poster of John Wayne. For Enrique, a subscription to *Playboy*. But the most astonishing presents were those given by Papá and Enrique. Papá's present to Teresa was his own handcrafted pair of bronze bookends to signify his shame at having shredded her books in the past. Enrique's present to Teresa was this: he had matriculated at the university.

Enrique cried aloud to get everyone's attention. "You have all sacrificed so much for me that I can never repay you. You, Teresita, have done the most to show me that the poor people have possibility. I am becoming the doctor of medicine. That is my present to you, my promise. Also I think the girls will be better-looking at the university!"

On Christmas afternoon Enrique drove us to the airport. Possibly instructed by Colonel Günter von Albensleben, the functionaries gave us no difficulties. We boarded the jet and sat by oval windows peering out at the tarmac. Although I had trusted Günter, intuition told me Teapot would not be arriving for take-off.

Woolpack appeared just before take-off escorted by soldiers who pushed him ahead of them, spun him around, and pushed again as if they were playing blindman's bluff. He covered his face with the hands of Masaccio's Adam.

I *knew* what had happened.

It was all there in Woolpack's face when he half stumbled down the aisle of the jet, solid, separate, and alone without our daughter. *If Woolpack dies before Grace dies, Christina will be released unharmed.* Words from a dream had divined the logic of Grace's revenge, leaving Christina to the mercy of Günter's honor and Woolpack to a choice between painful separation or suicidal splendor.

4

SIX years were to pass before Virgil Warbonnet and I stood on a bald rim of the Grand Canyon and scattered Woolpack's ashes to the wind...

Dying from cancers, he had dragged himself from the bed in his room at Paradise Ranch and stumbled outside in sub-zero weather in order to freeze to death. When I came home from Flagstaff, I picked up his trail in the snowpacked hills north of the ranch. The boots left inverted cones in the snow in a zigzag pattern. He wasn't drunk, I'm sure. During the five months he had lived with me and Teresa at the ranch, after he drank radioactive water, he had refused alcohol and pain relievers of any kind. And it had to be north, the direction he was headed. The Canyon lay in that direction about a hundred miles as the crow flies. As I followed his trail, I found places where he had fallen and rolled, vomiting blood in the snow. A blizzard was obliterating the higher elevations when I found his clothes piled neatly as if to mock forever the illusion of accommodated life, and then I found the emaciated body naked and prone in a drift, already stiffened with what was probably a kind of smile on blue lips.

I know now from everything Woolpack confessed to me about his life that he was coming full circle and that he went into the snow at last as if to close his life where it began, his life having begun not with a date but with an occasion half a century before.

Once in September of '28 a boy named Woolpack and called Boy visited the Grand Canyon. Most of the way he slept in the saddle behind his grandfather, hour after hour in the hot dry air amidst the steady clatter of hooves on a rocky trail, scents of sagebrush and piñon mingling with J. Byron Woolpack's strong odor, Boy lulled in and out of sleep. *Boy's coming with me to see the dam*, Grandpa had announced to John Junior and his wife, the silent woman called Woman, the peremptory tone echoing among timbers of the Scottish-baronial Great Hall on the walls of which buffalo, elk, and moose eyes gleamed. Dishes being washed by Chinese servants rent the silence and were sealed off again. Cigar smoke curled between lozenges of the chandelier above the eighteenth-century Jesuit Mission refectory table where the family had eaten. Now the silence was broken by Woman's racking cough. After the coughing, Boy's father rasped, *Time he did*, the blue eyes bulging unblinkingly as they had ever since the gas-green woods of the Ardennes entered them. *Make a man of him*. Boy hadn't any idea what to expect. He was going to the Canyon, he knew that, just as he knew that Grandpa's cold blue eyes and handlebar mustache had taken the measure of men and mountains when Arizona was still a Territory, just as he knew that his mother was dying of tuberculosis. But Grandpa didn't know how Boy would make a man. Then he was wakened by the snorting of the horse to his presence on a rim of light-grey limestone but a few feet away from a chasm of appalling depth in which clouds drifted in the belly of the wind and flat-topped mesas floated like an archipelago. He slid to the ground. Grandpa vaulted from the saddle, tethered the horse, came and took Boy to that rim of what seemed the outermost and innermost sublimity.

Grandpa pointed vaguely southwards to masses of color—purples, reds, yellows, blues—above abysmal black through which a thin river ran. "See there, Boy!" Grandpa's voice, for once, could not contain exuberance. "That's where we're putting her, by dom and thunderation! Four times higher than the Empire State with more stone in her than all the pyramids, more steel than all the naval vessels of the world! She'll make the wonder of the ages! Far as the eye can see—water, blue water, Lake Woolpack, greatest man-made lake in creation—an ocean, Boy, an ocean right here lapping at your feet! And down a ways further, by dom, we'll excavate so much the Panama Canal will dry up with envy. We're taking water to the cities, Boy. One day, tens of millions of folks will wake up in a tropical paradise instead of a dom furnace and say to themselves one word of regeneration like a god's!" He paused and gripped Boy by the back of the neck. "What d'ye think the word is, Boy?"

Half a century in the future we stood on the awesome height, Woolpack and I. He spat blood and answered his grandfather's question as his soul might have done in childhood could it have spoken: "No! The word was no. Not only no, but Hell, no!"

Back then, Boy speechless and Grandpa standing and staring like Moses on the Mount, a clap of thunder burst below them and reverberated through the Canyon, a giant's mad dance on a drum. Bolts of lightning slashed pinnacles and spires.

"What's the word, Boy?"

He had to answer, but Grandpa answered for him. "Opportunity," he muttered and sucked upper lip until its smacking sound exploded. Then Grandpa seized Boy's wrist in a vise-like grip and dragged him to the rim. "Opportunity, Boy. Look around you." He swept his free hand across the sky, like an eagle's wing. "All is open to the shrewdest and the boldest... We're building here the greatest dam the world has ever seen, me and John Junior," he went on in a kind of rapture, then frowned and lowered his voice. "Soon's we get the capital, of course. But we'll get it by hook or crook, by thunder and lightning we will! And that's where you come in, Boy. If you grow up man enough... I may not live to see Woolpack Dam and Lake Woolpack. John Junior may not live to see them. *You* will. *You*'ll be rich. *You*'ll build her. Huh? What d'ye see out there? Tell me, Boy. What d'ye *see*?" Grandpa tightened his grip with one hand and pointed with the other. "Water! Water, water everywhere! Look there, look! *Water*!"

All of a sudden Grandpa swooped and, after seizing Boy's other wrist, began to swing Boy in a clockwise circle of centrifugal force, each 360-degree turn becoming faster and more unsteady than the previous one, Grandpa shouting, "Say *water*! Say you see *water*!" and Boy saw, like a strobe light going berserk, the abyss illuminated by spiderwebbed lightning, high and multicolored buttes blurred into a phantasmagoria of titanic upheavals and subsidences. "Say *water*, ye dom fool!" Boy neither spoke nor screamed. The last thing he remembered before he fainted, he fell in a world of white light. The first thing he saw when he woke in the cactus where Grandpa had flung him was a face peering down, black with the poison of its lunacy. "Disgrace!" the face said.

Disgrace, Grandpa would later be saying to John Junior in the Great Hall. *I saw water right away, didn't I, Pa*? John Junior said. *Never thought a son of mine would be a weakling. Send Boy with the Woman back to England. But get him out of my sight...*

Not long ago on that bald rim of a Golgotha that drops off into unimaginable layers of the Earth's evolution—seas become mountains, mountains become seas, over and over—Virgil and I pondered Woolpack's circular journey in life. Longhaired Virgil answered in silence the question I had not even uttered: *Why*. Because the answer was already woven in a Joseph's coat of rocks, already orchestrated for the point-counterpoint of man and the earth when destiny had been fulfilled, Woolpack born to the imperative of beauty, faithful in his radiant ashes to the soul of a boy's unspoken imperative of love, repudiating everything that his father and grandfather had dreamt of and worked for in their ecstasy of profanations.

Paradise Ranch is in a mountain valley some thirty miles from Flagstaff. Built in 1911, the ranch house is a three-story mansion of salmon-colored rock and has thirty rooms, including a Presidential Suite where Teddy Roosevelt slept and where my father-in-law, Augusto Rico de las Golondrinas, now sleeps with his poultry in Chicken Heaven. Woolpack's grandfather, when he left his English father's estate and copper mines in Pacífica in order to seek fortune in the American Southwest, acquired the ranch, then ten thousand acres, by marrying a cattleman's daughter, who died giving birth to John Junior in 1895. J. Byron Woolpack, however, was not interested in cattle. His educated engineer's eye told him that under northern Arizona and northwestern New Mexico lay water, oil, and mineral resources of fabulous proportions. He surveyed the land, took out leases, and waited, living as a cattleman until finally he inherited his father's wealth and business, enough to begin mining operations and to build his mansion in the wilderness. Here came sporting gents and financiers, Rough Riders and Rugged Individualists, boosters and buckaroos, and consumptives, these latter advised by physicians back East to breathe the salubrious air of almost inaccessible places. Here at Paradise Ranch, Earthco was sired by the stud of empire upon the mare of greed and ridden over arid deserts first by J. Byron Woolpack, then by John Woolpack Jr., who in 1921 begat John Woolpack III, upon an English nurse he had married after his service with the A. E. F. in the First World War. The birthdate seemed propitious: exploitation of the land was gathering momentum toward a day when a new oasis civilization of the West, as large as Western Europe, would dominate the Pacific Ocean from Panama to the Philippine Islands and beyond. Paradise Ranch would be one of the focal points of enterprise. John Junior had a Latin inscription carved on the mantelpiece of the inglenook-sized fireplace in the Great Hall. It read: EGO WOOLPACK.

The expulsion of Woolpack when he was seven was intended as a temporary one, the playing fields of an English boarding school being calculated as the appropriate place to crush Boy's effeminacy. To a man of John Junior's way of thinking, the English gentleman combined a cool sense of natural superiority with a relentless will to impose order on chaos. He had been impressed with the behavior of English gentlemen in the war, and an English gentleman from Cambridge, Charles Darwin, had established the principle of Survival of the Fittest upon the foundation of The Jungle. It was John Junior's duty as a father to prepare Boy for life in The Jungle, but if in the process of natural selection the child was predestined for failure, so be it—by dom! At first the reports from Woman, Boy's dying mother, and from the grammar school were favorable: in a rugby match Boy had bitten off the earlobe of an opponent in the scrum and in a boxing match had broken his opponent's jaw, first round. Woman died, but reports from the school continued to be favorable: in a drunken brawl in a pub Boy had thrashed a dark-skinned student from Calcutta who had had the impertinence to argue for Home Rule in the colonies and in a gang-bang in a village hayloft Boy, together with other high-spirited young gentlemen, had earned a mild dose of the clap. The Man was on his way, by dom! A little more polish and John Woolpack III would come home to assume directorship of the newly created New York headquarters of Earthco.

However—reports were vague—Boy had no sooner matriculated at Darwin's very own university than he became associated with decadents and radicals, traitors really, commies certainly, evolutionary throwbacks who denounced Great Britain's entry into the Second World War as a conspiracy of the ruling classes. Preposterous! Boy wrote an essay, published as a pamphlet priced one penny, "The Human Use of the Human Environment," incomprehensible for the most part, arguing that all wars were promulgated to prove all enemies as monsters whereas the only future of mankind lay in nonviolent cooperation. Before John Junior could recover from Boy's debasement of moral coinage, Boy was imprisoned for conscience—another word for cowardice.

Well, to Hell with Boy! Earthco could carry on without him, and Earthco did, expanding wartime and postwar operations in Southwestern and in South African uranium. John Junior himself moved to New York, selling to developers all but 500 acres of Paradise Ranch. When Boy married Grace Littlehale and brought his bride to New York for a reconciliation, John Junior studied his cards for blackjack. His twenty-one-year-old daughter-in-law was both to the manner and to The Jungle born, no redundancy for a slip of a gal with a heart of stone. By dom, if she had been his *blood* relation, he would have bequeathed her everything! As it was, he would go the limit with Grace, just hedging the bet in case a true Woolpack were born of this union. And, just to show Boy what might have been his had he played his cards right, Boy would inherit one measly jackpot: Paradise Ranch.

Surrounded by thickly forested, high mountain plateaux, the ranch is reached by a switchback dirt road that ascends past majestic peaks and wild gorges to a pass at the 9,000-foot elevation, dips into rolling pastures, crosses a plank bridge over Kachina Creek, and rises to a knoll of ponderosa pines amongst which are the mansionhouse, a barn and stables, woodshed and power-generating plant, and assorted outbuildings. The house is cleverly situated to receive the sun. Through a V-shaped canyon sliced by the creek out of precipitous sandstone bluffs to the east, the first morning rays sluice in, yellow gold. Often I rise before dawn and stroll across the creek to take in the view, light my first pipe of the day. Scarves of gauzy mist unravel through cottonwoods and fluttering aspens. Magpies shriek, strut about. Rabbits nibble, freeze, hop. Squirrels pump their tails, send shrill signals. Mule deer graze, lift their heads like startled philosophers while cattle lurch from wallows. Everywhere the rippling gurgle of mountain water, then peaks turn lavender that finally, suddenly, is a yellow blaze of molten coals pouring over crepuscular barrancas and fathoming with a linear fall of brilliance the drowsy haze. Then I about-face to see the house take romantic fire, my concave radio-telescope receiver like a meteor arrested in flight and the windows of gables and meretricious corner turrets like quicksilvered shields. Then my castle dwindles down to what it really was, the ramshackle folly of a tacky tycoon.

But it's home to quite a few people in fact—one Hungarian-American and his Pacifican wife, their twin sons who are in kindergarten, two Pacificans who quarrel incessantly and two Navajos. And now my beautiful seventeen-year-old daughter, Christina. It is home to Virgil's horse and to assorted cats and dogs and sheep and cows and lizards and scorpions and chickens, these last having converted the oak-paneled Presidential Suite into a lime-encrusted zoo of squawk and cock-a-doodle. Don Augusto sleeps with the chickens. Mamá cooks. Hosteen sees to the sheep, the horse, and cows. Sun's Forehead weaves rugs. Once in a while Virgil, Txó and Little Horse come for a visit from their home in Gallup, New Mexico, two hundred miles away where Virgil works for an agency that provides services for relocated, alcoholic Indians. Christina is recuperating from her ordeal. Teresa teaches psychology at the university. After leaving the army, graduating from college, and earning a teacher's certificate, I'm an elementary school teacher, also the proprietor of and general factotum for Paradise Ranch, Coconino County, Arizona. After a day of teaching, chauffeuring Henry and Attila to and from school, shopping for groceries, chopping firewood, shoveling snow, repairing cars, waxing the floors, feeding the animals, dusting the buffalo-elk-moose trophies, balancing the checkbook and, when Woolpack lay dying, feeding, bathing, and providing companionship for a man whom I loved as a father, I'm often too tired to shower, shave, and put on clean Levis and shitkickers to greet Teresa when she comes helling home in her pickup truck expecting cocktails, a hot meal at a table set with damask cloths and candlesticks, Mozart on the stereo, the washer humming and the dryer flip-flopping in what used to be a billiards room for empire-builders. But we're all doing what we want to do, given the circumstances of our lives and the Bluebeard's room of our minds just behind the wallpaper of forgetfulness. For even with Christina safe at home, there is still terror, still the remembrance of Günter's threat to find and eliminate my family if any word of Bluejean's disappearance is ever leaked to the authorities.

I often slip away in the dead of night to the musty solitude of the attic. It was here that the Woolpacks stowed their Chinese servants smuggled across the Mexican border. The pine planks are a wailing wall of indecipherable inscriptions. It is here, now, where I write my memoirs for eventual safe-deposit with Virgil should the long arms of PRED extend operations into the United States and Günter's threat be carried out. It is here, too, that I have set up my radio receiver. My days of precognitive experience apparently ended seven years ago, but I still spend hours tuning in to the buzz and blip and whine of cosmic energy, feeling calm in the mystery of infinity.

Woolpack, Teresa, and I left Pacífica on Teapot's birthday, Christmas, 1973, her fate sealed for an indeterminable future, our lips sealed accordingly. During the flight to Miami Woolpack sat rigidly in isolation. Only after much persuasion from Teresa did he accept an invitation to stay as our guest in Colorado Springs rather than leave at once for his ranch. Until you decide what to do, we said. Sell the ranch, invest the proceeds, get a job, start a new life, we said. We said nothing to him of Bluejean, Teapot, Grace and Günter.

"Oh," he said cryptically, "I'm starting a new life."

He didn't want our advice, but after a month at our house he dished some out for me and Virgil, who was having dinner with us one night. "You two," he declared in an irritable tone from Woolpack territory, "you two army lifers are nursing too many grievances. One of you is an Indian who wanted to be a white man and now wants to be an Indian again but can't go all the way back. The other wanted to use his brains to be of some good to people and now wants to have a boot in his face and complain he's being pushed. You're both lacking the solidity of definite intention. You're not full-blooded men moving to a visible world. By the way." He paused and met Virgil's flaring gaze. "What kind of joke are you pulling, naming your son with a birth defect Little Horse?"

"One must hate someone with a mighty hate not to love someone named Little Horse," Virgil replied evenly, then laughed his wonderful laugh.

"Horse feathers," Woolpack cut in scornfully. "You're mad as hell because the same government you serve in a demeaning capacity supports the uranium-mining industry that produces low-level radiation that is causing and will cause more and worse birth defects than were caused by both atomic blasts at Hiroshima and Nagasaki. So what do you do about it? You give your son a name to make him a laughing stock... My advice to you two is to muster out of the army."

Virgil and I could not refrain from grinning. I explained to Woolpack that the term was *process out*. Woolpack got angry and shot back. "If you wait too long to be processed out, you'll have no more feeling left than a sausage or a piece of cheese."

"We have to bring home the bacon," I snapped. "You've never done that in your life."

Woolpack's face did not change expression. It was strange, his having blue eyes and perennially boyish visage, his sounding a Western note. "A man has to do more than bring home the bacon," he enunciated with a kind of drawl. "He has to *dream*."

He left for Flagstaff a few days later. I wasn't sorry to see him go. Teresa began to avoid my eyes. Finally I said to her one night, "He's right."

"I'm sorry to tell you," she said, "but he's right. You forgot to fight back when Grace and Mr. Simonini defrauded you of entrance to university."

"Yes."

"Then quit the army. We'll manage."

"How?"

"I have faith in God."

I said nothing.

"You, too," she went on. "You have faith in a mystery without a name."

A month passed. One morning a letter arrived from Woolpack. He had deeded his ranch to me and was, he said, "hitting the trail."

> *You can sell the ranch, or live there. It's a gift outright but don't thank me. Say it's a gift from Bluejean and Christina. If you decide to live here at Paradise, you'll find plenty of elbow room. I'm not trying to confine your life, as others have tried. I have a selfish motive: I'm hitting the trail. Two more things. I don't think Flagstaff is a good place for Virgil's parents. You can't raise sheep in Flagstaff. The other thing is, the university has a junior position in psychology opening in the fall. I have spoken with some of the people there about Teresa's research in mind-brain theory and the social implications for world peace inherent in that theory. I think they're interested. Take it easier.*

"Hitting the trail!" I exclaimed, appalled, to Teresa. "He's at the vanishing point, and he hits the trail!" I had Woolpack's fate nobly determined for him—his Socratic sacrifice, his immemorial crucifixion. I was expecting another Attila *alias* Oszkár to put things aright by upholding the honor of living and bequeathing positive beliefs upon which a truly human set of values could be erected, but here, it seemed, another Malakov was being revealed, another mass of impotence, another cracked soul.

Teresa, by now, had grown accustomed to my outbursts, my distinct and obsessional vocabulary revolving around such words as abyss, vanishing point, disappearance, and disrepute, all my sense of human descent from previous high esteem. "Everything will turn out for the best," she said with that kind of finality which acts upon my nerves like a sudden emanation of radiance.

So in time I processed out of the army, Teresa received a tenure-track appointment to the university in Arizona, and we moved to Paradise Ranch.

And six years passed before Woolpack died.

I had collected, that afternoon, the twins from school. When we got to the ranch in late afternoon, the sky was like Woolpack's eyes, a kind of milk curdling the blue. A foot of snow had fallen in the night. Dust-devils of powder danced across our valley and vanished into mountaintop marriage with the naked wind. The creek gossiped in the hush, then a faint jangling of bellwethers came from the barn. Somewhere in the house there was a muffled shout—"*¡Hijo de puta!*" I sent the boys to have tea with their grandmother in the kitchen and ran up the creaking staircase to Woolpack's room, the Santa Fe Room.

It was empty. Yellow *vigas* gleamed with dying light of embers in the belly of a fat adobe fireplace. I switched on a lamp. The four-poster bed had been made with clean linens and Navajo blankets, and a sheet of paper pinned to a pillow, a message inked in a trembling, spidery hand like King Lear's:

Christina can come home now.

For some time he had been too weak to do more than crawl to the bathroom on all fours, there to spit and excrete blood and to cool his skin in a Victorian bathtub. I found his pajamas and dressing gown there, then opened the closet. Boots, jeans, Pendleton shirt, ski parka and astrakhan cap: all were gone. With what torques of pain he had dressed himself and tidied the bed, I could but imagine after five months of nursing him, but of one thing I felt sure: he would never permit himself a scream unless, in torture akin to that suffered by my father in the old days, he ceased to be human.

He couldn't have gone far, I thought that. Perhaps he was in the house.

Up in the Presidential Suite on the third story I found The Greatest Man in the World trying to hypnotize a chicken. "*¡Hijo de puta!*" I didn't stick around but went to the kitchen where Mamá was serving the twins some slices of freshly baked bread smeared with strawberry preserves. She smiled upon the twins adoringly. On to the Navajos. They have the west end of the first floor all to themselves, including a kitchen with wood-burning stoves and a greenhouse for growing corn and for rug-weaving. I couldn't go rushing up to them to ask if they'd seen Woolpack. I went through the Great Hall. It was freezing cold. I'd have to build a big fire soon to warm the spread antlers, like a palm reader's sign, of the elks and the fiend-eyes of shaggy buffaco. I exited the house and went around to the west end's entrance. There I stamped my feet and blew steam from lips for ten minutes to ward off *tchindees*—evil spirits. I turned and went into the barn where Hosteen stood among his belling sheep.

"Seen Mr. Woolpack?"

He tilted cowboy hat from weather-wrinkled face. He came and squinted at me, shook his head and said in bewilderment, "They lie me now."

"I know," I said. "They took your land."

After a while Hosteen removed a Bull Durham bag from his Pendleton shirt, sprinkled some cornmeal on his gnarled hand, and made his hand tremble. Then he motioned for me to follow him outside.

"Mebbe him liked it that way," he said, nodding in a general northerly direction.

"*Ake'he*," I said. I began to run in that direction as snow on the land blossomed into knowledge.

5

WITH the last of Grace's money that had lured Bluejean to death and Christina to captivity Woolpack bought a used Ford pickup, converted it into a camper, and took to the road, his eyes no longer fixed on rapturous prospects or even on a destination. His only inheritance, the ranch, had been repudiated—the long dream of sudden riches with which to redeem the land, lost. Life would be whatever turned up around the bend of the road in the parched solitudes of places where silence and desolation enfolded his own estrangement. He avoided as much as possible the electric hum and Interstate throb of the West's instant, ephemeral cities, preferring to accumulate fleeting glimpses of glittering civilization from the perspective of shanty towns, backwoods campsites, and fugitive trailer parks, and at first, without destination or purpose, he was like a schoolboy on a holiday moving inside a halo of wonder at the miracle of wilderness: the Grand Canyon, dark chasms and wild arroyos and buttes capped by wind-carved statues, and blue-shadowed valleys and sagebrush-and-yucca plateaux and ragged juniper trees twisting in the winds of time, and the silver-lined puttybark of aspens, and peaks leaping into clouds, and shadows undulating over snow above timberline where hungry winds withered the bones of boughs, and elflike cones of spruce, and blue forget-me-nots and wild pink lupine and lustrous columbine like hummingbirds arrested in flight, and the sky crammed with the jagged mountain ranges of immeasurable America. Save, perhaps, for the incongruity between his rapidly whitening mane of hair and the raw-burned stockiness of his physique, he was little noticed, but something of himself, he perceived, was mirrored in the faces of strangers, something filled with an unspeakable loneliness and despair. It was this perception, shaped to the need to eke out a living, that brought him eventually to work as an itinerant laborer; and even the work, at first, was romantic. He was at Lake Cariboo in British Columbia when he landed his first job driving a dumptruck, dumping tons of semi-tundra down a sluice from which a grizzled old sourdough prospector extracted, each day, a few thousand dollars worth of gold nuggets. Then, each night, he and the prospector fried up salmon from the lake and got drunk listening to the whispering forest and watching the eerie flashing luminosity of the aurora borealis. Work and drink became two sides of the same coin of escape, itself now seeming the purpose of his existence, and with this purpose he wandered on, a few weeks here, a month there. In Minnesota he unloaded freight cars singlehandedly, slinging hundred-pound sacks of sugar, as if they were beanbags, on the loading dock of a jam factory. In Kansas he followed the wheat harvest. Farmers with shovel beards hired him to drive a tractor or a semi over the mosquito-plagued seas of golden grass, and after work he joined the rednecked, plumb-wore-out crews at communal tables heaped with chicken-fried steak, cornbread, potatoes and hot peach cobbler before he went out into the stubble to drink himself into oblivion while storms of heat-lightning burst upon the night like shattering domes of black foil. He lived for a while in Alva, Oklahoma, where grain elevators held up the lid of hot sky and the whistle-moan and shuddering clank of freight trains echoed inside him as the agonies of a monster coiled in a pressure cooker. He worked the conveyor belts inside a grain elevator. He was there in the unventilated and quiet dust, the temperature 120 degrees, the air thick with dust, his body drenched in sweat and covered with powder, his goggles and bandana giving him the appearance to himself of a fetus lost in a lime-pit. And he lived for a while in places like Lubbock, Texas, where oil pumps bobbed snouts like giant black-iron grasshoppers. And the road lengthened and looped but gradually took him to places where he settled for six months or a year if only because he and time were now strangers, but these places had something in common: they were places where yellowcake was being mined from the Grant's Mineral Belt, places where he might be the only non-Indian down in the pits breathing the deadly air, filling his canteen from puddles of contaminated water. And then in 1979 he turned up in Gallup, New Mexico, as a truck driver hauling and dumping radioactive wastes.

One day in Gallup, Woolpack was recognized by Virgil.

Virgil peered over his bifocals through the bars at the old bum crumpled in a corner of the cell next to the toilet bowl speckled with vomited beans. It was a man with long white hair and a handlebar mustache that reminded him incongruously of Buffalo Bill save for mudcaked boots, torn Levis, and a construction worker's hardhat nearby. The man's sun-blistered face betrayed a deathly pallor, and his body, even as he slept, twitched violently, like that of a dog with a severed spine. The sight held little novelty for Virgil. Although he was more accustomed to finding young Indians than old whites here at the jail, a town like Gallup had a history of accumulating the dregs of society, plucking them out of gutters where they lay with a bottle of muscatel clutched in fist, and shutting them in with a reverberating clank. The odor of dereliction was always the same, as if the lid of a septic tank had been propped open in a greenhouse.

"Sleeping it off?" he said by way of sharing a sort of detached commiseration with Chavez, the keeper, whose uniform was blackened under the armpits from airless July heat.

Chavez half shrugged. "Some bizarro. They picked him up on Railroad Avenue stoned out of his mind. Brought him in before some of you boys could find him and clean him out."

Virgil laughed, just enough to humor someone useful without flattering his stupidity. He resettled his bifocals and turned to view other cells. "What are you keeping Slim Derryberry for this time?"

"Drunk and disorderly."

"He's harmless," Virgil said.

"He had a knife."

"What's that supposed to mean?"

"Don't ask me. I'm not the judge."

"You're letting the bizarro go. Why not let Slim go? Let us take him over to rehab. Hey, man, he's relocated. Can't go back to the res'... Okay?"

He knew Chavez would release Slim Derryberry without charge or fine. Whether it was Slim or some other Navajo who had been forced off the reservation only to have his new home repossessed for lack of mortgage payments, there was more to be gained by putting them into the clinic for alcohol rehabilitation than having them serve time for misdemeanors. The source of the problem, as everyone knew, lay far away in Washington where an uninformed Congress had passed the Relocation Act in 1974, thereby depriving thousands of The People of their ancestral homes without providing adequate funds for a new life. In fact, Chavez himself had, as usual, notified him at the rehab clinic that Slim, a habitual drunk, was in custody. Virgil grinned and tapped Chavez on the shoulder. "So hey, man, what's new?"

Chavez relaxed, spread the palms of his hands out. "Ah, Chihuahua," he sighed, "you find out, you tell me."

Virgil turned again to study the old bum. He knew somehow that he'd seen him before. "So what's his name?"

"Shakespeare."

Chavez lifted his eyebrows and puckered his lips.

"Really?"

"That's what the man said. I was checking the stuff in his pockets before the fingerprinting, y'know, and he's drooling from the mouth, and he gets this big shit-eatin' grin on his face and fingers me to lean forward and says, 'Know who I am? Shakespeare,' he says, and I look at his driver's license—John Woolpack, it says—and I say, 'Shakespeare, huh, say something in poetry,' and he wipes the drool off his mouth with the back of his hand and says something like he could of had many a knave come into the world, meaning bastard, I guess, and—I remember this—'good sport at the making.' Horny old bizarro." Chavez giggled in his throat.

"Tell you what, man," Virgil said after a pause. "Mind if I use your phone before I check Slim out of here?"

Virgil's call had me and Teresa driving over from Flagstaff late the next afternoon, which was Sunday the fifteenth of July. Although my old Caddie's days were numbered, its pale-ale paint was still faithful to Bluejean's eyes, and so it seemed the proper vehicle for chasing Woolpack down. We drove east on 40 for four hours. On the outskirts of Gallup we passed the Rio Puerco, which at that time of year is little more than a dry gulch with a few Navajo children playing in the water and some stray cattle grazing where the stream veers around a flat, black lava bed. Usually there are strong winds blowing around this little city near the Navajo Indian Reservation, and it is not unusual to see the hills crawling with trucks and tractors dumping dirt from the uranium mill at nearby Church Rock, the dust swirling everywhere. But this was Sunday, nothing was happening, and the streets off Interstate 40 were quiet.

As I watched the dust in which Woolpack had been working, I was alarmed. For I knew about the liquid and solid wastes from the process of refining yellowcake from uranium ore, knew about radioactive gas wafted across the country, and about tailings ponds which have an acidity equivalent to that inside a car battery. Virgil had told me about probable causes of Little Horse's birth defect.

But what I didn't know was this:

Next day before dawn a twenty-foot section of a tailings dam near the uranium mill at Church Rock was going to burst and send 100-million gallons of radioactive liquid and 1,100 tons of tailings tumbling into the Rio Puerco, causing a flashflood that would flow sixty miles into Arizona and make it possible for contaminants to reach the Little Colorado River, the Colorado River, and Lake Mead, major sources of water for the Southern California area. What I didn't know was that hours after the spill a sampling of the "Perky" would be made that indicated that the level of radium was 120 times above normal and the level of thorium 6,000 times higher than normal; and that, whereas safe drinking water is calculated to be 15 pico curies per liter, the "Perky," the day after my arrival, was going to give a measurement of 100,000 pico curies per liter.

But, as I've said, all was quiet that Sunday as we drove through Gallup and, following the directions Virgil had given us, found our way to a trailer park where Woolpack's Ford pickup, a crude camper, squatted in silhouette against a burnt-yellow sky. In the distance, neon signs blinked, and street lamps decorated hills with artificial crystals. An eighteen-wheeler on Interstate 40 clutched down, snorting to make a grade. And there near a culvert out of sight of the trailers, sat Woolpack, his hard hat askew over long white hair and a bottle in a paper bag perched on the kneecap that poked from Levis.

We had already decided to bring him home to the ranch. It was his home, ours only as an impulsive gift six years earlier, and we had been keeping the Santa Fe Room ready for his occupancy. Moreover, he was part of the family, at least to Teresa's way of thinking. However, no such purity of motive was mine to claim. It was not that I wished Woolpack harm but that I wanted him confined. Six years I had lived in dread, six years had passed without my knowing whether he were alive or dead, whether Teapot would come home or vanish forever. If Woolpack died, our daughter would live, and if he prolonged his life, her chance to live was by that very measure diminished.

Woolpack rose, doffed his hard hat, and made an unsteady bow. "What may this mean that thou revisit'st thus the glimpses of the moon? Are we dressing for dinner?"

Teresa and I exchanged glances. Crazy or cutting up? Teresa spoke first. "We've come to take you home, Mr. Woolpack."

"It's your home," I chipped in. "You were born there, for Christ's sake."

"Huh," he grunted, as if giving the situation thought. He squinted at the setting sun, and a faint smile tugged at the corner of his mouth. "Not for Christ's sake," he muttered. "Because my father had another sake in mind for his unholy loves... I see him now, eyes bulging, boots creaking on the stairs, head swimming in the Grand Canyon. He was a man who would flood the Sistine Chapel to get a better look at the ceiling... " He lurched toward me, the weather of his levity turned grave and flashing from red-rimmed eyes, his body reeking of spicy sweat and his breath of undigested liquor. "You've come to tell me she is dead."

"No," I said after a pause. "There's still time."

He backed away, ran thickish fingers through the matted hair at the back of his neck, and closed his eyes. "I'm not worthy of this wonderful news. She must be—"

"—Sixteen," I offered.

"I knew her once. A pretty child." He nodded to himself as if confirming a dim remembrance. Then he clapped his hands and brightened. "We leave in the morning, I presume?"

We made arrangements to meet him at six o'clock the next morning at our motel. I gave him a twenty-dollar bill. "Buy some gas," I said. "Get something to eat."

He pocketed the money and winked. "Haven't been drunk in ages. Believe I'll fall to the occasion."

There was a thumping on the motel room's door at five thirty. Through the window I could see two men in the early light. One was Woolpack, dressed in shabby clothes. His hard hat was pushed back at an odd angle. He was supporting the slumped figure of an emaciated Indian whose long black hair fell in dishevelment to his shoulders. I pulled on Levis and opened the door.

"This here's Slim Derryberry. Him and me's partners,"

Woolpack declared in a dialect laced with a kind of hilarity. "He drinks like a fish, stinks like a goat, and has an announcement to make of great social import. Tell 'em what we just seen, Slim, old buddy."

Slim opened an eye as red as a wet autumn leaf. His head flopped sideways and was righted long enough to mutter, "Tchindees."

"Atta boy, Slim. Now you rest your perturbèd spirit. Innerspring mattress and all mod con." Woolpack steadied Slim through the door and dumped him on the unused double bed as if he were a ragdoll. "Relocated," Woolpack said after blowing air. "Poor son of a bitch."

"Do you *mind*?" Teresa snapped from our bed.

Woolpack seemed to ponder the question a long time. "Oh," he said finally. "Slim Derryberry won't bother anybody. He *couldn't...* " Woolpack went on in another voice, "Hell's empty and all the devils are here."

"*Here*?" Teresa snapped. She was furious. Woolpack also was furious. His face was flushed, but his eyes flared with more than liquor. His voice exploded, "The sonsabitches built a tailings dam and overloaded it fifty per cent of design capacity and the dam's busted loose into the Perky and the river is hot and overflowing and probably has been for hours and Slim and I just saw the whole goddam thing down by the mill and nobody's doing fuck-all!" He whirled from the room and slammed the door.

A few minutes later we vacated the room. I wondered whether Slim Derryberry would catch pneumonia from the air conditioning but decided to leave it on. It was going to be a scorching day. I clipped the Do Not Disturb notice to the outside doorknob.

Some cherry-top patrol cars were parked outside the restaurant. Although the officers had apparently gone inside, a dispatcher's squawk-box was blatting away, clearing metallic sinuses. Woolpack was listening. I joined him.

"*Wffst...* report on puddles 40 West what have you got? *Wffst.* Kids playing... *Wffst...* Clear the area, got it? *Wffst.* Bunch of Indians... *Wffst.* Lupe get some off-limits posted. *Wffst...*" That was all I heard before Woolpack ran toward the restaurant. I ran too, past patches of grass like Welcome mats, past imitation stagecoach lanterns aswirl with moths, through swinging glass doors and into pleasant odors of coffee urns steaming and hashbrown potatoes frying. Flat-faced waitresses scurried, fat tourists in baseball caps masticated pancake stacks, four brown-uniformed policemen sat at a private booth, sipped coffee and looked about with a proprietary air. Woolpack was speaking to them through clenched teeth, saying something about enough water for 50,000 people. The police looked edgy.

Suddenly Woolpack banged both fists on their table, spilling a coffee cup. "*¡Las madres de Ustedes no son más que putas gringas!*" he shouted in an ecstasy of indignation and flung away as I arrived and just as an officer was rising, hand on the butt of his revolver.

"Sorry, fellas," I said quickly, "he's just upset, doesn't mean what he says. I'll take care of him. Have a nice day."

Woolpack had swept past Teresa and out the door. I grabbed Teresa's hand and said in low voice, "He called them sons of white whores. I've never seen him this way!"

When we reached the parking lot, the Ford pickup was already burning rubber and swerving to avoid an aluminum camper hauling a huge outboard motorboat. I turned the ignition of my old Caddie on and sped in pursuit. He had headed west. We barely glimpsed him about a quarter of a mile distant, entering the ramp of the Interstate.

I was still confused about what was going on and why Woolpack was behaving like a lunatic. "He says the water's hot. Radioactive?"

"That seems to be what he means," Teresa agreed, "but why are the police so calm if there is an emergency?"

"Look!"

We had left Gallup and were crossing a bridge over the Rio Puerco. Instead of a thin trickle in a gulch fifty feet below the bridge, now the river surged in a black glistening torrent less than ten feet below it. "He's right about the flood!" I floored the accelerator.

And began braking a few miles further west where Woolpack had pulled off the road and stopped at a place where the river, not fifty yards from the road, had spilled over its banks and left large puddles.

In which some little brown-skinned children were playing.

And even as I parked and sprang from my car, I saw Woolpack crazily waving his arms at the children and shouting, "Get out! The water is sick! *¡Aléjense! Esa agua es peligrosísima...* Evil spirits! *¡Tchindees! ¡Tchindees!*"

And the children ran from the puddles, stopped, stared, shrieked with laughter as the madman lunged toward them, and the children ran to the bank of the river—and giggled over their shoulders.

The children had stopped by the riverbank. Woolpack ran, stumbled, fell, got on his feet again without his hardhat, and ran, and when he grabbed each child, one by one, he flung the child like a sack of sugar away from the water's edge until one child remained, a little pig-tailed girl paralyzed with fright, backing away from the white monster, and then he grabbed her, too, just as she was falling into the torrent—and as he flung her to safety, he lost his balance on sleek lava, clawed the air, and fell spread-eagled into the sun-quivered river, shattering its panels of cathedral glass.

He went under, then came up twenty yards downstream, clung to a rock and pulled himself gasping and coughing into muddy rushes speared by Indian paintbrush.

He heard my approach and made a halt sign. "Don't

touch me, Paul," he panted quietly. "Get my blanket from the truck... Don't let the police see me, if they come. And, for godsakes, don't call a bloody doctor."

Woolpack sat propped in bed in the Santa Fe Room. Hosteen had finished talking. "Them in Washington say a man doing a good job there in the war, say that land nobody ever taking it away," he had said, moistening his lips and nodding his head. "They lie me now."

"We're all waiting for something beyond our control to happen," said Woolpack. "Perhaps it is not too late." He lapsed again into feverish semiconsciousness.

Most of his hair was gone. His skin lay tight against the skull aflame with sores. The mouth was puckered as the tightly scaled lines of the sea turtle's. Eyes burned behind their milk. Each movement was a torque of pain. During the interlude of feverish sleep, his horny nails fidgeted with the hands, fiddler crabs burrowing before a rushing wave.

He surfaced again. "She'll come home now," he said.

There was a lurch in my chest. "Yes."

"She's almost seventeen. Isn't that remarkable, son?"

"Yes."

He held out a skeleton hand. I grasped it. "You'll look after her well," he said. I understood him to be making a kind of statement. He squeezed my hand and said before he swooned again to sleep: "The honor of our hands will prevail."

So I hadn't seen Christina in seven years when I telephoned the Earthco people down in Ciudad de Pacífica.

The line was clear. A man with an American accent answered. I gave him a message for delivery to Colonel Günter von Albensleben. The message was: "The judgment of the Chalk Circle has been carried out." The man said he would deliver the message. Before an hour had passed, the telephone rang, and someone with a deep voice—also an American accent—asked was I Paul Szabo? I sucked air. "Speaking." The man said, "Christina Szabo has the visa." And hung up. Next day I found an envelope on my desk at the elementary school where I teach. Inside the envelope was Teapot's itinerary.

The sky over the airport at Phoenix was the blue mantle of a nurturing earth goddess. When the plane arrived, the weight of thirty-five years was like a tense muscle unclenched.

There she was. I saw her emerging up the ramp, walking awkwardly on high heels in the manner of seventeen-year-old girls.

"She's beautiful," Teresa murmured in a gasp.

She was that. The lambent azure of soft, wild eyes peered from the soul of things.

"Oh Daddy," she cried against my neck, leaned back in my arms and brushed away tears. "Who are we cheering for this year? Raiders or Redskins?"

"Redskins," I said. "How's Grace?" I asked cautiously after a pause.

"Didn't they tell you?"

"Tell me what?"

"When the colonel gave Grace the news of my father's death, she had a party and invited everyone, including President Scarpio and the American ambassador. She drank too much *pichuncho*. That night she almost choked to death."

Christina—who now must have the dignity of her proper name—tossed her hair in the breeze and gazed serenely as another Soul.

"Almost choked?"

"She's fine now. She sends you her love."

"She *does*?"

"And Tío Günter. He has been *so* wonderful to me."

"He *has*?"

"When he was saying good-bye, he cried and said he would always miss me... So sweet. He said, '*En casa del herrero, cuchillo de palo*,' which means, 'In the house of the blacksmith, there is a wooden knife.'"

"The hard worker leaves nothing for himself," Teresa interpreted.

"Well," I said, "I'll be—"

I was looking at the sun. Right there. I was looking at my feet. Right there. Nothing was vanishing, and in the silence of the drifting planet I heard at last the sound of articulate infinity.

Now all the acts of human love and sacrifice proclaimed their brightness on the other side of dread, and a mortal splendor calmed my soul.